ILLINOIS!

The eighteenth fabulous adventure in the *WAGONS WEST* series—an exciting mixture of history and action in one of America's most turbulent decades, a time of new frontiers, new fortunes, and new heroes to inherit the pioneer legacy of vision and courage.

WAGONS WEST

ILLINOIS!

When Nature's fury destroys a city and a dream, it takes a special breed of pioneer to fight, to strive . . . to win

TOBY HOLT—

Tragedy shatters this fighting man's life, but courage sends him toward a new challenge on the tough streets of Chicago . . . where a dark shadow lurks with deadly intent, and a terrible conflagration can consume a man, a city, and all his dreams.

JANESSA HOLT—

The legacy of a night's careless passion, this rebellious young girl is none other than the secret daughter of Toby Holt, a child with a special gift and an indomitable heart.

LT. HENRY BLAKE—

A young officer far from home, his assignment as an American spy makes a beautiful German baroness his mission . . . and her embrace makes her the obsession he fears but cannot resist.

CINDY HOLT—

The high-spirited sister of Toby Holt, she impatiently waits for the return of her beloved Henry, but the wedding bells she dreams of may never ring.

★★★★★★★★★★★★★★★★★★★★★★★★★★★★

KARL KELLERMAN—
As big and powerful as he is cruel, he lives for one moment—the moment he pulls the trigger to shoot down Toby Holt.

GISELA—
Voluptuously beautiful, this German aristocrat's lust for gold is second only to her desire for young Henry Blake.

TED TAYLOR—
Strong and courageous, his quick draw can make the difference between whether Toby Holt lives or dies.

MARJORIE WHITE—
Brilliant and lovely, her talent for photography makes her aim her lens at a dangerous scene . . . and her heart at an impossible love.

TIMMY HOLT—
The irrepressible four-year-old son of Toby Holt and his late wife, Clarissa, his future may bring tragedy and guilt to his father's tormented heart.

★★★★★★★★★★★★★★★★★★★★★★★★★★★★

Bantam Books by Dana Fuller Ross
Ask your bookseller for the books you have missed

INDEPENDENCE!—Volume I
NEBRASKA!—Volume II
WYOMING!—Volume III
OREGON!—Volume IV
TEXAS!—Volume V
CALIFORNIA!—Volume VI
COLORADO!—Volume VII
NEVADA!—Volume VIII
WASHINGTON!—Volume IX
MONTANA!—Volume X
DAKOTA!—Volume XI
UTAH!—Volume XII
IDAHO!—Volume XIII
MISSOURI!—Volume XIV
MISSISSIPPI!—Volume XV
LOUISIANA!—Volume XVI
TENNESSEE!—Volume XVII
ILLINOIS!—Volume XVIII

WAGONS WEST ★ EIGHTEENTH IN A SERIES

ILLINOIS!

DANA FULLER ROSS

™ **BCI**

Created by the producers of
White Indian, Children of the
Lion, Stagecoach and
America 2040.

Chairman of the Board: Lyle Kenyon Engel

BANTAM BOOKS
TORONTO • NEW YORK • LONDON • SYDNEY • AUCKLAND

ILLINOIS!

A Bantam Book / October 1986

Produced by Book Creations, Inc.
Chairman of the Board: Lyle Kenyon Engel
ISBN 0-553-26022-7

Published simultaneously in the United States and Canada

Bantam Books are published by Bantam Books, Inc. Its trademark,
consisting of the words "Bantam Books" and the portrayal of
a rooster, is Registered in U.S. Patent and Trademark Office
and in other countries. Marca Registrada. Bantam Books, Inc.,
666 Fifth Avenue, New York, New York 10103.

PRINTED IN THE UNITED STATES OF AMERICA

KR   0 9 8 7 6 5 4 3 2 1

O'LEARY STABLE
(ORIGIN OF FIRE)

SOUTH BRANCH
CHICAGO RIVER

CHICAGO RIVER

LAKE MICHIGAN

MAIN
HARBOR

© BOOK CREATIONS INC. 1986

St. Paul

MICHIGAN

WISCONSIN

MINN.

LAKE MICHIGAN

Madison
Milwaukee
Muskegon

IOWA

Chicago

MICH.

ILLINOIS

Springfield

INDIANA

Missouri River

St. Louis

N

Wabash River

Ohio River

MISSOURI

MISSISSIPPI RIVER

0   50   100
MILES

KENTUCKY

NORTH BRANCH CHICAGO RIVER

TO THE RAIL YARDS

LINCOLN PARK

TO NORTH HARBOR

Chicago on the Eve of the Great Fire, 1871 •

RON TOELKE '86

★ ★ WAGONS WEST ★ ★

★ THE HOLTS ★

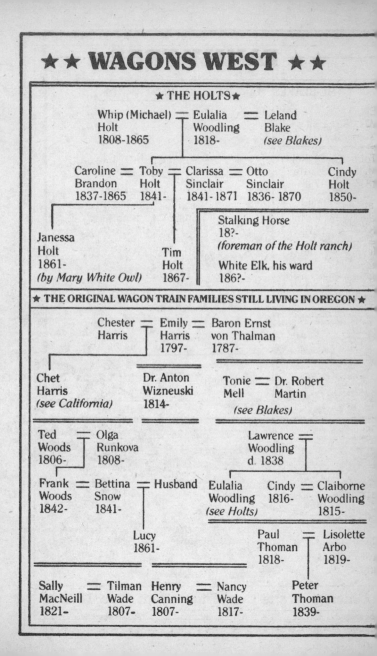

Whip (Michael) = Eulalia = Leland
Holt — Woodling — Blake
1808-1865 — 1818- — *(see Blakes)*

Caroline = Toby = Clarissa = Otto — Cindy
Brandon — Holt — Sinclair — Sinclair — Holt
1837-1865 — 1841- — 1841-1871 — 1836-1870 — 1850-

Janessa
Holt
1861-
(by Mary White Owl)

Tim
Holt
1867-

Stalking Horse
18?-
(foreman of the Holt ranch)

White Elk, his ward
186?-

★ THE ORIGINAL WAGON TRAIN FAMILIES STILL LIVING IN OREGON ★

Chester = Emily = Baron Ernst
Harris — Harris — von Thalman
— 1797- — 1787-

Chet Harris
(see California)

Dr. Anton
Wizneuski
1814-

Tonie = Dr. Robert
Mell — Martin
(see Blakes)

Ted = Olga
Woods — Runkova
1806- — 1808-

Lawrence =
Woodling
d. 1838

Frank = Bettina = Husband
Woods — Snow
1842- — 1841-

Eulalia
Woodling
(see Holts)

Cindy = Claiborne
1816- — Woodling
— 1815-

Lucy
1861-

Paul = Lisolette
Thoman — Arbo
1818- — 1819-

Sally = Tilman — Henry = Nancy
MacNeill — Wade — Canning — Wade
1821- — 1807- — 1807- — 1817-

Peter
Thoman
1839-

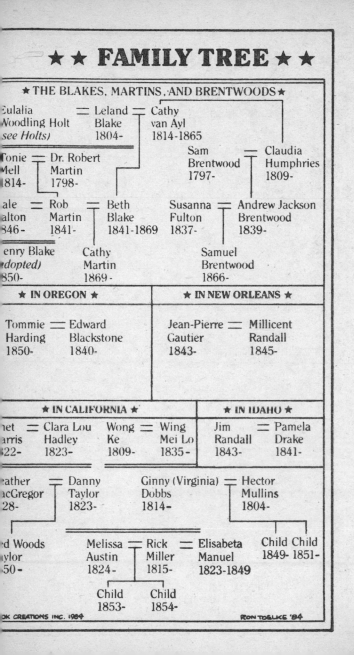

★ ★ FAMILY TREE ★ ★

★ THE BLAKES, MARTINS, AND BRENTWOODS ★

Eulalia
Woodling Holt
(see Holts)
— Leland =
Blake
1804-
Cathy
van Ayl
1814-1865

Sam
Brentwood
1797-
— Claudia
Humphries
1809-

Tonie =
Mell
1814-
Dr. Robert
Martin
1798-

ale =
alton
846-
Rob
Martin
1841-
— Beth
Blake
1841-1869

Susanna =
Fulton
1837-
Andrew Jackson
Brentwood
1839-

enry Blake
(adopted)
850-
Cathy
Martin
1869-

Samuel
Brentwood
1866-

★ IN OREGON ★   ## ★ IN NEW ORLEANS ★

Tommie =
Harding
1850-
Edward
Blackstone
1840-

Jean-Pierre =
Gautier
1843-
Millicent
Randall
1845-

★ IN CALIFORNIA ★   ## ★ IN IDAHO ★

net =
arris
822-
Clara Lou
Hadley
1823-
Wong =
Ke
1809-
Wing
Mei Lo
1835-

Jim =
Randall
1843-
Pamela
Drake
1841-

eather =
acGregor
28-
Danny
Taylor
1823-
Ginny (Virginia) =
Dobbs
1814-
Hector
Mullins
1804-

d Woods
aylor
50-
Melissa =
Austin
1824-
Rick =
Miller
1815-
Elisabeta
Manuel
1823-1849
Child Child
1849- 1851-

Child
1853-
Child
1854-

OK CREATIONS INC. 1984   RON TOELKE '84

ILLINOIS!

I

The man appeared suddenly, leaping out of the brush beside the trail and into the firelight. White Owl, a young Cherokee woman who was called Mary by the white people, looked up in shock at the ragged, grizzled intruder.

A glance at his face told her that he was a brutal, callous man. Chilling fright gripped her, but her apprehension was not for herself. Her fear was for her daughter, sitting on the other side of the fire.

A spasm of dry coughing seized her. "Who are you?" she gasped, trying to control her cough. "What do you want?"

"It don't make no difference who I am!" the man barked. "I'm here and nothing else counts. And I want whatever I can get!" He laughed harshly, his grin a savage leer.

Coughing hoarsely, Mary darted a glance toward the bundle in which she kept her pistol. It was too far away to reach. The days of solitude on the trail between Idaho and Oregon, as well as the feverish lassitude from her advanced stage of consumption, had made her careless.

"Take our food," she said, pointing to the pot of rabbit and wild onions boiling on the fire. "Take our mule and our belongings. Take whatever you wish, but leave us in peace."

The grimy, heavyset man grinned maliciously. A drifter and a petty thief, he had left everything behind when he

1

had fled Portland a step ahead of the police. Now, he reflected gleefully, his luck had changed.

The rangy mule hobbled near the trail would do until he could steal a horse. The smell of the food cooking made his mouth water. Best of all, he had happened upon a woman to use in any way he wished. Yes, he thought in lustful anticipation, his luck had changed.

Then, looking at the Indian woman more closely, he noted her thin, feverish face. Her otherwise youthful features were pale and drawn. "Are you sick?" he growled.

"I am dying," Mary replied. "Now take whatever you wish and go."

"I'll decide when I'll go!" the man snarled. "And I don't need you to tell me that I can take anything I want!"

Looking at the girl on the other side of the fire, he frowned. Unlike the woman, she revealed no fright. She seemed indifferent to his presence. And strangely, she had blue eyes, light brown hair, and typically white features. "Who is this girl?" he demanded. "She ain't no Indian."

"Her father was a white man," Mary replied, still coughing. "She is my daughter. Her name is Dawn Star—Ka-nessa in Cherokee. White people call her Janessa. And she is not yet ten years old."

"She's old enough for me," the man growled, leering at the small, thin girl. "I reckon I'll just have a look at her directly and see if she's white all over."

"She is only a small child!" Mary shouted in alarm, climbing to her feet. "Do what you wish to me, but leave her alone!"

"You sit back down!" the man snarled in savage fury, jerking out a knife. "I'll do whatever I want to you *and* to your kid!" The long, keen blade flashed in the firelight as he put it to Mary's throat.

While the man raged at her mother, Janessa opened a small gourd that she had taken from a bag beside her. She had been waiting for the man to be distracted. The lid on the gourd was tightly fastened to prevent its contents from contaminating the other containers of herbs, roots, and preparations in the bag. A pinch of the powder in it produced a lethargic state; more had a far different effect.

As the girl leaned over and emptied the gourd into the pot on the fire, Mary glimpsed her daughter's movement. She stopped arguing with the man and sat down again. The man, thinking only that he had cowed the woman into submission, grunted and nodded in satisfaction as he put the knife back into his belt.

"That's better," he grumbled. "If you and your kid are smart, you won't make me angry." He looked at the boiling pot of rabbit and onions, then moved it off the fire. "That's cooked good enough for me. I ain't had enough to eat these past two days to keep a bird alive."

Taking out his tobacco and cigarette papers, he sat down beside the fire and rolled a cigarette to smoke while the food cooled. Her face expressionless, the girl continued staring at him.

Her lack of fear made him uneasy. Accustomed to bullying everyone he could, he usually avoided those who showed courage. It touched a vulnerability deep within him, a point of weakness that was also the source of his gleeful triumph when he humiliated someone.

Finishing the cigarette and tossing the stub into the fire, he laughed harshly. The girl, he mused, would stop staring when she began screaming in pain and terror. He snatched up a spoon from the utensils beside the fire and began eating from the pot.

A few moments later, a numb light-headedness gripped him. His face felt as if it were swelling, growing enormously large. The campfire became an immense conflagration that filled the heavens and the earth. In the next instant, the fire was gone, and darkness surrounded him.

Out of the darkness came the girl's eyes. Blue and shining, they were gigantic. Their fixed, penetrating stare was a searing torment, boring into a raw, naked defenselessness within him. Then other fears began emerging, multiplied infinitely and bearing down upon him.

Dropping the pot and springing to his feet, the man bolted and ran headlong into a tree. He bounced off the tree and sprawled onto his back. Blood spurting from his mouth and nose, he screamed as he began thrashing about in a convulsion.

Coughing hoarsely, Mary put a hand on her chest as she smiled at her daughter. "What did you put in the stew, little one?"

"The mushrooms of dreams and visions," Janessa replied. She reached into the bag beside her and handed her mother a half-pint whiskey bottle. It contained a mixture of infusions of arnica and of the inner bark of mountain birch that had been boiled to a thick syrup. "He is seeing his soul," Janessa said. "He is doing to himself what he has done to others."

Mary's coughing stopped when she drank from the bottle, then Janessa replaced it in the bag and went to the mule. The man's screaming was making the mule stamp nervously, loosening a bandage that held a poultice over a wen on one of the animal's forelegs. Janessa tightened the bandage, then stepped back to the fire and gathered up the pot and spoon to take them to a nearby stream to wash.

A few minutes later, she walked back through the thick darkness to the campfire, the pot refilled with water. The man's screams had died away to quiet moans, and the peaceful murmur of the forest was restored, crickets chirping and the hooting of an owl echoing through the trees. Janessa began cutting up another of the rabbits that she and her mother had snared during the day, tossing the pieces into the pot.

"What happened was my fault," Mary said, reaching for the bundle that contained her pistol. "I should have kept the pistol close at hand."

"It isn't your fault there are evil people."

"It may not be my fault, but it is something that I know well, little one. So if I let myself be unprepared, what happens is my fault."

Janessa shrugged, acknowledging the point but unwilling to blame her mother for what had happened. Mary tossed more wood onto the fire and huddled closer to its warmth. Flames leaping up, the firelight shone brightly on the small, thin girl as she worked busily, cutting up the rabbit and putting wild onions into the pot.

Gazing at her daughter, Mary felt a deep admiration as well as love for the child. All her life, Mary had been a practitioner of herbal medicine. Because of her widespread reputation, she had been hired to work in a Union hospital during the Civil War. But Janessa had been born with a much greater innate talent as a healer. The girl was already far more skilled than many adults who were herbal medicine healers.

That talent had made great demands on the girl, however, and Mary's pride in her daughter was mixed with sadness. Janessa had never known a childhood. While other children laughed and played, Janessa had stood the deathwatch. Her power was a great burden for a small, thin girl. As a result, she was too quiet and reserved for a child, old far beyond her years.

"We have very little salt left," Janessa commented, placing the pot on the fire. "We need other things as well."

"What we have will be enough, my little one," Mary replied. "Our journey will be over within another two or three days. Then you will be safe, and I will be at peace in my mind."

Looking up at the stars through the dark branches overhead, Janessa sighed. "We should have stayed in Memphis."

"No, not for you to work as a midwife or to doctor only farm animals," Mary said. "You might not do any more than that in Oregon, but at least you will be with kin. We are doing the right thing."

"It has been years since you knew my father."

"It has, but that does not make any difference. In all the ways that are important, he is by far the finest man I have ever met."

"He didn't love you, and he left you pregnant."

Mary hesitated; with a thorough knowledge of intimate relationships between men and women, the girl approached the subject with a bluntness that was disconcerting. "He did not feel the same about me that I did about him," Mary admitted. "But when he was a patient in the hospital where I worked during the war, he needed me. That was enough for me. When he left, neither of us knew I was pregnant. I've told you all this before."

The girl shrugged, dismissing the subject. She stood up and walked over to the man, who was now silent and motionless. As she bent over him, Mary called out to her. "Don't take anything that belongs to him. He'll probably die, and it wouldn't be right to take his things."

Displaying one of her rare, wide smiles, Janessa held up the man's tobacco and cigarette papers. Mary started to shake her head, then changed her mind. The girl had little enough enjoyment. Smoking was one of her few pleasures, although some regarded it with deep disapproval. Mary nodded her permission.

Smiling gleefully, Janessa rolled a cigarette and lit it with a twig as she sat back down beside the fire. Then, as she smoked, she became pensive again. Returning to the subject that she and her mother had been discussing, she commented quietly, "Maybe he won't want me."

The soft, plaintive remark brought sudden tears to Mary's eyes. She looked at the small girl, whose shabby coat was pulled close against the evening chill. Wisps of her brown hair hung loose around her face. The girl was clearly frightened of being left all alone among strangers who might view her only as an embarrassment, as the outcast, bastard product of an indiscretion committed years before.

"That kind of talk is silly," Mary scoffed. "Your father is a good man, and any man would want a daughter as pretty and smart as you."

Janessa, puffing on her cigarette and inhaling deeply, made no reply. She exhaled smoke through her nostrils as she stared into the fire, her attitude skeptical. Mary sighed and looked away, less certain herself on the matter than her words had indicated.

The girl's father would undoubtedly have a family, she mused, and there might be problems. Also, Janessa could be difficult. Most of the time, she responded to persuasion; but any attempt to exert authority over her was met by an unyielding wall of resistance.

At the same time, Mary reassured herself, the girl was the very image of her father. Strangely, she even had many of his personality characteristics. Thinking back across the years and remembering the man she had loved, Mary was sure she was doing the right thing. She could die in peace, knowing that her daughter was safe. Toby Holt would accept his daughter, and he would love her and provide her with a good home.

Thick darkness and heavy rain turned the scene outside the train window into a blur of passing lights and formless shadows, but Toby Holt knew he was near his destination. Having traveled the route many times, he knew that the train was approaching Memphis.

The clacking of the wheels against the rails seemed to keep rhythm with his thoughts as he wondered why Martha had sent the telegram. Consisting of a single sentence—asking him to meet her in Memphis—it had been strangely cold. Their marriage plans were still tentative, and they had previously agreed to meet within two months to make definite plans.

At their last parting, she had been the warmly affectionate, beautiful Martha whom he loved. Her last letter had referred to their forthcoming marriage and had ended with a comment, punctuated by exclamation points, on how slowly time passed. A long silence had followed that letter, with no reply to two that he had written. Then the telegram had arrived.

Looking out into the rainy darkness, Toby reflected that he would soon have answers to the troubling questions that had haunted him all during the journey. And a tiny voice inside his mind whispered a warning. Things had not always gone smoothly between him and Martha.

The train slowed and took on a weaving motion as it passed over switches. The brakes squealed, and the lights of the station brightened through the rain and the gloomy darkness ahead. Then the conductor hurried along the aisle. "Mem-*phis*! Mem-*phis*! Mem-*phis*!"

The train shuddered to a stop; wind whipped the heavy rain and coal smoke along the platform, making the lanterns sway. Toby joined the people filing off the train, others around him hurrying to get out of the rain.

A movement in the shadows beside a pilaster near the restaurant entrance caught his eye. He stopped, rain pattering on his hat and trickling off the brim. Martha, wearing a long, hooded rain cape, was standing beside the pilaster. He walked toward her with long, eager strides.

"Martha!" he called. "What are you doing down here in the middle of the night? I didn't expect you to meet me."

"Expected or not, I intended to, Toby," she replied. "I received your telegram, so I knew when you'd arrive."

Her beautiful face was framed by luxuriously thick red hair peeking out from her hood. She smiled at Toby, but the smile was forced. And when he put his arms around her to kiss her, his lips found only her smooth, soft cheek, cool and damp from the rain.

Taking his arm, she pulled him toward the overhang at the side of the platform. "Get in out of the rain, Toby. After I sent that telegram, I felt very guilty about putting you to so much trouble."

He shook his head as they stepped into the shelter of the overhang. "No, I had to go to Chicago, so I just came by way of Memphis."

"Chicago? Yes, that's right, you wrote that you were going to meet a man there, didn't you? Well, I don't feel so guilty now. You also wrote that your sister Cindy is keeping house for you and taking care of little Timmy, didn't you? How is she doing?"

"She's doing fine. Cindy is stricter with Tim than Clarissa was, but she loves him, and I'm not going to try to tell her how to do her job."

Her smile false, Martha listened and nodded with an interest that was only a pose. When Toby started to broach the subject of her telegram, Martha cut him off with a question about the affairs of his horse ranch. When he finished answering and again tried to bring up the matter of her telegram, Martha quickly posed another question. "And how is—"

"Martha, why am I here?" he asked bluntly, interrupting her.

Her artificial smile and forced cheerfulness crumbled. She pointed toward the restaurant. "Could we get a cup of coffee?"

Toby nodded and shrugged. They walked along the platform and went into the grimy restaurant, which smelled of burned grease and of the omnipresent coal smoke. At the tables were a few rumpled, weary people who ate in grim silence. Toby brought cups of coffee to the table.

Martha did not speak for a long moment. Then she said, "I'm going to marry Red Leary." She lifted a hand as he started to reply. "Toby, I've made up my mind. When we're together, I can't think. But reason comes to bear when we're apart. It just wouldn't work for us."

"Doesn't love count for something?"

"It doesn't count for everything," she shot back. "We have nothing in common, and I'm not about to spend my life on a horse ranch in Oregon. Canal Street in New Orleans and Alexander Avenue in Baton Rouge are the only kinds of places where I can live and breathe, Toby."

He shook his head, explaining that they could compromise. She disagreed, mentioning other points of conflict.

"Your mother can't stand me," she said. "Neither can your sister Cindy. It's nothing personal, I know that. It's just that they don't think I'm the one for the scion of one of the first families of Oregon. And do you know something, Toby? They're absolutely right!"

This was a difficult point, Toby reflected, because his mother and sister had indeed been distant toward her. "If you're still thinking about that reception you weren't invited to when we were at West Point," he said, "that was for army wives, Martha. We've been over that before."

"Sure, and I keep getting explanations that mean nothing. Cindy went, and she isn't even married. She's just engaged to that Blake kid."

"He's an officer in the United States Army, Martha,

which rules out his being a kid. And Cindy's stepfather is a major general, which is accepted as middling good credentials among army wives."

Martha sat back, dismissing the specific as well as the broader subject with an impatient gesture. "Toby, you don't raise the ante when all you're holding is a pair, and you don't stay when you don't help the pair on the draw. You've got to know when to fold, and now I'm throwing in my cards. It was a nice game, Toby, but I'm out. And that's final."

Her green eyes reflected pain and regret; but they also mirrored her unyielding will. From experience, he knew that it was pointless to try to sway her when she was resolved on a course of action. After a long moment, he nodded. "I'll take you home, Martha," he said.

"I have a carriage waiting," she replied, standing up. She hesitated, then drew in a deep breath and spoke again. "Good-bye, Toby."

"Good-bye, Martha."

A moment later, she was gone. He sat and numbly looked at the cold, untouched coffee on the table. What had been an important part of his life was gone. He got up from the table and went outside.

The rain had stopped, and the sound of drops falling from the eaves over the platform was loud in the quiet. He went inside the station to the ticket counter, where he bought a ticket to Chicago from the sleepy clerk. Then he went to the baggage counter to make out new labels for his luggage.

After checking his bags back in for Chicago, he looked at the schedule. The train would leave at ten the next morning—too soon to make it worth the bother of going to a hotel but still seeming a dismal eternity before he could leave Memphis.

He went back outside and sat on a bench on the dark, quiet platform. Fatigue settled upon him like a crushing weight. He tugged his hat down over his eyes and pulled his coat closer against the cool, damp breeze. Then he fell sound asleep.

A bump against his feet and a man's voice awakened

him to instant awareness. To his surprise it was bright daylight. The voice had the lilting rhythm and rich, thick brogue of Ireland. "Sure and see what ye did, Meggie!" the man exclaimed. "Ye've wakened him and all and all. Can't ye watch where ye're walking, me sweetie?"

Toby sat up. Meggie was a charmingly pretty girl of about six, with a scarf tied tightly under her chin. Her blue eyes looked up in dismay at her father. There were two other small children with the man and woman. The family was loaded down with heavy bundles, and their clothes were threadbare but clean. All of them had red hair, freckles, and sparkling blue eyes.

"People shouldn't stick their feet out in the road, should they, Meggie?" Toby chuckled, then nodded politely toward the man. "I'm Toby Holt."

"Paddy Rafferty's me name, and here's me good wife Colleen and me little ones," the man said cheerfully. "We've just arrived here in the United States, in New Orleans, and now we're on our way to Chicago."

Exuberantly friendly, a constant smile on his face, the man continued talking as he and his family put down their bundles and sat on the bench. Toby stretched as he listened. The hours of sleep had refreshed him. He felt alert and energetic, as well as ravenously hungry.

The day itself was invigorating. The rain the night before had cleansed everything, and the sun beamed down from an azure sky in which fleecy clouds floated. Chattering birds played in the eaves above, and the breeze was sweet with the scent of green, growing things. Along the tracks, buttercups and bluebells were rich splashes of color, and even the gleaming rails seemed to beckon to new interests and opportunities.

Paddy Rafferty's buoyant spirits were infectious. He and his family had come by steerage on a leaky windjammer to New Orleans, then upriver by freight barge. But his home in Ireland and the journey received only scant mention. He was a man who looked toward the future, and he talked about his prospects in Chicago. He and his family were the hardy, enduring type of people who energized the nation in its burgeoning growth.

"Yes, I've been through Chicago several times," Toby said, replying to a question. "I'm going there on business now."

"Ye are, are ye? Well, we can keep each other company. I'm never short of talk, mind. Me sainted mother—may God treasure her soul for the precious jewel that it is—often said that I bit off a piece of the Blarney stone instead of just kissing it. But about Chicago . . ."

He continued, talking about a leaflet that had been distributed in Ireland, describing the city of Chicago and the jobs available there. His wife, reserved and very pretty, began rummaging among the bundles. The children watched her with silent, intense interest as she took out a small, covered pail that apparently contained food.

Toby nodded as Paddy mentioned the time that the train was scheduled to leave. "Yes, ten o'clock," he said. "We have plenty of time, and I'd be pleased if you and your family would be my guests for breakfast."

Silence fell, the woman flushing as she lifted her chin and looked at Toby indignantly. Paddy's habitual smile turned stiff, and his blue eyes were icy. "Sure and we've no need for charity," he said softly. "I provides for me family. If there's aught I don't have to hand, they can make do wi'out for a time."

"I know you don't need charity," Toby replied. "I wasn't offering it. You can have my address so you can repay me when you've found a job. I'd like for us to travel together, and I'm hungry enough to eat a horse. But if I went in there to eat and left those children out here, I wouldn't be able to look at myself in a mirror when I shave."

Paddy hesitated, his resentment fading. He looked at his wife, but she was suddenly inspecting the clouds, the decision his. The children's attention was riveted on their father, with the same hungry intensity with which they had looked at the bucket containing food. Paddy finally answered. "Aye, I'll have yer address and repay ye, then," he said. "Ye're a good man, Toby Holt, and it's me that's thanking ye."

"No need for thanks," Toby replied, standing up. "It's a loan, and I'd like to see you get your money's worth.

Breakfast here is a quarter for all you can eat. We have plenty of time, so let's see if those children can't hold a dozen eggs and a pound of bacon each."

Paddy laughed as he stood up. "Twenty-five cents for all ye can eat?" he exclaimed. "Aye, there's a fair bargain and all and all. The little ones here will do it justice. It's been a while since they've had a sit-down to a proper good feed."

As he glanced at his children, his smile faded. Then he looked into the distance along the tracks. "But they'll be fine now," he continued softly. "The very first minute I put foot on this soil, I knew I'd done right by them. And every minute since then has proven it. This is a great, grand country, isn't it?"

"Yes, it certainly is that," Toby agreed quietly. "I've been fortunate enough to have had opportunities to serve it, and I hope I will again." His expression abruptly changing, he smiled briskly and pointed toward the restaurant. "Now let's see how much bacon and eggs those children can hold."

Cindy Holt, standing in the doorway of the new addition to the ranch house, was torn between pride and worry. The Portland Water Closet Company had finished the last of the work the day before, and as a gesture of goodwill, the owner had ordered his men to tear down the privy behind the house, cart it away, and smooth out the ground where it had been.

There was ample reason for pride: In the new addition, white porcelain and shiny brass gleamed against the warm glow of hardwood. The bathtub on its claw feet set on glass balls was large enough to be comfortable for the tall, rangy Toby, and the sink was set at a height that would be convenient for him. The fixture that had been the cause for disposing of the privy was of the most expensive design, with a hardwood back and armrests, as well as a rack on one side for magazines and newspapers.

There was also ample reason for worry, since the total expense had been somewhat more than the cost of building two houses of moderate size. Although Cindy was engaged to be married to a man whom she loved, she measured all other men against her brother. He was the hero of her life, a man of unyielding principles and sterling qualities. She wanted to provide him with the most comfortable and orderly household possible—but she hadn't realized what the total cost of the bathroom would be.

A nagging headache pulsing in her temples, she stepped to the commode and pulled the chain. The water from the tank near the ceiling coursed down through the brass pipes with a satisfying gurgle. Then, hearing a knock at the kitchen door, Cindy stepped back out of the room. Since visitors came to the front door, she assumed it must be one of the ranch hands.

The past few days, the bathroom had created ribald amusement among the ranch hands, who joked about how genteel the Holt household was becoming since Cindy had taken charge of it. Anger made her headache swell to a painful throbbing as she walked through the house with a long, quick stride. If a ranch hand had found some excuse to talk to her so he could make a sly, grinning remark about the bathroom, she thought grimly, he would regret it.

As she opened the door, her frown faded. An Indian woman and a girl were standing there in front of a bony mule. The woman was thin and flushed, obviously ill. Both she and the girl were clean and neat but ragged. At first Cindy thought they were indigents seeking food and shelter. She started to speak, intending to offer what they needed before the woman had to ask for it—but then she looked at the girl again.

Something more than shock seized her. It was an uneasy shudder in the very foundation of her being, making her want to doubt the evidence before her eyes. Her brother was human and made mistakes. But he always faced his mistakes squarely and rectified whatever wrong may have come from them, regardless of what it cost him.

The one thing that Toby Holt would never do was father a child and then abandon it. But obviously he had. Those large blue eyes, cherubic features, and particularly the proud uplift to the girl's chin and determined line of her mouth screamed her bloodline to the heavens. This small girl was a Holt.

The Indian woman spoke politely, controlling a cough. "Ma'am, I was told that this is the Holt ranch. Is the man of the house nearabout?"

Cindy forced her eyes away from the girl, shaking her head as she turned to the woman. "No, he's away on business. I'm Cindy Holt, his sister, and I keep house for him."

"He is away?" the woman echoed, her thin, feverish face reflecting alarm. "Could you tell me if he will be gone much longer?"

Cindy drew in a deep breath and squared her shoulders. This was a family matter, and her brother was not the only one with a strong sense of right and wrong. "It'll be several days more," she replied, opening the door wider. "But I can see what the—the situation is, and you have my word that it will be dealt with fairly. Please come inside."

"We are most grateful, Mistress Holt," the woman said in relief as she and the girl carried their bundles of belongings into the kitchen. "Truly, we are most grateful for your kindness."

"I'm doing no more than you're due," Cindy replied firmly. "Put your things down, and we'll get you settled in a room as soon as you've eaten. I'll have someone take care of your mule." Leaning out the door, she summoned a ranch hand to take the mule to the barn. As she stepped back into the kitchen and closed the door, the woman introduced herself and her daughter, still addressing Cindy formally.

"I am very pleased to meet you both," Toby's sister replied. "Please call me Cindy." Still unable to comprehend how her brother had done something so unlike him, she thought about the girl's age. "I take it that you knew Toby some years ago."

"Yes, when he was in the hospital early in the war," Mary replied. "I do not want you to get the wrong idea about what happened, Cindy. The fact is, Toby does not know about Janessa. When he left the hospital, neither of us realized that I was with child and—"

"Yes, well, we can discuss that later," Cindy interrupted her. Although she was immensely relieved and wanted to hear more, she felt the conversation was becoming entirely inappropriate for the ears of a small girl. "Sit down at the table and I'll prepare something to eat. Then you can rest, Mary. You look like you don't feel too well."

Nodding in gratitude, Mary reflected that the tall, strikingly attractive young woman had a rigid and perhaps even somewhat prim sense of propriety. While that would create friction between her and Janessa, the same quality would make her feel responsible for the girl. There might be clashes, but Janessa would have a good home.

"I have consumption, and I am dying," Mary said, sitting down at the table with Janessa. "That is the reason I brought Janessa here. But I can go in peace because I know that my Janessa will be safe with you."

Tears stung Cindy's eyes. Mary looked ashen and drawn, yet the remnants of her once radiant beauty were still evident, and her eyes reflected a strong will. Youth and health had fled her, but fortitude remained. When her own time came, Cindy thought, she hoped that she could face it with the same unflinching courage. The woman's struggle to find a home for her child before dying was heartrending.

"Now, let's not have any more talk like that," Cindy said gently. "After you've eaten and rested, you'll feel much better. In any event, if there's anything to discuss, it's best that you and I talk about it later, isn't it? We don't want to upset little Janessa."

Mary started to reply that it was difficult to upset Janessa, but changing her mind, she silently nodded.

As Cindy stepped to the stove, she glanced again at the young girl. She was remarkably indifferent, Cindy mused, considering what had just been said in her presence. She seemed a strangely quiet, most unusual child. Dismissing the thought, Cindy began preparing a quick meal. Her headache seemed even worse.

After shredding part of a tender, leftover beef roast into a pot of broth she had been simmering, Cindy added some pearl barley also left over from the previous day's dinner. While the contents of the pot heated, she cut thick slices of homemade bread and toasted them in the oven, then neatly set the table. In a few minutes she dished up the rich, hearty soup.

Janessa began eating without ceremony, but Mary commented on the delicious soup. Cindy sat down at the table, shrugging off the compliment and confessing that she had such a bad headache that she could hardly concentrate. Abruptly Janessa put down her spoon and got up from the table. The girl took a cup from the cabinet, then dropped something in it from the bag she carried. She added hot water from a kettle on the stove and put the cup in front of Cindy, then sat back down.

"It will help your headache," Mary explained. "Like me, Janessa is a healer. That is what I have done all my life, and it is how I came to be working in the hospital during the war."

Dismissing it as an Indian superstition, Cindy nevertheless took a sip from the cup to be polite. It was some kind of herb tea, the taste not unpleasant, and Cindy continued sipping it as she talked with Mary about her long journey from Memphis.

The door flew open as Toby's son, Tim, came in from playing with his kite. Large for his age, he was a boisterous, sturdy boy of four. He slid to a stop and looked at Mary and Janessa. "Timothy, please close the door," Cindy said. "This is Janessa and her mother. They'll be staying here now. Mary, Janessa, this is Toby's son, Timothy."

The boy was courteous to a fault, partly because of Cindy's unremitting efforts since taking charge of him. He touched his forehead and greeted the woman and her daughter. Mary smiled and replied to him, then remarked to Cindy what a handsome boy he was. Janessa merely glanced at him and continued eating.

An amiable boy, Tim approached Janessa and asked her if she wanted to see his new kite. The girl's only response was a long, cool stare. Tim pulled up a chair for himself and sat down.

Controlling an impulse to speak sharply to the girl about her manners, Cindy excused herself and went to the stove to get a bowl of soup for Tim. He was always hungry.

When she returned to the table and put the soup down, Cindy realized that her headache was gone. For a moment she thought about the herb tea that Janessa had made for her, but she refused to believe that it had actually cured her headache. The headache had simply stopped as suddenly as it had begun.

When Janessa finished eating, she got up from the table—without excusing herself, Cindy noted—and stepped out of Cindy's line of view as she went to the stove. A moment later, Tim gasped as he looked in the direction of the stove, his eyes wide with shock.

Turning to look, Cindy was speechless with outrage. Janessa had rolled a cigarette and was lighting it with a sliver of wood. The girl tossed the sliver into the stove and closed the firebox door. She began puffing contentedly on the cigarette, inhaling deeply, then exhaling smoke through her nostrils. She sucked her teeth, patted her stomach, and smothered a belch.

Cindy finally found her tongue. "Janessa, put that cigarette into the stove this instant!" she snapped.

The girl's face flushed, and her eyes narrowed with anger as she threw the cigarette into the stove. She opened and closed the firebox door more forcefully than necessary. Mary apologized quietly, and Cindy forced a polite smile. "That's quite all right, Mary," she said. "But I won't allow a woman to smoke in this house, much less a young girl. It's simply not acceptable behavior. If you've finished eating, maybe you'd better rest now. You must be very weary."

Mary nodded, then went to the bundles near the door. Cindy helped her gather up her things as Janessa, still stiff with anger, picked up her own bag. Then they walked through the house toward the guest rooms.

Throughout her life, Cindy had never flinched from a

conflict of wills with any man or woman. But as she glanced down at Janessa and saw the girl glaring back, Cindy felt uneasy. Taking a firm hand with this child would be difficult. As she thought of the difficulties ahead, she felt her headache returning.

II

The rich, nutty fragrance of coffee boiling and the hearty scent of smoked bacon frying in a pan awakened Toby Holt. The smells were even more appetizing in the crisp, fresh air of the Wisconsin forest. On the other side of the campfire, Frank Woods was cooking breakfast.

The son of a blacksmith who had helped blaze the Oregon Trail, Frank had inherited his father's huge, muscular frame. His deep voice was like a rumble of kettle drums. "I wondered if I was going to have to turn you out of your blanket," he commented, smiling.

Toby laughed as he stood up and stretched. "When I'm in the forest, I sleep like a baby and eat like a pack of wolves."

"There's enough here to feed a pack of wolves," Frank said, turning the bacon. "It'll be ready by the time you've washed up."

Carrying his towel and soap, Toby walked through the trees to a clear, fresh stream that was dappled with early morning sunlight streaming through the foliage. He glanced around at the trees as he knelt beside a pool and began washing. Much of his life had been spent in surroundings such as these, in the service of his nation. His assignments had ranged from surveying routes for railroads to the governorship of the Idaho Territory. But personal business affairs had brought him here.

Toby had been involved in logging ventures in the

Washington Territory for some years now, in partnership
with Rob Martin, a longtime friend and associate. Frank
Woods had been in charge of the actual logging operations. Most of the mature trees on the Washington land
had already been harvested, and after seedlings had been
planted so that the forest could renew itself, Frank had set
out to find a new area for another logging operation. His
search had brought him here, to the virgin stands of fir
and pine in the deep Wisconsin forests.

Toby had another reason for coming to Wisconsin.
Since the death of his wife, Clarissa, his life had been
coming apart, and he was trying to put it back together.
His sister Cindy had helped immensely by taking charge
of his household and his small son, but now his plans to
marry again and begin rebuilding his life had been shattered.

Whatever Martha's reasons, it was done. She was
going to marry Red Leary. At least the trip to Wisconsin
now offered him an opportunity to be alone for a time, to
clear his mind of the past and to look to the future.

Frank was dishing up the food on tin plates when
Toby returned to the fire. Alongside the thick slices of
smoked bacon he spooned out large scoops of potatoes that
had been boiled and then fried with onions in the bacon
drippings. Steaming sourdough biscuits, which Frank had
baked on a flat rock, were next, served up with strong
black coffee. A hint of wood smoke made everything more
delicious, and they ate hungrily.

After breakfast, Frank carefully extinguished the fire.
"This is the big danger here," he commented. "One spark
in the wrong place could burn thousands of acres and kill
scores of people."

"I can see how it would," Toby replied as he helped
Frank. "There would be no way to escape, either. All of
the roads I've seen so far are through thick forest."

Frank nodded. "There are logging camps west and
south of here, and I hear they fire lumberjacks quicker for
careless smoking than for anything else."

The fire extinguished, the two men loaded the
packhorses and mounted up. As they rode through the

forest, Frank pointed out the more valuable stands of
timber.

The tract, belonging to a land speculator, comprised
several grants that the owner had bought from individuals.
Here and there were small, rotting cabins and clearings
that indicated that crops had been grown, but for the most
part the land was covered by thick, virgin stands of towering trees. By midmorning, Frank and Toby had looked
over most of the timber and were riding toward the side of
the tract that fronted on Lake Michigan.

"Logging rights in Wisconsin sell for up to ten dollars
an acre," Frank explained. "But this land is a long way
from the lumber mills at Madison and Milwaukee, so it'll
go a lot cheaper."

Something about Frank's manner betrayed an idea
that he was keeping to himself until the right moment. Toby smiled. "What do you have up your sleeve,
Frank?"

Frank grinned boyishly, but he remained silent until
they rode out of the trees at the edge of a high bank
overlooking Lake Michigan. For all practical purposes the
lake was an inland sea, its vast surface stretching away to
the horizon. Rolling waves lapped the shoreline at the foot
of the steep bank, some fifty feet below.

At last Frank began explaining his idea, proposing
that they build a dry chute on the bank and have the logs
dumped into the lake, collected in a catch boom, then
towed to the lumber mills in Chicago. Logging rights here
could be purchased at a low price, and towing the large
rafts of logs down the lake would cost less than hauling as
many logs on drays for even a short distance.

"That's the reason I've been staying in Chicago instead of Milwaukee," Frank continued. "The man who
owns this land has his office in Chicago, but I've also been
looking into setting our business up there. The charges at
the mills in Chicago are a lot more reasonable than here in
Wisconsin. And there are plenty of steam launches in
Chicago to tow the logs."

"You've come up with a very good idea, Frank," Toby
said. "But if we go to that much trouble, we should

examine the possibility of getting the logging rights to other land in the vicinity."

"I've already looked into it," Frank replied. "The tracts all around here are owned by speculators. If we could get the rights to several of them, I could put the main logging camp right here, move my family here, and settle in for the next few years."

Toby had seen and heard enough. Reining his horse back from the edge of the bank, he nodded and said, "Let's get on back to Chicago and start making some preliminary arrangements to organize this."

Frank grinned happily as he reined his horse around. He led the way inland to a narrow trail that gradually turned into a road through the forest, paralleling the lakeshore. They rode along it at a canter.

When they camped beside the road that night, Toby and Frank discussed the potential for the venture to become far larger than they had first contemplated. Toby believed that Rob Martin would be interested in investing in it, and he also thought it likely that another friend, Edward Blackstone, could be counted on as well. Both men were in New Orleans with their wives, and Toby decided he would write to them and ask them if they wanted to become partners in the venture.

As they continued along the road the next day, Toby brought up another possibility. During his trips across the Great Plains by train, he had seen that some farming families still lived in sod houses because of the scarcity and cost of lumber there. Even if he had to sacrifice some profit, he wanted to ship lumber west and make it available to the farmers on the plains. Frank agreed.

Late in the afternoon, they reached Chicago. Its sprawling stockyards and equally expansive rail yards worked in concert, providing a flow of livestock to all parts of the East and the South. The stockyards had spawned a burgeoning meat-packing industry, as well as tanneries and glue factories. Readily available work had drawn the jobless, and the presence of a large labor force had attracted other industries. During the past three years alone, Chicago had tripled in size to a population of over three hundred thousand.

The city, divided into three sections by the Chicago River and its two branches, was also an attractive place in which to live. Its streets were laid out mostly in a grid, with numerous large parks and botanical gardens. Theaters, fine restaurants, yachting clubs, and other forms of entertainment were readily available. But the explosive growth of the city had also brought problems.

Most of the buildings, Toby noticed, were wooden. The thirteen miles of docks along the mouth of the Chicago River were also made of wood, as were the paving blocks used on the streets. Riding along the busy streets with Frank, Toby felt that the situation was similar to that in the Wisconsin forests: A spark in the wrong place could result in disaster.

Since it was on the way to their lodgings, Toby and Frank reined up in front of the office of the man who owned the land they had inspected.

The man, whom Frank introduced as a Mr. Pomeroy, was overweight and overly hearty, his manner matching the loud, checked wool suits and striped shirts that he wore. Toby disliked him because his only apparent interest in his land was in wringing every possible dollar of profit from it. He had never even seen it.

Toby wanted a year's option to buy the logging rights on the land, and he wanted the option to include the right to clear roads and construct buildings so a logging camp could be set up. "That will amount to improvements and increase the value of the land," Toby pointed out.

The man shrugged and shook his head. "I don't care if it's improved or not—but you can do as you like. I'll sell you the option for a hundred dollars to buy the logging rights for seven-fifty an acre."

"That's completely unreasonable," Toby replied flatly. "You know as well as I do how far that land is from Milwaukee and how much it'll cost to dray the timber to the lumber mills there. I'll pay a hundred for the option to buy logging rights at four dollars an acre."

The man knew how costly it would be to haul the

timber to Milwaukee, but never having seen his land, he was unaware that Toby and Frank had found an inexpensive way to get the timber to the lumber mills in Chicago. After hesitating for a moment, he nodded and reached for pen and paper to write a contract for the option as Toby counted out a hundred dollars in gold. A few minutes later, Toby folded and pocketed his copy of the contract, and he and Frank left.

Increased business activity had made lodgings scarce in the city, but Frank had befriended a man named Aaron Ward, the owner of a dry goods store. Toby and Frank had been using the empty rooms above the store, for which Aaron had so far refused payment. The store was on Dekoven Street, on the west side of the city, with a restaurant conveniently nearby. A short distance away was a stable that rented horses, a business owned by a family named O'Leary.

When Toby and Frank reined up in front of the store, Aaron Ward was supervising the unloading of merchandise from a wagon. A brisk, amiable man in his late twenties, he smiled cheerfully as he waved. "It's good to see you back," he said. "I hope your business worked out well for you."

"It did," Toby replied. "The only trouble I'm having is in getting my landlord to accept rent money for my accommodations. Fair's fair, and you're a businessman, Aaron."

Aaron laughed and shook his head as he turned to go into his store. "I'm not in the hotel business, and I hope the day never comes when I can't do a favor for a friend."

"It's more than a favor, and I hope to repay you sometime," Toby said. "I'll be down to talk with you when I've seen to a few things."

The merchant nodded and waved as he went inside. Frank lifted the packs off the packhorse, then took the reins of all the horses. "I'll return the horses to the stable," he said.

"Very well," Toby replied, gathering up the packs. "I'll go up and get started on those letters to Rob Martin and Edward Blackstone while it's still light. When you get back, we'll have dinner and discuss how to proceed from here. I'll leave the rest in your hands and head on back toward Oregon within the next day or two."

Frank nodded as he led the horses away. Toby carried the packs up the outside staircase to the rooms over the dry goods store. Leaving the packs in the hallway, he went into the front room overlooking the street and took his writing materials out of the luggage that he had left behind.

Sitting down at a small table beside a window, he began writing. But it was difficult for him to concentrate on the letters; already he was eager to return to his home and to those he loved.

Three days after her arrival with her daughter at the Holt ranch, Mary died of consumption. The funeral was a simple affair, attended by Cindy's relatives. Janessa seemed to bear up well, although it was hard to tell what the girl was thinking or feeling. Her resemblance to Toby Holt had already become a topic of discussion on the neighboring farms.

It was also rumored that Cindy Holt was having trouble controlling the girl, but everyone who knew Toby's tall, strong-willed sister dismissed that as idle gossip. Certainly a woman whose temper gave pause to even the rowdiest hands on the Holt ranch could deal with a nine-year-old girl.

Horace Givens had heard all about it from his wife. But nothing was further from his mind as he ran through the predawn darkness toward his house, a cow lowing in pain inside the barn behind him. The cow was one of three prize Jerseys that he had brought in from California at great expense to improve the bloodlines of his dairy herd. It was having extreme difficulty calving, its frantic lowing shattering the early morning quiet.

Horace ran into his house. His wife, in the kitchen, frowned anxiously as he told her about the cow. The calf seemed to be too large, as well as turned the wrong way in the birth canal. They conferred in whispers because their two teenage daughters were in the next room. Suggestive of human sexuality, the breeding of animals and the birth of their young were too indelicate to mention in the presence of girls.

"Go over to the Holt ranch and fetch back Stalking Horse, that Cherokee who's the foreman over there," his wife suggested. "He knows a lot about animals, and they never lose a colt or a mare."

"The Holt ranch is a far piece from here," Horace replied. "The way that cow is taking on, somebody over there might hear her and come to help, but it'd take me too long to get there and back. I think I'll go fetch Cletis Johnson. He's done some doctoring on animals."

"Yes, that's probably best," his wife agreed. "Go on, then, Horace. Hurry, but be careful you don't fall down and hurt yourself in the dark. That cow ain't worth having a broke leg."

Muttering in doubt on that point, Horace ran out of the house. Suddenly he remembered that he had left his lantern burning in the barn, and he glanced back over his shoulder. Then he stopped and looked. In the feeble light of the lantern inside the barn, a silhouetted form seemed to move across the doorway. Dismissing it as a shadow caused by the wind, he decided it would be safe to leave the lantern for a few minutes. He turned and ran.

The loud, wailing lows of the cow echoed across the fields as Horace hurried through the darkness toward the Johnson farm. Then, as he approached the farm, the cow's lowing was drowned by the squealing and cackling of guinea fowl roosting in a tree in front of the house—a far more effective warning of intruders than the most alert watchdog. Their uproar sounded deafening in the quiet as he knocked on the door.

Cletis, a heavyset man with a thick beard and mustache, peered out sleepily, and Horace asked him to come and help. Nodding, he closed the door. A few minutes later he emerged, carrying a lantern and shrugging into his coat. They ran toward Horace's farm, the clamor of the guinea fowl fading behind and the cow's lowing becoming audible again.

As they hurried through the fields, the lantern mak-

ing a bobbing pool of yellow light, Horace explained what
he thought was wrong. Cletis's assessment of the situation
was less than reassuring. "You might be eating some mighty
costly beef," he commented gloomily. "I've never heard of
one being saved when that was the trouble."

"Don't tell me that," Horace groaned. "If you knew
how much that cow cost me, you wouldn't even think it."
He listened, then shook his head. "And she ain't mooing
as loud now. She must be losing her strength."

"She sounds plenty loud to me," Cletis said, puffing
from their run. "She also sounds to me like she's fixing to
calve."

"How could she be?" Horace replied worriedly. "I'm
telling you, she's locked up tighter than a drumhead. That
calf is caught sideways."

Cletis shrugged and fell silent, concentrating on keeping up with the younger man. The first light of dawn was
showing in the eastern sky as they ran past Horace's
house. Panting heavily, they crossed the yard to the barn.
There they froze in astonishment in the doorway.

Illuminated by the lantern that Horace had left behind, the cow was lying on its side in a stall, and a girl was
kneeling behind it. With a burlap bag wrapped around her
to protect her dress, she had an arm in the cow's birth
canal almost up to her shoulder. She had pulled the end of
a rope into the birth canal and was putting a loop around
the calf's forefeet, the traditional way to assist a cow in a
difficult calving.

Horace and Cletis looked at each other in silent amaze-
ment, the scene almost too strange to believe. Then they
looked back at the girl.

"Well, come on," the girl said impatiently. "She was
in such a bad way that I could hear her at the ranch. The
calf is laid right now, but I'm not big enough to pull it out.
Take the rope and get ready to pull."

Horace and Cletis almost stumbled over each other as
they ran forward and knelt behind the girl, taking the end
of the rope. Her lips were pursed in concentration as she
groped inside the cow with the other end of the rope.

Looking at the girl and thinking about her reference

to the ranch, Horace suddenly realized who she was. While she showed no evidence of Indian blood, she was undeniably a Holt. And she was obviously an extremely unusual girl.

"Get ready to pull," Janessa said, nodding in satisfaction. "The rope is on, and I'll guide the head out. It won't be but a minute . . . no, she's starting to squeeze now. Now! Pull! Pull!"

The two men gripped the rope and leaned back against it as the cow tensed and began lowing. The sound became a loud shriek, the cow quivering and the rope sliding out of the birth canal. Janessa winced with effort, her arm coming out with the rope. The forelegs of the calf suddenly emerged, then the head slid out, the girl gripping an ear.

Janessa quickly untied the rope from the calf's forefeet and tossed it aside. "Get ready to pull it on out," she said. "She should begin squeezing again in just a—no, not by the legs! You'll hurt its legs! Pull it out by the shoulders!"

Horace released the calf's legs as the girl shouted, and he and Cletis gripped its shoulders. The cow tensed and began contracting again, lowing hoarsely. Horace and Cletis pulled, and the calf slithered out of the cow and onto the barn floor.

What had threatened to be the certain loss of a valuable cow, Horace reflected numbly, had turned out to be a calving that was somewhat easier than usual. The cow scrambled to its feet and began licking the calf as it moved feebly, both of them perfectly healthy. Nodding in satisfaction, the girl removed the burlap she had wrapped around herself and went to a rain barrel outside the barn door. She dipped water out of the barrel and began washing her hands and arms.

Horace and Cletis exchanged a silent glance and looked back at the girl. Dawn was breaking, the early morning light streaming into the doorway as she methodically dried her hands and arms, then rolled down her sleeves. Her manner suggested that the situation was completely normal, which served to make it that much more extraordinary to Horace.

Janessa stepped back into the barn. "You bred that cow to a bull that was too large," she said. "She's a good, healthy cow, but Jerseys are small."

Horace and Cletis stiffened in shock, their mouths falling open and their bewilderment changing to embarrassment.

"If she has that much trouble calving again," the girl continued, "she might begin casting her calf bed. Then she wouldn't be worth nearly as much as a breeder, would she?"

The girl's casual reference to the possibility of the cow's having a prolapsed womb was too much for Horace. He looked at Cletis in a silent plea to say something. But the older man was examining the rafters in the barn loft, his face crimson.

Horace struggled to think of something to say. "Will you take butter and eggs," he choked, motioning toward the cow and calf, "for—what you did?"

The girl shook her head and shrugged off payment; then she thought again. She looked up at Horace hopefully. "Would you happen to have any extra tobacco and cigarette papers?" she asked.

Vastly relieved to get the girl's mind off the cow, Horace quickly took his tobacco and cigarette papers from his pocket, then pushed them into the girl's hands. He vaguely wondered why she wanted them—then his mouth dropped open again. He watched numbly as the girl separated a cigarette paper with a practiced flip of a thumb and poured tobacco into it.

When she started to return the tobacco and cigarette papers, Horace motioned for her to keep them. "Thank you," she said, pocketing them.

The two men watched in stupefaction as the girl expertly rolled a neat, tight cigarette, her small fingers moving nimbly. She put it between her lips and felt in her pockets. Then she looked up at the men expectantly. Her glance galvanized them into a frantic search for matches. Cletis found one first and struck it with a thumbnail.

His hand trembled as he held the match for the girl to light her cigarette. Then he took out four more and

gave them to her. "Thank you," she said between puffs,
tucking the matches into a pocket. Sighing in satisfaction,
she exhaled smoke through her nose. "Well, good morning to you," she said.

Horace and Cletis stammered a reply as the girl walked
out of the barn and into the early dawn light. They looked
at each other again in stunned silence. Then, on a common impulse, they hurried to the barn door. Standing
there, they gazed in wonder at the small girl as, puffing
contentedly on her cigarette, she walked across the dewy
pastures in the direction of the Holt ranch.

Mount Hood, its snowcapped peak glistening white in
the summer sunshine, was the dominating feature in the
distance at the Holt ranch, and it was a symbol to Toby
that he was home. The large, rambling house, originally
built of logs but converted to a brick-and-clapboard structure during its expansion over the decades, still retained a
rustic appearance. Toby was surprised to see a new addition on one side, and he wondered what it was.

Cindy met him at the door. Although she was smiling
and obviously happy to see him, she appeared to be
somewhat distraught. They embraced and kissed, then
Toby asked about his son, his mother, and his stepfather,
General Leland Blake. When Cindy said they were all
fine, he broached the subject of the addition. "Yes, I have
something to show you," she said. "Come along."

Carrying his luggage, Toby followed her down the
hall to a new door that she threw open. He stepped into
the bathroom and looked around. It seemed more than a
bit pretentious, but he loved his sister deeply and wanted
her to do as she wished in the house. He smiled and
nodded enthusiastically. "This is really pretty, Cindy," he
said.

"It only cost a little over seven hundred dollars," she
blurted.

With an effort, Toby kept from wincing. Seven hundred dollars was a lot of money, particularly when he was
preparing to make an investment in the logging operation.
He nodded again. "It's worth every penny of it, Cindy,

and you're spoiling me with the way you see to everything. If I don't let you get married and keep you here,
you'll only have yourself to blame."

Cindy smiled as she took his bags. "I'll just set these
in your bedroom for now. I'll sort out everything later,"
she said. "There's fresh coffee on the stove."

Her smile was strained, Toby noted. He had thought
that the nervous edge in her manner was concern over the
money she had spent, but it was something else. Then he
noticed a strange, not particularly pleasant odor in the
house. "Something smells different," he said.

"It's herbs and roots," Cindy tossed over her shoulder
as she carried his bags toward his bedroom.

"Herbs and roots? What herbs and roots?"

"Go pour yourself a cup of coffee, and I'll join you in
a minute," she said, going into his bedroom.

While he wanted an immediate answer, he knew that
Cindy would deal with things only in her own way and her
own time. After all, she was a Holt. He went through the
house to the kitchen, where he filled a cup with coffee and
sat down at the table. A few minutes later, Cindy joined
him. Taking a deep breath, she began telling him about
Mary and Janessa.

Sharp, poignant memories of Mary returned to him
across the years as he listened; memories of a beautiful,
loving woman who had filled a central role in his life for a
time and then had sent him on his way. He felt intense
remorse and a sense of guilt. "Cindy, I had no idea that
she was with child," he said. "None whatsoever."

"Of course you didn't," Cindy replied quickly. "Mary
herself told me that neither of you knew when you left."

"The girl must have taken it very hard when her
mother passed away."

Cindy hesitated, then nodded. "Of course," she said.
"But you'd never know it, Toby. She keeps everything
inside her, and the only time you know what she's thinking is when she gets angry."

"She's been a handful, then?"

Cindy nodded ruefully as she began talking about her
attempts to control the child. While the girl never replied

with a point-blank refusal to do anything, she did only what she thought she should. After futile attempts to get her to attend school, Cindy had personally taken her there twice. In both instances the child had been back at the house before Cindy.

The girl also persisted in acting as if she were some kind of "healer." In addition to assisting in a calving at the Givens farm—a scandalous undertaking for a young girl, according to Cindy—she had doctored various ailments among people and animals at a few neighboring farms and ranches. Her room was filled with the roots and herbs that she brought in from the fields, giving the house its strange smell.

"I saw old Jake Higgins yesterday," Cindy said. "Janessa had given him something for his aches and pains, and he said that she knows more than Dr. Martin and Dr. Wizneuski put together."

"If brains were dynamite, old Jake Higgins couldn't blow a mosquito's nose," Toby observed. "But if the girl was trained as a medicine woman, that could be the problem. Some of them spend most of their time with their heads in the clouds, even though Mary wasn't that way."

Cindy shook her head firmly. "Janessa isn't either, because she's practical—too much so for her age. She's also a worker. I haven't been able to wash a dish or scrub a pan in this house since she came. Mama and the general met her at the funeral, and I took her with me when I visited them last week. They're very taken with her."

Toby nodded; they would be, he thought. Major General Leland Blake commanded the Army of the West from his post at Fort Vancouver, across the Columbia River from Portland. He had married Toby's mother several years before, which had been a perfect match for the couple in their autumn years. The general and Toby's mother, Eulalia, were very fond of children.

"And you say she smokes tobacco?" he said.

"I just can't stop her," Cindy replied, nodding. "I tried taking it away from her, but people give her more. There have been so many other things, Toby, that it was coming to the point where I was nagging at her all the time." Cindy's eyes were filling with tears. She pressed her lips together, blinking rapidly and trying to control herself. Then she shook her head. "I'm not going to browbeat that sweet little girl, Toby," she said, her voice breaking. "I know how she must be feeling inside."

"You won't have to, Cindy," Toby said, patting her hand as he picked up his hat and stood up. "I'll talk to her and see if I can't do something with her. Where is she?"

"She'll be out on the ranch somewhere," Cindy replied, stepping to the door with him, "grubbing roots and plants to carry into her room. It seems so strange for a little girl to be doing what she does."

"No, not among Indians," Toby said. "Their medicine women start at an early age." He paused at the door and turned to Cindy. "I'm sorry all this was put on you while I was gone, Cindy."

The young woman sighed. "It wasn't your fault, Toby, but it was a difficult time for me. Watching poor Mary fade away was a torment, and I've been at my wit's end trying to deal with Janessa. But all I want right now is for her to let me love her. That's all I want."

Toby looked at Cindy fondly. She was strong-willed and spirited, as well as stubborn at times, but she was also a very warmhearted woman, and he loved her deeply. Taking her in his arms, he held her close for a moment, then he put on his hat, opened the door, and went out.

Stalking Horse, the Indian who had been foreman ever since Toby's father, Whip Holt, established the ranch, was working near the barns. Looking up and seeing Toby, he waved and began to walk toward him. Well into his sixties, he was wearing dusty boots, denims, and a western hat. He was like aged rawhide, tough and enduring.

Their handshake was the firm, warm grip of old friends. He and Toby talked about the affairs of the ranch for a moment, and then their conversation turned to Janessa. "She certainly knows a lot about herbs," Stalking Horse said. "But she is a quiet girl, and she keeps to herself."

"Yes, Cindy told me more or less the same thing. From what she said, the girl isn't much like a medicine woman."

Stalking Horse shook his head, his leathery face creased in a smile. "She does not even look or act like she is part Indian. No, she is like any little girl you would meet, except that she is very quiet, she knows a lot about herbs, and she has a mind of her own."

"That mind of her own has been giving Cindy some problems, as I guess you know. Do you have any idea where she is?"

Stalking Horse pointed. "In that thicket at the head of the creek. She is cultivating roots, collecting them, and planting them in patches. Do you want a horse to ride over there?"

"No, if she can walk there, I guess I can. Where's Timmy?"

"In the east pasture with his kites," Stalking Horse replied. He chuckled. "He is making his own kites now, and he is doing a good job of it for his age. Josh is over there looking after him."

Toby nodded and walked away as Stalking Horse returned to the barns. Thinking about what the foreman had said, Toby reflected that his son's former enthusiasm for ponies had turned entirely toward kites and mechanical things. But certainly that was not unusual. The boy was still very small, at an age at which it was normal for his interests to change rapidly.

Knowing every inch of the ranch from having explored it as a boy, Toby still took deep pleasure in wandering about on his land. There was a verdant beauty in its rolling hills and copses of trees, and the herds of horses grazing the deep grass gave him a sense of pride. But more than that, this was where his father had planted the family roots. This was home.

The girl was standing at the edge of the thicket at the head of the creek. Small and slender in her dark muslin dress, she had her back to him and was surveying her patch of herbs, several mounded furrows in the damp, cool shade of the trees. Smoke eddied up as she puffed on a cigarette. Hearing his footsteps, she turned.

In that instant, a subtle but profound change occurred in Toby's attitude toward her. Before, she had been the subject of a conversation. She had been an unknown entity, something that had reached out of his past and across the years to touch him in the present.

Now she was very real; she was his daughter. In the first instant that he saw her small, pretty face, he felt deep love for her and intense pride that she was his. It came easily, because she was Holt from the tips of her small shoes to the sandy blond hair on her head.

Her cigarette was so incongruous that he had to stifle an impulse to laugh. He pointed to it. "Put out the cigarette, Janessa," he said.

His tone was brusquer than he had intended, and the neutral, guarded expression in her eyes turned into resentment as she dropped the cigarette and put her foot on it. Realizing that he had made a poor beginning with her, Toby smiled as he spoke again. "I'm your father, Janessa."

"I know who you are," she replied, unsmiling.

Toby hesitated, then smiled again, folding his arms and looking down at her. "We can't have you smoking here, you know."

"You needn't have me here at all," she said woodenly. "You can send me back to Memphis. Or you can give me back my mule and my mother's gun, point out the road, and I'll go there myself."

The girl's large blue eyes were unflinching as she stared up at him, and Toby began to understand the problems Cindy was having with her. He pointed out a ledge of rock along the bank of the creek. "Let's go over there," he said. "We've got off on the wrong foot, so let's sit down and talk."

Her expression still resentful, Janessa nodded. They walked through the deep grass to the flat outcropping of rock. Toby sat down on the edge of the rock next to Janessa as she settled the folds of her long skirt.

"Children and their parents usually don't have to get used to each other," Toby began. "As boys and girls get old enough to notice the world around them, they become accustomed to their parents without realizing it. By the same token, as they develop personalities, their parents gradually get used to them. Does that make sense?"

After thinking for a moment, Janessa nodded. "Yes."

"Now, you and I should already be used to each other, but it's just as though we came around a corner and ran into a total stranger. Each of us is going to have to get used to the other before we can understand each other, but we're going to have to work on it together. Neither of us can do it alone."

Janessa was silent for a moment again. Then she looked up at him, her expression curious. "You think about things a lot, don't you?" she said.

"Sometimes I'd rather chop wood," he replied, laughing. "But I do think when I have to, and I do want us to get along with each other, Janessa."

The girl sighed and looked away again. "I want to get along with you, too, and with the others. But it's so different here, and everything I do is wrong. Maybe it would be better if you just sent me to Memphis."

"No, I'm not going to do that," Toby said. "You're not going anywhere, Janessa. I'm going to keep you right with me."

Janessa almost smiled as she glanced up at him, but then she looked away. "What do I have to do to get along?" she asked.

Toby shrugged. "That's the hard part, because there's no set of rules, as far as I know. It's a matter of treating others the way you want to be treated, and some give and take. For example, others don't like the smell of the herbs that you bring into the house. I have a shed where you can put them, where they won't bother anyone. That way, we both give a little, and everyone will be happier."

"That's all right with me," Janessa said. "I'll move them to the shed when I go back to the house."

There were, Toby reflected, many other things; but it would be better to end for the present on a note of agreement. Her smoking, school, and other matters could be dealt with one by one, in time. Accord would be easier once a solid bridge of love was formed, and for him that bridge was already firmly in place. In spite of, or perhaps because of, her willful disposition, he also intensely admired the small, pretty girl.

"I'll give you a hand with the herbs," Toby said as he stood up. "The shed might need cleaning out, so I'll help you with that as well. And we'll be having a lot more talks like this one, Janessa."

Janessa, unmoving, looked up at him. "Will we always talk only about what you want to? Or sometimes will we talk about what I want to?"

Tugging on his hat brim, Toby looked away. Then he sat back down. "What would you like to talk about, Janessa?"

A long moment of silence followed as Janessa stared down at her hands on her lap. "Do you really want me?" she finally asked softly. "Or are you keeping me just because you think you should?"

As he started to reassure her, Toby thought again. The girl had more self-control than many adults, and he realized that her question had been the bare whisper from an anguished wail deep within her. Suddenly he had a glimpse of the tragically lonely little girl she was. She desperately needed to be wanted.

"I want to keep you," he said, "for two reasons. The first reason is that you're my daughter and I want to have you with me. Now, do you understand that's only the first reason?"

Still staring at her hands, Janessa silently nodded.

"As to the second reason," he continued, putting an arm around the girl and pulling her closer, "during my life, I've seen hundreds of girls of about an age to be my daughter. If I had my pick of all I've ever seen, I'd take you first by so far that the distance couldn't be measured." He leaned down and kissed her forehead. "And that's because I just happen to like you that much better than any other girl I've ever seen."

Janessa's knuckles were white, her hands clenched tightly on her lap. She drew in a deep breath that was almost a sob, and for an instant Toby thought she was going to start crying. Then she pulled away from him and slid off the rock.

Her eyes shone with tears, and her small mouth trembled. She blinked rapidly and lifted her chin. Then she was composed once more. As he stood up, she tentatively put out a hand. Toby took her small hand in his, and she held on tightly as they walked toward the house.

III

Because of Janessa's reserved personality, the immediate visible change in her was slight. Yet also because of her personality, the fact that there was change at all was profoundly significant.

After the roots and herbs had been taken to a shed, Janessa and Cindy prepared dinner while Tim showed Toby his new kite. The girl conversed with Cindy as they worked—something she had never done before—and Cindy was content with that, viewing it as progress.

The solution to the problem of getting Janessa to attend school came the next morning, and from an unexpected quarter.

There was a knock at the front door as the family was finishing breakfast, and Toby went to answer it. The visitor was Dr. Robert Martin, the father of Toby's friend and business associate Rob Martin. One of the travelers on the first wagon train to Oregon, the doctor was in his early seventies and stiff and shrunken with age.

Leaning heavily on his cane, he greeted Toby and followed him into the kitchen. Cindy placed a chair at the table for him and offered him breakfast. He shook his head, blinking nearsightedly at her. "No, thank you, my dear. No breakfast, but I will have a cup of coffee, if it isn't any trouble." He peered around the table, then pointed to the empty space beside Janessa. "And I wonder if I might sit here."

"Certainly, Doctor," Cindy said, moving the chair.
"I'll get your coffee. How is your wife?"

"Quite well, thank you," the doctor replied, stiffly
sitting down and propping his cane against the table.
"More able to get about than I am, but then she's younger. Toby, I trust I haven't called too early in the morning. Don't let me interrupt anything you were doing."

"You're welcome here at any hour, Dr. Martin," Toby
said firmly. "You aren't interrupting anything, and we're
delighted that you called. I don't believe you've met my
daughter Janessa."

Taking spectacles out of his waistcoat pocket, the
doctor shook his head. "No, I haven't, and I must confess
that meeting her is the main reason for my visit." He put
on the spectacles and peered benignly through them at
the girl. "So you're Janessa Holt—and a colleague of mine,
I believe. We have a patient in common, Dr. Janessa—
one Jake Higgins."

There was a momentary silence. Cindy darted an
embarrassed glance at Toby as she put the coffee in front
of the doctor. Janessa, unabashed, nodded placidly. "Yes,
sir. He has rheumatics."

"Indeed he has," the doctor said, chuckling. "On the
more pedantic side of the profession, we refer to it as
rheumatism, but I see that you and I agree on the diagno-
sis. I saw him yesterday, and he told me that your pre-
scription was very effective. Could I ask what it was?"

"Infusion of jopi weed."

The doctor's smile became thoughtful. Lifting his eyebrows, he said, "And if there had been swelling present?"

"A poultice of dried blue lupine in goose grease."

The old man pursed his lips, nodded, and sat back in
his chair. "There are various treatments for rheumatism,"
he said to Toby. "Dr. Janessa has just named two of the
principal ones from the official pharmacopoeia. *Eupato-
rium purpureum*, or jopi weed, to be taken internally.
And in the event that swelling is present, *Themopsis
rhombifolia*, or blue lupine, is to be applied externally."
He looked back at Janessa. "I take it that your dear late
mother instructed you on herbs?"

"Yes, sir," Janessa replied. "But she always told me that doctors knew a lot more about healing people than she did."

"Did she, now?" The doctor chuckled. "That's an unusual thing for an herbal healer to say. She must have been an unusual woman. And I must say that you're an unusual girl." He took a sip of his coffee. "I understand you've been away, Toby."

Toby nodded and began telling the doctor about his trip and the fact that he had invited the doctor's son to invest in the logging venture. Rob Martin had been partners with Toby in a gold mine in Dakota, which had since become unprofitable and been closed. The old man sipped his coffee and listened, but Toby could see that he was only being polite; he couldn't be less interested in the trip and in his son's investments. His faded blue eyes kept moving back to Janessa as he studied her curiously. The girl returned his gaze. Toby noted that she had addressed the doctor with great respect.

Presently, Dr. Martin took a final sip of coffee and put down the cup. "That's very interesting, Toby," he said. "I trust that it will work out well for you and Rob." He turned to Janessa and smiled. "Would you like to come with me and see my surgery, Dr. Janessa?"

"Yes, sir," she replied eagerly.

It was the most interest that Toby had seen the girl display about anything. He nodded when the doctor glanced at him questioningly. "It's fine with me, Dr. Martin," he said. "But I don't want Janessa to be any trouble to you or to interrupt your work."

"No need to worry about that," the doctor said, taking his cane and getting stiffly to his feet. "When you're as old as I am, Toby, you'll find that the aged are trouble to the young, not the other way around. As far as work goes, I let Anton Wizneuski and the younger fellows in Portland do most of it now. Come along, Dr. Janessa."

Toby followed the old man and the girl through the house and watched as they climbed into the doctor's buggy, Janessa helping the doctor in. Toby noted with satisfaction that the girl took the reins, which would be far safer for both her and Dr. Martin. It was a standing joke that the doctor's buggy was a moving hazard, the horse always plodding along on the wrong side of the street and the old man frequently asleep in the seat.

Indeed, as soon as the buggy began moving along the road, the doctor felt drowsy. It was an automatic reaction. During his working years, he had done much of his sleeping while returning through the night from delivering a baby or calling on a critically ill patient.

But his drowsiness passed, his conversation with the girl keeping him awake. She made him regret that he had no daughter, for in addition to being pretty, she had an exceptionally keen mind. When the superstitious nonsense that she had learned was weeded out from the rest, the child was a walking encyclopedia of herbal medicine.

A train of thought also kept him awake. His visit to the Holt ranch had been out of curiosity and suspicion that he was the victim of one of Jake Higgins's tall tales—this one about a miracle rheumatism cure that a girl had provided in exchange for tobacco and cigarette papers. Then, upon meeting the girl, he had found what was possibly a long-awaited opportunity.

One of the responsibilities of a physician was to pass along knowledge and experience so it could continue to be of benefit. His son had chosen a path other than medicine—which was best if he had no penchant for it. Dr. Martin believed that too many entered the profession solely to earn a living and that it would be better in all respects if they had chosen law or carpentry instead.

The girl had more than a penchant. It was a unique talent that he had never before seen. Like a tangible force, her vast potential seemed to be exploding out of her, searching thirstily for fulfillment. To go with it she had a precocious maturity, a reserved personality, and a brilliant mind. She was perfect.

Others had been either dullards or those seeking only a livelihood; *she* was the one for whom he had been searching. But there were two problems. The first was a difficult one: He would have to live another ten or twelve years to see her on her way, which was a doubtful proposition. The second appeared insurmountable: She was a girl, and as far as he knew, the accredited medical colleges accepted only men.

Arriving at his house, a neat, comfortable brick dwelling on a quiet residential street, Dr. Martin led the girl up the walk toward the door. His office and surgery were in the front rooms, the living quarters in the rear, and a sign on a post in the front yard gave his name, with the symbol of the medical profession above it.

"It's called a caduceus," he offered, when Janessa stopped and gazed at the sign. "Two snakes entwined around the winged staff of a messenger. It goes back to the days of the Greeks."

"I know what it is, sir," Janessa replied as they walked on along the path, a trace of asperity in her tone.

When they went inside, Tonie Martin came along the hall from the rear of the house. Her hair, tied in a neat bun, was snow white, and her face was wrinkled, but her step remained light, and her radiant personality made her more vital and beautiful to the doctor than she had been the first day he met her.

He introduced Janessa, and Tonie greeted her with warm affection. After expressing sympathy over the death of the girl's mother, Tonie adeptly changed the subject, smilingly clicking her tongue in disapproval as she continued, "But I've heard that you've been giving Cindy some trouble about going to school. You should mind what Cindy says, my dear."

"Yes, ma'am," the girl replied. "But school is a waste of time."

The blunt statement took Tonie aback, leaving her without a ready response. The doctor laughed heartily. "Dr. Janessa is a Holt, Tonie," he said. "And you know how the Holts are. That isn't always bad, though, because we wouldn't be here if Whip Holt had listened to those who told him that a wagon train couldn't make it through the wilderness to Oregon."

Tonie laughed and nodded in agreement. She invited Janessa to stay for lunch, then went back along the hall toward the living quarters as the doctor took Janessa into his surgery.

As the old man opened the door, a new and wonderfully exciting world opened up around Janessa. An examination table occupied the center of the room, and the walls were covered with shelves and cabinets that contained a vast array of instruments and preparations. She was unable to turn and look around rapidly enough; everything seemed to draw her gaze at once.

Dr. Martin began leading her around and explaining the uses of various things, and Janessa listened in rapt fascination. From what her mother had told her about doctors, she knew she had found her way into an inner sanctum that contained the vital secrets of the universe. The proof was before her eyes as the doctor pointed to drawer after drawer of instruments and talked about procedures that the most adventurous herbal healer would never even contemplate.

The pungent odors of the medicines were like sweet perfume to her, and the polished instruments had a more alluring gleam than gold. An hour or perhaps even two later—Janessa had lost track of the time—the doctor was called away to talk with a man about repairs to the roof. Janessa continued looking around and went through the next door into the office, where shelves filled with books lined the walls. Taking down a thick tome at random, she put it on the edge of the desk and opened it. Before her was an illustration of all the bones in the human body. Yet another new world had opened up for her.

To Janessa, setting a broken arm or leg had always been a nightmare of trying to fumble a bone back into its natural configuration without a precise knowledge of that configuration. But these drawings showed everything clearly. On the following pages were enlarged, detailed illustrations of individual bones. Then there were illustrations of the organs, muscles, blood vessels, and other things she did not even recognize.

The doctor, returning while the girl was poring over the book, was pleased; he saw a perfect opportunity to make an essential point. Sitting down in the chair behind the desk, he reached over and tapped the explanatory text beside an illustration. "There's the important part, Dr. Janessa," he said. "Read that aloud."

The girl studied the text, then slowly shook her head. "I can read some, but I can't read that."

"Then you'll have to go to school to learn how, won't you?"

"I tried in Memphis, and it was a waste of time. It didn't take very long for my mother to teach me to read, write, and calculate some."

The doctor reflected that it was not easy to sway the mind of a Holt. "Dr. Janessa," he said, "your problem was that you needed to be let fly, not made to crawl with other children. The principal of the school here is a patient of mine, and I'll arrange for you to be advanced as rapidly as you can absorb the instruction. You should be finished and ready for college when you're fifteen or so."

As the girl pondered what he had said, he opened a desk drawer and took out a cigar. Rooting in her pockets, Janessa took out tobacco and cigarette papers. Then she looked at him for a reaction.

Dr. Martin sighed. He knew that Toby would disapprove, but the girl, he decided, belonged to humanity more than she did to Toby Holt.

He moved the ashtray closer to her and placed a match beside it for her. The keystone of the relationship between the aged man and the young girl had fallen into place; a bond of compromise and of mutual respect and trust had been formed. The doctor struck a match and lit his cigar as Janessa rolled a cigarette and lit it.

Exhaling smoke through her nostrils, Janessa picked a shred of tobacco off her tongue. "May I come here after school?" she asked.

"Yes, of course," the doctor agreed quickly. "I want you to do that so we can look through books and talk. The school isn't far from here, so you can put your horse in my stable. I'll go with you tomorrow morning to talk with the principal about you."

"Thank you."

"I want to do it. Bring the book over here."

The girl moved the anatomy book and stood beside his chair as they turned the pages, discussing the illustrations. She had an eager mind, quickly grasping explanations. The more he learned about her, the more perfect she seemed for him to sponsor in the profession.

At the same time, he wondered if he was overreaching his grasp. He wondered if wishful thinking was leading an aged mind into senile foolishness. Envisioning a medical doctor in a small child was absurd. And the problems of his age and her sex remained.

It was during lunch that a possible solution to the thorniest of the two problems occurred to him. Tonic's social talents were even up to drawing out the reserved Janessa in conversation and getting her to talk about Memphis. Listening to them absently, the doctor suddenly remembered a man to whom he had lent money to attend medical college.

The man's name evaded him—Hendon? Hinton? Swindon?—but he had written several times. He was instructing at the medical college in Providence, Rhode Island, and had mentioned that he believed he would be made dean of medicine within a few years. The college required a liberal arts degree for admission, which the girl would have when she was about nineteen, and the school was one of the best in the nation.

The man's letters had always mentioned the loan with gratitude. Dr. Martin decided to find the letters and to write back, just to keep in contact. Then, when the time came, he could demand a favor in return for the loan. The girl had the right personality to bear the ridicule that she would have to endure. And if the ivy on the venerable portals of Providence Medical College wilted somewhat from having gingham among the pinstripes passing through them, then so be it.

During the afternoon, he had reason to believe that the problem of his age was less of an obstacle than he had at first thought. Ordinarily, he slept after lunch, but that afternoon he felt wide awake and alert as he and Janessa thumbed through books and talked. The noxious fumes from the cheap tobacco the girl smoked made him cough occasionally, and he resolved to buy her some better tobacco at the first opportunity. But other than that, he felt better and more energetic than he had in years.

He knew the reason. Since he had curtailed his practice, he had only a few patients and nothing to interest him. He had been creeping down an incline toward a grave. Now he had something in life to occupy his thoughts and to energize him.

The idea became a goal in his mind; the wish turned into determination. His own race finished, he decided to try to survive long enough to see her through her preparations, then to give her what advice and encouragement he could to sustain her during her own long, hard run. When that was done, his responsibility to his profession would be fulfilled.

The idea occurred to the girl, too. Dusting cigarette ashes off the open page in front of her, she suddenly looked at him and broached the subject. "Sir, could I be a doctor like you?"

"I don't know whether you could or not, Dr. Janessa. But I believe that I could give you a *chance* to be a medical doctor."

"That's all I need," she said quietly, puffing on her cigarette and turning a page in the book. "If I have a chance, then I'm going to be a doctor."

When Dr. Martin brought Janessa back to the ranch, Toby and Cindy immediately noticed the change in the doctor. While he was weary from his active afternoon, something of his young companion's vitality seemed to have been communicated to him. He appeared more fit than he had in years, with more color in his wrinkled face, a lighter step, and a more vibrant voice.

The friendship that had developed between the old man and young girl was obvious, as was the professional interest that the doctor had taken in Janessa. It came as a pleasant surprise when Toby and Cindy learned that the girl was now eager to attend school, and Toby promptly agreed to allow her to visit with the doctor every day after school.

The doctor also mentioned that he would like to have Janessa come to his house the next day so that he could escort her to school. "I'll talk with the principal about her tomorrow," he said. "We want to make certain that she's placed in the correct form and advanced according to her ability."

"It's very good of you to help her, Dr. Martin," Toby replied, "but certainly that will be a lot of trouble for you."

The doctor smiled. "No, it won't be any trouble at all, Toby. My house is near the school, so it'll be convenient for her to leave her horse in my stable."

With a sudden flash of insight, Toby perceived that the old man had little to occupy his mind and time, and now he had found something to do. Agreeing to allow Janessa to go to the doctor's house before school, he thanked the old man again for his interest. Dr. Martin shrugged off the thanks, made his farewells, and left.

The problems with Janessa seemed to be melting away. While the girl would never be outgoing, she conversed with Cindy far more than before while they were preparing the evening meal and cleaning up afterward. But when she came to kiss Toby good-night, the girl reeked of tobacco. That problem would be difficult to resolve, he reflected.

Early the next morning, Janessa left for school on a gentle mare. Toby and Cindy decided to visit their mother and General Blake, so after Toby had helped move a herd of horses from a pasture that had been overgrazed, he saddled a mare and gelding and led them to the house. With Tim behind his saddle, Toby rode with Cindy into Portland to take the ferry across the river to Fort Vancouver.

The city of Portland, astride the Willamette River and nestled against the backdrop of the Cascade Range, seemed to have grown each time Toby returned, after even a short absence. The docks teemed with activity, cargo lighters plying between them and ships anchored out in the river. At the ferry terminal, Toby paid their fares and handed the horses over to a deckhand to take below as the passen-

gers finished loading for the trip across the Columbia
River.

At Tim's insistence, the three of them took a place at
the rail. Cindy was pensive as she stared across the river,
and Toby knew why. She was engaged to a young man
whom their mother and the general had adopted, Hank
Blake. As he thought about the name, Toby automatically
corrected himself: *Henry* Blake, which the young man
preferred to be called now that he was an army officer.
But most people, except for Cindy, still referred to him as
Hank.

The wedding was supposed to have taken place after
Henry's graduation from West Point, a few months before;
but the new second lieutenant had been assigned to a
special mission in Europe with Colonel Andrew Brentwood,
whose family had long-standing associations with the Blakes
and the Holts.

Toby knew Cindy was hoping, as she did each time
she visited Fort Vancouver, that General Blake would
know of developments that might bring Henry home.
"Penny for your thoughts," he said, as the ferry pulled
away from the pier.

Cindy flashed him a quick smile, then shook her
head. "They're worth far more than that, Toby. Do you
think Papa will have any news this time?"

"It's hard to say, Cindy. It hasn't been very long since
you visited them with Janessa."

"Yes, but dispatches can come in from Washington at
any time, can't they?" she said. Sighing, she pulled Tim
back from leaning over the rail. "Well, I hope he's had
some news."

"So do I, Cindy. Perhaps he has."

His words expressed more optimism than he felt. The
reason Henry Blake was in Europe was rooted in the fact
that the German states had recently been unified into the
German Empire under Wilhelm I. That had constituted a
major shift in the world balance of power, and Washington
had been turning its attention outward as the United
States gained in prominence as a first-rank power. To
obtain information about the combined German armies,

Washington had assigned additional personnel to the military attaché section of the American embassy in Berlin—among them Colonel Andrew Brentwood and Henry Blake.

With Germany and France now at war, however, and the German armies crushing the French and presently besieging Paris, Henry and the colonel had been sent as observers with the German forces surrounding Paris. Months had passed. The Germans were unwilling to destroy the city, and the French still showed no indication of surrendering. Toby knew there was no chance that Henry would come home before that situation changed.

Cargo lighters veered away from the long, bulky ferry as it foamed its way across the main river channel after passing between Hayden and Tomahawk islands. Its whistle hooted as the landing slip on the opposite shore drew near. The ferry nosed into place, and the gates opened. People, horses, and wagons flowed off it, then those waiting to go to the other side of the river filed on board.

Toby retrieved the horses and helped Cindy mount. Then he picked up Tim and climbed lightly into the saddle of his own horse.

A few minutes later, they were approaching the large, comfortable house that was provided at Fort Vancouver for the commander of the Army of the West. Their mother came out the front door to greet them as Toby and Cindy dismounted and tethered their horses. In her early fifties, she retained the beauty that had once drawn young men from distant cities to her father's plantation in South Carolina.

Eulalia embraced Cindy and Toby, then picked up Tim and carried him into the house, making the boy squeal with glee as she bounced him in her arms. "Where is little Janessa?" she asked over her shoulder. "Why didn't you bring her with you?"

"She's in school," Cindy replied. "Mama, has Papa learned of anything that could mean Henry might be coming home soon?"

"No, I'm sorry, he hasn't," Eulalia said, stopping and smiling sympathetically at her daughter. "And I'm also sorry I made you ask. I should have thought to tell you."

Cindy sighed in disappointment. "I suppose I'm like someone asking the time every five minutes. It's only been a few months, but it seems as though he's been gone forever."

"I know, Cindy," Eulalia said, patting her shoulder. "But you'll have to get used to that, dear. Army wives spend much of their time waiting for their men to come home." She turned. "Come, we'll sit on the back porch. I'll send someone to tell Lee you're here. He's probably looking for an excuse to get out of his office."

Toby and Cindy followed their mother through the large house, which approached being luxurious in its tasteful furnishings and decorations. It had a small staff and guest quarters for visiting senior officers. Eulalia paused in the hallway to glance into a room and tell an orderly to go and inform the general that Toby and Cindy had come over from Portland; then they went out onto the back porch.

Over the years, the military post of Fort Vancouver had gradually spread outside the log walls of the old fort originally built by the British. The quarters for officers were on a small rise nearby, and there was a pleasant view of the river from the cool, shady back porch of the general's house.

As they sat down around a wrought-iron lawn table, Cindy told Eulalia about Dr. Martin's interest in Janessa and how the girl was becoming much more manageable. "Words won't express how pleased I am about the change in her, Mama, because I do want us to be close. It's easy to be fond of her."

"Indeed it is," Eulalia agreed emphatically. "I've never seen a more adorable child in my life. I'm delighted that she's becoming easier for you to deal with, but I must say that I could understand it if she was totally uncontrollable, considering what she's been through." She turned to Toby. "I realize that you didn't knowingly leave that poor woman with a child, Toby, but still it does you little credit."

The words were in a light tone and accompanied by a smile; but it was a reminder that he had temporarily abandoned the principles that she and his father, Whip

Holt, had instilled into him during his formative years. "I
know that as well as you do, Mama," he said. "I'm only
thankful that we have Janessa with us now so we can love
her and care for her."

"As I am," his mother replied, smiling warmly as she
reached over to pat his hand. "And I'm sure you would
have gone to the ends of the earth to claim that child if
you'd known about her, Toby. But now we have her with
us, and she'll enrich our lives at least as much as we will
hers." She turned, listening. "I believe I hear Lee."

A moment later the general opened the door and
stepped out onto the porch. He was in his late sixties, his
hair snowy and his tanned face creased deeply with age,
but he remained a healthy, active man, tall and spare in
his neat uniform with twin stars on the shoulders. After
greeting Cindy and Toby warmly, he picked up Tim and
placed the boy on his lap as he sat down at the table.

"The flag isn't down the staff yet," Eulalia said, stepping toward the door, "so we'll have lemonade for refresh-
ment. If you can stay until later, Toby and Cindy, we'll
have some of the California wine that General Cummings
at the Presidio kindly sent to us."

She went inside, Cindy following her to help with the
lemonade. Lee Blake asked Toby about his recent trip,
and Toby enthusiastically described the Wisconsin forests
and the countless millions of board feet of timber that he
had seen. Then he explained the plans that he and Frank
Woods had made. He also told the general about his plan
to send lumber to the plains.

"That was one of the benefits I envisioned when I was
surveying routes and maintaining order while the railroads
were being built," Toby continued. "In the interest of making the nation more united, the resources from every
region should be made available to all."

"Yes, we have that potential now," the general agreed.
"But it's possible only because people like you make it
possible, Toby. What did you think of Chicago?"

The women had come back out with glasses and a
pitcher on a tray, and Cindy poured the lemonade. She

handed Toby a tall, frosty glass, and he took a sip before he replied.

"In a way it's a picture of the nation as a whole," he said. "It's growing by leaps and bounds, and there's activity at all hours of the day and night. But a lot of the buildings are made of pine and crowded together, and streets are paved with pine blocks. Until those buildings are replaced with more permanent stone or brick structures, fire will be a danger."

"Yes, particularly during dry weather," Lee Blake commented. "Rapid growth can bring growing pains and problems in cities as well as in children. Let's hope that problem can be overcome quickly." He turned to Cindy. "I'm sorry I don't have anything encouraging to tell you about Hank, Cindy. But there's been no change in the situation over there."

"That's what Mama told me," Cindy sighed. "I do wish we could have been married before he left, but I know that Henry's duty comes first."

Eulalia smiled as she sipped her lemonade. "I'm gratified to hear you say that, Cindy," she remarked, "because it lets me know that I haven't failed entirely as a mother. We have ourselves to think about, but we must also be prepared to make sacrifices."

"It's a good assignment for him," Toby said. "It amounts to an intelligence mission that must be carried out with discretion."

"The utmost discretion," the general agreed emphatically. "The secretary of state and the secretary of war need to know everything possible about the situation there and the German forces. Our military attaché personnel are accorded diplomatic status by the host nation, but if they engage in traditional espionage techniques, such as recruiting agents, they'll be ordered out of the country."

Toby smiled wryly. "That certainly limits the information they can obtain," he observed. "But I'm sure that Hank and Andy Brentwood will do the best possible job."

"Yes, and they'll be back as quickly as possible," Eulalia added, speaking to Cindy. "We all realize how you feel, dear, but you know that you have us to love you and to keep you company while Henry is gone. You had a daguerreotype made to send to him, didn't you?"

"Yes," Cindy replied. She sighed heavily as she looked out from the porch. Below the rise on which the house stood, the bright afternoon sunlight beamed down on the broad surface of the Columbia River and the dense copses of trees along its banks. "I do hope it pleases him. . . ."

Second Lieutenant Henry Blake adored the daguerreotype, which stood in a prominent spot on the desk that almost filled his cubbyhole office. Not only was it a photograph of the beautiful young woman whom he had loved for years, it was also a breath of home, evocative of the known and familiar while he endured surroundings that were alien to him.

The sausage and brioches he had eaten for dinner had been tasty, but they were unlike the ham and bread of home. Outside his window he heard a babel of foreign tongues as people passed by. The detachment from the military attaché section of the American embassy in Berlin was in the village of Vittel, three miles outside the German lines surrounding Paris. Manned by two officers and five enlisted men, the detachment was housed in a small cottage, with offices on the first floor and living quarters upstairs.

The cottage faced the main road through the village, which was also a connecting road between the German lines and rear area supply depots. Military attaché personnel and journalists from many nations occupied houses in the village, the German command staff having provided all the necessary facilities. These included a telegraph office that the detachment used to exchange coded messages with the embassy in Berlin.

Supply wagons and caissons trundled past the cottage at all hours, as did horse and foot traffic. Cafés established in the village by enterprising Germans were open around the clock. They were centers of noise and activity as journalists and military officers ate, drank, and chatted in a mixture of languages.

It was a bustling, exciting scene, at the focal point of

history in the making. Henry Blake was also acutely aware of his responsible position, charged as he was with the duty of obtaining information of vital importance to his nation. But in quiet moments he sometimes longed for more familiar sights, especially the woman he loved.

A corporal knocked on the doorjamb and stepped into the office, saluting. "The colonel would like to speak with you, sir," the man said as Henry returned the salute.

Henry nodded, straightening his tunic as he stood up and followed the corporal out. The front room of the cottage, with white plaster walls and thick beams crossing the low ceiling, was provided with several small tables at which the sergeant and the corporals worked. They were all decorated career soldiers of the most sober, trustworthy character. Henry stepped across the room to the colonel's office and rapped on the doorjamb.

At thirty-two years of age, Colonel Andrew Jackson Brentwood was one of the youngest officers of his rank in the United States Army. Dark-haired and with strong, chiseled features, he had the decisive manner of the professional military officer, mixed with a polished urbanity. "Come in and sit down, Henry," he said. "I've just been reading your report on your last conversation with this Captain Richard Kochler. It's very interesting. Apparently you're becoming good friends with him."

"Yes, sir," Henry replied, sitting on the chair beside the desk. "We get along fine. He has a lot of fun finding officers who think they're marksmen and challenging them to a shooting match with me."

The colonel chuckled dryly; Henry's prowess as a marksman was well known. "I'm sure you have very little trouble convincing them that they're not as good as they thought," he observed.

Henry smiled and nodded. "I don't have any trouble beating them with my service pistol. But if we use rifles, I have to borrow a Mauser."

"Yes, that was a very good report you wrote on the Mauser rifle, Henry. You think it's that much better than ours, then?"

"Yes, sir. I don't know why, except that it must be in

the manufacturing process. But their standard issue military weapon is the equal of the best handmade sporting rifle manufactured in the United States."

"Needless to say, if you ever hear anything about the Mauser manufacturing process, take due note of it," the colonel said, looking back down at the report. "Is Captain Koehler quartered in Thieux by any chance?"

"No, sir. He's quartered in the cantonment area."

"Yes, I thought he would be." Andrew frowned. "That's too bad, because I'd like for us to have some reasonable excuse to visit Thieux, where the senior German officers are quartered. We need to find out how the Saxons, Prussians, and so forth actually get along with each other. Also, we need to know if there's friction between the infantry, artillery, and cavalry. Any scrap of information such as who the dinner companions are among the senior officers would tell us a lot, but we can't just go to Thieux and wander around." He reached for a sheet of paper and handed it to Henry. "And that's why. We received that dispatch from the embassy today."

Henry read the dispatch, which one of the enlisted men had decoded in pencil. It was terse and to the point: Three Russian military observers had been ordered to leave the country because of activities inconsistent with their diplomatic status. The communication also amounted to a further message that was unwritten: Be careful.

"They must have tried to bribe someone," Henry commented, handing the paper back. "That makes seven Russians who've been ordered to leave since we came. They should get the point sooner or later."

"Yes, that's right," the colonel agreed. "They were doing more than snooping around in Thieux, of course, but we want our relations with the Germans to remain completely cordial. Above all, we must be very circumspect in what we do." He handed another sheet of paper to Henry. "That also came in from the embassy today."

The subject of the second dispatch was communications procedures. Dispatches from the detachment were transmitted onward to Washington from the embassy, usually with added comments or other information. The military attaché functioned as both a military affairs specialist and a staff member of the embassy, so his dispatches were sent simultaneously to the secretary of war and to the secretary of state.

The dispatch directed that if information of a vital nature was obtained whose value to Washington would be jeopardized by the delay of sending it through the embassy, the detachment would transmit it directly to Washington. Rereading the dispatch, Henry was puzzled. The same instructions were contained in one of the detachment operating procedures that had been prepared by the military attaché staff at the embassy.

Henry commented on that fact as he handed the message back. Andrew put the message aside. "Yes, it's only a reminder," he said. "What they're actually telling us is that if we find out when the French are going to surrender, we're to inform Washington directly instead of wasting time by going through the embassy channels."

"But that would take only a few hours, sir."

"That's a few hours too long. There are diplomatic initiatives and many other things being held in abeyance in Washington, pending the outcome of hostilities here. The first minute that Washington knows that the situation here is changing, any number of actions that are being held up will be put in motion on a priority basis."

"Yes, I see," Henry said. "And if we had the information before the British, Dutch, Spanish, and others, that would give us a head start on them. But I don't see how the embassy thinks we could find out."

The colonel sat back in his chair and shrugged. "We've had a stalemate here for months. I would think that when the Germans find out the French intend to surrender, the activities of the senior officers should be revealing. But the fact that some German generals are happy will hardly be conclusive evidence about anything." He chuckled wryly. "And I *don't* think it would be a good idea to send dispatches to the secretary of war or to the secretary of state without being absolutely certain that all our facts are correct."

"No, sir," Henry agreed. "I'd like to see Cindy again

as soon as possible, but getting kicked back home isn't the
way I want to go about it. In any event, the negotiations
between the French and the Germans are being carried
on at the foreign ministry level, aren't they?"

"Yes," Andrew replied, then laughed heartily. "The
way things are now, we can't even find out which German
generals are dining together, never mind what the foreign
ministries are up to."

Henry laughed too. "You're right, sir. I don't believe
we'll find out anything that they don't want us to, unless
we have an amazing stroke of luck."

IV

A few fleecy clouds made slowly moving shadows on the landscape in the bright forenoon sunlight as Second Lieutenant Henry Blake and Captain Richard Koehler stood and talked. The skyline of Paris filled the horizon, while in the foreground were the trenches occupied by Captain Koehler's infantry company. Off to the right and left were other infantry companies that were links in the solid chain of German military forces surrounding Paris.

The bivouac areas for the infantry companies, rows of tents, were set back from the trenches. Much farther back, and at wide intervals, were the clustered, upraised cannon barrels of the artillery emplacements. The terrain was farmland, with the remains of stone fences, ruined houses, and orchards scattered here and there.

In contrast to the martial appearance of the scene, the atmosphere was relaxed and cheerful. Women camp followers laughed shrilly as they bargained with off-duty soldiers in the tents behind Henry and the German officer. The soldiers in the trenches were gathered in clusters to laugh and talk. For months, the Parisians had been waiting inside the city while the Germans had been waiting outside.

Captain Richard Koehler was explaining the German strategy to Henry, as he had done before. Their objectives were to force Paris to capitulate and to install a new, friendly government, not to destroy the city. "We could march in and take it within a day, Heinrich," the captain said. "But what soldier wants to kill civilians?"

"I wouldn't want to be in such a battle," Henry commented.

"Nor would I," Richard agreed emphatically. "Or we could bombard the city until they flee. But we have no desire to turn Paris into rubble. The people of Paris are only being stubborn."

"They are probably also hungry by now," Henry observed.

Richard laughed. "More than probably, my friend. I heard from a reliable source that they have eaten all the animals in the zoo and they are catching rats along the Seine."

Making a mental note of the remark, Henry reflected that it was either gossip or it indicated that the Germans had informants inside Paris. If other comments could be gleaned that supported the latter view, the subject would make a report that would be well received at the embassy.

The captain, an affable, muscular man of thirty, continued talking. His uniform was that of the Prussian dragoons: a gleaming spiked helmet, a pale blue tunic with white facings, and shiny knee boots. Henry wore a plainer, dark blue uniform, with contrasting stripes down the seams of his trousers, a diagonal belt across the chest and one around the waist, and a campaign cap.

Taking out his watch and looking at it, Richard changed the subject. "My widowed aunt, the Baroness von Kirchberg, has recently arrived here from Saarbrücken. She wished to see the lines, so she said she would bring a lunch and visit me today. You must stay and eat with us."

"No, certainly not," Henry said. "I wouldn't think of intruding upon your visit with your relative."

"Heinrich, you must stay," Richard insisted. "The baroness is my relative, but she is not one of whom I am particularly fond. However, she will bring good food, and there will be more than enough."

Deciding that the young man was being sincere rather than merely polite, Henry nodded. "Thank you, and I'll look forward to meeting your aunt. I wasn't aware that your family has a title, Richard."

"We don't," the captain replied. "She is my father's sister, and she married the Baron von Kirchberg, who died a few years ago. Perhaps she poisoned him. She has little fondness for men, and she . . ." His voice faded as he looked toward the city. He pointed. "I see the French are taking another look at us."

A hot-air balloon was rising above the skyline of trees and buildings. Henry was barely able to see the man in the gondola under the expanse of the balloon. As it continued rising, he saw that it was not on a cable, as the occasional observation balloons were; it was floating free. "No, he's taking a trip, not a look," Henry said.

Richard smiled and nodded. "Either he broke his cable or he's a very brave man."

The wind began catching the balloon as it continued rising, sweeping it directly toward Henry and the German officer. By now Henry could see the man in the gondola; he was stuffing straw into the fire basket in a desperate effort to increase the heat and climb more rapidly.

Then a movement on the edge of Henry's vision caught his attention. At a distance and to one side was the regimental headquarters of the infantry companies in the immediate area. It consisted of a cluster of tents, with poles for signal flags in front of them. Flags were fluttering up the poles, signaling the captain's company to open fire.

The noncommissioned officers in the trenches, also seeing the flags, began bellowing orders. The soldiers scrambled to their positions, taking up their weapons. Then the sergeants looked at the captain, who continued to watch the balloon.

Regretfully, Henry spoke up. "Richard, your regiment is ordering you to open fire."

"They are?" the captain replied in a bemused tone, his eyes on the balloon. "No, you must be wrong, Heinrich. I see no such signal."

Henry smiled in understanding, and the captain chuckled. The balloon continued rising rapidly as it approached. The soldiers in the trenches waited and watched the captain as he watched the balloon. When it was directly over the trenches, it was a tiny dot high in the sky.

The captain turned and looked toward the headquarters tents. "Heinrich, my regiment has ordered me to open fire," he announced gravely. Cupping his hands around his mouth, he shouted a command to open fire.

The sergeants repeated the order, and the troops began firing. As the rifles crackled, the sergeants looked at the captain and waited for the order to cease fire, for by now the balloon was hopelessly out of range. After a moment, Richard shouted the order. The rifles stopped firing, and the balloon continued to rise and drift away, unharmed.

A man came into view, running toward the trenches from the regimental headquarters. Henry pointed to him. "I believe your colonel has sent someone to invite you to come and talk with him."

"Yes, I believe so." The captain chuckled wryly. Taking out his watch, he looked at it. "He's given to being long-winded when he's angry, and it's almost time for my aunt to arrive. Would you make my excuses to her and entertain her until I return?"

"Certainly," Henry replied; then he laughed. "I'd rather entertain your aunt than attend your meeting with your colonel for you."

Richard chuckled ruefully. "Yes, I don't blame you. But if a man is brave enough to soar up to the clouds on some rags with a straw fire under them, I won't shoot him down." Sighing in resignation, the captain began dusting his tunic in preparation to report to his colonel.

The messenger from regimental headquarters, a lieutenant, approached. He exchanged salutes with the captain, relating the colonel's order to report to him immediately. Richard exchanged salutes with Henry and walked away, smiling.

Watching the two men depart, Henry knew that the incident would make a good report to forward to the embassy. It was an example of flagrant disobedience of orders, which reflected on the morale and discipline of the

German forces. Liking the captain, he almost regretted the point of view that his duties required him to take.

At the same time, he wondered if the German officer had a similar point of view. It had been remarkably easy to form an acquaintance and then friendship with Captain Richard Koehler. There was at least a possibility that the captain had been ordered to watch him—which, in any case, still allowed latitude for friendship. They both simply had their duties.

The two German officers had been gone for only a few minutes when Henry heard the rumble of a carriage and the jangle of harnesses. A large, expensive landau drawn by a matched pair of spirited bays was approaching along the road through the bivouac area.

As the carriage stopped, the window in the door slid down. Henry stepped up to it. Inside was a woman wearing a gown and an elegant matching hat made of costly green brocade, with a heavy green veil concealing her face. Henry touched his cap and bowed. "Baroness von Kirchberg? I am Lieutenant Henry Blake," he said. "Captain Koehler asked me to convey his regrets, but he was summoned by his colonel. He should return presently."

The woman was motionless and silent for a few seconds. Then she unlatched the door and pushed it open. Henry stepped forward to help her down from the carriage. Ignoring his outstretched hand, she gathered her full, heavy skirt to one side with a green-gloved hand and stepped nimbly down. Still ignoring Henry, she looked around at the trenches and tents as she lifted her veil and tucked it up on her wide hat.

Expecting a dowager widow, Henry was surprised to see a woman no more than ten or twelve years his senior. Her large eyes were deep blue, the long, thick hair piled up under her hat a gleaming blue-black. She wore no cosmetics except rouge on her lips, and she needed no more. The long, thick lashes around her eyes dramatized them more than any amount of kohl; her softly rounded features were an artist's model of beauty.

The woman clearly had a forceful personality. She

was also angry, which made it more pronounced. Strangely, Henry felt both drawn to her and repelled by her; but most of all he was fascinated. She was completely different from any woman he had ever met.

She turned to Henry, her full lips pressed together in a straight line and her blue eyes sparkling with pique. "And so," she said flatly. "You are an American. An American spy."

Taken aback, Henry frowned and shook his head. "No, Madam Baroness, I am not a spy. I am an American military observer."

The baroness moved her lips in a silent, sarcastic comment on the distinction. "And so. Are you enjoying your sojourn among the civilized peoples of Europe? Or do you yearn for your native wilderness, Indians to fight, and a lump of a wild animal for your dinner?"

"Madam," Henry said, restraining his temper with an effort, "I met you at the request of my friend, Captain Koehler, to convey his regrets over his absence. I told him that I would remain with you until he returns. But if you persist in insulting me, and particularly in insulting my nation, then I shall have to withdraw from your presence."

Gisela von Kirchberg struggled to control her temper. She was not angry—she was furious. Out of exasperation over the interminable wait for the French to surrender, she had decided to look at the German lines herself, to find if that would convey a sense of when the wait might end. It had been a waste of time; the wait would continue, the seething fury of impatience within her continuing to mount. And her nephew had failed to meet her.

The young officer in front of her was, she reflected, a boy, but he conducted himself well. He was tall and handsome, with a strong, masculine appeal. Thinking of him in that sense, she experienced a sudden flush of erotic sensation, a physical reaction that surprised her. Her pleasure in life came from the sensuous feel of heavy gold coins and from wielding power; men as men were usually nothing more than a nuisance to her.

On an impulse, she took off a glove and put out her hand. "I apologize for being rude," she said. "I was annoyed, and I vented my anger on you. May we begin again?"

The hand extended to Henry Blake was soft and perfumed, but there was nothing coquettish about the woman. Her attitude was much like that of a man who, with full self-respect, was apologizing for an offense. He told himself that he was making peace with her because she was his friend's relative; but he knew it was because of the compelling tug that he felt toward this beautiful, unusual, and fascinating woman.

The civilities over, the woman looked up at him from under the veil of her hat. "You are my worthless nephew's friend?" she said. "But it would appear that you are different. For example, your German is excellent. You must have studied hard, which he wouldn't do."

"I certainly don't enjoy studying," Henry said, smiling. "But I did study hard, yes. I also had a good instructor in German."

The answering smile on her face almost took his breath away. She was an attractive woman under any circumstances, but her smile made her indescribably lovely. Henry was overwhelmed.

Glancing around again, she pointed to the camp followers. "You should be careful about them," she remarked. "Many of them are diseased."

"I have no need to be careful about them," he replied, thinking of Cindy. "I merely avoid them entirely."

The reference to sex stirred images in Gisela's mind. Years before, out of boredom, she had read a book on sexual technique from her husband's collection of pornography. Envisioning herself and this young man in the positions of the illustrations in the book, an erotic, melting glow suffused her, possessing her.

Bewildered, she also felt enraged with herself for reacting to the young man as if she were a cat in heat. Sex was a waste of time—time that was needed for serious matters. Then she thought again. She was doing nothing now but writhing in an agony of impatience while she waited. For once, she had time. Sex would be different and unusual, even entertaining.

Motioning to the driver, Gisela announced that she and Henry would eat. Henry smiled and shook his head. "Richard asked me to keep you company," he said, "not to have his lunch."

"There will be more than enough," she assured him. "You and I will eat, and we will talk. And so, we are friends. You must address me as Gisela, and I shall call you Heinrich."

The driver, Henry noted, had reacted to the snap of the woman's fingers with considerable energy. Having leaped down from the box, he took a small folding table and stools from the carriage, then set them up in the shade beside the vehicle. Gisela began chatting with Henry, telling him that she had taken a small apartment in Thieux.

The town, a few miles east of the village where Henry's detachment was located, was where the senior German officers were quartered. Immediately interested, Henry asked how she had managed to obtain an apartment in a place where accommodations were in such great demand. "With money," she replied bluntly. "It is very inadequate— two rooms over a shop—but it will do for as long as I need it. Come, Heinrich, let's sit down."

A white cloth covered the tiny table, and Henry felt his knees touch Gisela's as the two of them sat on the stools. Gisela dismissed the driver with a wave of her hand, then opened the large food hamper on the carriage step beside them, taking out glasses and a bottle of wine. She opened the wine and poured a splash into a glass for Henry to sample.

Compared with even the most expensive wine he had ever tasted, this tart, full-bodied white was nectar. Gisela reached into the hamper and took out pots of caviar and pâté, several varieties of spicy sausages, small loaves of dark bread sliced into rounds, and other delicacies. They began eating as they continued talking.

One of the sausages was similar to but much better than sausage he had eaten in one of the German-run cafés in the village. When he mentioned it to Gisela, her nod suggested that she knew about the cafés, but she shook her head when he asked if she had eaten there. "No, but the managers are my employees, and what they sell comes from my firm in Saarbrücken. But let's not discuss business. Tell me how such an interesting young man as you came to know my worthless nephew."

As he began relating how he and Richard had met, Henry recalled that there had been a French café in Vittel that had been forced out of business. He wondered if Gisela had had something to do with it.

A few minutes later, Richard returned, accompanied by the lieutenant who had been sent to summon him. Richard's face revealed speechless surprise mixed with pleasure when he saw Henry and his aunt chatting and addressing each other in familiar terms. Recovering himself quickly, he bowed and greeted his aunt.

"And so," Gisela said, pouring wine for the two German officers. "You had an appointment with me, but you preferred to visit your colonel."

"It was not out of choice, Madam Baroness," the captain said, laughing. "Let me introduce you to my companion."

The lieutenant bowed and made a gallant remark as Richard introduced him. Gisela responded with a disinterested nod, handing glasses of wine to him and the captain. After she gave them sausages and bread from the hamper, the two officers withdrew to one side to eat and drink, laughing as they discussed between themselves the reprimand Richard had received. Turning her attention back to Henry, Gisela spooned caviar onto a round of bread and gave it to him.

Replying to her questions, he had been telling her about his native country. Now she changed the subject, her voice becoming softer as she told him that she had been having dinner in the best restaurant in Thieux and had overheard numerous conversations between senior German officers. Then she began relating what she had overheard.

Henry could hardly believe his luck. Even the names of the officers who had been dining together were important —but there was far more information. A cavalry training school was being established near Frankfurt, where officers would receive the same instruction as the men. Recruiting and shipbuilding were being undertaken to expand the German Navy by one third. A study group had been formed to improve the command structure of the army.

There was more, and the baroness's voice was a soft whisper as she continued. Frantically trying to make mental notes of all the names and other facts, Henry suddenly realized why the woman was giving him the information. She was courting him, winning him over.

It was as different from the usual flirting of a woman as she was from other women. Rather than a display of feminine wiles, this was more of a businesslike, masculine pursuit. Gisela von Kirchberg was proceeding as she did toward any other objective, with energetic determination.

Immensely flattered, Henry also felt overpowered by her alluring beauty and the force of her personality. A long moment of silence followed after she finished talking. Then he spoke quietly. "Perhaps I could come to Thieux and have dinner with you soon."

In reply Gisela picked up a pot from which she had scraped the pâté with a tiny silver spoon. Wiping a finger around the inside of the pot, she gathered up the remaining pâté, then leaned across the table. The taste of perfume on her soft finger blended with the spicy, delicious flavor of the pâté as she put her finger in his mouth.

Sitting back, Gisela then put her finger in her own mouth, her eyes staring into his, her lovely face flushed and unsmiling. "I'll send you a note within a day or two," she said softly. "It will be soon."

Reaching into the hamper again, Gisela took out wedges of cheese similar to cheddar and offered them, with more bread, to the German officers. Then she took out a single, small slice of a different cheese.

The cheese that she had given to her nephew and the lieutenant was like that of Oregon, a wholesome yellow that was evocative of healthy cows grazing in lush pastures under sunny skies. The small slice, in contrast, was a pallid gray, shot through with veins of green.

As she divided the slice, her attitude was one of sharing some secret delight. Her knees touching his under the table, she looked at him with a fixed gaze, her eyelids heavy and her blue eyes shining with bold, torrid promise. "The cheese that Richard and his friend have is merely food to nourish the body," she said in a sultry whisper. "This is a treat for the adventurous. It is unusual and different, and exquisite pleasure when one becomes accustomed to it. Join me, Heinrich."

The cheese looked unappetizing, and its odor was unpleasant, but Henry ate it. It had a sticky consistency and the musty, dank taste of the cave where it had been ripened. But it was still warm from Gisela's soft, perfumed fingers. With her knees touching his, eating the cheese became a heady experience.

Then, the meal finished, Gisela stood up and straightened the folds of her long, green brocade skirt. In response to her beckoning motion and a snap of her fingers, the driver leaped into a flurry of putting things back into the carriage. Gisela made her farewells to her nephew and the lieutenant, and Henry handed her into the carriage.

As she stepped up, she paused, her face near his. She had saved the best tidbit of information for last. The tips of her white, even teeth shone as she spoke softly. Her sweet breath was warm and damp against his face. The alluring scent of her perfume combined with the warmth of her shapely body and the feel of her presence, an array of bewitching sensations. The impact was overwhelming.

And what she told him left him thunderstruck.

"At dinner the night before last," she whispered, "I heard Colonel General Frommel and General Brunner discussing a report on German artillery that had been prepared by the American military observers. They agreed that it was a very accurate and penetrating report."

Unable to voice a reply, Henry nodded. He was all too familiar with the report, since he himself had helped prepare it. Gisela had just told him that the Germans had broken the code being used by the detachment and were reading the dispatches being sent to the embassy. Her beautiful face wreathed in a smile, Gisela waved to Henry as her carriage jerked into motion and rumbled away. Numbly, he managed to lift his hand to his cap.

It was the time of day when reports prepared during the morning were taken to the telegraph officer. Henry felt a compelling sense of urgency, but he knew it would be the worst folly imaginable to rush off. That would be tantamount to admitting that Gisela had told him something of importance.

The two German officers were again discussing Richard's reprimand, the lieutenant howling with laughter as the captain mimicked his colonel's speech and mannerisms. As a military officer, Henry felt a sense of disapproval over the nature of the conversation, but it was amusing.

Then the captain broke off. With hands on hips, he stepped forward and began surveying Henry closely, a droll expression on his face. "Tell me, Erling," he said to the lieutenant, "what is there about this American officer that I failed to see?"

"I don't know what you mean," the lieutenant replied.

"I mean that he has done the impossible," Richard said. Folding his arms, he shook his head and smiled. "Heinrich, my aunt has always been impervious to men. She is attractive, so men have tried to win her over. But even those who could inspire passion in a nun's heart have failed. What did you do?"

"I did nothing," Henry said. "We simply talked."

"Simply talked!" Richard echoed scoffingly. "She was acting like a schoolgirl over you, and she's old enough to be your mother."

"My mother?" Henry exclaimed. "She is not! Gisela is a bare eight or ten years older than I am, no more."

The captain, a knowing smile on his face, turned to the lieutenant. "Observe how quickly he leaps to her defense, Erling," he said. "Also observe that he refers to my aunt by name, while I am obliged to use her title." He turned back to Henry and slapped his shoulder in a friendly gesture. "She's thirteen years older than you, Heinrich, which should make no difference. Perhaps you will be able to make her more human. All she ever thinks about is business and money."

"I gathered that she's a businesswoman."

The captain nodded as he began talking about his aunt. Her father, the captain's paternal grandfather, was a lawyer whose financial situation had been modest when Gisela was a girl. Some fifteen years before, she had married Baron von Kirchberg, a moderately wealthy man of her father's age. The baron had died ten years later, leaving his money to her.

"I'm sure she's multiplied it many times over," Richard said. "But she never discusses her business affairs. My father once said that she was snubbed by wealthy girls in her school, and that may have driven her to have more than anyone else. She's undoubtedly here on business, but I can't imagine just what that would be."

Remembering what Gisela had said about the cafés in Vittel, Henry decided to treat it as a confidence. At the same time, he strongly suspected that far more than the cafés had brought her to France from Saarbrücken. He also felt that the captain, not understanding his aunt, was taking a harsh attitude toward her. "Perhaps she's lonely," he said.

"Lonely?" Richard exclaimed, then began howling with laughter. "No, Heinrich, no. She has her bags of gold to keep her company."

The lieutenant took out his watch and looked at it. "Apparently she will have more than that now," he commented. "It is past time for me to report back to duty, so I'd better leave."

"I must leave as well," Henry said. "I hope to see you again tomorrow, Richard. And you, Erling."

After the three officers exchanged salutes, Henry walked along the road past the tents, to the picket line where the officers tethered their horses. He mounted and began riding toward Vittel at a slow canter. When he passed over a hill, out of view from the German lines behind, he spurred his horse to a run.

Old, mossy stone fences lined the road, and farmland stretched away across rolling hills. In places the gathering of the armies had created ripples in the centuries-old ebb and flow of life on the land. Farmers were replowing fields where caissons had made ruts and soldiers had marched; they would plant turnips and marrows to mature during the winter. Elsewhere, the rhythm of life on the farms was undisturbed.

A squad of German soldiers was working at the side of the road on a huge machine called a road vehicle, with three large steel wheels and a steam engine. Scores of them were in use by the logistics divisions of the German armies, and Henry had written a report on them. Each one was capable of doing the work of several teams of horses, but they broke down frequently and were so heavy that they easily became mired in the mud.

As the village came into view ahead, Henry slowed his horse to a canter. The thick bundles of telegraph wires leading into town looked anachronistic among the ancient houses with slate roofs, low doorways, and deeply inset leaded windows. As usual, the street bustled with activity, the cafés were busy, and journalists and military officers from many nations milled about.

As he rode into the village, Henry saw the sergeant from the detachment going into the telegraph office, a folder under his arm. Quickly, and without drawing attention, he spurred his horse forward and called to the sergeant. The man turned and followed Henry back to the cottage.

The other enlisted men looked in surprise as the sergeant, still carrying the dispatches, came into the cottage with Henry. Henry crossed the room to the colonel's office and knocked on the doorjamb.

Andrew glanced up from the papers on his desk; then his gaze moved to the sergeant behind Henry. "The dispatches should be at the telegraph office now, Sergeant," he said. "I want the attaché to have them today."

"I stopped him, sir," Henry said, stepping into the office. He glanced at the window and lowered his voice. "The Germans have deciphered our code, and they're reading our dispatches."

The colonel frowned in concern, telling the sergeant to wait outside and Henry to sit down. Taking the chair beside the desk, Henry quickly related the principal facts of his meeting with Gisela von Kirchberg. When he finished, the colonel was silent for a long moment, pondering. Then he stood up and began opening the safe behind his desk.

He took out the code book, then a new code book in its sealed wrapper. Returning to his desk, he opened the old code book to the last page. On it was an otherwise meaningless phrase that was the signal to the embassy that a change was being made to the new code book.

Writing the phrase on a sheet of paper, Andrew called in the sergeant. He gave the sergeant the paper, telling him to take it to the telegraph office for immediate transmission to the embassy. Then he handed him the new code book and told him to have the corporals encode all of the day's dispatches in the new code. The sergeant saluted and left.

"As I've mentioned," Andrew said, sitting back in his chair, "one of the dangers here is that we'll meet an *agent provocateur*—that is, someone who will try to lead us into an indiscretion and then expose us."

"I'm sure that isn't the case in this instance, sir."

The colonel nodded firmly. "I am as well. When you first mentioned this woman, I considered that possibility. Then I dismissed it. For one thing, such an agent would probably be someone other than a German, since we're in competition with several nations here. This looks like it's a gold mine of information, but I don't quite understand why this woman is helping us. Now, start at the beginning and tell me all about it."

His previous explanation had been brief. This time Henry began relating in detail what had happened, and after a few sentences Andrew Brentwood began smiling widely. "Now it's becoming clear to me," he remarked, chuckling. "How old is the baroness?"

"About thirty-five, sir."

The colonel smiled. "So it's simply a case of a woman being attracted to a handsome young devil who is younger than she is, isn't it? Very well, go on, Henry."

While he disagreed with the colonel's conclusion, Henry saw no point in debating the matter. He continued telling what had happened, omitting the more personal details. When he finished, the colonel was sitting bolt upright in his chair, listening with rapt attention. "A cavalry training school?" he said. "And they're expanding the navy by one third? Good lord, Henry, this *is* a gold mine! And she lives in Thieux?"

"Yes, sir. We're to have dinner there within a day or two."

Andrew shook his head in wonder. "Henry, you've scored a coup that could even conceivably get us both promoted. I want you to develop this source as rapidly as possible. If you need more time away from the office, petty cash, or anything else, just let me know. For now, go and write down what she has told you today while it's still fresh in your mind."

"Yes, sir," Henry replied, standing.

"From what you've told me about the lady's appearance," Andrew commented dryly, "this shouldn't be an unpleasant assignment for you."

"No, sir," Henry agreed, laughing as he left the office.

Crossing the front room, he went into his own small office and sat down at the desk. He took out pen and paper, mentally organizing his thoughts to write down the information in logical sequence. Then his glance fell on the daguerreotype in its metal case on his desk.

Intense guilt replaced his sense of satisfaction. The eyes in the beautiful face in the daguerreotype seemed accusing. He picked up the case, folded it, and put it in a desk drawer. It was, he told himself, no more than removing a distraction that kept him from concentrating. Cindy Holt was the woman he had loved for years, the one he intended to marry.

V

On a Sunday morning, Henry Blake woke to the sensuously smooth feel of silk sheets against his skin. Gisela's long, thick black hair was touching his face, a feathery, tantalizing sensation. As he breathed, the fragrance of her hair blended with her perfume and the other alluring scents of her boudoir. Her thigh resting across his, she lay beside him, asleep.

It was a pleasantly familiar situation, Henry having slept here nearly every night since the first evening they had dined together, more than two weeks before. By now, he felt that he almost knew Gisela von Kirchberg. A woman of keen intelligence who was wary of most men, she was vicious when her quick temper was aroused. But she had gradually begun to trust him, and toward him she was warmly affectionate.

With ledgers and correspondence scattered about her apartment, and Gisela often poring over a sheaf of papers while he was there, it had not been difficult for him to learn about her business affairs. She had even begun using him as a sounding board for her ideas, leading him deeper into the bewildering maze of her speculative ventures.

Gisela was in France because in Paris there was a vast amount of gold and other valuables, but no food. In Saarbrücken she had warehouses filled with tons of food. Having calculated everything to the smallest detail, she knew that when Paris surrendered there would be, at

most, one week during which she could virtually set her
own prices for whatever food she brought into the city.
Then ample supplies would begin arriving from elsewhere,
prices would tumble, and she could sell the remainder at
only a substantial profit. But during that first week, if her
plans materialized, she would become one of the wealthi-
est women in Europe.

As Henry lay there and woke slowly, he felt a throbbing in his temples from too much wine the night before.
On Saturday nights he and Gisela stayed up late and rose
late the next morning. Their frenzy of lovemaking after
going to bed was a vague blur in his memory. He was
content to leave it dim and formless. Gisela, often taking
the initiative, was as inventive as she was abandoned. And
when she took the initiative, their passions sometimes
strayed onto eccentric paths.

The rhythm of her slow, steady breathing changed as
she stirred. Turning onto her back, she stretched luxuriously
and yawned, then pulled her hair away from his face and
smiled into his eyes. "Good morning, my loved one," she
whispered. "How do you feel?"

"I have a headache," he replied.

Pursing her lips in exaggerated, affectionate sympathy, she lifted a hand to his forehead and stroked it gently.
Her dark blue eyes were warm and smiling as she gazed at
his face. "And so," she murmured, "my lovely young man
has a headache. Shall I cure it for you?"

"It will go away."

"I will make it go away more quickly."

He smiled, shaking his head. "That will make it worse."

"No, it won't," she replied softly, pushing the covers
down. "Look at me, Heinrich, and you will forget your
headache. Then when you do what you wish with me,
your headache will go away and stay gone."

The silk sheets pushed down to her feet, she lay and
smiled at him, inviting his gaze. More plump than slender, she had high, heavy breasts, rounded arms, and full
thighs and hips, but her waist was tiny. Her large nipples
and the black hair at her thighs contrasted sharply with

the milky white of her soft skin. To Henry she seemed almost unreal, a vision of perfect beauty.

"If you would like to," she whispered, her eyelids heavy, "you could tie my arms and legs to the bedposts with the sashes from the drapes. Then you could do anything to me that you wish, and I would be unable to resist. You could also tie a handkerchief over my mouth to keep me from crying out, and I would be entirely at your mercy. I would be defenseless, every part of my body yours, to use according to your whims."

The sultry whisper was in a whimsical, half-bantering tone to give him the choice of how to react. But now the passion racing through Henry's veins was unmixed with wine to smother inhibitions and veil memories that were uncomfortable when clear. He chose to treat her suggestion as a jest, smiling as he reached out. Accepting his decision, she smiled in turn and wriggled into his arms, pulling him over her.

There was no fumbling, both of them completely accustomed to each other and both of them eager. Their lips touching and her mouth opening warm and damp under his, she arched up strongly to meet him. Then time froze as they met in a pulsing rhythm that slowly quickened and became urgent. Her fingers bit into his back, and her murmurs and moans became louder. Then she tossed her head back in a cry of triumph that lifted him and took him with her.

A sheen of perspiration made their bodies cling together damply as they breathed heavily and kissed, smiling into each other's eyes in the mutual happiness of lovers. Gisela ran her fingers through his hair as she pulled his head closer, her lips opening wide on his mouth and her tongue caressing his. Then she pulled back from him and smiled. "How is your headache?" she asked.

"What headache?"

Gisela laughed softly, then glided out of bed. Shrugging into her robe and pushing her feet into slippers, she disappeared into the lavatory. When she emerged a few minutes later, Henry got out of bed and gathered up his clothes.

After he had washed and dressed, leaving his tie off and his collar open, he joined Gisela in the other room, where she was making coffee and heating water on a kerosene stove. As he sat down on a chair beside a table, Gisela put small towels into a basin, sprinkled scented toilet water over them, then poured hot water into the basin.

She plucked a towel out of the hot water and wrung it out with quick squeezes. Then she stepped to Henry and wrapped the steaming, scented towel around the lower part of his face. He closed his eyes and relaxed, enjoying the sybaritic pleasure of having Gisela shave him.

"I learned to shave a man by shaving the baron," Gisela remarked. "While he was with a whore, he had a seizure that paralyzed him. After that I had to shave him, bathe him, and attend to all his personal needs. Then, a few months later, he died."

"He was a fool," Henry said, opening one eye.

"For going to a whore?" Gisela replied, glancing over her shoulder as she tossed a hot towel from hand to hand and wrung it out. She shrugged. "Perhaps there was something he needed that she gave him." Changing the towel on his face, she leaned over and touched the tip of her tongue to the end of his nose. "But you would be a fool, Heinrich," she said softly. "I'm older and more understanding now. If there is anything you need, you have only to tell me. You know that."

Stepping back to the basin, Gisela dropped the towel into it. She picked up the razor and began stropping it on a leather strap hanging on the wall beside the stove. "I wish you would let me buy you a good watch, Heinrich," she said. "A pretty one in a gold case."

The subject had come up before, although Henry always tried to avoid it. Gisela's wealth was something he preferred not to think about. While the apartment was modest—only two rooms and a bath—it was crowded with sumptuous furnishings that she had brought with her from Germany, furnishings that were more valuable than the entire building. "I don't want you to give me presents, Gisela," he said. "It is I who should give you presents."

"No, no, dear Heinrich," Gisela replied, smiling as she put down the razor. "I must court you and give you presents because I am more fond of you than you are of me." She sprinkled scented toilet water into the shaving mug, then poured in a splash of hot water and began whipping up a lather. "That is the way things are between us, and I accept it. But I have become so fond of you that it frightens me."

Looking at her, Henry reflected that their relationship had changed rapidly during the past days. Initially self-serving for both of them, it had become a web of subtle, complex attachments, difficult for him to comprehend. While his feelings for her were not love, her personality seemed to have become firmly implanted in his very being. "It shouldn't be frightening to be fond of someone," he said.

"Whenever I am vulnerable in any way, it frightens me," Gisela replied, changing the towel on his face again. "You are a great joy in my life now, Heinrich, but everything exacts a toll." She smiled as she placed the razor and shaving mug on the table beside him. "And nothing is simple. I am very fond of you, but in a small way I resent you. While I should be attending to my affairs, I am playing with you and enjoying you."

Henry smiled, thinking of several of her employees she had recently summoned to join her; they were crowded into a drafty barn on the edge of Thieux—undoubtedly very different accommodations from what they had enjoyed in Saarbrücken. "It will give your employees a rest," he said.

Gisela nodded as she took the towel off his face and began lathering him. "Some of them. But others are still working busily. I am trying to arrange another loan, and several are working on that. It is proving to be difficult, but I must have the money."

The subject of loans had come up before. Apparently Gisela had invested all her available cash in massive stocks of food and then borrowed money to stockpile more food. But she had never mentioned having problems in obtaining a loan. "Why is it proving difficult?" he asked.

"There are two reasons," she replied, perching her pince-nez on her nose and starting to shave him. "One is that I have already mortgaged everything I own to secure previous loans, and banks aren't eager to extend credit under such circumstances. The second is that the government has instituted *Kulturkampf*, a return to traditional German culture. Protestant German culture, that is. A lot of Catholics and Jews are leaving the country, a number of whom are bankers."

"It must be very difficult for them to leave their homeland."

"Yes, it must be. It is also bad for business, but the government is too stupid to see this."

The second remark was said in the scornful tone she reserved for ultimate evils. Stretching the skin on his chin between her thumb and forefinger, she carefully scraped away the stubble with the razor. "I may also lose my source of choice beer."

The reference, Henry knew, was to the beer that was sold in her cafés for several times the price of other beers. Brewed in limited quantity, it was more than worth the price, the most delicious beer that he had ever tasted. "Because of the *Kulturkampf*?"

Gisela nodded, wiping the razor on a towel. She lifted his chin and began shaving under it. "The master brewer is a young woman named Maida Oberg. Her father had no sons, so he trained her. But her mother is Catholic, so they may leave the country." She sighed as she shaved his upper lip. "As I said, it is bad for business."

When she had finished, Gisela removed her pince-nez, then took a damp towel and wiped the rest of the lather off his face. She mixed drops of scented toilet water with a splash of witch hazel on her palm, patted it onto his face, then combed his hair. Finally she stepped back and looked at him. "There is a handsome young officer any corporal should be proud to salute," she said in satisfaction. "I'll prepare breakfast now."

As she moved back and forth, pouring cups of coffee and putting things on the table, Henry thought about what she had said concerning her need for more credit.

"Gisela, what will happen if your agents are unable to obtain a loan for you?"

"The loans I now have will be called in, and I will be ruined," she replied. "I am now within a very few days of losing everything I own and of being left heavily in debt."

It was his first inkling of how near she was to disaster. Her smile was placid, but for the first time Henry realized the turmoil that she had to be suffering inside. Her outward steely calm was, he reflected, at the very least the equal of a troop commander's when facing a far more powerful foe.

Breakfast consisted of cups of hot, strong coffee with clotted cream and honey stirred in, boiled eggs, fruit, and brioches topped with shredded cheese. On one side of the plate was a small square of the cheese veined with green mold that they sometimes had.

Seeing Henry glance warily at the cheese, Gisela laughed. "You ate freely of it last night," she said.

"I had too much wine, and I don't remember."

She shrugged. "You wanted it, so I gave it to you. I'm always pleased when I can give you what you want, my love. And you can't drink too much wine when you're with me. I will attend to you."

"Don't try to mother me, Gisela," he said, chuckling.

"No, I won't," she replied. "But I am older than you in years, and in other ways. As a child, you walked roads that had been forest a short time before. I grew up on cobblestones that had been trod in joy, in grief, and in sin by countless generations before America was discovered. I have old wisdom, Heinrich, that can make your days more profitable. And I know old pleasures that can make your nights more joyful. Yes, I am happy to please you in ways that would make other women you have known flee in terror or disgust." She smiled. "I will attend to you in all ways, loved one."

When they had finished eating, Gisela went into the other room and returned with his tie, cap, and tunic. She helped him put on his tie, then he buttoned his tunic and put on his cap. At the door, she lifted her lips to his. They

kissed, her hands guiding his under her robe. Then he
went down the stairs to the stable behind the building.

His horse knew the route well between Vittel and
Thieux, having traveled it nearly every day the past two
weeks. During that time, there had also been a steady
flow of dispatches from the detachment's cottage to the
military attaché section in Berlin. The value that the attaché placed on the information Henry had gleaned had
been evidenced by an order a few days before to change
the code book each week as a precaution.

While having dinner with Gisela at the restaurants in
Thieux, where his presence had become accepted, Henry
had been hard-pressed to remember even half of what he
had heard. More had come from Gisela, who lunched in
one of her cafés almost every day. But along with all he
had seen and overheard of value, there had been tantalizing hints of even greater riches waiting to be revealed.

In one instance, two senior officers at an adjacent
table had been discussing the Mauser Arms Works, but
Henry had been unable to make out any details of the
conversation. Later, when he had talked with Gisela about
it, she had made an enigmatic comment about possibly
being able to help him find out all he wanted to know.
Then she had abruptly ended the discussion, declining to
talk about it further.

The fields to either side were deserted this Sunday
morning, and there were only a few riders and vehicles on
the road. As Henry neared Vittel, the activity increased,
with people strolling about the village. When the cottage
where the detachment was quartered came into view, he
saw a carriage parked near the door and the sergeant and
corporals loading luggage into it.

As Henry reined up, the sergeant saluted and informed him that the colonel was leaving for several weeks.
Surprised, Henry hurried inside and climbed the stairs to
the living quarters. Andrew was in his room, putting
belongings into a traveling bag.

"My father is seriously ill, Henry," he said. "I received a dispatch from Washington about it early this morning."

"I'm very sorry to hear that, sir. You have my deepest sympathy and my hopes that he'll soon be well. You're authorized leave, then?"

The colonel nodded, his face drawn with worry. "Yes, but I'm afraid there's little room for hope. The dispatch amounted to an order to take leave. Washington hasn't forgotten that President Andrew Jackson asked my father to set up a supply station in Independence to provision wagon trains."

"I don't think anyone west of the Mississippi has forgotten it either, sir. After all, your father devoted a good portion of his life to helping those people or their parents to get where they are."

"Yes, that's true," Andrew said. "I suppose I'm going to Independence both as my father's son and as a representative of my government." He closed the bag and picked it up, glancing around the room. "Well, that looks like everything. I'll have the men put this with the rest, then I'll be ready to go."

Henry followed the colonel out of the room and down the narrow staircase. "How long do you think you'll be gone, sir?" he asked.

"About six weeks, more or less," Andrew replied. "The military attaché in Berlin knows I'm leaving, but I'm not sure whether another senior officer will be sent here right away. Probably not." Reaching the bottom of the stairs, he handed the bag to a corporal and turned to Henry. "I do know they don't have anyone readily available, and they're well aware that most of our dispatches have been coming from you. Also, there's no reason to believe that this deadlock between the French and Germans will change anytime soon. In any event, you should receive a dispatch from the attaché today on what to expect."

"Yes, sir. Have your travel arrangements been set up?"

Andrew nodded, stepping into his office to get his cloak and cap. "I went to see General Ritter early this morning. The general was very helpful." He came back out of his office, putting on his cap. "His staff issued me a priority train pass to Le Havre. There's a steamer leaving for New York tomorrow, and they've sent a telegraph message reserving a cabin for me."

"Those are very good arrangements, sir. If you have a fairly new steamer, you should be there in little more than two weeks."

"Yes, about that," Andrew agreed. Smiling wearily, he placed a hand on Henry's shoulder. "I'm glad you got here when you did, Henry. If I'd had to wait to talk with you, I could have missed my train. And you smell as good as you usually have these past couple of weeks."

Henry smiled. "Yes, sir. Gisela likes to throw that toilet water around. If you see any of my friends when you get to Independence, please give them my best regards, sir."

"Yes, I'll do that," Andrew said. Turning toward the door, he added, "Well, you know the safe combination, and you know the drill on everything, Henry. I'll see you in a few weeks."

"Yes, sir. Godspeed, sir."

The colonel nodded, going outside. The sergeant and a corporal climbed onto the box of the carriage, the other corporals standing at attention as the colonel came out and got into the carriage. Henry stood at attention in the doorway of the cottage and saluted. The colonel returned his salute as the carriage moved away.

A dispatch from the military attaché in Berlin arrived during the afternoon. It stated that until and unless there were indications of a change in the situation between the French and German governments, no officer would be sent to replace Colonel Brentwood. For the present, Second Lieutenant Henry Blake would be in command.

It was as Andrew had predicted. Yet reading in an official dispatch that he had been assigned responsibilities previously borne by a colonel gave Henry pause. He could remember many times when he had needed and sought Andrew's advice.

However, the day ended uneventfully, and another

week began without a single crisis arising to test Henry's ability to meet his sudden new responsibilities.

He had to spend more time at the cottage, approving release of dispatches, opening the safe, and attending to mundane administrative tasks. Otherwise, there was little reason for change in his routine. He briefly contemplated sleeping in his quarters again Monday night, but he dismissed the idea. The sergeant knew where to find him in an emergency.

When he returned to Thieux, Gisela seemed artificially bright and cheerful. He knew that under her façade of good spirits was a turmoil of anxiety, for the perilous state of her business affairs remained unresolved. Henry spent Monday and Tuesday nights with her, returning each morning to Vittel.

Wednesday began the same as the two previous days, but it abruptly changed as soon as Henry settled down to work back at his office. He had been at his desk for only a few minutes when he heard a man enter the front door and ask for him. Stepping to the office door, he saw that it was one of Gisela's employees. The man handed Henry an envelope, bowed and clicked his heels, then hurriedly left.

Going back to his desk, Henry tore open the envelope. It was a note from Gisela. She always wrote in German script—the form and several of the letters completely different from the English alphabet—but he usually had no trouble reading her writing, because she had a smooth, neat hand. This note, however, was scribbled. Obviously it had been written in a hurry.

With some effort, he finally deciphered it. He was to meet her beside the road east of Thieux with all haste. Under no circumstances was he to tell anyone where he was going, and he was not to attract attention by running his horse where he would be seen by anyone.

Henry was puzzled. He had left Gisela's apartment only a short time before. What could have happened since then?

He put the note back into the envelope. "Sergeant!"

he called. "Have my horse brought back around. And quickly, please."

"Yes, sir!" the sergeant replied. "Harrison, go get the lieutenant's horse for him! Get a move on!"

The front door slammed as the corporal ran out. Henry tucked the envelope into a pocket, put on his cap, and went out into the front rooms. "I'll be gone for a short while, Sergeant."

The sergeant saluted and nodded. As Henry went out the door, the corporal was hurriedly leading his horse around from the stable at the rear of the cottage. It had not yet been unsaddled from its morning ride. Taking the reins, Henry mounted and set off toward Thieux.

It was still very early. Some of the journalists and military officers in Vittel were not yet up and about, while others were still having breakfast. Henry rode through the streets at a slow canter. Then, when the village fell behind, he spurred his horse to a gallop.

The powerful gelding breathed deeply from the long, hard pace. Henry leaned forward, the wind brushing his face and pockets of mist on the road whipping past. He was thinking about how to get past Thieux without riding through the town at a pounding run.

Then he remembered a rutted country lane that circled north of the town, rejoining the main road on the other side. When he slowed for the turnoff, the horse fought the bit, accustomed to going straight into Thieux; then he turned onto the side road.

Five minutes later, Henry could see the buildings of Thieux come into view through the thin mist off to the right. A few farmers at houses set back from the road moved about doing chores, ignoring him. Then the road began curving, Thieux falling behind. The junction where the rutted lane rejoined the main road came into view as the horse crossed a rise. Henry spotted Gisela's carriage parked to one side, and he stared at it in surprise. Three teams in tandem were hitched to it, the driver trying to keep the young, spirited horses calm.

Gisela, pacing the grassy verge near the carriage, seemed even more agitated than the horses. Strikingly beautiful in an expensive brown brocade traveling outfit with yellow piping, she was wearing a bonnet and short cape that matched her long, flared gown. The mist was eddying around her as she took short, quick steps in one direction and then wheeled to pace back.

Seeing Henry, she turned toward him and waited impatiently, her gloved hands clenched. The teams hitched to the carriage began rearing and plunging in excitement as his horse galloped up, the driver clinging to their bridles and shouting at them. Henry reined his horse to a sliding stop beside Gisela and leaped from the saddle.

"And so!" she barked, lifting a hand as he started to speak. "You are finally here. Finally! I have no time to waste, so you are to listen to me carefully. Do you understand?"

Nodding, Henry felt concerned for her. The woman had iron self-control; when she displayed temper, it was usually because she had no wish to control it. Now she was wrought up to a frenzy. Her dark blue eyes were wide in her pale face. She trembled, and her breath was short.

"One," she said, lifting a gloved finger. "I have received a telegraph message from an informant in Berlin that a delegation from the foreign ministry departed the city last night. They are en route to observe a special session of the French Assembly at Bordeaux on Friday afternoon. Now, do you understand that?"

Henry nodded again.

"Two," she continued, lifting a second finger. "Not an hour ago, I overheard two generals discussing an order from the highest level for all senior officers to be at headquarters in dress uniform on noon Friday for a special ceremony. Two of my employees overheard mention of the same thing while they were having breakfast. Do you understand that?"

Nodding once again, Henry pursed his lips musingly. Gisela waited for a reaction, then frowned impatiently. "And so!" she snapped. "Either you have lost the power of speech, or you are unable to understand what would be evident to a mentally deficient child. I will explain. The French have come to terms. On Friday afternoon, the

Paris government will be formally dissolved, and the city
will capitulate. Now do you understand?"

"I understood your meaning to begin with, of course,"
he replied. "But it appears to me that you're leaping to
conclusions. And just how reliable is your informant in
Berlin?"

Anger flared, and for a moment Henry thought Gisela
would explode in rage. Then the flush subsided from her
cheeks, and her expression became tense as she turned
away and put a hand to her lips. Swallowing and drawing
in a deep breath, she appeared to be fighting nausea.

"My informant in Berlin is totally reliable," she finally
replied in a soft, strained voice. "He is my father, who is
one of my employees."

"Even so, the French Assembly could be meeting for
any number of reasons," Henry said. "And those generals
look for excuses to wear dress uniforms. This might be no
more than—"

"Then ignore what I have told you!" Gisela shouted,
wheeling on Henry. The horses stamped and tossed their
heads nervously at this outburst, and she stepped closer to
him and stretched up, shouting in his face. "Fool! Idiot! I
have relays of horses waiting to speed me to Saarbrücken,
where I have warehouses bulging with tons of food that
must be loaded onto drays and on the road to Paris within
hours! I wasted precious time to tell you what I have
found out, and your only gratitude is an argument. Ignore
what I told you, and be damned to you!"

As she spun and stamped toward the carriage, Henry
hurried after her. "Gisela, don't take that attitude," he
said. "I am grateful, but I can't help but question your
conclusion."

Stopping so suddenly that he almost ran into her,
Gisela put her hands to her temples. She turned back to
him, her face distraught and tears in her eyes. "I cannot
leave you with harsh words between us," she whispered in
distress. "I love you, Heinrich, but I must tell you that I
also hate you. You have made me weak. I should now be
speeding toward Saarbrücken, but I delayed to talk with
you. You possess my very soul, loved one."

"Gisela, please take hold of yourself," he said in concern. "I've never seen anyone in such a state. You're a strong, healthy woman, but I'm afraid you'll bring on a seizure."

"But it is so close, Heinrich!" she replied softly. Her eyes shining, she lifted her clenched, trembling fists. "Now it is almost within reach of these hands! Wealth you cannot imagine. And power! I will buy those bankers who refused me loans and nail their testicles over my fireplace. When I have an appointment with Chancellor von Bismarck, it will be at my convenience, not his. Wealth, Heinrich! Power!"

Henry shook his head doubtfully. "Gisela, I hope you aren't headed for a fall. I hope you aren't making a mistake."

She tossed her head back and laughed, suddenly becoming more like her normal self again. "I'm not," she said. "On the contrary, I've found out in time to have my drays at the gates of Paris when the road opens. I'll be there days ahead of others, and my profits will be immense. Now kiss me good-bye, my love."

Her smile became sultry as he took her in his arms. Lifting her lips to his, she moved a hand down his body and fondled him. "Think of me night and day," she whispered against his lips. "Think of my naked body, loved one, and gather within yourself a torrent of passion for me. When I return, I'll drain it from you so eagerly and in so many rapturous ways that I will give you ecstasy such as no man has ever known."

He held her close and kissed her, then smiled down at her. "I'm pleased to see you've got something on your mind now to take you out of that state you were in," he remarked. "How long will you be gone?"

"Only a few days," she replied. "When I return, I'll be very busy for a week or two, but I'll make time for my loved one." Her open lips caressed his. "But it will be over soon enough, and then we'll have plenty of time together. And if you yearn for your Oregon in America, I'll buy it and have it brought to Germany for you."

"No, I don't think you'll do that," he said, chuckling. "You don't know how large Oregon is, Gisela."

"You don't know how wealthy I will be. Kiss me again, loved one."

She pressed herself against him as they kissed, her thighs squeezing one of his through their clothes. Her open lips were warm and damp, pressing urgently to his mouth as her tongue caressed his. Wriggling away from him, she gathered up her skirt and hurried toward the carriage.

At her orders the driver released the bridles on the lead team and ran for the carriage. He leaped up to the box and gathered the reins as he seized his whip. Gisela bounded into the cab and slammed the door behind her. The driver's whip snaked through the air over the long line of horses and snapped back with a shattering crack.

The six horses snorted and whinnied as they turned into a bucking, plunging mass. Eyes glaring and manes flying, they charged onto the road, the carriage swerving after them, Gisela clinging to a strap as she waved to Henry. In a seeming instant, they were gone, the carriage careening precariously around a curve, then disappearing from view.

In the quiet beside the roadside, Henry mounted his horse and began riding back toward Vittel. The responsibility for decisions that the colonel had borne was now his. And suddenly it had become a crushing burden.

There was no time to consult the military attaché. Thinking back to his conversation with Andrew of almost three weeks before, on the day that a dispatch about communications procedures had arrived, Henry recalled what Andrew had said. Washington needed to be informed immediately whenever the stalemate between the French and Germans began to change.

Not only hours but minutes counted. Diplomatic initiatives of the most vital importance were being held in abeyance pending the outcome of the conflict. If Washington knew before London, Madrid, Moscow, and other world capitals, the information would be of inestimable value. Henry was in a position to render a priceless service to his nation.

He was also in a position to blunder seriously. If the information was wrong, it could result in confusion, disruption, even irreparable damage to affairs of state. And if the information was correct and he failed to communicate it, he might still, through inaction, harm his nation's interests. A decision had to be made and acted upon. It could not be avoided through excuses about his rank and lack of experience.

On any matter of lesser importance, Henry thought, he would promptly accept Gisela's judgment without question. At times during their conversations, he had been astonished by the dazzling speed with which she assimilated information and arrived at logical conclusions. The woman had a brilliant mind. However, she was human. During the past days, she had been tormented by anxiety over her debts. That could have affected her judgment. And her conclusion had been drawn on extremely scanty evidence.

Still undecided, Henry arrived at Vittel and went into the cottage. He sat at his desk, acutely aware that precious minutes were trickling away while he agonized in indecision. Weighing all the facts a final time, he forced himself to make a decision. He went to the safe and took out the code book and communications procedures manual.

Sitting back down at his desk, he wrote two addresses at the top of a sheet of paper. Then he started on the text of the dispatch, which began with a series of letters that identified the code book he was using so the message could be decoded. Next was a series of letters that designated the priority at which the dispatch was to be handled. Looking in the procedures book, Henry chose the priority for reporting sudden outbreaks of war, calamitous natural disasters, and deaths of heads of state.

The message itself consisted of only two short sentences. Leafing back and forth through the code book, Henry quickly encoded them and printed the five-letter groups of jumbled letters on the form. Then he put the code book and communications procedures book back into the safe. He would have plenty of time later to notify the attaché in Berlin of what he was doing.

Carrying the dispatch, Henry went through the outer office and told the sergeant that he would return within a few minutes. He walked quickly down the street toward the telegraph office, avoiding the gaze of others. He did not want to have to stop and converse with anyone.

"Lieutenant Blake!" a voice called.

Henry cursed his luck. Commander Stephen Wyndham, a British naval officer and his country's chief observer, was heading across the street toward him. Henry had met Wyndham before and liked him immensely, but this was not the time he wanted to chat with him.

Wyndham eyed the folded dispatch. "You aren't running your own errands now, are you, Henry?" he asked, returning Henry's salute. The commander's expression was amiable, but his eyes were curious and watchful.

Henry smiled as he shook his head. "No, sir. I felt like getting some air, and I thought I'd drop this off and get some coffee. Would you like to join me?"

An instant of silence passed, the commander's keen blue eyes studying Henry's face. Then he shook his head. "Sorry, but I can't. Have to run back to London for a day or two, and just thought I'd let you know. I heard that Colonel Brentwood left for the States."

"Yes, sir, but he'll be back." Henry briefly told Wyndham about Sam Brentwood's illness, then the two of them exchanged farewells and Wyndham left. Henry breathed a sigh of relief and continued down the street.

At the telegraph office, the clerk behind the counter took the dispatch and filled out a line on the dispatch registry. After Henry signed the registry, the clerk carried the dispatch through a doorway into a busy room, where telegraph operators sat at keys in front of an array of equipment with rows of switches on it.

Henry watched the clerk hand the dispatch to one of the operators. He controlled the sudden impulse to shout at the clerk and tell him to bring the dispatch back. As the telegraph operator flipped switches and began tapping on his key, Henry turned toward the door. His hands felt damp, and his mouth was dry.

Back at his office, he sat numbly in his chair, thinking

about the length of time it would take for the dispatch to reach the addressees. It would go by transatlantic cable and reach Washington within thirty minutes or less. The priority on the dispatch would separate it from others for immediate processing and decoding, which would take no more than fifteen minutes.

Looking at his watch, Henry was surprised to see that it was still early in the day; many hours seemed to have passed. On the East Coast, the sun would not yet have risen.

Henry knew that, within the hour, couriers from the government telegraph office in Washington would be racing through the night to the homes of the secretary of war and the secretary of state. Those high officials would be roused from their sleep by fists thumping on their doors. No doubt they would become wide awake when they read what the couriers had brought.

Then activity would spread through the Washington night like ripples from stones cast into a pond. The quiet would be broken by horses and carriages clattering along the otherwise deserted streets. Silent buildings would stir with life. Dark office windows would begin glowing as lamps were lighted.

Disheveled aides and staff members would collect in hallways and whisper as senior officials conferred on courses of action to pursue. By the time the sun rose over the Potomac, the wheels of government would be grinding at full speed—and all because, on the following Friday, Paris was going to capitulate.

Or at least Henry hoped. If he was wrong, then all the savage fury of outraged Washington officialdom would turn on a second lieutenant in France.

Henry wondered if he had ended his army career before it had hardly more than begun.

VI

The general, Toby Holt reflected, dealt with everything as though it were a military campaign. As Toby rode with Cindy and Tim up to the house where his mother and stepfather lived, he saw Dr. Robert Martin's buggy and a carriage belonging to Ted Woods parked out in front. The doctor and his wife, as well as Ted and Olga Woods, Frank's parents, had evidently received notes from General Blake similar to the one a sergeant from the fort had delivered to the horse ranch some two hours before.

Eulalia, her mood subdued because of the news from Independence, met them at the door. After greeting her daughter and son, she took Tim's hand. "I'll have one of the orderlies look after him," she said. "Lee and the others are in the parlor, and I'll join you in a moment."

As she led the boy away, Toby and Cindy went into the parlor. Lee Blake, seated in his chair by the fireplace, was talking quietly with the two couples. Greeting everyone, Toby and Cindy found chairs. Years of labor as a blacksmith had given Ted Woods a burly frame, and his Russian-born wife was his female counterpart. Now in their sixties and healthier and more active than many people half their age, they were the owners of a good-size inn, as well as a smithy in Portland that employed several men.

The doctor and Tonie Martin were seated on a couch, Janessa between them. The girl and her frail, aged mentor were constant companions, and Dr. Martin had discussed with Toby his ambition for her to be a doctor. Toby supported the idea because that goal fitted his daughter's interests and personality; but he also felt that the doctor was looking very far into the future. Janessa was still quite young, and Toby envisioned serious problems in getting her into a medical college.

When Eulalia rejoined the group, the general began talking about the purpose of the gathering. Listening to him, Toby thought again about how systematically and efficiently Lee Blake approached everything. It would be surprising for him to do otherwise, Toby decided, considering his lifetime of military service.

Lee spoke of the letter that he and Eulalia had received from Claudia Brentwood in Independence about her husband's sudden illness. "The doctors diagnosed it as a heart seizure," he said, turning to Dr. Martin. "That's very serious for someone Sam's age, isn't it, Robert?"

"It's serious for anyone of any age," the doctor replied quietly. "But particularly for someone of Sam's age, yes."

"Claudia sent a telegram to General Aberly at the War Department," Lee continued. "He's an old friend of Sam's, and I've known him for years as well. He replied by telegram, informing Claudia that a telegraph dispatch would be sent to Andrew in France, informing him of his father's illness and authorizing him to take leave."

"Do you think he'll take leave, General?" Ted Woods asked.

Lee Blake nodded firmly. "No doubt about it," he said. "If I know Jason Aberly, Andrew received an *order* to take leave. Also, there's no reason to believe that the standoff between the French and the Germans will change any time soon, so I'm sure he's on his way home by now." Putting the letter from Claudia aside, he glanced around at the group. "Eulalia and I decided to go to Independence, so I asked you here to find out if any of you wish to go. If you do, we can all travel together."

There was a murmur of affirmatives, everyone intending to go. "If it wasn't for Sam Brentwood, we probably wouldn't be here," Dr. Martin observed. "Gold rush or not, the entire West is a far more settled region as a result of his provisioning the wagon trains. Yes, Tonie and I certainly want to go—don't we, Tonie?"

As his wife stated her agreement, Janessa looked up at him. "What about my school?" she demanded.

The old man smiled and patted her hand. "I'll talk to the principal about it, Dr. Janessa. You can study during the trip."

Lee turned to Toby. "You mentioned the other day that you intend to return to Chicago soon, Toby," he said. "Will this conflict with the arrangements you've made?"

"No, sir," Toby replied. "Rob Martin and Edward Blackstone have replied to my letters and expressed interest in the Wisconsin venture. We were going to meet in Chicago, but they and their wives will go to Independence as soon as they hear about Sam. I'll meet them there, and then we can travel on to Chicago together."

"Very well," the general said, glancing around the group again. "That leaves the questions of when and how we'll set out on the journey to be decided. Robert, you and Tonie are bothered by seasickness, and Eulalia didn't feel very well the last time we took the steam packet up from San Francisco. I suggest we go down the coast by carriage and leave tomorrow morning."

"The sooner the better," Ted Woods commented, and the others nodded in agreement. "Phelps Livery Stable has carriages, and John Phelps is a good friend of mine, so I can make the necessary arrangements."

A consensus was quickly reached; the group would leave early the following morning for the long trip by road to San Francisco. The general offered to send wagons from the fort to collect the group at the Portland ferry terminal, where he and Eulalia would join them. Other details were discussed and quickly agreed upon.

It was late afternoon when Toby and Cindy returned to the Holt ranch. Janessa accompanied the Martins home to get the horse she rode to school and arrived back at the ranch a short time later. She and Cindy packed for the journey while Toby talked with Stalking Horse about what was to be done on the ranch during his absence. By nightfall, their arrangements had been completed.

The wagon from Fort Vancouver was at the ranch well before daylight the next morning, and the corporal who drove it helped load the luggage. Toby lifted Cindy and Janessa up into the back, then handed Tim to Cindy. The boy was still sleeping. The corporal shook the reins, and they set off on the road to Portland, passing dark, quiet farmhouses.

The stars glittered brightly overhead, and the snow-cap on Mount Hood gleamed in the light of the setting moon, the clear sky promising a fair day on which to begin the journey. After they had passed through the deserted center of the city, the brightly lighted ferry terminal came into view. The two hired carriages were there, the drivers standing around a small fire to ward off the chill. Ted and Olga Woods had already arrived, and they greeted Toby and Cindy as the drivers came over to take the luggage out of the wagon and load it onto the top of a carriage.

The doctor and Tonie Martin arrived a few minutes later. They would ride with the Woods and Janessa. As dawn began breaking, the shrill hoot of a whistle signaled the approach of the Vancouver ferry, its rows of bright lights appearing through the darkness lingering over the river.

With bells jangling and its engine throbbing, the ferry docked. As General Blake stepped off it with Eulalia, the soldiers hurried to carry their luggage to the carriage they would share with Toby, Cindy, and Tim. The dawn light was brightening, and the sun was starting to rise when the last rope on the luggage was securely tied and the party was ready to leave.

As the carriages moved off, Cindy's eye was caught by a newspaper boy who was on his way to the terminal. "Wait! Wait!" she cried. "What does the headline on those papers say?"

Lee Blake, letting down the window in the door, called to the driver to stop. He shouted at the boy, "What's the headline, son?"

"The latest news from Europe, sir! Paris went belly up to the Germans! Read all about it for three cents!"

Cindy exclaimed in gleeful delight as both Toby and Lee reached into their pockets. Toby got out his change first, handing the boy fifteen cents through the window and taking four of the newspapers. Cindy snatched one of them and began scanning it eagerly as Toby handed copies of the newspaper to his mother and the general.

The carriage swayed into motion again, following the other one along the street. Lee raised the window and took his spectacles out of a waistcoat pocket. Eulalia shifted the sleeping Tim on her lap and removed her own spectacles from her reticule. There was silence for several minutes as everyone read the news from Europe.

Cindy was the first to finish, and she began talking excitedly about the possibility that Henry would be returning soon. Lee shook his head cautiously. "Don't get your hopes up, Cindy," he said. "This doesn't necessarily mean Henry will be able to come home right away."

"What does it mean, then, Papa?"

Lee was noncommittal, telling her that it would be better to wait and discuss it with Andrew Brentwood, who would have a more complete understanding of the situation. Absently listening to their conversation, Toby turned to the inner pages of his newspaper to read about other developments. Not surprisingly, the biggest story was a tawdry account of the murder of the assistant secretary of the treasury, James Martinson, who had been stabbed by his mistress, a woman named White. Toby frowned and turned to another story.

Some of the details of the government's negotiations with Canada over boundaries and offshore fishing rights were still unsettled—not necessarily in dispute, but simply unresolved. Washington had formally proposed that Wilhelm I of Germany arbitrate the matter—a proposal that implicitly affirmed the confidence of the United States in the German government to make a balanced judgment.

The diplomatic move had no apparent connection with the recent German victory over France, having been made two days before the outcome of the hostilities had been known. The German government, in the circumstances, had favorably received the proposal, which had already resulted in a broadening of contacts between the two governments on a range of issues. The Germans were eager to discuss purchases of coal and other commodities that the United States wanted to sell. Closer contact between the armed forces of the governments was also to be discussed in the near future.

Toby pointed out the article to the general. "It looks as though the people in the State Department had unbelievable luck in approaching the Germans at just the right moment," he said. "If they had delayed a couple of days, it would have appeared that we were only currying favor. As it is, with Germany having increased stature and influence for at least a time, their goodwill means a lot."

Lee Blake frowned as he read, then looked at Toby over the top of his spectacles. "Yes, that's right," he agreed. "It was unbelievable luck. Or perhaps it was good intelligence, Toby."

Toby nodded. "Yes, it could have been that," he said. "Do you think Andy might have had anything to do with it?"

"Well, I suppose it's conceivable," Lee replied doubtfully. "But extremely improbable. The host country usually keeps military observers well insulated from such high-level matters. Even colonels."

"Perhaps Henry had something to do with it," Cindy offered.

Both Lee and Toby burst into laughter. Eulalia looked over the top of her newspaper as she also began laughing. Cindy flushed hotly and lowered her head, embarrassed by the hilarity created by her remark, which had been made in all sincerity. Then a smile gradually broke through on her face, and she joined the laughter.

Lee took out his handkerchief and removed his spectacles. Still chuckling, he wiped his eyes, then put his spectacles back on. "Cindy, Cindy," he said in amusement, shaking his newspaper to straighten it. "No one can say that you don't have faith in Hank. Well, I do as well, because he's a fine young officer. But the lad is a second lieutenant, Cindy, so let's let him get a little more experience before we expect him to start dabbling in international affairs."

The party's last overnight stop before reaching San Francisco was at Fort Ross, a former fur-trading outpost that the Russians had abandoned a generation before. The workers at the outpost at the time had also been abandoned, and the few of them who had remained in the area conversed with Olga Woods in her native Russian. The children, however, were typical native-born Americans, speaking only English.

South of Fort Ross, the road leading to San Francisco passed through fertile valleys, with cultivated fields extending as far as the eye could see. The lure of gold had once drawn fortune seekers to the hills east of here, but these valleys were now inhabited by a different breed—people of the land.

Over the past twenty years, they had transformed the countryside. Virgin forests and grassland had been turned into farmland, and fertile marshes had been drained and put under the plow. Where lawlessness had been rampant, law and order now prevailed. Those who had come to California in search of gold were fighting to preserve their unrestricted way of life, but they were losing.

Toby Holt looked out at the passing fields, thinking about a newspaper article he had recently read. It stated that in the previous year the gold mined in California had been worth ten million dollars, a vast fortune. But the California wheat crop for the same year had been worth twenty million dollars. The people of the land, he reflected, were winning on all fronts.

It was late afternoon when the carriages reached the Presidio, the military post in San Francisco and part of General Blake's command. The carriages were met by Brigadier General Cummings, the commander of the Presidio, and his wife, Wilma. A dapper, portly man of fifty, General Cummings talked with General Blake as Wilma greeted Eulalia and the others.

The brigadier general explained that he had arranged

for the party to stay in the visiting officers quarters if they wished to rest after the long trip. "Or," he continued, "I have an officer standing by to reserve compartments on a train that leaves at eight this evening. That will allow plenty of time for a leisurely meal at the officers' mess, and carriages can take you to the train station."

Leland Blake, still neat and alert after the days in the carriage, glanced around at the party. The trip had taken a toll on some of the others; Dr. Martin, in particular, looked weary. "How do you feel about it?" he asked the group. "Shall we rest for a day?"

"We can rest on the train," Dr. Martin replied, and the others nodded and murmured in agreement. "By all means, let's be on our way."

"Very well," Lee said, turning back to the brigadier general. "John, if you would be good enough to make the arrangements, we'll have a meal here and leave on the train this evening."

"Yes, sir," General Cummings responded briskly, beckoning an officer who had accompanied him. "Captain, go and reserve five compartments for General Blake and his party, and have their luggage taken to the train station. General Blake, if you, Mrs. Blake, and your friends will come with me, I'll escort you to the officers' mess."

The two generals and their wives chatted as they led the way toward one of the fort's original Spanish buildings. The interior of the officers' mess was quiet and softly lighted, combining the orderly efficiency of a military facility with the atmosphere and appointments of a fine restaurant. After the travelers had freshened themselves, they went into a vast, richly carpeted dining room furnished and paneled in oak. Hangings on the walls complemented the carpets, and the soft light of the chandeliers gleamed on the snowy linen and sparkling silver on the tables.

The travelers stood around a large table with the Presidio commander and his wife to raise glasses in a toast to the President. Then they seated themselves and waiters moved silently around with the first course, a thick, hearty soup. It was accompanied by a tossed salad made of crisp,

fresh lettuce, tomatoes, and bits of diced green pepper
and celery.

The fish course consisted of thick, boneless slices of
hake that had been smoked over smoldering hardwood
until pale brown and permeated with the flavor of the
smoke, then steamed to a tender, flaky consistency. The
fish was followed by the main course, juicy, generous
sirloin steaks accompanied by mashed potatoes covered
with rich gravy, and cauliflower dressed with cheese sauce.

After a dessert of apple pie accompanied by cups of
hot, strong coffee, the two generals argued good-naturedly
about which of them was going to pay the bill. Ted Woods,
flushed and drowsy after the large meal, joined the conversation. "I ate more than anyone," he said. "By rights I
should pay for the dinner."

As Toby and Dr. Martin spoke up, also wanting to
pay, the two generals firmly refused. "This is a military
post," Lee Blake said. "Civilians are not allowed to pay."
He turned back to the brigadier general. "In any event,
John, I still owe you for that wine you and Wilma sent to
Eulalia and me."

"Then we owe you for the salmon you and Eulalia
sent to us," Wilma Cummings replied. "I think we're at a
fair draw on that."

"So do I," General Cummings said. "That being the
case, I'll host this time, and you can host the next, General Blake."

Lee Blake smiled and nodded in agreement. After
taking out his watch, he pushed his chair back, commenting that it was time for the party to leave for the train
station. There was a stir as everyone got up from the table
and followed the generals and their wives back out.

Darkness had fallen, and the carriages waiting outside
had their lamps glowing brightly. After exchanging farewells with John and Wilma Cummings, the party climbed
into the vehicles, which rumbled away from the fort and
into the crowded evening streets of San Francisco.

The captain from the Presidio, waiting dutifully at the
train station, escorted the party to the compartments he
had reserved for them. Toby Holt arranged his bags in the

compartment he would share with Tim, then took out his folder of letters and other materials pertaining to the logging venture. As the train moved out of the station, he thumbed through the papers and looked at the pages on which he had calculated costs and estimated profits.

From its beginnings as a modest investment, this venture had grown to a major undertaking that could yield very large returns. Tentative inquiries had indicated that landowners in the area Toby had visited in Wisconsin were eager to sell logging rights totaling tens of thousands of acres. That made it more economical and potentially far more profitable to build a lumber mill in Chicago than to pay to have the timber sawed into lumber.

A major problem that Toby foresaw was management. Frank Woods was unexcelled as a logging camp superintendent, more than capable of dealing with lumberjack crews and making efficient use of equipment. But the man was not a manager. When the additional operations of transporting the logs and building and running a lumber mill were considered—together with the mountains of bookkeeping and other related paperwork that would be involved—Toby knew that Frank would be unable to handle it.

Cindy came in to put Tim to bed, then returned to the compartment she shared with Janessa. Toby turned the shade on the lamp to keep the light away from the boy's bunk. Continuing to look through the papers as the wheels clacked and the train rushed through the night, he once again arrived at a conclusion he had drawn before. If the venture expanded to the scope that appeared likely, he might have to go to Wisconsin and stay there for at least a time to manage it himself.

The train slowed, weaving across switches as it changed tracks, then stopped. Toby glanced at his watch and pulled the window curtain aside to confirm what he surmised, that the train had stopped in the Roseville yards to couple on a second engine for the long, hard pull over the Sierra Nevada. Yawning as he put his folder of papers away, he decided to stretch his legs before going to bed.

The corridor of the compartment car was empty, all

the doors closed and everyone settled for the night. Upon
entering the vestibule at the end of the car, he stopped in
surprise. Janessa, wearing her coat over her long night-
gown, was standing there with a cigarette between her
lips, frowning impatiently and searching her coat pockets.
"Hello, Dad," she said, her frown changing to a smile. "I
don't have any matches."

He looked down at her, half annoyed and half amused.
"Janessa, are you asking me for a match to light that
cigarette?" he demanded.

"Please, Dad," she begged, smiling up at him brightly.
"I don't want to wake Dr. Martin. He's tired, and he
needs his sleep."

Toby hesitated, then sighed in resignation and felt in
his pockets. "Janessa, you're going to have to stop that
smoking," he said, taking out a match and handing it to
her. "You know what Cindy and your grandmother think
about it, and it isn't right. What are you doing out here
anyway? You shouldn't be wandering around at this hour."

"All that jarring when the train stopped woke me,"
she replied, lighting her cigarette. "I'm not used to being
rich, riding on trains and things. And I didn't want to
smoke in the compartment, because Aunt Cindy would
wake up and get mad. I don't like to make her mad, you
know."

"Come on, you can sit in my compartment," he said,
opening the door. "I don't want you wandering around at
night, Janessa. If you aren't with Dr. Martin, then you
come and get me." Following her through the door into
the corridor, he noticed the smooth, mellow odor of the
tobacco that she was smoking. "What kind of tobacco is
that?"

"Select Virginia crimp."

"Select Vir . . . that's better tobacco than I smoke!"

"Shh!" she hissed, a finger over her lips. "You'll wake
everyone up, Dad." Her smile changed to a wide grin as
she puffed on her cigarette again. "You should get some of
this. It's pretty good."

Toby chuckled and playfully pushed her ahead of him
along the corridor. The girl spent most of her time with

the doctor, and while she remained very quiet and reserved, she would now converse freely with her grandmother and Cindy. But it was only with him that she displayed a sense of humor, which to Toby was gratifying in a way that he had never before known.

They sat in his compartment and talked as she finished her cigarette. Then she kissed him good-night and went to her compartment. As he prepared to go to bed, Toby thought about her smoking. There were, he mused, much worse things than tolerating her smoking. He might never have met his daughter, thus missing a world of joy.

As he went to bed, the train pulled out of Roseville, and he fell asleep to the laboring of the engines up the steep incline of the Sierra Nevada. The next morning, the train was racing across the flatlands east of the range, and Toby and the others settled into a routine. They had breakfast and lunch together in the dining car, then went to a passenger car and sat in adjacent seats to look at the passing countryside. After dinner they retired to their compartments for the night.

As he sat with the others and looked out the windows, Toby occasionally saw features in the terrain that he recognized. They brought back memories of when he and Rob Martin had maintained order among the crews laying track. Where he and Rob had ridden slowly along on horses, the train now sped in a rush of iron and hiss of steam.

Looking at the older members of the party as they gazed out, Toby knew that his progress had been rapid compared with theirs, when they had come westward on a wagon train. Forging into an unknown wilderness, ten miles a day had been good progress. More often it had been five miles or less because of broken axles, lame animals, and other problems.

However, both generations had faced unique problems, and both had overcome them. His own son, merely bored with the journey, had been born to a generation of even faster progress, the inheritors of the railroads. But his generation would have its problems and challenges.

The most recent addition to the circle of family and

friends, the small, quiet Janessa, was already confronting her challenges. Sitting with Dr. Martin, she studied tirelessly. In addition to helping her with her schoolwork, the old man was teaching her the rudiments of Latin and Greek. At other times the two pored over thick tomes the doctor had brought along, books containing illustrations that Cindy and Eulalia viewed as ranging from the outright obscene to those merely unsuitable for a young girl to see.

Soon the snowcapped peaks of the Rocky Mountains lay behind, and the train was crossing the vast spaces of the Great Plains. From here on in they would make good time, Toby knew, and in less than two days they would reach their destination.

It was late at night when the train pulled into the station in Independence. The platform was almost deserted in the yellow light of the lamps hung along it, and it was easy for Toby to spot those who had come to meet the party.

Rob and Kale Martin stood on one side of Susanna, Andrew Brentwood's petite, auburn-haired wife, and Edward and Tommie Blackstone stood on the other. All of them young, they were a handsome, well-dressed group. Kale's dramatic, honey-skinned loveliness complemented Tommie's fresh, fair beauty. Edward, the urbane Englishman, was dapper and stylish as he leaned on a cane. Rob was tall and solidly built, with strong features.

All of them wore bands of black crepe on their right coat sleeves. It was duly noted by the party filing down the steps from the train, and the greetings between the relatives and close friends were subdued as they embraced and shook hands.

"It happened this afternoon," Susanna Brentwood explained. "It was very peaceful. He just passed away in his sleep."

Leland Blake's chiseled, lined face reflected remorse and disappointment as he sighed heavily. "I'm sorry. . . ." he said, his voice trailing off.

There was a momentary silence, then Eulalia said, "How is Claudia holding up, Susanna? Well, I hope."

Susanna nodded. "Yes, quite well. It wasn't unexpected, of course, but it's impossible to be prepared for something like this. But she's doing quite well."

"Have you had any word from Andrew?" the general asked.

"Yes, he sent us a telegraph message as soon as his boat arrived in New York," Susanna replied. "His train's due in tomorrow morning. The burial will be the following day."

"Sam has been taken to a funeral home," Edward added in his crisp, precise accents. "He left very specific instructions as to what is to be done, but it would probably be better for Claudia to tell you about that. I'm sure you're weary after your long journey. We have hired carriages waiting."

He beckoned to porters who were waiting nearby, and they pushed handcarts over and gathered up the baggage. The group followed the porters through the doors to the waiting room and across the lobby to the front entrance of the terminal, where the carriages were parked.

It was a half-hour ride to the Brentwood home, an expansive Victorian mansion on the edge of town, on a street lined by other large homes. As the carriages turned in at the circular drive in front of the house, Toby recalled how Sam Brentwood, one of the early trappers and hunters in the Rocky Mountains, had found the prosaic life of operating a supply depot for wagon trains confining. But it had provided material compensations, the supply depot gradually expanding into one of the largest and most profitable shipping firms in the region.

Claudia Brentwood met them at the door, pale with grief but composed. At sixty-two she was white-haired and matronly, but her green eyes were those of a much younger woman. After quiet greetings were exchanged, a maid assisted Susanna, Kale, and Tommie in showing the new arrivals upstairs to their rooms. After the children had been put to bed, the others came back downstairs to the large, luxuriously furnished parlor.

A maid served cups of hot cocoa. Claudia waved her own cup away. "It's late, and I know all of you must be very tired," she announced. "I only wanted to talk with you for a moment about the arrangements that Sam wished, and then I'll let you retire for the night."

"There's no need for you to coddle us," Dr. Martin said. "It's you we're concerned about, Claudia."

Claudia glanced around at her old friends, her eyes brimming with tears, but she would not indulge her sorrow. Her bearing reflected the determination that had made her more than a passive bystander in the family's business affairs. She had managed first her father's business as a girl and then her first husband's as a young woman. It had been said of her that she would never find a man strong enough for her. She had, but now he was gone.

In a steady voice, she began detailing Sam Brentwood's last wishes. He had specified that no wake be conducted and that the funeral and burial be short and simple and attended only by family and close friends. Further, he had expressed the wish to be buried in a plain oak coffin in an unmarked grave a few miles along the Oregon Trail west of the city.

Everyone present could easily understand the first part of what Sam had wanted, for he had been an unpretentious man who disliked pomp and ceremony. But he had also been a man of deep but quiet religious convictions, having endowed several churches. For him to ask to be buried in an unmarked grave far from hallowed ground seemed completely uncharacteristic.

In the silence that followed when Claudia finished speaking, Toby and the others exchanged uncomfortable glances. The same thought was on all of their minds. In his last days, Sam Brentwood had been very ill—irrational at times, according to Susanna. Leland Blake, Claudia's brother-in-law through his first marriage, voiced the common concern.

"Claudia, we want to do what Sam wanted," he said gently, "as well as what you think is appropriate. Now, I must ask you: Was Sam himself when he asked you to do this?"

"He was himself," Claudia replied. "His mind was as clear as on the first day I met him and Whip Holt in Cathy's house on Long Island in 1837. That's what he wanted, Lee."

"Then that's what we'll do," the general announced firmly, glancing around as he sat back. "You'll have our full support in fulfilling Sam's wishes."

Claudia smiled faintly in acknowledgment of the murmur of agreement from everyone. Then her eyes filled with tears again. "I'll have to ask you to excuse me, please," she said softly. "Susanna . . ."

After she had gone, Toby filed out with the others and climbed the stairs to the guest room where he was staying.

The maid had opened a window to air out the room, and the lamp on the nightstand was flickering in the night breeze. Toby stepped to the window to close it.

As he did, he thought he glimpsed a man at the end of the circular drive. Peering into the darkness for a better look, he saw nothing.

Foot traffic was rare on the street of expensive homes, particularly at this late hour. Wondering if he had glimpsed a prowler, Toby watched the drive.

After a minute or so, seeing nothing, he shrugged and dismissed it, then closed the window and prepared for bed.

VII

Colonel Andrew Brentwood arrived early the next morning. Susanna, Toby, and General Blake went to meet him at the station, to break the news to him.

When their carriage returned to the house, Andrew went into the parlor with his mother. It was not yet noon when the entire group, dressed in mourning, boarded carriages and set off toward the center of town.

At the funeral home, Sam Brentwood's body reposed in the plain oak coffin he had specified. A large man, he somehow looked smaller to Toby than he had in life, when the force of his personality had blended with his physical appearance to make him a giant among men. Paying his last respects, Toby passed the coffin with the others.

In the hushed stir of activity as everyone was sitting down, Tim fidgeted until Cindy pointed a finger and turned her pale blue Holt eyes toward him in a warning glare. Toby noted that little Samuel Brentwood was also restless and that Susanna had pulled him onto her lap to quiet him. But the other child present, Janessa, was as decorous as any of the adults. Wearing a black dress and a small black hat that the thrifty Cindy had once worn, she was as solemn as her clothing.

After a time Andrew, holding his watch, leaned over and spoke to his mother. The governor, his wife, and a small group of officials had asked to call on Claudia at her home at one o'clock, to express their condolences. Claudia silently nodded, standing up. The others stood and followed her toward the door.

Outside, while the carriages were being brought around to the front, Andrew spoke quietly to Toby. "While we were at the house," he said, "my mother told me about the arrangements my father wanted." His voice reflected concern about burying his father in an unmarked grave in the countryside.

"What he wanted came as a surprise to all of us, Andy," Toby replied. "But your mother said that his mind was clear at the time, that he knew exactly what he was saying."

The colonel drew in a deep breath and sighed. "She told me the same thing, Toby. I would have greatly preferred to have a monument and a suitable place in a churchyard, but we intend to follow his wishes. I understand that Edward and Rob have made some arrangements."

The Englishman, standing nearby, stepped closer and joined the conversation. He had, he told Andrew, made arrangements for carriages and a hearse for the next day. Susanna, formerly a newspaper reporter and the author of several books, had been researching the Brentwood business records and writing a book on the Oregon Trail. Thoroughly familiar with the route of the trail, she had designated a suitable spot for the burial.

"It will take several hours to get there," Edward continued, "so we should set out fairly early tomorrow morning."

"By all means," Andrew agreed. "My mother mentioned that she would prefer to be well west of the city before the streets become crowded, so let's set out about an hour before daybreak."

"Very well," Edward said. "I'll make the arrangements accordingly."

Andrew nodded gratefully, turning to get into a carriage with his wife and mother. Toby and the others followed, the bustle of activity on the streets a jarring reminder that life continued in its normal patterns.

At the house, Claudia, Andrew, and Susanna withdrew to have lunch by themselves and await the arrival of the governor. The others had lunch in the dining room, then went out to the gazebo on the spacious, landscaped grounds behind the house. The governor and his party arrived, then departed thirty minutes later, and Andrew came out the back door of the house.

"My mother is lying down and resting now," he said, stepping into the gazebo. "Susanna is with her."

The others moved to make room for Andrew to sit down. In the awkward silence that followed, Cindy spoke hesitantly. "Colonel Brentwood," she said, "we've read about the recent developments in Europe, and I wondered if Henry may be coming home soon. I know this isn't an appropriate time to bring up the subject. . . ."

Andrew nodded in understanding. "No, that's quite all right, Cindy. I realize how you feel. However, it doesn't appear that the events in France will necessarily result in Henry's coming home soon."

As his stepdaughter sighed in disappointment, Lee Blake said, "Toby and I noted some interesting developments in the newspapers, Andrew. From the actions taken toward Germany by the State Department a few days before the surrender, it appears that Washington was either very fortunate in its timing or they had some good intelligence."

The colonel nodded. "I have some news for you, so I may as well tell you all now. It isn't privileged information, or obviously I wouldn't mention it. However, it isn't something to be discussed openly, particularly where it could be picked up in diplomatic circles. Is that understood?"

Everyone replied affirmatively as he glanced around the group. "When I came through New York," he continued, "I saw Colonel Bill Hanson, who is on the staff of the secretary of war. He told me that the secretary of war and the secretary of state were informed by priority dispatch of the impending capitulation of the French more than two days before the surrender. Those dispatches came from the hand of one Second Lieutenant Henry Blake."

There was a soft gasp of delight from Cindy and stunned silence from everyone else. General Blake shook his head and frowned. "Andrew, do you mean that Hank had access to the results of secret negotiations between the French and German governments?"

"No, sir," Andrew replied. "He must have observed and correctly interpreted actions taken by the Germans. As a matter of fact, our young Henry has been achieving some very extraordinary results. He's come up with reams of data on the senior German officers and other things. The rest of the attaché section put together can't hold a candle to him."

"But the secretary of war could see that the dispatch was from a second lieutenant," Leland Blake said. "Didn't his staff question the reliability of the source?"

The colonel nodded. "Yes, sir. The State Department staff apparently didn't, but the War Department staff asked the attaché section for a full clarification. The attaché section replied to the effect that the source had proved to be highly reliable."

"In other words," the general said in disapproval, "they shirked responsibility in the matter. They bowed off the stage and left it between the secretary of war and a second lieutenant."

"That's what it amounted to," Andrew agreed. "But at the present time, to my knowledge there isn't a second lieutenant assigned to the attaché section in Berlin. By order of the secretary of war, General Blake, your stepson has been promoted to first lieutenant."

The subdued atmosphere among the group completely dissolved. Cindy and Eulalia gasped in pleasure, while the others smiled and commented. "My word, that puts the lad three to four years ahead of his contemporaries," the general observed. "That certainly gets his career off to a running start. Considering the magnitude of the achievement, Andrew, you could also be in line for promotion. That is your command, after all."

"It could happen," the colonel replied. "When I was talking with Bill Hanson, he more or less said I was a strong candidate for the next promotion of a colonel to brigadier general."

The general smiled in satisfaction. Cindy, her curiosity merely whetted, asked what Henry did during his free time. The colonel explained that everyone at the forward post worked seven days a week.

"But surely he has some friends there," Cindy insisted.

"Yes, he's become quite good friends with an officer in the Prussian dragoons," Andrew replied. "Captain Richard Koehler. The captain is a few years older than Henry and outranks him, of course, but they spend some time together at least every day or two."

Cindy's manner was whimsical, but her eyes were direct as she persisted. "He hasn't become acquainted with any French ladies?"

The colonel shook his head. "Not even a speaking acquaintance. Captain Koehler has a widowed aunt, a Baroness von Kirchberg, and Henry knows her. But we don't come into contact with many French people, and our duties take up virtually all our time."

Her curiosity momentarily satisfied, Cindy fell silent. The others began questioning Andrew about France and the war in general, and as they did, Toby noticed a man come out of the house, a maid escorting him and pointing to the gazebo. In his early twenties, he was well-built and had strong, darkly tanned features. His boots and wide-brimmed hat added a western flavor to his neat, conservative brown suit, and a watch chain hung between his vest pockets. A slight bulge under his left arm indicated to Toby that he carried a pistol in a shoulder holster. The man seemed vaguely familiar, and Toby stepped out of the gazebo to meet him.

The others fell silent as the stranger approached. He removed his hat with a gravely courteous nod to the ladies, then extended his hand to Toby. "Mr. Holt? I'm Ted Taylor."

Toby nodded, recognizing the name; he was a lawman from California, his parents Danny and Heather Taylor. Despite his relative youth, Ted Taylor had a widespread reputation. One of a new breed of lawmen, he relied upon judgment and wits as much as weapons, and he was equally at home in polite company or in a shoot-out with criminals. "I've heard a lot about you, and I'm very pleased to meet you," Toby said as they shook hands.

"I'm pleased to meet you, Mr. Holt," Ted replied. "Needless to say, I've heard a lot about you."

"Then you should know that you don't call me mister unless you expect to have it returned," Toby said, smiling. "I'm Toby and you're Ted. Come on and meet my friends and relatives."

They stepped into the gazebo, and Toby began the introductions. The burly Ted Woods, who had been like a father to Danny Taylor, greeted the young lawman effusively and inquired about his parents. When it came Cindy's turn to be introduced, a faint flush rose to her cheeks; Ted Taylor was extremely handsome. As the lawman shook hands with Andrew, he explained his presence. "I didn't want to intrude upon you and your family, Colonel Brentwood," he said, "but when I heard about your father, I felt obliged to pay my respects. If I've intruded, I apologize, sir."

"No, you haven't intruded at all," the colonel replied, favorably impressed with Ted. "I view your visit in the same way it is intended. Toby, I take it you know of Ted?"

"Yes, indeed," Toby said emphatically. "You served an interim term as a United States marshal, didn't you, Ted? The last I heard, you were working with the California attorney general in breaking up phony gold investment schemes that were bilking people out of money."

"I finished that up a while back," Ted said. "The reason I'm out this way is that I was hired to be in charge of the guards on a gold shipment to St. Louis. I was headed back home when I heard about Mr. Brentwood."

"If you would like to accompany us to the burial service tomorrow," Andrew said, "you're more than welcome to do so."

"I'd be most honored, Colonel Brentwood," Ted said sincerely.

"We'll be honored to have you. The service will be a simple one, and we'll be leaving before daybreak. In view of that, you'd better stay here tonight. We have plenty of rooms, so if you'd like to go for your things, I'll have a maid show you to your room."

Ted hesitated only a moment. "You're very kind,

Colonel, and I do hope I'm not inconveniencing you in any way."

"No, not at all," Andrew assured him. "Just go to your hotel and get your things, and then you can join the rest of us."

Ted nodded gratefully, and he and Toby stepped back out of the gazebo. As they walked toward the house, Ted spoke quietly. "I'm much obliged to you, Toby," he said. "I could tell that it was through you that the colonel invited me to stay."

"I'm glad you accepted. We could use another good lawman in Oregon, and maybe I can recruit you. Do you have a horse?"

"Yes, a hired one," Ted replied. "I'll return it to the livery stable and catch a carriage back." He hesitated, then added, "When I came up the street, there was a man down near the corner who acted as if he'd rather not be noticed."

"What did he look like?"

"Big—well over six feet and about two hundred and fifty pounds. About forty or so, with a thick beard and mustache."

The description meant nothing to Toby, but it seemed characteristic of the young lawman to have been so observant; his steady gray eyes would miss little. "About the only thing you'll see on this street is carriages," Toby said, "with a few riders. I don't know what a man would be doing standing around on it."

"If he's still there, I'll ask him."

The comment was matter-of-fact, completely without bravado; Ted Taylor was obviously a man who would assume the authority to inquire into whatever appeared suspicious to him, to correct whatever was wrong. He was a leader, and Toby liked him. "I'll see you when you get back, then, Ted," Toby said.

Ted nodded, putting on his hat as he walked away. Turning back toward the gazebo, Toby recalled having seen something the night before at the end of the drive. He wondered if he had indeed glimpsed a man, perhaps the same man Ted Taylor had seen.

* * *

When the lawman returned, he made a passing mention of the fact that the tall, bearded man had been nowhere in sight. Then the subject was dropped.

With his quiet, courteous bearing, Ted Taylor fit smoothly into the group. He listened more than he talked, but when he did speak, his comments reflected a subtle wit and a quick, active mind.

The following morning everyone rose well before daybreak, and the minister, with the hearse carrying the coffin, arrived a short time later. Everyone filed out of the house, Claudia, Andrew, and Susanna getting into the buggy behind the hearse and the others finding places in the carriages. Then the vehicles moved slowly out of the drive and along the dark, quiet streets of Independence.

By dawn the procession had crossed the Missouri River into Kansas, leaving the city far behind. The weather was unsettled but not unpleasant. The sunshine brightened and dimmed as clouds scudded across the sky, pushed by a gusty wind that rippled the deep grass in the fields on either side of the road. There was a damp, fresh feel of approaching rain.

Nothing else moved along the narrow road as it wound over the rolling countryside. From time to time, the shining ribbons of the railroad came into view to the south, or an occasional farmhouse could be seen. Then, during midmorning, at a place that was much like any other stretch along the road, the hearse slowed. It turned off and headed north across a field, the buggy and the carriages following.

The horses strained harder as the vehicles swayed over bumps and ruts, the deep grass brushing past on either side. The line of vehicles moved across one low hill and then another, until the road, farmhouses, and other signs of life were left behind.

Finally, a half hour later, the procession halted on a low ridge above the old Oregon Trail. As the women waited by the carriages, the men carried tools down to a level spot overlooking the trail. Ted Taylor, silent and energetic, was the first to doff his coat and roll up his sleeves. He began cutting the sod into neat squares and stacking it aside so it could be put back into place and leave no visible sign when the grave was filled.

Once the sod was removed, Toby and the others began helping Ted dig the grave. They worked in silence for a long time, and not until they paused to rest for a minute did anyone speak. Ted indicated the trail with a nod. "This is the first time I've ever seen it," he said, "even though I've been back and forth to Missouri several times. This is the very first time I've seen it, Toby."

His voice reflected a sense of wonder, as well as bewilderment at having overlooked something of great significance. As Toby thought about it, he experienced something of the same feelings.

The trail had had a profound influence on him. It had brought his parents together and set the place, time, and circumstances of his birth. Because of the innumerable conversations he had heard about it from his early boyhood on, his mental concept of it was somehow more that of a vital, living force than of merely a place. Yet, like Ted, he had never before seen the Oregon Trail.

Now overgrown with weeds, it was still easy to identify. Out here on the prairie, nature built in flowing, curved lines, its forces following the path of least resistance. But human beings were single-minded. Among the rolling hills, the trail was a wide, deep road that led straight westward, cleaving completely through a low hill a short distance away and others farther on.

The deep grass on either side of the trail was littered with the remains of belongings that had been discarded long ago from overloaded wagons. A few yards away Toby could see a decayed, sun-bleached wooden bedstead. In its time it had probably harbored generations of young, lusty couples, women in the agony of childbirth, and the aged and ill in the despair of approaching death.

The grave finished, the men went back up the ridge. Toby, Edward, Ted, and Rob took the coffin out of the hearse and lifted it to their shoulders. Claudia, Andrew, and Susanna walked behind the coffin, and the others followed them down the slope to the grave. After the coffin was lowered into the ground, the minister took his place at the head of the grave.

The clouds swirled overhead, the wind fluttering the pages of the minister's Bible and stirring the women's long dresses and the men's hair. As the minister began reading, Claudia sobbed into her handkerchief, Andrew and Susanna holding her.

"I am the resurrection and the life, saith the Lord. He that believeth in me, though he were dead, yet shall he live. . . ."

The wind snatched the minister's first words from his lips, scattering them in the vast open reaches under the Kansas sky. But as he read on, something in the atmosphere of this place seemed to strengthen his voice. In the same way that the walls of a house that have sheltered generations in their grief and joy become something more than inert wood and plaster, this place had a life that those gathered around the grave could almost sense.

Too many had come this way, and too much human pain and struggle had been endured here for this patch of ground to be no more than lifeless, open prairie. These things lingered on the wind, faint whispers across the decades. They joined the minister's voice, and those whom Sam Brentwood had sent to a new life were a distant chorus bidding him Godspeed to eternity.

". . . earth to earth, and dust to dust. The Lord giveth, and the Lord hath taken away. Blessed be the name of the Lord."

As the minister finished and closed his Bible, Andrew and Susanna turned and began leading Claudia back up the hill. The other women and the children followed, and Toby and the men began filling the grave. At last Toby understood why Sam Brentwood had wanted to be buried here; and from the faces of the other men, he could see that they understood as well.

It was to this trail, made by the iron-rimmed wheels of countless wagons bearing a river of people westward, that Sam Brentwood had devoted the best years of his life. This trail was the realization of a duty he had been asked to perform by the leader of his nation. Now it was his monument.

Rather than lying in an unmarked grave, he had a monument that reached halfway across a continent. He would never be alone here, for the trail was alive with ghostly presences. And while it was far from any church-yard, Sam Brentwood had been laid to rest in hallowed ground.

Dark rain clouds moving in from the west followed the carriages back to Independence, and the storm broke over the city just as they reached the house. The change in the weather seemed to mirror a change in the atmo-sphere among the group. Sorrow and remorse remained, and Sam Brentwood would be mourned, but a new chap-ter had begun, new tasks lay ahead.

The first large, heavy raindrops were smacking down from the low clouds as the group went into the house. Claudia Brentwood, her face pale and her mouth set in a determined line, went into the study to lose herself in the account books of the Brentwood business affairs. The oth-ers began taking up where they had left off.

Janessa, walking up the stairs with Dr. Martin and Tonie, talked with the old man about Latin verbs. Leland Blake and Andrew Brentwood hung up their caps and went into the parlor, discussing planned organizational changes in the army. Toby, after telling Rob and Edward that he would meet them in the parlor in a few minutes, started up the stairs to his room to get the folder on the logging investment.

Ted Taylor, walking upstairs with him, took out his watch and looked at it. "Well, I have time to catch a train west today," he said. "But the way that rain is pelting down, I'd just as soon infringe upon the Brentwood hospi-tality for another night."

"I'm positive that the Brentwoods wouldn't call it infringing, Ted. If you don't have anything urgent await-ing you in California, you're more than welcome to come to Chicago with us."

As they paused in the hallway, Ted said, "I don't have

anything waiting that's as interesting as going with you might be, Toby," he said. "From what I've heard, things seem to happen around you. Yes, I'll come."

"We'll be glad to have you along," Toby replied in satisfaction. "When you've put your hat and coat away, meet us down in the parlor."

Toby stepped into his room for the folder of papers, then went back downstairs. As he sat down and began talking with Rob and Edward, their wives moving closer to listen, Ted joined them. Toby explained the investment, handing Rob and Edward the estimates he had prepared.

At length, the Englishman nodded. "Yes, this looks very interesting, Toby," he said. "Very interesting indeed. But it's much larger in scope than you indicated in your letter."

"The possibilities grew larger as we got farther into it," Toby explained. "It began as a more limited undertaking, about the size of what Rob and I had in Washington. Then it developed into this."

Edward looked at the papers again. "There's one thing that puzzles me, though," he said. "I'm not questioning your estimates, but the savings you show by owning our own sawmill versus paying to have the timber sawed are very substantial."

"The charges at the mills are high," Toby said, leafing through his other papers. Taking out the list of costs that Frank had made up on the mills in Chicago, he handed it to Edward. "That's what they charge in Chicago. But if you think that's high, take a look at what they charge in Wisconsin." He separated another paper and handed it to Edward.

Looking at the paper, the Englishman whistled softly. "My word, they do levy hefty charges, don't they? It looks as though they're taking a lot of the profits from the loggers."

"Maybe the mill owners are conspiring to keep the charges high," Rob suggested.

"Maybe," Toby said, letting his friends draw their own conclusions.

Edward handed the papers back to Toby. "Whatever they're doing, it would be of no concern to us. As I said, though, that is a very interesting proposal, Toby."

"It certainly has more potential for profit than the logging in Washington," Rob said. "Our shipping costs were high there because we were limited to shipping by barge. But Chicago is the major railhead of the Midwest. It sounds like a good investment to me." He looked questioningly at Edward.

Edward smiled. "I'd certainly like to take a look at it, Toby. You'll come along, won't you, Tommie?"

"Try to keep me from it," his wife replied, laughing.

Rob turned to Kale. She was extremely attached to Rob's two-year-old daughter, Cathy, and was obviously regretful when he told her that they would have to make arrangements to leave the child with a nurse at the Brentwood home. "From what Toby says, we'll be going through the forest for several days."

"Frank has a logging camp built now," Toby added, "and Bettina and Lucy are there. But the trip from Chicago is a hard one, with overnight camps along the way."

Nodding reluctantly, Kale agreed to leave the child behind. Toby then talked with Edward and Rob about travel arrangements. Frank was in Chicago, attending to details of the operation while he awaited word on when Toby would arrive with the others, and he could escort the two couples to the logging camp. They decided to set out for Chicago the following day, when those who were returning to Oregon were also leaving.

The next day began in a rush of activity, Ted borrowing a horse from the Brentwood stables and riding into the city to arrange for hired carriages to take everyone to the train station. Toby took a horse and went to send a telegram informing Frank Woods of the train that he and the others were taking. Shortly after he returned to the house, the carriages arrived.

At the train station, everyone sat together in the waiting room until the train to San Francisco pulled in. Then they went out to the platform, and Toby made his farewells with those going to Oregon. They were a closely knit group of relatives and friends, regretful over parting, but all of them also had their pressing private concerns.

The general was anxious to return to his post, while Ted and Olga Woods had to get back to their businesses in Portland. The trip had been fatiguing for Dr. Martin, and he and Tonie were looking forward to getting back home. Eulalia had bought a box of mechanical toys to entertain Tim on the trip, and Toby hugged them both as he said his good-byes. Cindy was involved in a conversation with Ted Taylor.

Toby saved his last farewells for Janessa. It had been too short a time since they had met, and every moment together had been a joy. Parting with her was difficult.

The platform teemed with activity as Toby talked with her, the conductor shouting and others boarding the train. Feelings similar to his were reflected on his daughter's small face. "I wish I knew Latin, Greek, or some of the other things that Dr. Martin does," he said. "If I knew something to teach you along the way, I'd take you to Chicago with me."

"If you think I haven't been learning anything from you, Dad, you're wrong," she replied. "But I have to go to school and study other things, so I couldn't go to Chicago anyway."

He smiled and nodded, kneeling down to hold her. As he kissed her good-bye, he detected, as always, a heavy odor of tobacco. "You've got to stop that smoking, Janessa," he said.

It had become a joke between them, and she smiled as she kissed him back. "Good-bye, Dad. Hurry home as soon as you can."

"Yes, I will. Good-bye, Janessa."

Its bell clanging and the engine puffing, the train was starting to move away. Janessa hopped up the steps and into the vestibule with the others, all of them waving. She leaned out to wave to her father. Cindy, taking the back of the girl's coat and holding it firmly to keep her from falling, waved to Ted, to Toby, and the others.

After the train was gone, Toby and his friends went into the station restaurant to get coffee and to wait until their train arrived. When it pulled into the station an hour later, they joined the other passengers going out to the platform.

After Edward, Rob, and their wives had boarded, Toby started up the steps, then paused. Ted was looking along the platform, his lips pursed in a frown. "What is it, Ted?" Toby asked. "Do you see someone you know?"

Ted glanced at Toby and then looked along the platform again. "No, apparently not," he said, following Toby up the steps. "I thought I glimpsed that man I saw loitering on the street where the Brentwoods live, but I must have been mistaken. He's a man who's very easy to spot, even in a crowd, and I don't see him."

Frustrated rage throbbed within Karl Kellerman as he stood with his back to the station wall, a cast-iron pillar between him and the train he had been watching. The first time he had seen the tanned, gray-eyed man in the brown suit and western hat and boots had been two days before, while waiting near the Brentwood house for a glimpse of his quarry.

The stony facial expression and penetrating, searching look were characteristic, and Kellerman had immediately sensed that the young man was some kind of lawman. He had fled, but not because he was frightened. He feared no one, including lawmen. His fear was that he would fail when he finally had a chance at his quarry, Toby Holt.

Now the lawman, apparently having joined up with Holt and the others accompanying him, had almost seen him again. The tanned face had been turning and the gray eyes moving toward him just as he stepped back behind the pillar. The seething fury within him was mixed with apprehension as he listened for boots approaching along the platform.

Then he relaxed as the conductor shouted the last call for passengers to board and the train started moving. When it began picking up speed, moving out of the station, Kellerman stepped from behind the pillar. Watching the train drawing away, he walked along the platform.

Others stepped out of his path. Three inches over six

feet tall, he weighed two hundred and forty pounds. But it was not solely because he was a large man that others gave him room. It was because of the glare of savage fury in his eyes, because of his unswerving, relentless stride. He was a man consumed by hatred, driven by a single, burning force in his life. He wanted to kill Toby Holt.

At an earlier time, Kellerman had been driven by other powerful forces. One was an overriding need to possess beautiful women and to bend them to his will before casting them aside. Another was a greedy hunger for wealth.

He had fulfilled those needs. In the aftermath of the Civil War, Mississippi had been fertile ground for one without principles or morals. Through one scheme after another, ranging across a variety of illegal activities, he had amassed wealth and had had the leisure time to pursue beautiful women. Then Toby Holt had come upon the scene.

Kellerman's world had collapsed. Through Toby Holt, he had lost everything and had barely escaped with his life. Then his purpose had become revenge. Knowing that he would fail if he went to Portland, where Toby Holt had many friends, he had waited. When he had read about Sam Brentwood's death, he had assumed that Toby Holt would come to Independence.

Disguised by a thick beard and mustache, he had been waiting at the train station the night Toby Holt had arrived. But others, who might have stopped the bullet meant for Toby Holt, had been in the way. Then, when the lawman had come upon the scene, Kellerman had retreated. His need for revenge was a raging hunger within him, but he was also patient. It had to be under the right circumstances. His one fear was of failure.

Reaching the end of the platform, Kellerman watched the distant train as it disappeared around a curve. His sense of disappointment was the angry frustration of a predator who misses on the first lunge, the quarry still within reach.

He knew that Toby Holt was going to Chicago. In a few hours, he himself would take a train to Chicago. There he would kill Toby Holt.

VIII

As the train approached a small, isolated station in the Illinois countryside, the red arm on the signal post beside the track was down. The train jerked as it suddenly began slowing.

Ted Taylor, who was talking to Toby, broke off in midsentence. The Martins and the Blackstones, sitting across the aisle, also fell silent; the next scheduled stop wasn't until Chicago. A weaving motion passed along the train as it crossed a switch and turned onto a stretch of track behind the station. Moments later, brakes squealed, and the train shuddered to a halt.

A hubbub of conversation rose, the passengers getting up and leaving the train to find out what had happened. Toby and his friends went with them, walking across the dusty yard toward the small station.

They joined the crowd gathering at the end of the platform, where the stationmaster was explaining the delay. He said that the Chicago and North Western and the Chicago and Rock Island railroads were competing for a mail contract, which was to be awarded to the line that could make a run between Council Bluffs and Chicago in the shortest time. North Western had made its run two days before, and the track was being cleared ahead of the Rock Island locomotive, which was due through shortly.

Most of the passengers were cheerful, their boredom relieved. A few, however, were annoyed over the delay. A flushed, heavyset man in a checked wool suit spoke for them. "How late will we arrive in Chicago?" he demanded angrily.

The gray-haired stationmaster, immaculately neat in his black uniform and cap, remained unruffled. "It ain't up to me to make prognostications, is it?" he pointed out. "It's the Good Lord who sees to the future, ain't it? But if'n nothing else happens to delay you, and you don't give yourself a seizure and take a lot longer trip than you planned, you ought to be in Chicago no more than thirty minutes late."

Red-faced and muttering, the man wheeled and stamped back toward the train as people laughed. Most of the passengers moved closer to the track to get a good view of the special train when it passed.

Inside the small station, the telegrapher sat at his equipment, watching it intently and waiting. Two youths, railroad trainees wearing ill-fitting railroad coats and caps, sat on a bench beside the door. Toby exchanged an amiable nod with the stationmaster, asking how long it had taken the North Western line to make its run.

"Might near thirty-five hours," the man replied. "But I knew that Rock Island had it hands down all the time."

"Why do you say that?" Toby asked.

The stationmaster started to answer, then broke off as the telegraph just inside the door began clattering furiously. When it stopped, the telegrapher sat up. "That was Hayward's Crossing, Mr. Tolbert!" he called excitedly. "She just tore through there, and old John Siler said she moved his station back into the yard by about two feet!"

The stationmaster took his watch out of his waistcoat pocket and looked at it. "All right, Jake," he replied. "Old John Siler is worser'n a little kid for getting agitated, though. She's just coming out of them hills, so she can't be going too fast." He replaced his watch in his pocket, turning back to Toby. "Rock Island is using the Silver Cannonball, and Pejoe Claiborne is at the throttle. No line in the world can beat that pair."

Toby had heard of the engine, built by the Grant Locomotive Works of New Jersey and displayed at the

1867 Paris International Exposition. The boiler on the huge, powerful locomotive was encased in German silver, and its headlights, whistles, and other fittings were solid silver.

The stationmaster continued, talking about the engineer on the train. "Percival Joseph Claiborne," he said, "but it'll cost you a knot on the head to call him anything except Pejoe. Nineteen years old and with nerves like boiler steel. He knows the rails and he knows his trains, and he gets the most out of both."

The telegraph began clattering again. Then it stopped, and the telegrapher called out, "Cedar Flats, Mr. Tolbert! She just shot past Cedar Flats, and old Tom Watson said that she sucked up all them shrubs that he planted by his station!"

The stationmaster took out his watch again. "Old Tom Watson sees a buffalo every time a mouse runs past him, so I don't . . ." His voice faded as he studied his watch. Then his dignified composure began evaporating. "By Jehoshaphat!" he exclaimed. "Old Pejoe is leaning on the throttle! Between Hayward's Crossing and Cedar Flats she was running near seventy miles in the hour!"

Toby exchanged an astonished glance with Ted, Edward, and the others. "She'll be here in a few minutes," the stationmaster continued, beckoning one of the youths. "Reuben, you've come to work early every day this week, so you can be the one to throw the switch on the signal and flag her through. You know what to do. When she toots for a clear track, give her the flag. Hurry up and get out there, son."

The youth raced into the small station and snatched up a flag, then ran back out and bounded off the platform, dashing toward the signal post. The stationmaster stepped to the end of the platform and called to the crowd of passengers.

"You folks stand back from them tracks!" he ordered. "When she's running with plenty of throttle, the Silver Cannonball stirs enough wind to suck you right under her wheels if'n you're too close. Now keep ahold of your children and stand well back!"

The people obediently moved away from the tracks. They watched as the youth reached the signal post, threw a lever dropping the green arm, then held his flag and looked down the tracks. The stationmaster glanced at his watch, his manner betraying growing excitement.

The telegraph began rattling again. The stationmaster looked toward the door and waited impatiently. A few moments later the telegrapher leaned out the door. "She'll be here in a minute!" he shouted. "She just went through Nortonville, scorching the rails! Elmer Giddings says that the wind off'n her bent his signal post!"

"As soon as she passes, send word on down the line!" the stationmaster replied, flushed and animated. "Tell them that we're going to need new shingles for our roof!" Wheeling, he shouted at the crowd, "Now you folks keep ahold of your kids!"

Toby looked down the tracks, the rails stretching in a straight line for a mile before they curved gently and disappeared over a low hill. Just then, a puff of black smoke rose at the crest of the hill. An instant later, the train came into view.

The sun gleamed on the brilliant silver engine, a thick column of smoke sweeping back from it. The train flowed rapidly along the rails toward the curve. In the distance the men in the coal car were tiny figures, struggling to stand on the shifting coal in the careening car as they heaved shovelfuls into the bin at the rear of the engine.

The train sped around the curve to the straightaway. The people on the platform stretched and craned their necks, their excited murmur blending with the distant, muttering roar of the massive locomotive. A white plume of steam cut through the thick smoke billowing from the stack, one of the whistles blowing a rising and falling interrogative note. The youth beside the signal post leaped into the air in a frenzy of excitement as he flapped his flag wildly.

Four more spouts of steam appeared, as all of the whistles on the engine sounded a warning to stand clear. Their varied notes blended into a piercing shriek that was joined by the frenzied tolling of the three silver bells atop the locomotive. The crowd waved and cheered in an outburst of glee that became smothered under the roar of the massive locomotive thundering along the rails.

The youth at the signal post, still leaping and waving his flag, disappeared into the dust boiling up alongside the train. Then the giant, gleaming locomotive was suddenly near. The shattering noise from it was numbing, almost a physical force. The platform under Toby's feet trembled violently as the roaring locomotive bore down on the station and towered over it like a shimmering silver mountain.

Gigantic and awesome, it passed in a fleeting blur of impressions: the men in the coal car frantically throwing coal across the gap to the bin; the brawny, sweat-streaked fireman heaving shovelfuls into the maw of the raging furnace; the engineer sitting in the window and gazing ahead, his cap turned backward, his chin set at a determined angle, his youthful face black with soot around his goggles.

Then it was gone, the station enveloped in dust and smoke, the deafening noise fading to a ringing in Toby's ears. The whistle on the sidetracked train hooted. Toby and his friends went down the steps and joined the laughing, excited crowd streaming back to the train. The beefy man in the checked wool suit who had complained of the delay was among them, chewing a cigar as he laughed and talked with a companion.

When the journey resumed, the passenger train seemed small, slow, and prosaic, its wheels clacking against the rails as it gradually picked up speed. A hubbub of conversation filled the car as people discussed the other train. Toby talked with his friends about it, but his main impression of the speeding train was a concept that he *felt*, not what he had seen.

In a way, the train seemed an embodiment of the American spirit. It was huge and powerful, and the men on it were risking a fiery death in a mass of twisted wreckage to achieve a far more lofty goal than the announced purpose of the run. The mail contract was irrelevant to them, and their destination was Chicago in only a very limited sense. Those men had been challenged. Having seized up the gauntlet, they were hurling their giant machine along the rails toward victory, not Chicago.

Toby gazed out the window as a tiny hamlet passed by. Near it were farms where people were doing their afternoon chores. A blacksmith worked at his forge in his open-fronted shop, and wagons were parked in front of the small general store. The town and its people, going about their daily activities in peace and freedom, was to Toby a scene of unsurpassed beauty.

He wondered if in succeeding generations speed and progress would inhibit feelings about this nation such as he had. It seemed possible. The tendency to become immersed in daily affairs, even in a world that moved at seventy miles an hour, was all too human. If contact was lost with the texture and the heartbeat of the nation, it would be easy to begin taking for granted the simple things that were unattainable dreams in nations where the many were ruled by the few.

In Chicago Frank Woods led the group through the train station to two rented carriages outside.

It was a warm late afternoon without a breath of wind, which made the crowded carriages seem even more close. Powdery dust hung in the air, and the traffic along the street kept it stirred up. Along with the dust and the varied smells of the city, there was a noticeable reek of pine resin from the wooden buildings.

Toby's carriage passed a burned-out building, a heap of charred timbers and ashes that had yet to be cleared away. The sight turned the conversation to the danger of fire in the city. "It's been weeks since the city has had any rain," Frank said, frowning. "There's plenty of water, of course, because the lake is the water supply. But the city is very dry."

"It certainly looks that way," Rob agreed. "I'm sure the loss of that building was a severe blow to someone, but a tiny step will be made in the right direction if it's rebuilt in stone or brick."

"It will be," Frank said. "Strict building codes have been put into effect to begin eliminating wooden buildings in the downtown area, and many businesses have been rebuilding in brick or stone. It was the sudden growth of the city that resulted in all these wooden buildings." He turned to Toby. "In fact, we may have problems building a sawmill. There's talk of a moratorium on new construction, until a planning commission is formed to oversee zoning and new construction within the city limits."

Toby frowned, concerned over costly delays. "When will this commission be formed?" he asked.

"I'm not sure," Frank replied. "But I've made you an appointment to see Mayor Mason tomorrow morning, and he's looking forward to meeting you. I talked to him briefly myself, but I didn't go into the issue with him."

Frank began describing the other things he had done. In addition to making inquiries about the cost of logging rights on properties adjacent to the logging camp, he had contacted the owner and captain of a steam launch who might be willing to tow logs down the lake. Frank said that Toby could meet him the next day, too.

The carriages stopped on narrow, busy Dekoven Street in front of Aaron Ward's dry goods store, and everyone got out. Frank began carrying the baggage up the outside staircase as Toby led the others into the store to introduce them to their host. Wearing a canvas apron over his neat shirt and tie, the merchant was as affable as always, shrugging off thanks for the use of the rooms over his store.

"As I told Frank when we met," he said, "my warehouse is near the edge of the city, convenient to the rail yard. The rooms upstairs aren't large enough to be of any great use to me, so they may as well be of use to someone. But I'm afraid they won't be large enough to make very comfortable quarters for your party."

"They will do excellently," Edward said firmly. "Most of us will be here only one night, so they will more than serve our purpose. But I must say that your generosity makes our visit here one we'll long remember."

"It's my pleasure to be able to help you," Aaron replied. "Besides, the company Frank brings here adds gentility to my surroundings, which is worth far more than coin." He bowed to the two ladies. "And I must say that the gentility of this company is of a high standard indeed."

The two women smiled, returning the compliment. Then Toby and the others went back outside and climbed the staircase to the second floor. The two rooms over the store, with a lavatory at the end of the hall, had been originally intended as a small apartment. Kale and Tommie took the smaller room, leaving the other for the men. Dusk was gathering when they finished arranging their belongings and went back outside to walk to a nearby restaurant for dinner.

The restaurant was one that Frank frequented, as had Toby during his previous visit. Serving good food in pleasant surroundings, it was always crowded, and this evening was no exception. Others were waiting for tables when Toby and his friends arrived, so they took seats in the entrance foyer.

When a large table had been vacated, the headwaiter escorted Toby's party into the dining room. After they were seated, Edward stood back up and looked across the restaurant at the entrance foyer. "I believe I know that young lady who just came in," he said. "Yes, I'm sure she's Margie White. I met her in Boise."

"If you know her, ask her to join us," Tommie suggested. "There's more than enough room at the table, and it's always difficult to get single seating in a restaurant."

With the others echoing Tommie's suggestion, Edward crossed the room toward the entrance foyer. Upon his first glimpse of the woman, he had almost failed to recognize her. Although it had been only a couple of years since he had known her, she had changed. When he first met her, she had come west from her native New Hampshire to be married, but the man had deserted her in Boise. Out of sympathy, Edward had sent her to Boston to work as a receptionist, giving her a recommendation to a senior partner in a law firm that had handled a number of business matters for him.

Apparently the arrangement had been good for her. The shy, helpless girl he had known in Boise had been replaced by an attractive, briskly self-confident young woman who seemed in complete control of herself. Wearing a dark brown dress with a matching hat and short cape, her clothing somewhat dusty and wrinkled, she looked as though she had been traveling. Certainly she had not attempted to enhance her attractiveness with finery.

As Edward approached, she was firmly telling the headwaiter that she could be served in the kitchen. The level gaze from her blue eyes turned toward Edward, and after an instant's hesitation she smiled in recognition. "Edward!" she exclaimed. "I'm so pleased to see you again!"

"I'm delighted to meet you again, Margie," he said. He turned to the headwaiter. "The young lady is a friend of mine. Could we have another chair and place setting at my table, please?"

"Certainly, sir!" the headwaiter replied emphatically, relieved to be rid of this unusual young woman who wanted to eat in the kitchen. He beckoned to a waiter. "I'll have it seen to immediately, sir."

As he led his friend toward the table, Edward was intrigued by what she had been saying to the headwaiter. "You didn't actually want to be seated in the kitchen, did you, Margie?" he asked, chuckling.

The young woman tilted her head to smile up at him from under her wide hat. "It's *Marjorie* now, Edward. I've turned over a new leaf. And what's wrong with eating in the kitchen? I came here for food, not to be fussed over and waited upon. And I certainly didn't come here to sit down and wait. Does my lack of convention offend you?"

Edward laughed at this little speech. "Absolutely not. In fact it's most refreshing. But you do seem to have become a most extraordinary young lady, and I must hear all about what you've been doing. But first let me introduce you to my wife, Tommie, and to my friends."

The men at the table stood up, and Edward introduced Marjorie to everyone. The waiter brought another chair and place setting during the introductions, then Marjorie sat down and began relating what she had done since she had last seen Edward. After working for a time at the law firm in Boston, she had found other employment.

"It was at a shop that makes likenesses," she said. "I've always been fascinated with that, and I visited the shop every spare moment I had after I made friends with a woman who worked there. At length, I was hired and became a photographist myself."

"How interesting!" Kale exclaimed. "Do you have a business here, or have you come here to start one?"

Shaking her head, Marjorie explained that she was now in partnership with a man in Boston who had been a photographer until he had been badly burned and partially paralyzed in an accident. She traveled about and made plates for stereopticon slides, sending them to the man, and he prepared the slides and sold them through a catalog dealer.

"I apologize for my appearance," Marjorie added, brushing at the dust on her cape. "I accompanied a cattle drive from San Antonio to Abilene, then came here on the train with the herd to photograph the train and the stockyards. The owner of a photography studio down the street rented me his darkroom to develop my plates, and I've been working on them since I arrived here two days ago. I haven't had time to see to myself."

Frank smiled, making a gentlemanly, reassuring comment about her appearance. "You traveled on a cattle drive with cowboys?" he continued. "Didn't you find them to be rowdy company for a young lady?"

Marjorie laughed and shook her head. "Cowboys are rowdy company, but not with ladies," she said. "They were perfect gentlemen almost without exception, and the rest of them always stood ready to deal with the exceptions. During my travels, I've found that for the most part one will be treated like a lady if one has the deportment of a lady."

As the other two women at the table emphatically agreed, Edward looked at Marjorie thoughtfully. This young woman, he observed to himself, now had an aplomb about her that would enable her to face down most men who made advances. And for the rare circumstances that could be truly dangerous, she had taken adequate precaution: Under the right side of her cape, he noted, was a slight bulge that almost escaped detection—a pistol in a shoulder holster.

Ted Taylor had also noticed it. He smiled as he pointed. "Is that a thirty-two or a thirty-eight?" he asked.

"A thirty-eight," Marjorie replied, laughing. "I'm a poor shot, so I bought one that makes enough noise to scare people."

Everyone laughed, and the conversation continued as the waiter brought the food to the table. It was a home-style dinner of fried steak, mashed potatoes with rich gravy, and well-seasoned vegetables. The portions were generous and were served with hot rolls and cups of coffee. As they began eating, Marjorie replied to questions from the others about the places her work had taken her.

"Wasn't it difficult to make photographs of a cattle drive?" Kale asked. "The cattle and everything would be moving all the time."

"Movement doesn't blur as much in the photograph if the camera is positioned properly," Marjorie replied. "It should be at a distance from the subject, with the line of motion either directly toward or away from the lens. On bright days, however, the exposure of the plate can be so brief that a slow movement makes no difference. Also, by doing the developing myself, I can underexpose and over-develop the plates to an extent."

Taking a sip of coffee, Marjorie began warming to her subject. She explained that the most sensitive plates were those coated with wet collodion; but they had to be used while damp, which required taking along a portable dark-room. However, her partner had devised a means of increasing the sensitivity of dry gelatin plates by exposing them to bromine fumes, making the emulsion almost as sensitive as wet collodion.

As she began describing the chemical reaction of the bromine in the emulsion, she broke off and glanced around the table. Everyone was looking at her in total lack of comprehension. "I'm sorry," she said. "I forget myself when I start talking about my work."

"There's no need to apologize for being interested in your work," Tommie said. "Where are you staying, Marjorie?"

"I'm using a storage room in the rear of the studio."

"Then you must stay with us," Tommie said, and Kale agreed. "You can't sleep in a storage room. Accommodations are scarce here, but not that scarce!"

Marjorie shook her head, smiling. "Thank you, but no. It's not as bad as it sounds, and I've cleaned up the room. It's better than other places I've stayed, and I need to finish my work."

"But you're through for the day, aren't you?" Tommie asked.

"No," Marjorie replied. "I'll work some more tonight. My partner must have the plates as soon as possible, and I don't need much sleep."

"You certainly do enjoy your work," Kale commented. "I was thinking—some of us are leaving tomorrow to go to a logging camp in Wisconsin. The trip takes two days, but if you would like to visit the camp, that might make a good subject for stereopticon slides."

Marjorie glanced around the table with a smile of thanks as the others echoed the invitation. "That's very kind of you," she said. "I'll send my partner a telegram and ask him about it when I send my plates to him. He picks the subjects, because he knows more about the market than I do. He's been trying to make arrangements for me to go on a whaling voyage, but without success so far. In view of the fact that I'm this close to Wisconsin, he might suggest that I go there."

"If you decide to go," Toby said, "you can go with Ted and me. I have some business to attend to here in Chicago, so we won't be leaving for a few days yet."

Marjorie thanked him, and the conversation continued. She ate in silence and listened as the others discussed the camp and travel plans.

Tommie was also silent, thinking about Marjorie. She suspected that Marjorie and Edward had once had an aborted romantic relationship, but her twinge of uneasiness on that account had been completely allayed in the first few minutes.

Although Marjorie was undeniably a beautiful woman, her dark brown muslin dress was unbecoming. In addition, she wore not a trace of cosmetics. Indeed, instead of being perfumed, she had a scent of chemicals about her. The tiny lines of fatigue at the corners of her eyes and mouth belied her claim that she needed little sleep; she simply did without. Marjorie White, Tommie concluded, was so totally involved in her work that she had no interest in any man.

It appeared, though, that at least one man at the table found her attractive. Ted Taylor was a man who revealed little of what he was thinking, yet every time Marjorie wanted the salt or something else, Tommie observed, Ted immediately noticed and reached for it to hand to her.

Large servings of sweet, juicy peach cobbler completed dinner. When the waiter brought the bill to Frank, Marjorie opened her reticule and took out her purse to pay her share, but Frank shook his head. "Toby and I have an account here," he said. "You're our guest, Marjorie."

"No, that wouldn't be right," Marjorie protested. "I'm here on business, just as you are, and—"

Her words were drowned in a chorus of objecting voices. She nodded in thanks and put her purse away, silently sighing in relief. After Frank signed the bill and handed it back to the waiter, everyone stood up and walked toward the door. The men told Marjorie that they would escort her to the photography studio, since the streets were dark and it was late. Although she looked vaguely distressed, she accepted the offer.

In her conclusions about Marjorie, Tommie had been both right and wrong. Marjorie was totally involved in her work and at present had no special feelings for Edward, other than deep gratitude for the help he had at one time given her. Having been betrayed once, she was resolved never to be vulnerable to another man. However, all that had been before she met Toby Holt.

Leaving the restaurant with the group, Marjorie walked between the two women. When they reached the studio, both the women and the men turned in at the dimly lighted alley to escort Marjorie to the back door, the one for which she had a key. Marjorie kept her eyes averted from Toby Holt, the source of her quaking uneasiness.

A quiet but cordial man, one who would be a valuable friend but a deadly enemy, he had a tall frame that seemed to be composed entirely of sinew and muscle. He was boldly masculine, but he also had a gentle quality about him. Among other men, he seemed like an oak among saplings.

He was different from any man she had ever met. He was also a complication, a danger that she would make herself vulnerable again, and a threat to her work. Her work was a demanding master, leaving no time for anything else. She regretted having gone to the restaurant and met him.

Minutes before, there had been another reason why she had regretted having gone to the restaurant. Income from her most recent slides had been meager, and she had little money—a fact that in itself was only a nuisance, since money meant little to her. But wanting a bowl of soup and a roll for five cents, she had gone into the expensive restaurant by mistake. The meal had probably cost fifty cents or more, and the generosity of the people she had met had saved her from having to economize even further.

At the back door of the studio, Toby Holt struck a match. "Let me have your key, Marjorie," he said.

Still avoiding his eyes, Marjorie took the key out of her reticule and handed it to him. As he unlocked the door, she turned to the group as a whole. "It was very pleasant meeting you and talking with you, and I enjoyed the meal very much."

"We enjoyed your company," Kale said. "Please do try to come to the logging camp, Marjorie. We would certainly like to have you there with us."

"I'll do my best," Marjorie replied. "If I do come, perhaps I can make likenesses of all of you."

The two women nodded agreeably, but the response from the men was silence. Many men who could unflinchingly face gunfire were intimidated by a camera lens. Toby struck another match, then handed her the key. "We'll wait out here until you close the bolt inside, Marjorie," he said, quickly changing the subject.

"Thank you, and good night, everyone."

There was a murmur of replies as she closed the door and, shot the bolt. Leaning back against the door, she heard the men and women talking quietly, their voices becoming fainter as they walked away. Marjorie drew in a deep breath, inhaling the familiar, comforting smells of the chemicals. Toby Holt faded from her mind, her greater love possessing her.

Going into the storage room, Marjorie lit a lamp. She changed into her work smock, then carried the lamp down the short hall to the darkroom. It was neat and clean, all of the chemical tanks and other equipment in tidy order, which was the result of a few hours of furious work on her part before she had begun her developing.

The past days had been a blur of hard work and little sleep, and the large meal made her fatigue feel like a heavy weight. Lighting the darkroom lamp with its red globe and blowing out the other one, Marjorie consciously summoned her will and shrugged off her fatigue. A darkroom could be a lethal place for the careless or inattentive.

One of the chemicals used in fixing the images was potassium cyanide. Inhaling too much of it or some of the other chemicals could cause anything from hallucinations to a stupor that would last for hours. Her partner, Clayton Hemmings, was disfigured for life, the left side of his face a mass of scar tissue and his left arm and leg almost useless. While he had been preparing wet plates coated with collodion, a volatile mixture of guncotton, ether, and alcohol, a spark from some unknown source had ignited it.

The lamp cast a ruby glow as Marjorie moved about the small room. The plates she had developed before going to dinner were almost dry, the oblong glass negatives standing in a wire rack. With only a few more plates to develop, Marjorie decided to do something she had been saving.

During the cattle drive, she had exposed six daguerreotype plates. They were an extravagance, but the daguerreotype was her favorite process, and they were for her private collection. With most of her work done, she decided to reward herself and develop the daguerreotypes.

Marjorie lit the kerosene heater under the tank of mercury and put the shield into place over it so that no stray light would escape. Then, while the mercury began heating to the point of vaporizing, she took out her notes on the exposures and peered at them in the ruby light.

When the mercury was hot, she removed one of the plates from the holder, opened the tank, and placed the plate over the mercury. She looked at her watch. Photography was mostly a matter of judgment, which she had developed to a precise degree. Presently, she looked at her watch again, then took the plate off the tank and carried it to the light.

As always, a perfect daguerreotype created a tight feeling in the back of her throat and a stinging sensation in her eyes. While developing supreme technical skills, she had not become detached from the result. It was still wondrous to her. Decades would pass, and a moment in time would remain fixed, immutable. The process was mechanical and chemical, but the result reached into another plane, becoming fascinating and magical.

The day she had exposed the plate had been very bright, so the exposure had been brief. The image was crisp and clear, without a blur. It was a scene of cowboys around their campfire, with the chuck wagon, horses, and cattle in the background. But in addition to being a scene, to Marjorie it was something else, a different framework for reality.

The chuck wagon had been old, and the trail boss had talked about abandoning it in Abilene. Gunfire had been an intermittent sound all of the time she had been in Abilene, and some of the men around the campfire could be dead by now. Some of the horses could have gone lame and been shot. All of the steers would have already been slaughtered and butchered. But that was only in one reality. The daguerreotype provided another.

In the reality of the daguerreotype, that chuck wagon would always be on the Chisholm Trail, would always be a magnet where the cowboys gathered. These handsome young men would never be killed or become old and die. These horses would always be healthy and spirited. These steers would contentedly chew their cud through eternity, never seeing a slaughterhouse.

Tonight, as on other nights, Marjorie labored while others slept. She was accustomed to meals that were often skimpy, and she often slept on a bench in a railroad station to save money for a part for one of her cameras or a carton of emulsion plates. She endured burning heat, freezing rain, and other hardships as she went from place to place.

But all those things were nothing more than minor inconveniences. They were a small price to pay for the rapture she felt as she stood in the ruby glow of the lamp and looked at her creation. Fate had smiled upon her and given her the means to reach out and freeze magical moments in time. She had her dream, and she wanted nothing more.

Frank Woods snored resoundingly, and Toby could hear Rob's deep, rhythmic breathing as he slept on his pallet. Ted was either awake, or his breathing was inaudible. The cigar Edward was smoking made a bright red spot in the darkness.

The cigar glowed brighter as Edward puffed on it. It made an arc through the darkness as he flicked the ash into a dish beside his pallet. "Are you awake, Toby?" he asked softly.

"Yes."

Edward moved on his pallet, turning toward Toby. "I'm still thinking about Marjorie," he said. "You know, I can't get over the change in her. She's an entirely different woman."

"From what you said, she's a lot better off now."

"Oh, definitely," Edward replied, laughing softly.

"She's much more capable of taking care of herself. And she's more spirited now."

"It's probably because she found a trade that interests her. I've seen the same thing happen to others. It takes away self-doubts and makes people aware that they're worth as much as anyone else."

"Yes, I'm sure that's what happened," Edward said, taking a last puff on his cigar. He exhaled the smoke, then put the cigar in the dish beside his pallet. "Well, good night, Toby."

"Good night, Edward."

Lying and looking up into the darkness, Toby thought about Marjorie. She was a beautiful young woman, even though she made no effort to be beautiful. When Edward had introduced them, Toby had felt for a moment as though there was something more than an ordinary interaction between them. Then it had passed. Marjorie had devoted no more, and perhaps less, attention to him than to anyone else. He had forced the thought out of his mind.

It was, he decided, too soon after his parting with Martha even to contemplate a romantic relationship. His primary concern should be to build up an estate for his children. The logging venture, a major step in that process, would be a long, difficult undertaking. Until he had provided for his children, he would have no time for personal concerns.

The scent of Edward's cigar hung in the air, its smell vaguely reminiscent of the tobacco Janessa smoked. Thinking of Marjorie again, it occurred to him that some of her personality characteristics were similar to Janessa's. They both had the same single-minded determination, the same unswerving dedication to whatever they set out to do.

IX

The next morning, Frank took Toby to meet the captain of the steam launch. As they rode their hired horses out of the trees in Lincoln Park, Toby took in the view of Lake Michigan.

It was a busy scene, with vessels of all sizes and descriptions in sight, ranging from large cargo ships to smaller craft that plied between the cities on the shores of the lake and its connecting waters. Some were sailing ships, the October morning sunlight gleaming on their spreads of canvas. Others, with steam engines to supplement their sails, had trickles of smoke wafting away from them on the gentle westerly breeze. The steamers among the ships looked comparatively naked and unfinished, with only smokestacks and masts for cargo booms jutting up from their hulls.

The main center of activity was some two miles south of Lincoln Park, at the mouth of the Chicago River. Railroad docks and huge grain elevators lined the waterfront there, and the river with its two wide branches gave ships access to docks and warehouses in the heart of the city. Toby and Frank rode north along Lake Shore Drive, a broad avenue that on warm Sunday afternoons was the meeting place for eligible youths from good families.

On this day the drive was almost deserted as Toby and Frank rode along it. North of Lincoln Park, however, were numerous small warehouses and piers, and the traffic increased again. This was the general location where Toby wanted to have a lumber mill, and he discussed it with Frank.

"From what I understand," Frank said, "the Board of Trade owns most of the lakefront property here."

Toby frowned, puzzled. "The Board of Trade, Frank? That's a government body that conducts and regulates trade. It isn't a commercial organization, so I don't see how it can own property."

"Toby, I'm just telling you what I heard," Frank said. "For all I know, a board of trade is a wooden plank that men sit on to make deals. I'll run the logging camp and leave all that up to you."

Toby chuckled. "I'll discuss it with the mayor when I meet him. Probably he'll also know all the details about the moratorium on construction."

Frank took out his watch and looked at it. "It'll take us longer to ride to those temporary offices the city is using than it would to get to the old city hall. But we still have plenty of time before your appointment with the mayor, and the pier where Captain Crowell keeps his launch isn't far from here."

Toby nodded. He had heard that the old city hall was being demolished to be replaced by a larger and more modern structure, and that in the meantime the city government was occupying temporary offices near the outskirts.

As they rode along a busy street, Frank wondered aloud why Ted Taylor had not come with them. Toby had expected Ted to want to see the city, but instead the young lawman had elected to remain behind to help the Martins and the Blackstones sort out the baggage they would take with them to the logging camp.

When they reached the end of the pier where the steam launch was moored, Frank and Toby dismounted. "He doesn't have a lot to say about things," Frank commented, still talking about Ted. "But what he does say is worth listening to, and he's as fine a young man as I've ever met. He's also quick to help out. Still, I don't think Edward and Rob need help in deciding what baggage they'll take with them."

The same thought had occurred to Toby, and he had decided that the young lawman must have had some private reason for remaining behind. In any case, Toby thought, Ted was entirely within his rights to do as he wished and to have private reasons for doing so.

The steam launch at the end of the pier was a stubby, ungainly craft, wide in the beam for its length. With a tall wheelhouse and a cable winch at its stern, it was basically a large, powerful engine to tow massive barges, with enough hull around it to be able to weather the sometimes dangerous storms that swept the lake. Two crewmen were carrying boxes on board from the pier as the captain moved about the deck checking equipment.

Noticing Toby coming along the pier with the tall, heavyset Frank, the captain walked down the short gangplank to meet them. He was a portly, muscular man of about fifty who walked with a rolling gait, his nautical cap pulled down firmly on his gray hair. He shook hands with Toby as Frank introduced them.

"I'd ask you to come aboard and sit down to talk," the captain said apologetically, "but I'm just getting ready to cast off. A barge is being loaded down at the city docks for me to tow to Muskegon, and it'll be ready and waiting by the time I get there."

"That's quite all right, Captain Crowell," Toby replied. "I have an appointment to meet with Mayor Mason, and I wouldn't be able to stay very long in any event. Frank is leaving today for our logging camp, and I only wanted to meet you before he left. I'll be here for several days, so we'll be able to get together and talk at length when you return."

The captain nodded agreeably. "I'll be back late tomorrow afternoon, and I have some work to do on my launch that should keep me here for at least a day or two. If you want to come back then, we'll have a cup of coffee and talk about the towing that you want done. Frank said it'll be rafts of logs from the west side of the lake."

"Yes, that's right. I don't have precise estimates yet on just how many there will be, but we can discuss it in general terms."

"That sounds fine to me," the captain said. "At this point I'd rather keep it in general terms myself, because I've never towed any logs on the lake. And as far as I know, no one else has, either. So we'll want to take our time and come to an agreement that'll be fair for both of us, won't we?"

"We certainly will," Toby agreed. "If this venture works out, it should help a lot of people. The charges levied by the lumber mills in Wisconsin make the lumber from there expensive both here and wherever it's shipped."

"It's unreasonable, that's what it is!" the captain exclaimed, shaking his head. "With all those trees in Wisconsin, lumber should be cheap here, but it costs just as much as it does in the big cities in the East. If you can put lumber on the market here at a reasonable price, you'll have all the business you can handle." He shrugged, dismissing the subject, and shook hands with Toby again. "Well, we'll get together in a couple of days to discuss things."

"I'll look forward to it," Toby replied.

The captain went back onto his launch as Toby and Frank returned to their horses. As they mounted, Frank commented that he had briefly talked with two other launch captains and could take Toby to meet them if he wished. Toby shook his head, replying that he had met the right man. Captain Crowell's handshake and gaze had been firm, and he had talked about coming to an agreement that was fair for everyone. Such a man was the right man.

Riding southwest across the city toward the temporary city hall, Toby and Frank were delayed for a short time at the northern branch of the Chicago River, where a swing bridge was open to allow a ship to pass. The bridge closed, and an hour later they had crossed the city and were approaching city hall. The large, three-story wooden building was located on a wide street along a low ridge some two miles west of the downtown.

The ridge was the only elevation for several miles in any direction; the surrounding terrain was flat prairie.

From the grassy courtyard in front of the building, where Toby and Frank tethered their horses among the other horses and carriages, they had a panoramic view of the city. Church spires and taller buildings jutted above the general level of the dense mass of structures, and the expanse of streets stretched for miles, fronted by the shimmering surface of Lake Michigan.

The police constable on duty at the entrance stepped forward as Frank and Toby mounted the steps. Young and earnest, he peered up at Toby suspiciously from under his tall helmet. "Excuse me, sir," he said curtly. "Are you armed?"

Wearing the wool suit, white shirt, and tie appropriate to the occasion, Toby had a Colt in a shoulder holster under his coat. "Yes, but I promise not to try to rob anyone," he said, smiling. "My name's Toby Holt, and I have an appointment to see Mayor Mason."

The young police constable's stern bearing suddenly dissolved into youthful awe. "Toby Holt?" he gasped, grinning boyishly and putting out his hand. "I'm Johnny Whittaker, Mr. Holt. I've certainly read a lot about you in the newspapers."

Toby smiled, shaking hands. "My name's Toby, Johnny. And if you'll take my advice, you'll remember that newspapers are in business to sell newspapers. So you can forget half of what you read in them and take the other half with a grain of salt."

The police constable laughed. "Yes, you're certainly right about that, Mr. . . . Toby. I didn't mean any offense when I stopped you."

Toby shook his head as he and Frank stepped toward the entrance door. "No offense taken, Johnny," he said. "You're doing your duty, and you're doing it right. No one should take offense over that."

Inside was an entrance foyer flanked by a staircase. Toby and Frank went up the stairs to the top floor, then walked along a hall through one wing of the building. At the end of the hall, they went into the office occupied by the mayor's secretary, who immediately showed them into the mayor's office. It was an expansive, airy corner room, with large windows overlooking the city.

Mayor Roswell B. Mason, a dapper man of medium stature, had a commanding bearing. "You must be Toby Holt," he said, standing up from behind his desk and crossing the room. His handshake was firm and his smile warm. "This is indeed a pleasure."

"It's certainly a pleasure for me as well, Mayor Mason."

"No, none of that," the mayor said, cordially insistent as he raised a finger. "I am Ross, and you are Toby, all right?" He smiled and nodded as he shook hands with Frank. "Please sit down, gentlemen."

Returning to his desk, the mayor asked about Toby's family. Thoroughly familiar with Toby's deceased father by reputation, he also knew all about Toby's public service as governor of Idaho Territory and in other posts. They talked for several minutes about Toby's family and general subjects, and then the mayor asked Toby where he was staying in the city. When he replied, the mayor shook his head.

"No, that won't do at all," he said. "Our hotel construction hasn't kept up with the pace of our business activities, so accommodations aren't always immediately available. But we can do better than that. I'll contact one of the hotel managers and make arrangements for your party."

Toby smiled and shook his head. "I'm very grateful, but that won't be necessary, Ross. We were a little crowded last night, but most of my party will be leaving today. In any event, the main reason we've been staying there is that Aaron Ward is a friend. He's made us his guests, and he absolutely refuses to accept a penny."

"Indeed?" The mayor lifted his eyebrows. "Well, that's generous, isn't it? Aaron Ward, you say? I don't believe I know him."

"I'm sure you will in time. It wouldn't surprise me if he became one of the leading merchants of the city. He certainly has the qualities, and he's a credit to the business community here."

"Well, his generosity is a credit to the city," the mayor commented. Sitting back in his chair, he changed the subject. "Now, I understand you're contemplating going into business here yourself, Toby. What are your plans, and how may I help you with them?"

Toby briefly explained the logging venture. "We're still in the preliminary stages," he said, "and my partners haven't fully committed themselves yet, but I think it's going to be a profitable undertaking and will be of benefit to the whole nation. I think I can put lumber on the market here at a competitive price, as well as ship it to the plains for sale at a reasonable price."

"Yes, I'm sure you could," the mayor said, stroking his chin. "No doubt you know what the mills in Wisconsin are charging."

"We do," Toby said. "That's what started us thinking about operating out of Chicago. Then the scope of our plans grew to the point where we'll be going from standing timber to finished lumber. But I understand there's a moratorium on construction now."

The mayor nodded, explaining that the planning commission was completing new zoning and building code procedures for his approval and would probably begin accepting applications for building permits within the next three or four days. "Once they get started," he said, "processing the applications shouldn't take more than a week or ten days. So that won't hold you up very long. Where do you contemplate building your mill, Toby?"

"I was thinking of the area north of Lincoln Park, and I've heard that the Board of Trade has something to do with it."

Again the mayor nodded. "Indirectly. Several of the members happen to have extensive holdings along there. If you like, I'll send a message about your plans to Charles Horton, the chairman. He should be able to put you into contact with the owner of a suitable property."

"I would appreciate that, Ross," Toby said. "And as a prospective businessman in the city, I stand ready to fulfill my civic responsibility and assist you and your staff in any way I can."

Smiling mischievously, the mayor opened the inkwell on his desk and jotted a note on a piece of paper. "Toby,

I'm going to accept your offer," he replied, his eyes twinkling in amusement. "I'll send a message to Charles Horton this afternoon, and you can see him anytime tomorrow morning at the Board of Trade Hall. Then, tomorrow afternoon, there is something I'd like you to do for me."

"Certainly, Ross. What do you have in mind?"

"Governor Palmer is arriving here this evening to spend a few days in Chicago and will be working with me on several things. If he heard that you're in the city and I didn't arrange for him to meet you, he would never let me forget it. I'd like you to come here tomorrow afternoon to meet him."

"That's hardly a chore," Toby said, laughing as he stood up. "I'll be here without fail. Frank is leaving for Wisconsin this afternoon, but if you don't mind I'll bring along Ted Taylor, a young lawman from California who accompanied me here."

"I'll look forward to meeting him," the mayor said as he stood up. Farewells were exchanged, and Toby and Frank left the office.

Belatedly, it occurred to Toby that Ted might decline to accompany him, as he had that morning. Once again, Toby wondered if there had been some private reason why Ted had chosen to remain behind.

There had indeed been a private reason, which Ted Taylor was just then in the process of acting upon. But as he walked along the street near the dry goods store in the crowded bustle of midday, he was uncharacteristically hesitant, torn by indecision. There was even an icy feeling of apprehension in the pit of his stomach.

It was not, he told himself, that he was shy with women. He was unable to remember any other instance involving women in which he had felt anything like the uncertainty that possessed him now. No, the reason he felt this way was because a particular woman was involved, one like no other woman he had ever met.

Having paced back and forth along the street twice, hesitating and then passing the photography studio four times, he turned and walked toward it again. To remain

unsure of how she would react, even with the accompanying torment of suspense, seemed preferable to an unfavor-
able reaction. But the possibility of a favorable reaction
was a heady, alluring thought.

Images of her beautiful face formed in his mind; her
delicately molded features, her large blue eyes, her shining blue-black hair. The expressions that had mirrored her
changing moods were indelibly imprinted upon his memory. Everything about her was fascinating. Even her lack
of concern over her appearance was charmingly different.
When he had met Marjorie White, he had turned the first
page in a new chapter of his life. Nothing would ever be
the same again, he reflected. He had loved her from the
first moment he had seen her.

Reaching the front of the photography studio again,
he paused. In his mind raced the sensations that had
assailed him all morning—buoyant hope for success, followed by a swift, icy blast of dismal certainty of failure. He
seemed rooted where he stood, unable to walk on or to go
back in the direction from which he had come.

Then, suddenly, he had to know one way or the
other, whatever the result. And the thought of seeing her
again was irresistibly enticing. He opened the door and
went into the photography studio.

A bell overhead clanged, and a man came through the
doorway at one side. Middle-aged and chubby, he had
graying hair parted in the center and combed straight
down the sides. He smiled unctuously. "Good day, sir,
good day," he said breezily. "Do you want to have a
likeness made? These are the sizes, and we have the best
prices in the city." He waved toward frames on display on
a counter.

"No, I came to see the lady who's using your darkroom," Ted replied. "I'd like to speak with Marjorie White."

The man's ingratiating manner faded, but he remained
amiable. Studying Ted curiously, he said, "You want to
talk to Marjorie? Well, she's busy working in the darkroom right now, friend."

His uncertainty making him impatient with any delay, Ted said, "I'd still like to talk to her. My name's Ted Taylor."

"I'm Claude Leggett," the man said. "Well, go ahead and talk to her if you want to. The darkroom is through that hallway there, the second door on the right. Knock, though, and wait for her to open the door. Like I said, she's working."

Ted nodded and began walking toward the hallway. Then he hesitated and turned back. "It was my understanding that she had just about finished her work."

"Yes, she has," Claude replied. "She's completed her developing, and she's wrapping up her plates and boxing them for shipping. But she's also been doing some developing for me." He shook his head in wonder. "She's the best I've ever seen, bar none. With a camera or in a darkroom, that young lady flat beats anyone. She's one of the few photographists I'd call an artist."

"She's doing some developing for you? Is that part of the bargain she made with you for using your darkroom?"

"No, we settled that before I saw the kind of work she does. I had several customers who wanted the best and were able to pay for it, so I made another bargain with her to develop the plates. I'm giving her two cartons of glass emulsion plates for doing the work."

Ted nodded thoughtfully. As accustomed to observing nuances of behavior in others as he was to concealing his own, he had noticed the way Marjorie had handled her purse in the restaurant the night before. She was short of money. "If I were a photographist, how much would you charge me in cash for a carton of those glass plate things?"

The man pursed his lips, thinking. "About four dollars," he replied. "That's just a tad more than I pay for them, so it would be a fair price. But you don't want to buy any, do you?"

Digging into his pockets, Ted stepped back to the man. "Not for myself," he said. "Why don't you tell her that you're really pleased with her work and that you might have made the bargain a little on the sharp side for her." Counting out three silver dollars and a five-dollar gold piece, he handed them to Claude. "Give her four cartons of those plate things—but let's keep this just between us, all right?"

Claude grinned knowingly as he pocketed the money. "Whatever you say. Four cartons it is."

"I appreciate it," Ted said, turning and walking toward the hallway again. "I'll go talk with her now."

"Don't forget to knock on the door and wait for her to open it," Claude called after him. "Interrupting her when she's working in there is a little like dragging a badger out of its den by the tail."

The last remark was less than reassuring, and Ted's indecision and doubts began returning—but he was committed now.

He stopped in front of the second door in the narrow, dim hallway. The air was thick with the reek of chemicals. He took off his hat, smoothed his hair, and brushed the toes of his boots against the back of his trouser legs. After a last, lingering second of hesitation, he knocked on the door.

"Who is it?" Marjorie snapped impatiently from inside.

"Ted Taylor," he replied. "I'd like to talk to you."

Marjorie made a wordless sound of annoyance, and then the doorknob rattled. "Who?" she barked, snatching the door open.

Her short black hair was tied back, loose wisps hanging around the sides of her face. She was wearing a shapeless smock that had stains and bleached spots on it from chemicals. Her face was lined with fatigue from too little sleep. But it was also bewitchingly lovely, and her blue eyes were like mountain lakes. She was the most captivating woman Ted had ever met.

Her frown was replaced by an expression of strained patience. "Oh, yes," she said. "Hello, Ted. What do you want?"

"It's almost midday, and Kale, Tommie, and their husbands will be getting ready to go to lunch as soon as Toby and Frank get back. I thought I'd come by and see if you'd like to join us."

A long second passed. Marjorie seemed to be trying to control her temper as she looked up at him. She shook her head. "No, thank you," she said evenly. "I'm working, Ted, so I'm not hungry."

He laughed. "Working doesn't have anything to do with getting hungry. People get hungry regardless of what they're doing."

Shaking her head, Marjorie pulled the ribbon out of the back of her hair. She began gathering her hair with both hands and tying it again, not to improve her appearance but because the loose wisps were bothering her. "No, I don't get hungry when I'm working," she said. "I get empty, and sometimes I get so empty that I become weak and have to get something to eat. But no, I don't get hungry."

"What are you doing right now?" he asked, stepping closer to the door. "If I could help you finish, then maybe you could—"

"No!" she barked, holding the door tight. Then she forced a smile to soften her reply. "No, I'm wrapping my plates, Ted. I've never chipped or broken one of my glass plates, but if I did, I'd probably knock my head against the nearest wall until blood flowed. If someone else ruined one of them, I don't know what I'd do. No, I don't want any help, Ted."

"Rob, Edward, and their wives will be leaving with Frank this afternoon," he said, trying another subject. "We'll have an empty room, and it would be a lot better than staying here."

"No, thank you. The room I have is fine."

"Well, it wouldn't have this smell. It's also a room that's meant for someone to stay in, not a storage room."

"What smell? I like this smell. And my room is fine."

Ted struggled to maintain his poise, his self-confidence starting to crumble. He decided to give up before she became angry. "You said that you would be sending a telegram to your partner about going to the logging camp, didn't you? When will you send it?"

"As soon as I ship my plates—perhaps tomorrow."

Her attitude conveyed as clearly as any words that she might be delayed even longer in sending the telegram if he continued to keep her from her work. Ted nodded and backed away from the door. "Perhaps I'll see you tomorrow, then," he said. "I certainly hope so. Good-bye, Marjorie."

"Yes, good-bye, Ted."

Closing the door and stepping across the darkroom to the workbench, Marjorie breathed a sigh of relief. She immediately returned to preparing her plates for shipment. The interruption and all of its implications were wiped from her thoughts as she resumed working.

It was a tedious but crucially important task. Each glass negative had to be wrapped in wax paper, because fibers of the cotton she used for cushioning could become caught in the gelatin emulsion and make dark lines on the stereopticon slides. Then sufficient cotton had to be placed around all the plates so they would be cushioned against damage even if a railroad porter threw or dropped the heavy wooden crate.

The plates, one hundred and twenty of them, represented several months' work, but many would never be used. The catalog company was selective; one dollar was the maximum price at which sets of slides were listed, and the company preferred them to be well below that.

Her partner would make proofs for a set of twelve or fourteen slides of the cattle drive to be listed for a dollar, but the company would probably approve only an eight-slide set for seventy-five cents. The box also contained a set of plates on the Alamo, a well-covered subject, but hers were far better than most. The company might approve a six-slide set on it to be listed for forty-five cents. There was one plate on a hanging—a certainty to be a single slide listed for fifteen cents—and a few other possibilities among the plates that the company might approve.

If there were many orders for the slides, she and her partner might realize a thousand dollars or more in profit, after expenses. If the slides sold only moderately well, the profit would be a few hundred dollars. Poor sales would barely pay expenses, but the important objective was to keep sets of slides listed in the catalog so a trickle of revenue would continue coming in.

As Marjorie was carefully folding wax paper over a

plate, there was another knock on the door. "Who is it?" she called, irritated.

"It's me, Marjorie," Claude Leggett said. "How is that last batch of ambrotypes coming along?"

"They're drying," she replied shortly. "Don't you have a watch? It hasn't been two hours since I started on them. I'll put them in the frames as soon as they're dry." She turned toward the door, her voice louder. "And clean the lens on your camera! It's covered with dust!"

Claude chuckled. "That don't make any difference. All you have to do is give her a little longer exposure."

"It does make a difference, because I could see it on the plates. Dust on the lens diffuses the light and blurs the image. Will you just clean the lens on your camera, Claude?"

"All right, Marjorie," he replied, laughing. "You know, you've been doing some really good work for me. If those ambrotypes are like the rest, I'll give you four cartons of plates instead of two for the work."

Marjorie stopped wrapping the wax paper, surprised and pleased. "Four cartons?" she exclaimed. "That's very good of you, and I appreciate it, Claude. I certainly can use them."

"I figured you could. Say, is that young man who came in here your fellow?"

"Don't be silly, Claude. My fellow is a Moore and Morgan camera with a Kleinhart lens. You know that."

Claude laughed. "Yes, I guess so," he said. "But I believe that young man would like to make some room for himself alongside that Moore and Morgan, Marjorie. Let me know when those ambrotypes are finished."

"Yes, all right."

As she put cotton around the plate, Marjorie thought about her conversation with Ted. It occurred to her that she had been both thoughtless and rude to him. There had been hurt in his gray eyes, a shadow of defeat and disappointment on his strong, handsome face.

Regret over what she had done rose within her. He was a quiet, unassuming man, and she liked him. Moreover, he was someone upon whom to fix her attention and draw it away from Toby Holt. Nodding to herself, she resolved to be more pleasant to Ted when she saw him again.

While they were having a late lunch at the restaurant with the others, Toby told Ted about his appointment with the mayor and the governor the next afternoon, asking him if he wished to come along. Ted replied that he would enjoy meeting them.

During lunch Ted gave no hint as to why he had remained behind, other than the reason he had already given. However, he was more subdued than usual, and Toby felt certain that something had happened to him that morning.

It wasn't until preparations were being made for the Martins and the Blackstones to leave that Toby found out what Ted had been up to—and then he found out only indirectly. Frank had gone to the O'Leary stable to get horses, while the other four men carried the packs downstairs. After Frank returned with the mounts, the packhorses were loaded up.

"You and Ted will join us at the logging camp within the next few days, won't you?" Rob asked, settling in his saddle.

"We're counting on it," Toby replied. "As soon as I've lined up the land for the sawmill and submitted the request for a building permit. Three days at the most, I hope."

Toby shook hands with his friends, farewells were said all around, and then the party set off, Frank leading the packhorses and riding in front. Toby and Ted watched them until they disappeared around a corner.

With part of the afternoon left, Toby thought it would be a good time to get more concrete commitments from the landowners for the logging rights on property adjacent to the logging camp. He asked Ted if he would like to come along.

The young lawman nodded, his attitude less than enthusiastic. "Yes, I'll go with you, Toby," he said. "You know, with the extra room we have upstairs now, Marjorie White would be able to have a room to herself."

His manner and tone were slightly too casual, conveying volumes of meaning. "She certainly would," Toby agreed promptly. "Let's see to that instead, then. I know that Aaron will be agreeable, but we should mention it to him. Then we'll go on down to that photography studio and bring her and her things back."

Looking away, Ted sighed. "Well, I've already asked her," he said uncomfortably. "She told me that she'd rather stay where she is."

The situation suddenly became clear to Toby, and he smiled. "So you've got your eye on her? Why didn't you say so, Ted?"

"It isn't a thing a man likes to talk about, is it?" Ted replied, then smiled wryly. "Particularly when he's got his wheels in the mud trying to do something about it. And mine are stuck up to the axles."

"That's when a man should talk about it to his friends," Toby said. "Maybe I can put my shoulder to that wagon and help you get it out of the mud. Come on and let's speak to Aaron. Then we'll go to the studio, and I'll help you argue with her."

Ted nodded, his attitude markedly more enthusiastic than it had been about accompanying Toby to see landowners. They went into the dry goods store to talk with Aaron Ward, who reacted as Toby had expected; then they headed down the street toward the photography studio.

"She was probably busy when you talked with her," Toby said as they walked along the crowded sidewalk. "And the way she is about her work, she wouldn't appreciate being bothered when she has her mind on it."

"I guess not," Ted agreed. "It did seem that she just wanted to get rid of me and get back to work. And the man who owns the place said she was busy. It didn't even occur to me to wait, because I was in such an all-fired rush to talk to her."

"Well, you can't make horseshoes out of cold iron," Toby observed. "You have to strike when the iron is hot. And sometimes you have to wait until it gets hot."

Ted nodded ruefully as he opened the door and they went into the studio. The bell clanged over the door, and the chubby owner reappeared through the same doorway as before. Glancing first at Ted, then at Toby, he chuckled merrily. "Brought you some reinforcements to try again, did you?" He nodded to Toby. "I'm Claude Leggett."

"I'm Toby Holt, and I'm pleased to meet you. Is Marjorie still busy, or has she finished her work?"

"She should be about through with everything now," Claude replied. "She finished packing up her plates a while ago, and she's been reloading her plate holders with new plates. Ted, she was mighty pleased to get those extra two cartons of plates. I handled it just like you asked, as though I gave them to her."

"I appreciate that," Ted said. "Well, Toby, we might as well go and talk to her. Is she in the darkroom, Claude?"

"Yes, but you'd better remember to knock," Claude said. "If she's still putting plates in the holders, you might ruin one if you open the door. And if you do that, mister, I'm just going to wait out in the street until things stop flying."

Ted laughed weakly and nodded. As they went into the dim, narrow hallway, the air was again thick with an acrid odor. Ted commented that the chemical smell was stronger than before. In front of the door, Ted took off his hat and then knocked.

"Who is it?" Marjorie called inside the room.

"It's me again, Marjorie," Ted replied. "Ted Taylor. I'd like to talk to you again, if you don't mind."

The door opened, and Marjorie smiled up at him. "I'm glad you came back, Ted," she said. "I'm sorry I was rude a while ago."

Ted smiled and shrugged. "I was more rude than you were, interrupting you while you were working. Toby and I came to see if we could talk you into changing your mind about taking that extra room where we are."

"The air is a lot fresher there," Toby added, smiling. "The chemical smell in here is pretty strong, Marjorie."

Her smile faded as she looked at him. "I've been fuming my plates with bromine to accelerate them," she said. Looking back at Ted, she smiled again. "I didn't mean to seem ungrateful, Ted. If my partner thinks slides of the logging camp might sell well, it would be better for me to be nearby so we could discuss travel plans, wouldn't it?"

"It certainly would," Ted agreed quickly. "Where are your things? Toby and I will carry them for you."

"I can't go out like this," she said, plucking at her smock. "I'll change, and then I'll bring my things out front. I've finished my work, so I'll only be a moment."

Ted nodded, then glanced at Toby with quiet triumph as they walked back along the hall. They waited in the front room, looking at the displays of photographs on the wall. A few minutes later Marjorie appeared, dragging a large wooden box and wearing the same dark brown dress, hat, and cape she had worn the night before. Leaving the wooden box, she went back down the hall and returned with two large cases containing her camera equipment, plus a carpetbag.

Claude came in, smiling amiably. "Well, are you fellows taking my border?" he chuckled. "Where are you headed next, Marjorie?"

"It's hard to say," she replied. "I may be going to a logging camp in Wisconsin with these gentlemen."

"Well, if you ever get back to Chicago, come and see me. The next time, the rent on the darkroom will just be cleaning it up."

"I appreciate that, Claude. Look after yourself."

"You do the same, Marjorie."

Toby took the wooden box containing her plates, Ted the two equipment cases, and Marjorie followed with the carpetbag as they walked along the street. When they had set her things in her room over the dry goods store, Ted and Toby left her alone to unpack.

By the time she had finished it was dinnertime, and Marjorie reluctantly gave in to Ted's insistent invitation to be his and Toby's guest at the restaurant down the street. During the meal, Toby observed with satisfaction that Marjorie appeared to enjoy being with Ted, smiling and talking with him.

Darkness had fallen when they left the restaurant. Marjorie walked between the two men. Although he was

attentive to Marjorie, Ted apparently remained keenly
aware of his surroundings, for as they started up the
staircase beside the dry goods store, he suddenly stopped
and stared into the darkness across the street. Toby asked
him what he had seen.

"I'm not sure," he replied quietly. "I thought I saw
someone on the other side of the street watching us. A big
man, tall and heavyset."

"He'd have to be the size of a mountain for me to see
him," Marjorie commented. "It's dark over there."

"He was silhouetted against a window," Ted said. "Or
at least I thought I saw someone silhouetted against a
window."

He continued looking into the darkness a moment
longer; then he shrugged and they continued up the steps.
As Marjorie and Ted went in, Toby hesitated a moment
and looked across the street.

A vague uneasiness stirred in the back of his mind, a
tiny voice whispering a warning. He sensed danger.

This feeling had come to him before in other places,
and more often than not it had been correct. He wondered if some old enemy of his was in the city, following
him around.

X

Although Chicago was built on marshy prairie soil along the lake, necessitating deep foundations under the larger buildings, the city was known for its wholesome climate. Normally, fresh breezes off the lake swept smoke from manufacturing plants away from the city and scattered it inland, providing a pleasant, healthful atmosphere.

This October, however, had been unseasonably warm, and the wind was from the west as Toby and Ted crossed the southern branch of the Chicago River and rode into the business center of the city. It was an oppressive, sultry breeze, from the parched inland prairies that had been thirsting for rain during the past weeks. The torrid breath of air carried with it the scorched odor of grasslands that had been consumed by raging wildfires during the drought.

However, the close atmosphere could not stifle Toby's high spirits. To him, the heart of the city, with its throbbing vitality and magnificent aspect, was always awe-inspiring. As he and Ted followed Aaron Ward's directions to the Board of Trade, Toby commented that the buildings around them rivaled the best that could be found in the old, wealthy cities of the East. Ted agreed. Most of the buildings in the central business district were of stone rather than wood, and nearly all of them reached at least five or six full stories. The Mercantile Building was of marble, but its grand appearance was no more impressive

163

than the Oriental Building, the Phoenix Building, and other large structures made of brick.

Clock towers soared far above gargoyles reaching out from elaborate cornices, and many buildings featured iron ornamentation wrought in elaborate Victorian designs. The buildings housed newspapers, banks, theaters, and hotels, along with jewelry stores, haberdasheries, and fine restaurants. Construction was under way on almost every street. The Grand Pacific Hotel, when completed, would fill an entire block between Jackson Boulevard and Clark and Quincy streets.

The Board of Trade occupied a large building adjacent to the Chamber of Commerce, on the corner of LaSalle and Washington streets. Toby and Ted mounted the broad steps in front of the building, went through the expansive foyer, then up the wide marble staircase to the chairman's office. The pace of activity in the building exceeded that of the teeming streets outside. Clerks rushed between the offices of brokerages, insurance firms, and the representatives of produce houses along the marble hallways. The hubbub from the vast stock exchange hall on the top floor filtered down the stairways in a loud murmur of background noise.

The chairman's office was an island of quiet in the scurrying activity. The chairman himself, a thin, immaculately neat man of about fifty, had an air of composed, unhurried competence. Looking up from papers on his desk as his secretary showed Toby and Ted in, he peered at them over gold-rimmed spectacles, then smiled, stood up, and stepped toward them.

"I've been expecting you," he said cordially, shaking hands with Toby. "I received a note from Mayor Mason yesterday afternoon concerning you." He shook hands with Ted, then gestured to the chairs in front of his desk. "Please make yourselves comfortable, gentlemen. It's very warm today, isn't it?"

"It certainly is," Toby agreed as he and Ted sat down. "There's a hot, dry breeze from the west, and it has a strong smell of smoke."

Charles Horton took off his spectacles, then looked

toward the window. For a brief moment his high forehead wrinkled in an anxious frown. "Yes, well, perhaps we'll have rain before long," he said optimistically, sitting back down. "We could certainly use it, couldn't we? Now, how may I assist you, Mr. Holt?"

Toby explained the purpose of his visit, describing the kind of property he wanted to acquire and the general location.

Horton thought for a moment. "I would recommend land farther to the north of Lincoln Park, because a syndicate of landowners is planning to build large, expensive apartments just north of the park. That could give you a problem with the building permit."

"That's just the sort of information and advice I'm seeking," Toby said. "I don't want any problems with the permit, and I certainly wouldn't want to put a sawmill anywhere close to someone's residence, be it expensive or modest. By all means, let's concentrate on the properties that will remain in an industrial area."

The chairman smiled and nodded, putting his spectacles back on. He opened his inkwell and began scratching notes on a piece of paper. "I'll have someone contact our members who are landowners in that area," he said as he wrote. "And I'll concentrate on those who own water rights as part of their land deeds, so you'll have access to the lake. That should present no difficulty, by the way."

"I'm pleased to hear that. If I could be put in touch with a landowner within the next two or three days, I would appreciate it. I plan to leave for Wisconsin within the next few days."

"It won't take nearly that long," Horton said. "A clerk will begin contacting the board members within the hour. If you'll return tomorrow afternoon, I'll have some names for you. They'll all be here in the building, so you can begin talking with them immediately."

"That will be excellent, and far more than I expected," Toby said, standing up to leave. "I'm very grateful for your help."

"It's my pleasure," Horton said, showing them to the door. "I'm most gratified that you're contemplating starting a business enterprise here, Mr. Holt. You're an individual who'll be invaluable to the business community. I'll look forward to seeing you tomorrow."

Toby thanked the man for his compliment as they shook hands. Then he and Ted departed.

After attending to some other business, Toby and Ted set off in early afternoon for their appointment with the mayor and the governor. As they rode westward across the sprawling city, they passed a wooden water tower. Its huge, weathered mass rested on an immense wooden framework rising from a cleared plot of land. A fence surrounded the base of the tower, a NO TRESPASSING sign on the locked gate.

As they rode past, Ted pointed to the narrow platform around the massive body of the tank. "While I was talking with Marjorie last night," he said, "she mentioned the walkway around the water tower. She wondered if we could get permission for her to climb up there and take photographs of the city. Do you think we could?"

Toby looked at the long, spindly wooden ladder that reached up to the platform from inside the fence. "Yes, I think we could," he replied. "We'll go to the Water Works tomorrow and ask them. And I'll help you get Marjorie up that ladder, if you need help. But when it comes to those big, heavy equipment cases of hers, you're on your own, Ted."

Laughing, Ted looked at the ladder. "Yes, that would be a job," he agreed. "I wouldn't want to try to climb up there with one of those cases, but I believe I could haul them up with a rope." He sobered, looking along the street again. "I wish she had let me help her take that big wooden box to the railroad station. She'll have a hard time getting it from the carriage into the station."

"She's taken care of those boxes plenty of times before, Ted," Toby said. "She strikes me as the kind who likes to do a lot of things for herself, and it would be a mistake to try to help her so much that she felt crowded."

Ted sighed heavily. "Yes, you're right, Toby. She

does like to do things for herself. I guess that's one of the reasons I think so much of her."

"It's a good reason. It means that there's a lot to her. Bedroom business between men and women takes a couple of hours every day or two, at the most. That leaves a lot of time, and there has to be something to fill it. Men who marry women who can't do anything but primp and look pretty, and women who marry men who can't do anything but boast and strut, soon find that they made a big mistake."

Ted nodded in agreement, and they rode on in silence. After a few minutes, they noticed a group of people who were talking and pointing down the street, across the rooftops. Reining up, Toby and Ted looked in the direction in which the people were pointing.

The hot breeze, as it had been all day, was carrying smoke from the prairie to the west. But a much darker smudge was rising from nearer by, indicating a large fire burning in the southwestern part of the city. Riding on toward the low ridge where the temporary city hall stood, Toby and Ted urged their mounts to a canter.

From the courtyard where carriages were parked in front of city hall, Toby and Ted had a clear, elevated view of the fire. It was among the neighborhood of tenements, ramshackle residences, and small shops south of Dekoven Street. The size of the column of smoke indicated that the fire had spread to a number of buildings.

As they watched, the base of the smoke column began thinning. It was obvious the pump wagons of the fire department were on the scene and extinguishing the flames. The warm breeze was dissipating the smoke over the lake as Toby and Ted tethered their horses and walked toward city hall.

News of Toby's visit the day before had apparently spread among the police constables; the guard at the entrance was a different one from the day before, but he touched the brim of his helmet and greeted Toby by name. Toby returned the greeting as he went up the steps and inside with Ted.

City employees were standing at windows, talking quietly and watching the smoke disperse. When Toby and Ted were shown into the mayor's office, they found the two officials also at a window, looking at the smoke. They turned to the visitors, the mayor introducing Toby and Ted to the governor. Governor John Palmer was a large, gray-haired man whose muscular frame was starting to turn to corpulence. He had a ruddy, beefy face that could both smile and scowl easily.

Now his face was wreathed in a wide, pleased smile as he insisted that Toby and Ted address him by his first name.

The four men sat in the comfortable chairs around the mayor's desk, and Toby nodded when the mayor mentioned the fire. "Yes, Ted and I saw it while we were on our way here. From the smoke that was rising, I would say that it must have destroyed several buildings."

"At least that," the mayor agreed. "With this long dry spell we've had, wooden buildings are almost like tinder."

"And that wind certainly isn't any help," the governor added. "It feels like the hot air out of a furnace. Well, Toby, Ross tells me that you're thinking about starting a business here."

Toby nodded, then briefly described the logging venture. He mentioned the help he had been given that morning by Charles Horton at the Board of Trade.

"Charlie's a good man," the mayor interjected. "Of course you are too, Toby, and that makes a big difference in getting things done right."

"It certainly does," the governor said. "And maybe, once your business gets going, we can get some lumber in here at a reasonable price. I've talked with Governor Washburn in Wisconsin a number of times about the cost of lumber up there. He can't explain it, because the truth of the matter is that he doesn't know the reasons for it any more than I do." He shrugged, the beginnings of a dark frown on his ruddy face fading as he dismissed the subject. "Toby, tell me how you went about settling the Indian troubles when you were governor of Idaho."

Toby related how, when he had been territorial governor, he had made peace with the Nez Percé and Shoshone and persuaded the Indians to remain on their reservations. The conversation then turned to other subjects, and an hour passed swiftly, both the governor and the mayor obviously enjoying the discussion.

During a momentary lull in the talk, Toby took out his watch and looked at it. "Well, I know you two have many other things to do. I've taken up enough of your time."

"Unfortunately, we do have other things at hand," the governor replied. "And none of them nearly as pleasant as chatting with you. With Chicago the size it is and Springfield as it is, Ross and I have to get together occasionally to work out ways for the tail to wag the dog as easily as possible." He pushed himself up from his chair as Toby and Ted stood up. "Toby, will you and Ted be free for lunch tomorrow?"

Toby glanced at Ted and looked back at the governor. "Yes, I believe we will."

"Then by all means let's get together at noon. Ross and I will be your hosts."

As he nodded, Toby observed the urgent signal Ted was conveying with his eyes. "We'd enjoy that very much," Toby said. "If we could prevail upon your hospitality, we'd like to bring along a young lady of our acquaintance. She's a traveling photographist, and I might add that Ted has developed something more than a passing interest in her."

"By all means, bring her along," the governor said jovially, as Ted's face reddened a shade. "If Ross and I see any way to assist you in your objective, Ted, you can be sure you'll have our full support."

Back outside, Ted asked Toby where he wanted to go next.

"Let's call it a day," Toby said. "By the time we get back, it'll be pretty late, and I'm sure you're impatient to see Marjorie."

Ted's grin was uncharacteristically boyish. As the two friends rode through the city streets, Ted began speculating aloud about the possibility that Marjorie's business partner would want her to go to the logging camp.

He also brought up another assignment Marjorie had mentioned. Her partner was trying to arrange for her to go on a whaling ship out of New Bedford, Massachusetts, to take photographs during the voyage. However, Ted added cheerfully, Marjorie had told him that many of the sailors on whaling ships were extremely superstitious about having women on board, and therefore such an arrangement was unlikely.

As they rode farther south, the air was thick with the smell of smoke from the fire of a few hours before. When they reached Dekoven Street, Toby and Ted rode past their lodgings to the O'Leary stable to return their hired horses.

The stable was a family business. Set back from a modest house, the weathered, ramshackle barn had stalls for a large number of horses, along with one for the family cow. One of the O'Leary boys took the horses, and Toby and Ted headed toward the dry goods store.

The day had been a busy one, but during quiet moments Toby had mused about the man Ted had seen—or thought he had seen—across the street the night before. At various times during his life, Toby had come into conflict with criminal elements and had made enemies. To dwell on that fact would make him see enemies lurking in every shadow. But to forget it would be foolhardy.

As he and Ted walked along the street, Toby again felt vaguely uneasy, just as he had the night before. A warning voice whispered quietly in the back of his mind. Glancing around the busy street, he saw nothing out of the ordinary.

He wondered if he was indeed imagining the feeling, if the oppressive, unseasonable heat was beginning to get to him. It was possible. In any case, the sagging weight of his Colt in his shoulder holster was comforting.

As they approached the dry goods store, Ted remarked that the windows on the second floor were open, indicating that Marjorie was there. His pace quickened. Toby smiled at Ted's eager anticipation. The two of them turned into the wide alley between the store and the adjacent building and began to climb the outside staircase.

Suddenly Toby saw the deadly blue of gunmetal. Ted saw it too, and he pushed Toby, shouting for him to look out as he himself leaped to one side. The warning was unnecessary, for Toby was reaching for his Colt as he jumped from the stairs and fell to the ground.

Toby's reaction was so rapid that the rest of the scene registered in his mind only after he hit the ground. The weapon was a double-barreled shotgun; a large, bearded man in the alley was aiming it. And the barrels were tracking Toby.

The weapon and bearded face disappeared behind smoke belching from one of the barrels. The hot breath of the muzzle blast pushed at Toby as the shattering clap of sound battered his ears. The buckshot ripped into the staircase beside him, showering splinters over him.

The hammer of his Colt was caught in the lining of his coat, and Toby jerked at the pistol to free it as he heaved himself in the other direction, rolling toward the adjacent building. The shotgun thundered again, and a geyser of dirt exploded from the ground behind Toby.

His pistol still tangled in his coat, Toby tugged at it frantically. Over the ringing in his ears, he heard the metallic clatter as the bearded man quickly reloaded the shotgun. Then the sharp, penetrating boom of a Colt rang out in the enclosed space between the buildings.

The rapid flow of action abruptly halted. Like a nightmare, every movement now seemed to drag out, taking forever. Ted, his tanned face set in stony lines, was holding his nickle-plated Colt at arm's length and aiming down it; smoke was rising from the barrel. The bearded man had recoiled a step, his eyes wide and dazed with shock. There was a hole in his coat right over his heart.

Wisps of smoke wafted up from the ejected shells on the ground at the man's feet. The shotgun, its hammers cocked, was partly elevated. The man surely was dead, his heart pulverized by the heavy .45 bullet that had ripped through it. Yet some savage determination kept him on his feet, gave him the strength to lift the shotgun another fraction of an inch.

The hammer on Ted's Colt made a soft, oily click as

he thumbed it back. Then the pistol roared and bounced in his hand, smoke boiling from its barrel. Another hole appeared beside the first one on the bearded man's coat. The impact of the bullet sent him reeling backward. As the man toppled and fell, both barrels of the shotgun fired into the ground with a thunderous blast.

The battering echoes of gunfire faded into the voices from the street, people shouting and gathering to see what had happened. As Toby walked with Ted toward the bearded man, he explained how his pistol had tangled in his coat. Replacing the spent bullets in his Colt, Ted nodded. "It can happen," he said. "And it can happen at the wrong time."

"That was certainly the wrong time for it to happen to me, and I'm lucky you were here. I owe you my life, Ted."

"You owe me nothing," Ted replied firmly. "I did no more than you would do for me, and no more than any man should do for a friend. But who was he, and why was he trying to kill you?"

As they stood over the body, looking down at it, Toby recognized Karl Kellerman's face behind the thick beard and mustache. He told Ted, briefly explaining the long-standing enmity between Kellerman and him. People were rushing into the alley and questioning Toby and Ted.

Abruptly a woman's voice rang out over the others; it was Marjorie, who was standing on the landing at the top of the stairs and asking Ted what had happened. He looked up at her and replied, and she hurried back inside.

Two police constables were pushing through the on-lookers, ordering the people to disperse. Moving back to the sidewalk, the people gathered into a dense crowd. Toby identified himself to the policemen and told them about Kellerman. Both men immediately nodded; there had seen wanted posters circulating on Kellerman for crimes he had committed in Mississippi.

One of the police constables shouted to men in the crowd and told them to go for a wagon; the other police-man jotted notes in a little book as he talked with Toby and Ted. A minute or two later, Marjorie came down the steps, struggling with one of her cases and a large camera on a heavy wooden tripod. Ted rushed to take her case, and she nodded in thanks.

Spreading the legs on the tripod, she pointed to the corpse and spoke briskly to the policemen. "Please set him up against the building there," she said, "with his gun across his lap. The light is fading rapidly, so we don't have very much time. Please hurry as quickly as possible."

Her tone and manner, suggesting that it was incumbent upon the police constables to cooperate fully and quickly, had precisely that effect. The policemen touched their tall helmets, then began dragging the body over to the building. The attention of the crowd on the sidewalk shifted to Marjorie as she extended the long lens bellows on the camera. A photographist at work outside the studio was as much a novelty as a shootout.

Both Toby and Ted had an aversion to having their picture taken. They exchanged apprehensive glances, wondering if Marjorie would want them in the picture. She did, motioning them over toward where the policemen were standing beside the body. As she directed the policemen to take off their helmets, she opened her case and took out a mirror, comb, and can of pomade for them to tidy up their hair and handlebar mustaches.

Marjorie positioned Toby on one side of the body and Ted on the other, his Colt across his chest. The policemen took their places beside Toby and Ted, Marjorie posing them with their helmets on their stiffly crooked left arms, right hands tucked inside their coats and left feet a half pace in front of right. Then she went back to her camera and focused it carefully.

Peering at the image on the ground glass at the rear of the camera, she adjusted a knob near the lens. Then she took a photographic plate holder out of her case, slid it into place in front of the ground glass, and pulled the dark slide out of the holder, exposing the plate inside the camera. Holding up the slide to signal all was in readiness to take the picture, she turned to the crowd. "Silence, please," she called. "Please be silent for a moment."

As quiet fell over the crowd, Marjorie looked up at

the sky. "The light is poor," she said to Toby, Ted, and the policemen, "so the exposure will take about thirty seconds. Please be absolutely motionless while the cap is off the lens. Are you ready? Now draw in a breath—not too deep—and hold it while I count."

Toby and the others drew in their breath, and Marjorie put her hand on the lens cover. As she lifted the cover off and began counting, Toby stared fixedly at the large, shiny lens surface, which he thought resembled a malevolent, gleaming eye. On the edge of his vision, he could see the people in the crowd craning their necks and gaping as they whispered to each other.

Thirty seconds seemed a long time; but Marjorie finally replaced the cover on the lens. A hubbub of conversation immediately rose from the crowd, Toby and Ted sighing as they relaxed. It had apparently been even more of an ordeal for the police constables, both of them almost exuberant with relief as they put their helmets back on.

The men who had gone for a wagon returned. Ted carried Marjorie's case and followed her up the stairs as the men put the body into the wagon. The policemen asked Toby to come to the station house with Ted the next day to make statements so that the matter could be closed.

Nightfall brought little relief from the heat. Toby, Ted, and Marjorie went to the restaurant for dinner. During the meal Toby noted that the young woman always seemed reserved with him. It bothered him mildly, because he liked her. But he was keenly pleased to observe that she appeared to return a degree of Ted's interest in her.

The air was still close and sultry when they went back to the rooms over the dry goods store. Toby lighted a lamp and sat on his bunk, to look through his folder of papers on the logging venture. Ted visited in Marjorie's room, talking with her and oiling the bellows from one of her cameras as she cleaned the metal and wooden parts. When the camera was reassembled, Ted came back to the room, and Toby put away his folder and began getting ready for bed.

The noises from the street outside had faded to silence when Toby and Ted were lying in bed in the dark room. They talked quietly, Ted mentioning Marjorie's delight over being invited to lunch with the mayor and the governor the following day. "I appreciate your giving me credit for getting her invited," Ted said. "You're supposed to go and see Charles Horton afterward, aren't you? And then some real estate dealers? It's going to be a busy day for you."

"Yes, it will be," Toby agreed. "Maybe you should talk with Marjorie in the morning and find out if there's anything in particular she wants to do, and then we can discuss our plans for the day."

"All right, Toby. Good night."

"Good night, Ted."

Toby listened to the night sounds of the city. Putting the incident with Karl Kellerman out of his mind, he thought about his appointments the next day as he slowly drifted off to sleep.

As it turned out, Toby was unable to keep any of the appointments. The next morning, noises from the street woke him well before daylight. As he opened his eyes, the glow of flames in the street filled the room with ruddy twilight. He sat up, reaching for his clothes. After pulling on his trousers and boots, he stepped to the window as he shrugged into his shirt.

The fire was a hundred yards or so down the street, well out of sight. People were scurrying around, carrying their belongings from adjacent buildings. A man came running up the street, his trousers pulled on over a nightshirt. As he passed under the window, Toby called to him and asked what was burning.

"It's the O'Leary stable," the man replied. "One of them was milking their cow, and it kicked over a lantern. The whole stable caught fire like it was a pile of tinder, but they got the animals out."

"Has the fire brigade been summoned?"

"Yes, it has," the man called over his shoulder as he

continued to run. "And they'll have their hands full when they get here."

Yawning, Ted sat up on his bunk. "What does it look like, Toby?" he asked. "Do you think it'll be a bad one?"

The warm breeze from the west was still blowing, brushing against Toby's face as he leaned out the window. Burning straw and hay were being wafted up from the blazing stable by the heat of the flames and settling on the roofs of nearby buildings.

Some of the roofs were of corrugated iron, but most were of wooden shingles that had been parched to brittle dryness during the past weeks of drought. As Toby watched, he saw shingles beginning to smolder and flames leaping up in the darkness.

The commotion had awakened everyone in the vicinity of the fire. People were handing up buckets of water to others on roofs to extinguish the flames. But there were only a few people, and too many fires.

"Yes, I think it'll be a bad one, Ted," Toby replied quietly. "I think it's going to be so bad we'll remember this day for a long time to come. You'd better get dressed and wake up Marjorie."

XI

"It's getting out of control," Ted said as he and Toby walked quickly along the street toward the fire. "They're going to have to use blasting powder to blow up some buildings and clear a firebreak."

Four pump wagons were stationed at the fire, the street a pandemonium of moving people and vehicles, the predawn darkness broken by the bright glare of flames. The men on three wagons were spraying water on the fire that was consuming the stable and two adjacent buildings. Farther down the street, the men on the fourth wagon were hosing water on the upper floor of a general store that had been set ablaze by the burning straw and hay from the stable.

People were fighting fires in other buildings, assisted by some among the crowd drawn by the commotion. They, as well as the firemen, were losing ground to the flames. Burning cinders eddying up from the roaring fires were carrying into other streets.

"I believe it's already out of control," Toby said. "These flying cinders are starting fires everywhere. The firemen should have begun by clearing a firebreak instead of hosing water on those fires."

Ted looked back along the street toward the dry goods store. "Well, if they don't stop it soon, it's going to spread down to Aaron Ward's store. We'd better get Marjorie out of there."

"Yes, we'd better," Toby agreed. "And there's no point in our staying here." He indicated the carriages for hire at the side of the street where the crowd of onlookers had gathered. "Bring one of those carriages to the store, and I'll get the baggage downstairs."

Ted nodded and hurried toward the carriages as Toby ran back along the street to the store. Marjorie, pinning up her hair, came out the door as Toby went up the steps. He explained the situation to her, and she quickly went back inside to carry out her equipment cases.

By the time the carriage arrived, Toby had carried most of the baggage downstairs. The driver climbed down from the box to calm the horses, which were dancing nervously in the glare and smoke of the fires. "Where do you want to go, mister?" he asked Toby.

"To the city hall," Toby replied. "The temporary one out on the west side of the city."

The driver smiled and nodded, pleased at the prospect of a long trip and a substantial fare. He began loading the baggage as Marjorie put her cases into the carriage. Ted went upstairs with Toby to carry out the last of the bags that the Blackstones and Martins had left behind.

A short time later Toby, Ted, and Marjorie were seated in the carriage, ready to leave. The driver had to scramble down again from the box, however, and hold his horses to keep them calm as two more pump wagons approached along the street.

The pump wagons rushed past in a clamor of clanging bells, pounding hoofbeats, and heavy wheels rumbling along the wooden paving blocks. A large freight wagon followed, kegs of blasting powder stacked in it. The carriage driver climbed back to the box and urged his horses on.

Moving a bag to make a more comfortable seat for Marjorie, Ted asked Toby why he had decided to go to the city hall. "To be on hand to help," Toby replied. "I think the mayor and the governor are going to need all the help they can get before this is over."

"You think it's going to be that bad, then?" Ted asked.

Toby nodded somberly. "Yes, I do. But I certainly hope I'm wrong."

"The fire department put out a fire yesterday that was about as bad as this one," Marjorie said. "It wasn't far from Dekoven Street, and several buildings were involved. What makes this one worse?"

"The way it started," Toby replied. "It got a big jump on the firemen right away, and the blasting powder should have been used sooner."

The conversation ended on that foreboding note, and the three of them fell silent as the carriage rumbled along, the glow of the flames gradually fading behind.

Then, abruptly, the light from the fire brightened again as kerosene, whale oil, or some other flammable material ignited and sent flames high into the sky. There followed a sudden, massive explosion that shook the ground under the carriage, a fountain of fire and burning embers erupting with a roar.

The powerful blast swept shingles off buildings all down the street and shattered windows. The carriage jerked and pitched wildly from side to side, the horses rearing and plunging in terror from the noise and the debris raining down around them. The driver shouted and cracked his whip, and the team began running, the carriage careening along the street.

The ruddy glare was almost as bright as daylight, and the fiery embers scattered by the explosion were dropping everywhere in showers of sparks. The horses were running full out, and Ted put his arm around Marjorie and held her as the carriage tilted and swerved dangerously. Then the crimson light faded once more, the carriage speeding along the street and leaving the smoldering firebrands behind.

As the horses began tiring and slowing, the driver shouted down and asked if everyone was all right. Toby leaned out the window to reply that they were, then sat back in his seat. Ted commented about the force of the explosion, saying that the entire wagonload of blasting powder must have detonated all at once.

"Yes, or at least a good part of it," Toby replied.

"That big flare just before the explosion must have touched it off. I certainly hope everyone was well clear of it and that the horses were unhitched from the wagon before it happened."

Marjorie and Ted nodded.

"I'm beginning to think you're right that this will be a really serious fire, Toby," Marjorie said. "I didn't think so at first, but it looks as though the worst combination of elements is present."

Her voice faded into a sigh as she looked out the window. The horses' hooves clopped hollowly against a long swing bridge over the southern branch of the river. Lanterns built into the bridge superstructure dimly lighted the roadway, and lamps on the docks and the moored ships below glinted on the wide expanse of water. The carriage cleared the bridge and turned onto a wide street leading north, paralleling the lake.

In this part of the city, the quiet of the dark streets contrasted with the tumult and roaring fires on Dekoven Street; the only movement was an occasional milk or ice wagon making its early morning rounds.

The first light of dawn was showing in the east by the time the carriage had crossed the vast city and reached the street leading up to city hall. Here the fire came into view again, a distant circle of bright red against the darkness, the tall column of smoke rising from it outlined against the lightening sky.

The young police constable Toby had met the first time he had come to see the mayor was on duty. Johnny Whittaker greeted Toby cheerfully. "You're calling a bit early this morning, aren't you?" he asked, laughing.

"Quite a bit earlier than I had intended," Toby replied. "We were a little too close to that fire for comfort."

The young policeman's smile faded as he looked at the fire. "Even from this distance it's bad enough. Worse than the one yesterday, isn't it?"

"It is. Do you have somewhere we can put our baggage?"

"Yes—yes, indeed," Johnny replied, a bit startled by

the request. "In the guardroom closet, just inside. I'll take care of it, Mr. Holt."

While Johnny busied himself with the bags, Toby paid the carriage driver. After apologizing for the hectic ride, the man frowned and looked at the fire in the distance. "My house isn't far from Dekoven Street," he said. "Guess I might go there and check on my family before I try to pick up any more customers."

"If I were you," Toby replied quietly, "I wouldn't waste any time checking. I'd go get them and take them to the outskirts of the city, and I'd do it without delay."

The driver looked at Toby. Then, without another word, he climbed to his box, gathered up the reins, and snapped his whip, turning the carriage around and driving rapidly back down the street.

Compared with the sprawling mass of the giant city, the fire seemed small as Toby, Ted, and Marjorie stood in the courtyard in front of city hall and looked at it. But it was steadily growing larger, and it was surrounded by miles of streets lined with wooden buildings. Already a myriad of smaller fires, spread by airborne cinders, could be seen burning outside its circumference. The wind off the prairie was driving the flames toward the heart of the city, the central business district. As the light brightened into dawn and the sun rose, a towering column of smoke was rising from the fire and bending toward the lake.

Well over an hour before their workday began, city employees began arriving. Gathering in a group near Toby, Ted, and Marjorie, they discussed the fire. Then the mayor's carriage pulled up, the governor's carriage following a short distance behind.

The two officials walked across the courtyard to greet Ted, Toby, and Marjorie. "Ted, is this the young lady we're having lunch with today?" the governor asked jovially, tipping his hat to Marjorie. "If so, it should be a very pleasant occasion indeed."

Ted smiled and nodded, then introduced Marjorie. The two officials lifted their hats and bowed as they exchanged greetings with her. Then, their smiles fading, they looked at the fire.

"I knew it was a bad one when I first noticed the smoke," the mayor said. "Those wooden buildings are as dry as matchsticks."

"Yes, they are," the governor agreed. "And this confounded wind only makes it worse."

Listening to them talking so casually about the fire, Toby felt uneasy. They didn't seem to regard it as a potential disaster. Their luncheon engagement that day seemed to be of more importance than the fire.

Toby was certain both men were efficient, capable administrators, and that as the morning progressed they would gradually realize what they faced; but any delay would be costly. "Ross," he said, "we have a lot more serious problem than just a bad fire. This is something on an entirely different scale."

"Do you think so?" the mayor mused, lifting his eyebrows. "What do you recommend we do, Toby?"

"I believe we should proceed on the assumption that this could be a serious threat to the city," Toby replied. "I think it would be a good idea to organize the city administration on an emergency footing, with a command post set up in your office. Then the police chief, fire chief, port master, and other officials could keep you advised of the situation and pass along your instructions on how to deal with it."

The mayor and the governor exchanged a glance, both of them obviously considering Toby's analysis as too pessimistic. "Well, the fire chief came to my house and talked with me just before I left there," the mayor said. "He told me that he would have every fire brigade in the city on the scene shortly and that they should be able to control it."

Toby shook his head doubtfully. "I sincerely hope that they will be able to, but I don't believe they can. The wind is carrying hot cinders too far ahead of the flames."

"Yes, that's what Chief Sloan told me," the mayor said. "But he's going to use blasting powder to clear a firebreak. We're going to have some citizens who are very angry because their property was destroyed, of course, but there's nothing we can—" A dull thud of an explosion carried across the distance, and he broke off and looked toward the fire. "That must be Chief Sloan's men blowing up a line of buildings now, so they should have the fire contained very shortly."

The thump of another explosion rippled across the city, followed by a series of explosions at intervals, sounding like a kettledrum in slow cadence. With each explosion, a puff of dust and debris rose in a line along the east side of the fire.

Toby and the others watched silently. The smoke and the distance made it difficult to distinguish any details, but minutes later it was obvious that the fire had crossed the firebreak.

The governor and the mayor looked at each other, the governor stroking his chin and frowning. "Ross, perhaps it wouldn't be a bad idea to do as Toby said. This is something more than an ordinary fire, and we would be organized to deal with whatever happens."

"Yes, you're right," Mayor Mason agreed. He turned to Toby. "I'll take your advice, starting with setting up a communications center."

Toby nodded. "On the subject of communications, I'm concerned that the fire might burn across the telegraph lines and cut off the city from the south and west. It would probably be a good idea to put in temporary wires from the edge of the city to a room near your office."

"That's a very good idea," the mayor said. "We should certainly at least find out where the wires are in the city." He glanced around at the people standing nearby. "The manager of the Atlantic and Pacific Telegraph Company office was supposed to come here this morning in connection with a building permit, but I don't see him. I'll have someone look for him. In the meantime, though, I'd like to ask you and Ted to stay here and assist us."

"Yes, by all means," Governor Palmer added firmly. "It's obvious that you're experienced in dealing with emergencies, Toby, and we could certainly use your and Ted's help."

Toby and Ted glanced at each other and nodded. "You can certainly depend upon us to do anything we can," Toby said.

"Let's go and get organized, then," the mayor said briskly, turning toward the city hall.

He called to his secretary and others among the city employees as he walked toward the building. He began giving orders rapidly. Three men were told to get horses and go for the fire chief, police chief, and port master. The mayor directed other people to bring a large map of the city to his office and to find the telegraph company manager.

In the mayor's office, everything began bustling with activity. Toby and Ted moved furniture out of the way so there would be an unobstructed view of the city through the large windows, and the mayor's secretary brought in sets of binoculars. A large map of the city was fastened to a wall.

The fire was a pool of red that continued to expand slowly, its thick column of smoke now reaching far over the lake. Toby stared at it, considering ways to contain it. The only remedy that occurred to him was a drastic one, and he knew that the mayor and the governor would refuse to agree to it.

The two had abandoned their schedule for the day. They were busily organizing the command post, clearing out an adjacent office for the fire chief, police chief, and port master to use. But Toby knew that they still lacked a complete grasp of the gravity of the situation.

On the vast, open prairies of the plains states, he had seen the phenomenon that he feared would develop here. A grass fire fanned by a hot wind could develop such intense temperatures that grass hundreds of feet ahead of the line of fire exploded into flame. Rocks shattered, and the sap in trees turned to steam and burst them open.

It was called a fire storm. One had to see it in order to appreciate fully its awesome destructive power. Toby had seen the effects of these fires; the mayor and the governor had not.

Toby's appraisal that the governor and mayor were treating the fire casually was proved correct when the manager of the telegraph company office arrived. He was a tall, thin man of about forty named Phelps. Toby, the mayor, and the governor talked with him as he stood in front of the map and pointed out the route that the telegraph lines followed in the city.

"It runs right along here," he said, drawing a finger down the north side of the southern branch of the river. "Now, if you tell me to, Mayor Mason, I'll close my office in the city and splice my lines into the city hall here. But it's going to cost me a lot of business."

"No, there'll be no need for that," the mayor said confidently. "The fire is on the other side of the river there, so the telegraph lines will be safe. What do you think, Jack?"

"Yes, I'm sure they'll be safe," the governor agreed. "The river's much too wide there for the fire to cross, even if our men don't stop it first. Do you agree, Toby?"

"I wish I could, but I can't," Toby replied. "I don't believe the firemen will be able to stop it before it gets to the river, and when it does, the way the river curves will put it almost directly downwind from the fire. I believe it'll get across."

Silence fell. The mayor and the governor stood looking at the map, thinking.

"Couldn't you get everything in readiness to run a line in here, just in case?" Toby suggested. "That would cut down on the time it would take in the event that the fire does get across the river and burn down the lines."

Phelps thought for a moment. "Yes, I could do that," he said. "It wouldn't interfere too much with my normal operations. And it would save a lot of time if you decide you want the lines run into here, Mayor."

"All right, let's do that," the mayor said. "Make whatever arrangements are necessary, Mr. Phelps. Then, if you would, stay in the building so we can contact you."

The man nodded, walking toward the door. As he went out, the police chief, fire chief, and port master came into the office, bringing with them the atmosphere of the frantic, losing battle against the fire raging in the city. Smudged with soot and cinders, they smelled of

smoke, and deep lines of strain and fatigue were etched
into their faces.

The mayor introduced the men to Toby and Ted,
then instructed them that he wanted them to work out of
the adjacent office, maintaining contact with their subordinates at the scene of the fire through mounted messengers. When he finished explaining what they were to do,
the three men pointed to the map and described the
situation at the fire.

The port master talked first, relating how he had
commandeered all the available steam launches to move
ships from the docks in the southern branch of the river to
the harbor. A few hot cinders were reaching as far as the
harbor, he said, so as a precaution he had instructed all
barges containing flammables to be moved to safety. He
had also warned all ships in the harbor to be prepared to
weigh anchor.

The police chief pointed to the area around and to the
east of the fire where his men were evacuating the buildings. Then the fire chief outlined on the map the present
perimeter of the fire. He also drew his finger along a line
where his men were planting blasting powder in another
attempt to make a firebreak, this one over a hundred feet
wide.

"That should stop it, shouldn't it?" the mayor said
optimistically. "The fire shouldn't be able to cross that,
Chief Sloan."

The fire chief, portly and graying, was hesitant. "I
think it has a good chance of stopping it, Mayor Mason.
I'd like to be more positive about it than that, but I can't."

"What do you mean?" the mayor asked.

"I thought that the first firebreak would stop it," the
chief replied. "But that's the hottest fire I've ever seen,
and even the wooden paving blocks in the streets are
burning. The cinders are shooting far out ahead of it and
starting fires behind my men, and I've lost a lot of hoses
and pump wagons they've had to abandon. We're steadily
becoming worse off while that fire is steadily gaining in
strength."

The mayor stared at the men. "Well, let's hope that

the firebreak stops it," he said. "If that doesn't work, what do you plan to do next?"

Chief Sloan frowned. "That'll be about all we can do, except fight it on the upwind side. On the downwind side, we'll have to abandon everything south of the southern branch of the river."

"Toby thinks it will cross the river," the mayor commented quietly.

The fire chief looked at Toby with a weary expression. "I hope you're wrong," he said.

"So do I," Toby replied.

The fire was turning out to be the worst the city had ever experienced. The people the police were evacuating had increased from scores to thousands. Toby, the mayor, and the governor discussed means of sheltering them temporarily, agreeing that the rolling-stock sheds at the rail yards were safe and suitably large. The mayor sent for the yard managers, who promptly agreed to clear the sheds; then policemen were dispatched with instructions to guide those streaming out of the city to the rail yards.

The port master reported at intervals on the ships and barges with dangerous cargoes that were being moved to safety. The police chief moved pins on the map to outline the areas being evacuated. The fire chief similarly indicated the perimeter of the fire and placed a steadily lengthening line of pins that represented the charges being planted to clear another firebreak.

The straight line of pins was a major focus of attention in the office. The fire chief finally placed one last pin on the map, then stepped over to the table where Toby was conferring with the mayor and the governor. "All of the charges for the firebreak have been set, Mayor Mason," he said. "They will be detonated within the next few minutes."

The mayor nodded in relief as he stood up. "Thank you, Chief Sloan. Let's all hope this firebreak will do the job for us. The city will be crippled for weeks as it is, and we certainly don't need to lose any more property to this fire."

Toby and the governor echoed the mayor's comments as they stood up from the table. Ted joined them as nearly everyone in the room went to the windows. The mayor's aides and others crowded around, quietly waiting.

Minutes later, the powerful explosive charges began detonating in rapid sequence. The mayor and others watched through binoculars, yet even without them Toby could clearly see the heavy timbers and sections of walls being hurled high into the air as the waves of concussion from the blasts rippled across the city and rattled the windows in front of him.

And even without binoculars Toby could see wisps of smoke rising from the north and east sides of the firebreak only minutes after the explosion; hot cinders carried by the wind were igniting roofs on the other side of the line of demolished buildings. After a few more minutes, there was no need to wait for a messenger to report on the success or failure of the firebreak. It had failed.

Nevertheless, a short time later, the fire chief came back in with a note rushed to him from the scene of the fire. The mayor, thinking that the message was about the failure of the firebreak, shook his head morosely. "You don't have to tell me what that says," he grumbled.

"This message isn't about the firebreak," the chief said. "It's worse news, I'm afraid. Fires are breaking out on the other side of the southern branch of the river. The division commanders are pulling all the men back north of the river before they're cut off from the bridges."

The mayor glanced at Toby with a look that acknowledged he had been correct in his assessment. Beckoning an aide, the mayor told him to go and find Phelps and have him move a telegraph line into the office, as planned. Then he turned back to the fire chief. "Will your men be able to stop the fire before it gets too far from the river?" he asked. "On that side of the river, it won't have the intensity it had before, will it?"

"No, it won't," the fire chief replied cautiously. "But the fire line will be just as long as before, if not longer, and we've had to abandon a lot of hoses and pump wagons. We've also had some men hurt, so we're not in nearly as good a shape as we were. But we're going to try another firebreak."

"Some of my men will help set the charges," the police chief added. "But in the event it doesn't stop the fire, I'm also having my men evacuate that area."

Mayor Mason nodded resignedly. "Well, we seem to be going from bad to worse," he commented. "But all we can do is give it our best, which we're doing. Perhaps the firebreak will work this time."

Only half listening, Toby was again thinking about a way of stopping the fire that had occurred to him earlier in the day. It was a drastic measure to take, and he was uncertain if it would work. But he was even more uncertain of whether the mayor and the governor would be willing to consider it. Finally, he thought of an indirect way to broach the subject.

"There are some things in the city that can't be replaced," he remarked. "Some of the documents in the museum date back to the early years of our nation, for example, and it might be wise to think about moving things of that nature to a place of perfect safety."

The suggestion was met with surprise and perplexity from almost all present. "The museum is in the center of the city, Toby," the governor said. "The central business district is the one part of the city that we don't have to worry about, since many if not most of the buildings are fireproof. Didn't you know that?"

Toby nodded. "Yes, I've heard it said, Jack. But having a fireproof building is like having a cattleproof fence. It can depend on the circumstances. If a whole herd is stampeding, the fence probably won't stop it." He turned to the fire chief. "Bob, have you ever seen what a fire storm can do?"

"No, I haven't," the fire chief replied. "I've heard about them, though, and apparently they're something to behold. But they only happen in forests and on the prairie. I've never heard of one in a city."

"We have a good size forest in this city," Toby pointed out. "The fact that it's been cut down and turned into houses doesn't alter its nature as far as a fire is concerned.

In fact, that makes it worse. The fire has a hot wind behind it, so we have all the circumstances for a fire storm to develop. Those supposedly fireproof buildings have wooden ceilings and floors, and I believe they'll burn if a fire storm develops."

The mayor started to shake his head and disagree. Then, thinking better of it, he sat back and turned to the governor. "Now I'm worried, Jack," he said. "If you think back over this morning's events, we've spent a lot of time telling Toby he was wrong on his predictions. And he's been absolutely right every single time. So now I'm worried."

Governor Palmer nodded soberly. "Chief Dougan," he asked, "have any of the managers of the banks asked for a police escort to move their funds elsewhere? Or have similar requests been made by jewelers or anyone else?"

"No, sir," the police chief replied. "It isn't a normal day in the center of the city, because the smoke is thick there and ashes are falling everywhere. But the stores are open, and none of the managers or owners are worried about the fire reaching them."

"And the hot ashes haven't started any fires there," the fire chief added. "For the most part the roofs are either slate or tile, thank goodness. Like Chief Dougan said, none of the people there are worried about their buildings. A lot of them are guaranteed to be fireproof, Toby."

Toby nodded and shrugged; he had seen that the men were not ready to entertain his idea for stopping the fire. "Still," he said, "I think it would be good for the police to have your authorization to commandeer hired carriages and other conveyances to transport valuable property, Ross. They might need the authority."

"They might indeed, and they will have it," the mayor agreed promptly. "Chief Dougan, you can pass the word along to your police captains that they are authorized to seize private conveyances for the purpose of transporting valuable property to safety."

The police chief nodded and left the room. The others began discussing the next attempt that would be made

to clear a firebreak. As they talked, Toby noticed that Ted
had disappeared.

When the meeting ended and the fire chief left, Ted
still had not returned. Toby walked down the hallway,
looking for him. He finally found him in the downstairs
entrance foyer.

Ted explained that he had been looking for Marjorie.
"Things got busy up there," he said, "and I suddenly
realized it's been a couple of hours since I saw her. And
now I can't find her anywhere."

"Well, she probably decided to go somewhere," Toby
said. "She can come and go as she pleases, can't she?"

"Yes, but this is a bad time for her to be wandering
around," Ted replied worriedly. "I think I'll look for her
outside."

"Ted, Marjorie is a grown woman. She's been on a
cattle drive and has done any number of things that prove
she can take care of herself. If you did find her, your
tracking her would probably annoy her. You know that as
well as I do."

Ted shook his head stubbornly. "I don't care if it
would annoy her. This is no time for her to be wandering
around."

"This is no time for you to be wandering around
either," Toby pointed out. "You're needed here, with me.
I have an idea that might just possibly be a way to stop this
fire, but I'm going to have to wait for the right time to
present it to the mayor and the governor. If they agree to
try it, I'll need your help." He could see Ted was still
unconvinced. "If we have to find Marjorie, we can get
Chief Dougan to send a man to look for her."

"I guess you're right," Ted agreed reluctantly. As he
and Toby walked toward the staircase, he suddenly laughed.
"If we sent the police for her, I wouldn't want to be the
one to face her when they brought her back."

"I wouldn't either," Toby chuckled.

Marjorie was moving along a street some two miles
east of city hall, much closer to the center of the city and

the fire. She had been walking at a good pace. Now she
was breathing heavily and almost staggering with fatigue.

All of the carriage drivers at city hall had refused to
take her where she wanted to go, so she had set out on
foot. The weight of the heavy equipment cases had become almost too much for her after a time, but now her
arms were numb.

The streets had been crowded in places, with people
moving in the opposite direction, fleeing from the fire. A
few times, trying to avoid the major thoroughfares, she
had almost become lost in the unfamiliar streets. But
now she was near her destination.

Another group of some twenty or thirty people who
had been evacuated from the path of the fire came along
the street toward Marjorie. Pale and harried, some of
them led animals and pushed carts as others carried bundles and pulled frightened, weeping children along.

As they approached, Marjorie moved to the inside of
the sidewalk to let them by. "You're going the wrong way,
lady," a man called. "Everybody is supposed to go to the
rail yards."

"Yes, I know," she replied. "I'll go there directly."

An old woman who was leading a mule hitched to a
cart beckoned to Marjorie. "Them suitcases is too heavy
for you to carry, honey, and we'll help you if you've got
separated from your family or something. Put your things
in my wagon and come along with us."

"That's very kind of you, but I'll manage," Marjorie
said. "Thank you anyway, and good luck to you."

The old woman and others with her returned Marjorie's expression of good will, then moved on. Like others
she had seen along the way, they were near despair,
homeless and without possessions except for the few piti-
ful things they had managed to take with them.

Yet, like others she had seen along the way, they
were universally ready to extend a helping hand. It was
the same response to dire circumstances that she had seen
during her travels. When the situation demanded it, the
very ordinary men and women of her country became the
most extraordinary of people.

Marjorie trudged to the end of the street, turned the corner, and abruptly halted. She had finally reached her destination, but the sense of victory that rose within her was stillborn. It turned into abject disappointment as she walked across the street and looked closer.

The gate in the wooden fence had a large, strong padlock on it. The fence towered over her to the height of ten feet, much too high for her to climb. And on the other side she saw a far more formidable obstacle as she looked up at the huge water tower, soaring above her on its thick wooden legs and crossbeams.

Having merely glimpsed the tower the previous day, she had not noticed the means of access to the high, narrow walkway around the base of the enormous tank. The only way up was a spindly ladder that was obviously meant to discourage boys who were adventurous enough to have climbed over the fence.

As she put down her cases at the gate and stared up at the ladder, Marjorie felt her weary arms throb with relief. But she knew that the toil of carrying the cases along the streets had been nothing compared with trying to hold on to one of them as she clung to the ladder and climbed it. It was braced at only one point, halfway up, where horizontal supports reached out from a crossbeam. That was the only place where she could rest a case for a moment during the climb.

It looked impossible. She was virtually certain that she would drop one of her cases, and it was probable that she herself would fall. Then, as a sense of defeat gripped her, she fought it. On the other side of that fence and at the top of that ladder lay the opportunity of a lifetime.

In the past, the catalog company that listed the stereopticon slides made from her plates had been critical and finicky. Sets of a dozen to fifteen beautiful slides that followed a logical sequence had been arbitrarily cut to eight or ten. The company had always refused to list any set at over a dollar, regardless of excellence or subject.

Now she was at a scene that would be of continuing national as well as international interest. If she made a series of twenty or even thirty plates for slides, the company would eagerly list the complete set. The price would be whatever people would reasonably pay, and a special supplement to the catalog would be immediately prepared to list the set.

In addition, newspapers and magazines all over the nation and the world would bid against each other for plates from her view camera to use in making etchings for their publications. Rights could be sold selectively, providing a steady flow of income for years.

On the other side of that fence and at the top of that ladder lay the end of makeshift repairs to cameras, skimpy meals, and sleeping on benches in train stations. Her cases would contain the best, most expensive equipment, and there would be money for all of the extras that would enable her to work more efficiently.

Marjorie glanced at the rickety ladder, at her equipment cases, then at the padlocked gate. It seemed that her entire life had led her to this place and this time. Both of her cameras were in good repair, and all of her plate holders had new plates in them, thanks to the two extra cartons Claude Leggett had given her. Circumstances had come together in such a way that she had been given an opportunity that few photographists ever had. All she had to do was get to the other side of that fence and the top of that ladder.

Picking up a large stone near her feet, Marjorie began hammering furiously at the padlock on the gate.

XII

Edward Blackstone smiled regretfully and shook his head as Bettina Woods offered him another serving of meat and potatoes. The venison roast was tender and juicy, and the spicy gravy accompanying it made it a delicious treat. The potatoes, baked in the pan with the roast, were succulent and savory.

The vegetables and fresh sourdough bread were just as delicious, but Edward had eaten all he could. "Everything is so tasty that I wish I could sit here and eat all day, Bettina," he said. "But I can't manage another bite."

His wife, Tommie, smiled at him as she took a sip of her coffee. "I don't believe you've offended Bettina about her cooking, Edward," she commented dryly. "You certainly did justice to the meal. And I did as well. Everything was absolutely delicious."

There was a chorus of agreement from Rob and Kale Martin, who were seated opposite the Blackstones, and from Frank Woods at the head of the table. "In any case, I didn't think I would be able to eat much after that large breakfast we had," Rob added. "Food like this and the comfortable guest cabins you've built here are certainly enjoyable after the ride from Chicago, Frank."

"I'm pleased that you like it here," Frank replied. "Traveling back and forth will be a lot faster and easier when we're completely organized. The steam launch that tows the logs will be making regular trips, and it will take

less than a day to get here. Also, I understand that someone intends to set up a livery stable in Wedowee, three or
four hours' ride west of here. If so, we'll be able to take
the train there and rent horses the rest of the way."

"That will certainly save a lot of time," Rob said.

As Kale commented that the weather was much warmer
than she had expected this far north, Edward, sipping his
coffee, sighed comfortably and sat back in his chair. The
trip from Chicago had been arduous, and everyone had
been weary when they had arrived the night before. But
after having slept late and spent a leisurely morning resting and talking, everyone was refreshed and in much
better spirits.

Certainly the setting was pleasant and relaxing. They
were seated around a long, heavy homemade table in the
large kitchen of the log house Frank had built for his wife
and their daughter, Lucy. There was a strong breeze, and
the shutters were open, letting in the fresh smell of the
surrounding forest. As well as rustic and informal, it was,
Edward reflected in satisfaction, very remote from the
pressures and the hectic pace of city life.

Lucy, a quiet, industrious girl of ten, stood up and
began clearing the table. Bettina took Tommie and Kale
outside to show them where she was planning to have
flower and vegetable gardens, and Edward walked around
to the front of the house with Rob and Frank.

The guest cabins were nearby, erected where a dense
thicket had stood only weeks before. Stumps littered a
wide clearing in front of the house and cabins, and a
corral, a dormitory, and other buildings were on the opposite side of the clearing. Four men were still working on
the dormitory.

The previous evening, when he had seen that men
had already been hired and preparations were in progress
to hire more, Edward had made a definite decision to
invest in the operation. Toby Holt was obviously intending to proceed with it, and Edward had absolute faith in
Toby's judgment.

As he crossed the clearing with Frank and Rob, Edward thought he smelled smoke on the wind. At breakfast

Frank had mentioned that one of the men, while working by the shore, where visibility wasn't limited by the screen of tall trees, had reported seeing smoke far to the south. Frank had said it was undoubtedly a forest fire, but too distant to be dangerous for those at the logging camp.

Edward put the thought aside as he listened to Frank describe his plans for completing construction at the logging camp.

"Those four men we have are good workers," Frank was saying. "We'll be ready to start sending a few logs down the lake before long. If you and Rob decide to invest in this, we'll go ahead with plans to build a lumber mill in Chicago, and we'll buy up the logging rights on all the land around here. If you don't, we'll have the logs sawed at someone else's mill in the city, and we'll probably build our own mill later, when we've accumulated enough profits."

"That makes sense," Rob commented. "According to the figures Toby showed us, you can sell lumber for much less than the mills in Wisconsin do."

"Yes, much less," Frank said.

"From what I've seen," Edward put in, "this looks like a very profitable investment—almost too good to be true. Aren't there any other logging operations around here?"

"No, the only other loggers in this area are well to the west, near the railroad lines," Frank replied. "Most of them use the railroad to haul their logs to the mills. Colmer, that little town we passed through yesterday, is the only settlement of any size within miles of here. It's a supply depot for the logging camps that use drays instead of the railroad. Other than that, there are only a few isolated homesteads."

"So apparently no one else has thought of rafting the logs down the lake to Chicago," Rob said.

Frank smiled. "Apparently not."

Edward pointed to the far end of the clearing, where the reflected light from the choppy surface of the lake gleamed through the trees. "Is that where you plan to put the chute to slide the logs into the lake?" he asked.

Frank nodded, then began detailing his plans as the

three of them walked to the steep bluff overlooking the lake. Although the lake could be rough at times, he said, the contour of the shoreline here was suitable for constructing a catch boom to contain the logs and for building a pier where the steam launch could dock.

"And I won't have to worry about logs sliding down the chute and getting stuck in the bottom," he continued. "There's a narrow bank at the foot of the bluff, then a straight drop-off just beyond the edge of the water. I used a forty-foot length of rope and a weight, and I couldn't touch the bottom with it. So I know it's deeper than—" He broke off as one of the men working on the dormitory across the clearing shouted to him. "What is it, Walt?" Frank called back.

"That smoke to the south is a lot thicker and closer now," the man replied. "And it ain't a forest fire. The smoke's too dark."

Frank exchanged a glance with Edward and Rob. Then the three men began walking rapidly toward the end of the clearing. They went through the stand of tall trees still remaining along the edge of the bluff and looked to the south. In the distance, a thick bank of dark smoke, towering high into the sky and blending with the clouds, covered part of the horizon. They stood and watched in silence for a long moment. Then Rob voiced what all three of them were thinking.

"That smoke is from burning buildings," he said. "Do you think it might be coming from Chicago, Frank? Or maybe Milwaukee?"

"Hard to tell for sure," Frank replied. "The winds around the shore eddy a lot, so it isn't always easy to figure where smoke is coming from. And the lake is unusually rough today. That certainly doesn't look like a forest fire, though, and I believe there's too much of it for it to be coming from Milwaukee."

"Yes, if the entire city of Milwaukee were burning, it wouldn't make that much smoke," Edward agreed. "So at least a large part of Chicago must be burning. But I don't believe there's anything we can do to help. By the time we got there, it would be all over."

Frank nodded. "There's no point in our setting out for Chicago now. But this might delay Toby and Ted for at least a few days."

"Yes, and Toby knows where we are," Rob added. "If there's anything we can do to help, I'm sure he'll get in touch with us in one way or another. So we may as well proceed with what we intended to do."

The three men fell silent for a moment, looking at the smoke and reflecting dejectedly on its implications. Then Frank sighed and shrugged as he turned away, echoing what Rob had said before. "Yes, we may as well do what we intended to," he said. "We'll saddle some horses, and I'll show you the stands of timber nearby. This is good timber here, but there's even better in all directions around."

As they started to walk away from the bluff, Edward noticed a tiny cinder that dropped through the air and settled on Rob's shoulder. He reached out and took it between his fingers, and the other two men stopped and looked as he showed it to them. It was a small bit of burned straw or some other substance that the winds had borne aloft with the smoke.

Hardly more than a black mote, the cinder was feathery light, turning into a smear of charcoal as Edward crushed it between his thumb and forefinger. But as a harbinger of what could follow, it was foreboding out of all proportion to its size. It was cold, but a hot cinder settling into the thick beds of evergreen needles reaching for miles in all directions could result in a conflagration, a sea of raging fire.

"I didn't think of that," Frank murmured, frowning as he looked at the smoke again. "Chicago is a fair piece from here, and it takes a very hot fire for the updrafts to carry hot cinders for any distance. But if a large part of the city is burning, that would be one of the hottest fires anyone has ever seen."

Rob looked at the clouds on the eastern horizon. "Those are rain clouds, aren't they?" he asked. "Do you think they'll reach this side of the lake, Frank?"

Frank shrugged. "I don't know. The wind will have to shift to move them in this direction."

Listening to the conversation between Frank and Rob, Edward was considering other possibilities. All the roads leading into the area were narrow tracks through dense forest—certain death traps if fires began sweeping across the area. That eliminated fleeing by land, and Frank had said that the lake was too deep to wade out into. "Are there any large clearings anywhere near here, Frank?" he asked.

Frank shook his head. "No, the largest within miles is at Colmer, and it's as closed in by trees as we are here."

Edward nodded toward the lake. "How long would it take us to build a raft out of logs?"

"A few hours," Frank replied. "But it would be a waste of time today. As heavy and unwieldy as a log raft would be, that surf would push it back to shore faster than we could paddle it out."

Edward was silent for a moment, reviewing all of the possibilities. Then he smiled as he wiped the smudge off his fingers with his handkerchief. "Well, I see no point in telling the ladies about this just yet, do you?" he said. "As far as going to look at timber is concerned, though, I'd rather stay with Tommie for now. In the meantime, I know of nothing we can do except wait and see what happens."

Frank and Rob nodded in agreement. To tell the women now about the danger would serve no purpose. The three men fell silent as they walked back toward the house.

Marjorie White had found a solution to the problem of how to get her equipment cases up the walkway around the water tower. The method she had adopted was excruciatingly painful, as well as perilously dangerous, but it worked—which was her only requirement. She had already made one trip up and down.

Now, with her belt through the handle of the remaining case and looped around her right shoulder, she crept up the ladder as the heavy wooden box rested against her back. Searing pains stabbed her shoulder, the leather belt digging into her flesh, and her right arm was becoming increasingly numb. Although she moved slowly and cautiously, the case occasionally bounced against her back. Its sagging, leaden weight increased when it bounced, threatening to jerk her off the ladder and plunge her to the ground.

Without the belt around her waist, her hem dropped below her toes, an additional hazard that she had to cope with. Each time she raised a foot to the next rung, Marjorie carefully lifted the hem with her toe, making sure the material remained above her shoe. Splinters in the rough wood dug into her hands as she slid them up the ladder. The splinters caused only minor twinges of pain, however, in comparison with the throbbing in her shoulder.

Each rung was a tremendous effort as she lifted herself with the heavy case on her back. It seemed that each one would be the last she could manage, but she continued finding reserves of energy. She was sustained by the knowledge that she could do it, because she had done it once already. Her left shoulder still ached, and her left arm tingled from the first climb, when the belt had been looped over that shoulder.

Keeping her eyes straight ahead, she tried to think of other things and not dwell on her pain, which threatened to overwhelm her. When she passed the thin brace at the center of the ladder, she felt a sense of disappointment, thinking she was much higher. Then she pushed it out of her mind and proceeded to climb a rung at a time, concentrating only on reaching the top.

After what seemed another eternity, the edge of the walkway was suddenly in front of her eyes as she hugged the ladder and started to take another step. But it was a moment of additional danger rather than an immediate relief. She had come within a chilling hairbreadth of toppling backward and falling when she had reached this point with the first case and had tried simply to climb on up to the walkway.

Gripping the base of a post under the railing around the walkway, Marjorie dragged herself onto her stomach on the platform. The heavy case crushed down on her as she wriggled farther onto the walkway, near her other case, which she had placed beside the black, mossy side of the tank. Lying full length on the boards, she turned and let the case slide off her back. As the numbness began leaving her right shoulder and arm, the pain increased. She flexed her fingers to get it over with more quickly.

The pain soared to an excruciating crescendo, and Marjorie gritted her teeth to keep from crying out. The throbbing agony was almost unbearable, but she continued flexing her fingers to make the pain peak and ebb more quickly. She was not yet finished with her preparations. One more task still remained before she could begin photographing the fire.

Her face was damp with sweat when the pain finally began subsiding. Taking out her handkerchief, she wiped her face and pushed wisps of her hair back, then crawled to the edge of the walkway and looked down at the street. The fire was on the opposite side of the water tower from the ladder. The narrow street below was empty, and she had apparently attracted no attention while climbing the ladder. But she knew she would when she went around the walkway.

Unfastening her belt from the case, she put it on and adjusted her hem to its normal length. Then she stepped over the side of the walkway to the first rung of the ladder and went back down it. When she reached the ground, she found a large rock. The foot of the ladder was nailed solidly to a thick beam set into the ground. Marjorie began hammering at the ladder uprights with the rock, driving the nails back out of the beam.

The long, shiny nails on one upright slowly pulled out the beam; then she hammered on the other upright and freed it from the beam. After removing her cape and fashioning it into a bag of sorts with which to carry the rock, she climbed the ladder to the brace halfway up. Intended only to stabilize the center of the ladder, the brace was composed of two thin boards extending horizontally to a massive wooden crossbeam.

One side of the brace loosened easily, the small nails pulling out as Marjorie hammered. Then, as she was moving the rock to her left hand, to free the other side of the ladder from the brace, she dropped it. Marjorie climbed back down and retrieved the rock, putting it in her cape with two others. Quickly she climbed back up and hammered the other side of the brace loose.

The ladder weaved insecurely from side to side as Marjorie climbed on up. When she reached the top and was on the walkway, she saw that the nails holding the ladder to the edge of the walkway were already partially loosened from the swaying of the ladder. Lying on her stomach, she hammered at the ladder with a stone. The stone slipped from her hand, taking a long time to reach the ground and slam into it with a solid thud. Marjorie took another large stone out of her cape and continued hammering at the ladder.

When the last nails were almost out, Marjorie tapped gently with the rock. Despite her caution, the ladder came loose suddenly and almost toppled away from the walkway. Snatching at it and reaching far out, she just managed to catch it with the tips of her fingers and pull it back. Holding it firmly, she drew in a breath, her heart pounding and her palms damp as she thought about how near she had come to watching the ladder break apart from its impact on the ground far below, thus stranding her on the walkway.

Gripping the top rung, Marjorie rose to a crouch and, using all her remaining strength, lifted the ladder and hooked the rung over the railing that projected over the opening. Gripping the heavy ladder again by the second rung, she lifted once more. Marjorie continued raising the ladder a rung at a time until she had hoisted some ten feet of it above the railing. The bottom end was now well out of reach of anyone on the ground.

She had finally finished her preparations. Wearily she picked up her cases and began trudging around the walkway.

The circumference of the huge water tank was even larger than it appeared from the ground. The walkway continued to curve on around ahead of Marjorie, dark and slippery in places where water was seeping from tiny leaks in the tank. The wide, busy street on the side opposite the

ladder came into view at last, and Marjorie saw people
hurrying along it toward the rail yards. Then, a few feet
farther along, the fire came into view.

Suddenly stopping, Marjorie gasped. The perspective
from the walkway was even better than she had thought it
would be, the distance from the fire and the elevation
perfect for photography. And the scene was overwhelming, so much so that Marjorie gazed at it spellbound for a
long moment. In terms of destruction, the fire was appall-
ing. But as a spectacle it was awesome, the most dramatic
scene she had ever witnessed.

The city was a vast panorama in front of her, distant
enough for her to view it with a sweep of her eyes, yet
near enough for her to see the details of the streets and
buildings with perfect clarity. Most of the southwestern
quadrant was a seething mass of flames, with an immense
column of boiling, black smoke rising from it and bending
away to the west. The fire had crossed the southern branch
of the river in places; the docks along it were engulfed in
flames.

As she watched, she could see the wall of flames
moving westward toward the tall grain elevators and warehouses along the southern waterfront. The actual sight of
the leading edge of the fire was spectacular and horrifying.
Liquid flames towered over buildings and swept down
upon them, almost like a giant tidal wave. Marjorie had
the eerie impression that the fire was sentient and malevolent, greedily devouring the buildings to feed its raging
appetite.

Tearing her gaze away, she bent over her cases in a
frenzy of activity, not wanting to lose another moment.
Her hands trembling as she worked, she took out the
pieces of her tripod and assembled it, sliding the bolts into
place and tightening the thumbscrews.

As she opened the other case, her hand hesitated
between her view camera and her stereo camera. She took
out the view camera, deciding to do first a set of plates
that could be used to prepare etchings for newspapers and
magazines. Placing the camera on the pan of the tripod,
she tightened the screw under it and extended the bel-

lows. She framed the scene in the ground glass, then took out a plate holder, inserted it, and removed the dark slide.

In addition to her having a perfect position for photographing the fire, all of the other conditions were ideal. The wind was pushing the smoke straight westward, clearing it from the scene, and the day was bright and sunny. The bromine accelerated plates would need only about a second of exposure.

Marjorie lifted the cover off the lens, replaced it, then pushed the dark slide back into place. Moving the camera to a different position, she took another plate holder out of the case. She jotted quick notes on the exposures, then exposed the second plate.

She had been working for only a minute or two when what she anticipated happened. People going along the street below, on their way to the rail yards, noticed her moving on the walkway. They began pointing and commenting. A few minutes later a police constable appeared. He shouted sternly.

Marjorie lifted her dark slide over her head. "Please don't disturb my concentration," she called. "I'm about to make a photograph."

The policeman's beefy face reddened with rage. Glaring, he stepped closer to the fence. "You're about to get down from there, and that's all you're about to do, lady!" he barked. "Now, you get down here where you belong!"

Marjorie lifted the cover off the lens and replaced it. "No, I will not," she shouted back.

"You get down here now!" the policeman bellowed. "If you don't, I'm going to come up there and bring you down, lady!"

Marjorie shook her head as she lifted her camera and moved it to another position. "No, you won't," she called.

"I won't?" the policeman shouted, enraged. He began running along the fence. "You just watch me, lady!"

The policeman disappeared from her line of view. The people on the street, eager for something amusing to lift their spirits, laughed at him and waved to Marjorie. She smiled and waved, then put a plate holder back into

her case and took out another. She positioned her camera
and slid the plate holder into it.

When she saw the police constable again, she had
finished her first series of plates and was resting her
notebook on the railing, catching up with her notes on the
exposures. "Lady, you put that ladder back down where it
belongs!" he shouted.

"Listen," Marjorie called placatingly, "when I'm
through here, I'll make a likeness of you, all right? Please
just don't disturb my concentration while I'm working."

"I'll disturb more than your concentration!" he barked.
"Lady, you're guilty of destroying city property!"

"No, I didn't destroy it," Marjorie replied patiently.
"I only moved it for a little while." She pointed to the
street. "Do you see those people there? They need your
help. But instead of helping them, as you should be doing,
you're disturbing me. Now do what you're supposed to be
doing and leave me alone."

"I don't need you to tell me what my job is!" he
roared. "And I'm going to put you in jail, that's what I'm
going to do!"

"Then you'll have to take me to Springfield, because
the Chicago jail is about to burn down," Marjorie retorted. "Now you may as well go away, because I don't
intend to talk to you anymore."

The policeman continued shouting and threatening,
but Marjorie ignored him as she finished her notes. The
man finally stamped away, crimson with rage. Putting
away her notebook, Marjorie removed the view camera
from the tripod and took out her stereo camera.

The wide, short camera had twin lenses that made
identical but slightly out-of-register images on its oblong
plates, giving an illusion of depth when the finished slides
were viewed in a stereopticon. Marjorie put it on the
tripod, then took out her view finder. While she was
accustomed to mentally dividing a panoramic scene into
sections to photograph, she wanted this series of views to
be perfectly accurate.

Looking through the view finder, she made mental
notes of where the lines in the instrument were on the

scene, planning to overlap each view with the adjacent ones. She put the view finder away and took out a plate holder, then slid it into place and positioned the camera for the first exposure.

During the morning, the explosions resulting from attempts to clear the firebreaks had been part of the turmoil around her, and at a distance they had not been especially alarming. Now, however, the force of the first explosion north of the river, when she was about to lift the cover off the double lenses, caught her completely by surprise.

In her unprotected position high on the side of the water tower, the sudden clap of noise was shattering. It was immediately followed by a concussion surging through the air with a forceful impact that staggered her and almost toppled her camera. The shock wave traveling through the ground rocked the water tower, and quaking fear stabbed within Marjorie as she heard the tons of water slosh and gurgle.

Even as she was steadying her camera and controlling her fear, she was observing and noting what happened. Huge beams and slabs of roofs and walls from two large buildings erupted and soared into the air. Then, just as they reached the apex of their upward arc and before they began their downward plunge, they seemed to hesitate for a long instant.

When the second thunderous explosion made the world shudder around Marjorie, she had the camera pointed toward it. Narrowing her eyes and bracing herself against the blast, she watched the debris soar into the air. When it reached the peak of its flight, she lifted the cover off the lenses and then replaced it.

While the debris was still settling, she worked frantically to replace the stereo camera with the view camera. With the fire at one side of the explosions, and the tiny forms of firemen and pump wagons in the streets on the other side, the scene was worth a small fortune as a plate to make an etching for a publication. By the time the third explosion rang out, she was ready, the view camera on the tripod and a plate in place.

As the explosions marched down the street, Marjorie exposed one more plate in the view camera and one more in the stereo camera to make certain she had perfect ones. Then, the explosions finished, she resumed her panorama with the stereo camera. While she worked, she noted that the fire had not been contained but had spread across the swath of demolished buildings.

After the fire crossed the opening, it seemed to gain in intensity. Large tenements and other structures were wreathed in fire within an instant, flames shooting from their windows and roofs exploding upward.

Shingles were sucked high into the boiling clouds of black smoke and disappeared even as they burst into flame in the searing heat. Preoccupied with her work, Marjorie barely noticed them. She failed to wonder where the eddying air currents over the lake might carry them, or to consider that they might be the fiery seeds of Chicago's destruction, ready to be broadcast many miles away.

Since Major General Leland Blake had returned to Fort Vancouver from Independence, he had worked late each night, yet his desk was still piled high with correspondence requiring his personal attention. There were proceedings of court-martial boards and lists of promotions to review and approve, reports on the levels of training and state of equipment in individual units to read and forward, and other thick bundles of papers, stacked one on the other.

All of them were important, but when the general read the priority dispatch his clerk laid on his desk, he immediately put everything else aside. Taking off his glasses, he picked up the dispatch and reached for his cap. As he went out, he told the clerk to saddle a horse and bring it to him at his quarters.

When he went into his house, Eulalia came along the hallway to meet him, surprised that he was home so early. Her smile of greeting faded as he handed her the dispatch. She took her glasses out of her pocket and put them on, gasping in dismay as she read.

"I'm sure Toby is in no danger," Leland said.

"No, of course not," Eulalia replied quickly. "He'll be in the midst of it, but he knows how to look after himself. But this is dreadful, Lee. . . ."

Her voice faded as she reread the dispatch. The general reflected that her quick dismissal of the subject of her son's safety might be interpreted as indifference by someone who didn't know her. But he knew that, on the contrary, it was a sign of how well she knew her son. She had full confidence in his ability to deal with any situation in which he found himself.

Although the lovely, mature woman who shared his home and his life had been his wife for years, she remained thoroughly a Holt. A generation of that bloodline had been nurtured in her womb, their blood and flesh within her forming her as much as she formed them. The attitudes and reactions of a Holt were uniform among the clan, even if they were often puzzling to an outsider. In this instance, her reaction was entirely predictable, because one of the Holts' foremost characteristics was intense, reverential patriotism. Always they thought first of the nation.

"It will take years to recover from this," Eulalia said sadly, "and the effects will be felt all over the country. But this isn't very specific about how much damage has been done to the city, Lee."

"Apparently the fire still hasn't been brought under control, so it'll probably be a day or two before we have full details. I'm sure the newspaper offices in Portland are being notified of this by telegram, so I'm going to ride over to the ranch and tell Cindy about it before she gets a garbled account. I'll reassure her and Janessa about Toby."

Eulalia nodded in agreement. "You may be getting more dispatches on it, Lee, so why don't you tell them to come over and have dinner with us."

"Good idea." Leland Blake smiled and kissed his wife, then went back outside. An orderly, waiting for him with a horse, saluted and handed him the reins. The general mounted and rode toward the river to take the next ferry to Portland.

While on the ferry, he pondered the implications of

the dispatch. Like his wife, he foresaw a detrimental effect on all parts of the nation from the disaster in Chicago. The city was the transportation and manufacturing hub of the Midwest, and it appeared likely that years would pass before it would recover from what had happened.

When the ferry docked, Lee disembarked, mounted his horse, and rode quickly through Portland. He turned onto the road leading to the Holt ranch. A few minutes later, along a straight stretch of the road, he saw a horse and a dismounted rider.

The rider was small, a child. Janessa Holt had seen him coming and had stopped to wait for him. And while she was waiting, she was smoking a cigarette.

Janessa dropped the cigarette and stepped on it as he approached. "Good day, sir," she said, exhaling smoke.

"Good day, Janessa," he replied, reining up. "I thought you'd be in school or at the Martins' house this early in the afternoon."

The girl gripped the horn on her saddle and sprang lightly onto her mare. "I usually am, but I heard about the fire in Chicago and decided to come home and tell Cindy," she said as they began riding. "Is that what you've come about, sir?"

"Yes, it is, as a matter of fact." Taking out the dispatch, he handed it to her. "It appears that the fire hasn't been controlled yet, but I'm sure your father is in no danger."

The girl was as impassive as usual, showing no reaction to what he said or to the dispatch as she read it and handed it back. They rode on side by side, talking, and while Janessa was courteous and respectful in her attitude and speech, her brief comments were punctuated by long silences.

The girl rode astride her horse, not sidesaddle, as Eulalia thought she should. Eulalia had complained of that to Toby, and she had joined Cindy in expressing strong disapproval of the girl's smoking. But both of them left decisions concerning the child to Toby, who considered her smoking, how she rode a horse, and other matters to be minor concerns.

For himself, Leland Blake was content to stay well out of disputes between the Holts. In any case, he liked Janessa.

At the ranch house, Cindy read the dispatch with obvious concern. "It was very good of you to come, Papa," she said, handing the dispatch back to him. "As you said, it will probably take them years to recover from this, and it will create problems all over the nation."

The general smiled in thanks as Janessa put a cup of coffee in front of him. Then he looked back at Cindy. The marked similarity between the two of them was a constant source of wonder to him. Their pretty faces were similar, and their hair was the same color, as were their eyes. They were like identical twins except for the difference in age.

"I may get more dispatches about it later today," Lee said, stirring sugar into his coffee. "Your mother suggested that you come over for dinner so we can keep you abreast of the news."

"Yes, we'll do that," Cindy replied. "I have a few things to attend to here, then I'll come over with Janessa and Timmy."

The three of them fell silent as they sat around the kitchen table, each of them lost in thought as they sipped their coffee. The general noticed that Janessa drank hers black. No one said a word about the danger Toby was in.

Finally Janessa spoke up. "Well," she said, "it could be much worse. They have Dad there to help them, so they'll be much better off than they would have been otherwise."

XIII

Toby stood looking out the window at the fire enveloping much of the southern half of Chicago. The clatter of the telegraph equipment in the adjacent office was a background to the explosions in the city.

The mayor and the governor were standing nearby, also watching. Instead of the hopeful anticipation with which they had observed the earlier explosions, their attitude was one of grim resignation.

Everything in the path of the fire, to as far as the center of the city, was being abandoned, and a firebreak was being cleared to prevent any damage to the tall, supposedly fireproof buildings there. It would not be long, Toby mused, until they knew whether or not the buildings were actually fireproof.

Donald Phelps, the telegraph office manager, crossed the room to Toby. "This is from the lieutenant governor in Springfield," he said, handing him a telegram. "They're loading all of their fire equipment and fireman on a train to send here."

Toby glanced over the telegram. "All right, I'll give it to Chief Sloan. Did you get all of those incoming personal messages stopped, Don?"

"Yes, I did," Phelps replied. "But we're also getting quite a few from newspapers. I'm having my operators give them that report you wrote to send to Washington." He smiled weakly. "Maybe I should pay you for it, since

212

we're charging them enough to make up for some of the business I've lost."

Toby smiled and shook his head. "No, there's no need to pay me for it, Don. I'm glad that it's doing you some good."

"My company headquarters is delighted that I'm still in operation," Phelps said. "They sent me a telegram of congratulations, and I informed them that it was all through you. If you ever need anything from the Atlantic and Pacific Telegraph Company, Toby, all you need do is ask."

Phelps left the room, and a moment later the series of explosions ended. The mayor and the others turned away from the window and crossed the office to the map on the wall, where Toby and Ted joined them. The mayor stared dismally at the line of pins. "What if this one fails, too?" he asked.

"I've put all the men I can spare to hose down the wreckage from the buildings," Chief Sloan answered him. "Everything that can be done is being done."

"Yes, everything that can be done is being done," the mayor echoed somberly. "But that's what we've been doing all day, and unfortunately it hasn't been good enough." He turned to Toby. "I'm still very concerned about your reservations as to whether the buildings at the center of the city are actually fireproof, Toby. What's your assessment now?"

"It isn't good, Ross," Toby replied. He pointed to the pins indicating the firebreak that had just been cleared, then to those showing the perimeter of the fire. "Notice how far the men have to get from the fire to set up a firebreak now. It's much farther than before."

"That's because the fire has become so hot," Chief Sloan interjected. "As hot as that fire is now, it would be suicidal for the men to try to get blasting powder any closer."

"Yes, and that shows the danger, Bob," Toby said. He pointed to the wide swath of streets between the perimeter of the fire and the firebreak. "It's going to come through the built-up area here completely unchecked. By the time it reaches the firebreak, I believe it'll be a fire storm."

A sober silence fell, the men looking at the map. Then the police chief, Charles Dougan, spoke quietly. "The merchants in the center of the city are getting nervous," he said. "Some of them have closed their businesses for the day, and a couple of jewelers and one bank have asked help in transporting their merchandise and cash. But it's far from becoming a widespread panic."

"That will change if Toby is as correct as he has been before," the mayor commented grimly. "Apparently, Toby, if this fire storm does develop, there's nothing at all we can do, correct?"

Toby exchanged a glance with Ted. An hour before, he had explained to Ted his idea about how to stop the fire, and the young lawman had agreed that the mayor and the governor would refuse to employ it. But now Toby felt that the time had come to tell them about it. "There may be something we can do," he said. "I'm not sure it will work, but I think it's our best chance for stopping that fire."

All of the men were suddenly looking at Toby eagerly. "By all means, tell us about it, Toby!" the mayor exclaimed. "The thing we need more than anything else is an idea—any idea that will work."

"We could set a backfire," Toby said. "That's the one certain way of stopping a fire in a forest or on the prairie, and a backfire will also stop a fire storm."

The momentary eagerness among the men dissipated suddenly, and they were even more sober than before. "Yes, but this isn't a prairie or a forest, Toby," the mayor commented. "It's a city, and we have buildings here that cost millions—not trees or grass."

"It might be something to think about, though, Mayor Mason," the fire chief said cautiously. He pointed to the streets of buildings between the fire and the firebreak. "These buildings are lost anyway, so perhaps we could set a backfire there."

"No, that wouldn't work, Bob," Toby said. "The space must be too wide for sparks and embers to cross, and that isn't. Also, the backfire must burn across a wide distance in order to become hot enough to make the main fire crown. When it does that, flames shoot high into the air and disperse most of the heat from both fires, and everything cools down."

"Where would you set a backfire, Toby?" the mayor asked.

Toby pointed to the south side of the main river channel, a wide, straight body of water that divided the center of the city. "Right there, on a street just south of the main channel. The buildings on the north side of the street would have to be demolished, and those on the other side would have to be set on fire with kerosene or something."

The mayor shook his head. "No, I can't authorize that, Toby," he said firmly. "In the short time I've known you, I've come to trust your judgment above that of anyone I've ever met. But you're talking about destroying millions of dollars' worth of property, and I simply can't authorize that."

"A further consideration, Toby," the governor added, "is the legal financial liability of the city and the state. If it could be established in court that Ross acted injudiciously, then the city would be liable for all damages as a result of his actions." He turned to the fire chief. "Chief Sloan, in your opinion, is setting a backfire such as Toby described the best course of action open now?"

"No, sir," Robert Sloan replied, glancing apologetically at Toby. "I think the firebreak we have now has a good chance of stopping the fire."

"So there you are, Toby," the governor concluded. "The mayor would be going against the advice of his own expert. And before the ashes cooled, we would have lawyers in here by the score, soliciting damage suits against the city from property owners."

"He's absolutely right," the mayor agreed. "Every shyster in the country would flood in here, and they would empty the state treasury. No, we'd better stay with our present course of action."

"Well, at least you'll have some help with it now,"

Toby said, handing the mayor the telegram that Donald Phelps had given him. "Firemen and fire-fighting equipment are being loaded onto a train in Springfield."

The mayor brightened visibly as he read the telegram. He handed it to the fire chief. "That's the first good news we've had today," he said. "I'm sure you'll be able to use the men and equipment, Chief Sloan."

"Indeed I will, Mayor," the fire chief replied, as he read the telegram. "If they get here in time."

The mayor turned back to the map. "A new fireproof building was recently completed on the street just north of the river," he said. "What was it called?"

"That's the Hawthorne Building, sir," the police chief replied. "It's seven stories tall, all stone, and has a tile roof. It replaces the last of the wooden buildings on that block." He pointed to the map. "It's the closest building to the firebreak."

"Yes, the Hawthorne Building," the mayor said. "Well, keep me posted, gentlemen, and let's hope that this nightmare will soon be over."

He walked toward his desk with the governor, as the fire chief and police chief filed out. Ted and Toby stepped back to the windows.

"We agreed that they probably wouldn't like the idea," Ted said quietly. "We were absolutely right about that. But if there ever was an army general who was as cautious as they are about acting forcefully, he wouldn't win many battles."

"That's true," Toby agreed. He was silent for a moment, then asked, "Did we get that smaller map of the city we asked for?"

"Yes, the city engineer brought it up a little while ago," Ted replied. "It's over here."

They went to a nearby table, and Ted unrolled the map and spread it out. Toby studied it. "I'm sure the fire will spread across the central business district," he said. "But if we could box it from the west and the north, we could save part of the city."

"Where would you set the backfires?" Ted asked.

"Here and here," Toby replied, drawing his finger

from the southern branch of the river clear across to the northern branch, then at a right angle to the waterfront.

"There are mostly houses and tenements in those areas," Ted said. "That would wipe out most of the housing that's left."

"It would also save the northern part of the city and the docks there," Toby said, "as well as the western and southern outskirts. The way it's going now, there won't be a building left standing."

Ted nodded. "Do you think the mayor and the governor will agree to this?"

"I don't think they'll have any alternative. Once the central business district starts burning, they'll see the whole city is doomed unless some forceful action is taken quickly."

As Ted looked at the map, he pointed to a symbol inside the area Toby had indicated for the western backfire line. "That's the water tower Marjorie was talking about climbing up with her things," he said. "You don't suppose she could be on that tower making photographs of the fire, do you?"

"She couldn't make photographs of anything without her equipment cases," Toby replied. "How would she get them up there, Ted? You know how heavy they are."

Ted nodded, but he still looked worried. Toby began studying the map, then thought again about Ted's question. Assuming that the mayor agreed to his plan, which seemed inevitable, Marjorie would be doomed to a fiery death if she was indeed on the walkway around the water tower.

Then, remembering the long, spindly ladder and the ponderous weight of the equipment cases, Toby dismissed the thought.

"The Hawthorne Building is on fire, Mayor Mason," the fire chief blurted as he entered the room. "This man brought the message from the division commander, and he was there when it started burning. His name is Jenkins."

Toby looked up from the map he was studying. A momentary silence fell. The mayor slumped in his chair and stared at the fireman. The fireman, wearing his protective canvas coat and carrying his helmet, was a tall, well-built young man, no more than twenty. But under the soot, his face was as lined with fatigue as that of an old man, and the intense heat of the fire had toasted his skin to the deep red of a severe sunburn. His lips were cracked and parched, and his red eyes mirrored the terror of the scene he had just left.

The mayor sat up straighter in his chair. "How far away were you, and how did it happen, Fireman Jenkins?" he asked.

The young fireman licked his dry lips and glanced around uncertainly. "My brigade . . . we were about two hundred yards away, Mr. Mayor," he replied in a hoarse, hesitant voice. "We can't get the horses any closer than that. And the building . . . every piece of wood in it must have caught fire all at once. . . ." His voice faded, and then he cleared his throat. "The iron trim on it melted like candle wax."

"What about the adjacent buildings, Fireman Jenkins?" the mayor asked.

The fireman started to reply, but his voice suddenly broke with a sob. He put his hands to his face and began weeping. "They're all going," he wailed. "It's beat us at every turn, and there ain't nothing we can do. It's taking the whole city from us, and we just can't stop it. . . ."

Toby's chair skidded back in his haste to get to his feet. He crossed the room with long strides and put a hand on the young man's shoulder. "You did your duty, and you did it well, Fireman Jenkins," he said firmly. "You and the other firemen stood up to impossible odds longer than anyone can be expected to. But they were impossible odds, and you certainly can't be blamed for that."

"Indeed not," the mayor added emphatically, quickly following Toby to the fireman. He patted the young man's shoulder. "I'm proud of you, and of every fireman in this city. But as my friend here said, you were up against impossible odds. Chief Sloan, please take Fireman Jenkins to your office so he can have a cup of coffee and rest for a while."

As the fire chief led the young man out, the mayor folded his hands behind his back and stepped to the windows. The governor joined him, and the two men stood and looked out in silence. Ted pointed to the map on the table and lifted his eyebrows in a silent question as Toby returned to his chair. Toby shook his head. He quietly told Ted that there was plenty of time to bring up the subject of a backfire again, since it would take the fire several hours to work its way across the center of the city.

A few minutes later, the fire chief, police chief, and port master came in for a reassessment of the situation. The police chief cleared his throat. "My captains are getting a lot of requests for help from the merchants now, Mayor Mason," he said. "A lot of them want help in moving money and valuables, and I've passed the word to my men to help them as much as possible."

Turning away from the window, the mayor nodded wearily. "Very well, Chief Dougan. Chief Sloan?" he prompted.

"I've ordered my men to assist the police in evacuating the streets being threatened now," the fire chief replied. "We're falling back on a line along the main channel of the river."

"And what action do you recommend now?"

The fire chief stepped to the map and pointed to the south side of the main channel. "The streets here are wide, and we would have a very wide firebreak if we combined two of them with the width of the river. We still have plenty of blasting powder left."

The look that the mayor and the governor exchanged made it clear that both officials considered yet another attempt to clear a firebreak completely futile. "How many casualties do we have now, Chief Dougan?" the mayor asked.

"About eighty, including those among the firemen," the police chief replied. "That's not many, considering the scope of this disaster."

"Yes, that's true," the mayor agreed quietly. "That's

true—but it's still eighty human lives. And we're not out of this yet. Chief Sloan, I have to assume that the condition of young Jenkins is now the rule rather than the exception among our firemen."

"I'm afraid so, Mayor Mason," the fire chief replied. "They've been working at the absolute limits of human endurance since daybreak."

"In that event," the mayor said, "we shouldn't have them working with something as dangerous as blasting powder unless we're certain it's going to do some good. Men who are weary are prone to mistakes, and a mistake with blasting powder could cost many lives." He turned to Toby. "Toby, I know you find no satisfaction in having been proved right in a situation such as this, but you have been. I suppose it's too late to set a backfire such as you described?"

"Yes, but we can still save part of the city by boxing the fire with backfires here and here," he said, stepping to the map and indicating the same areas he had pointed out to Ted. "The backfires should meet the main fire and make it crown somewhere near the northern edge of the central business district. The core of the city will be gone, but we'll save the northern part and all of the outskirts."

Frowning, the mayor closed his eyes.

"It would save at least a part of the city, Ross," Governor Palmer commented.

"Yes, it would," the mayor agreed, sighing. "It'll take us years to recover from this, but at least we would have something to build on. We still have fires burning upwind in the western part of the city, though. Could you handle those, Chief Sloan?"

"Yes, sir," the fire chief replied confidently. "As soon as my men make certain that the backfires won't spread in the wrong direction, I can put them all there. And we'll have the reinforcements from Springfield by tonight. But while Toby's suggestion is our only hope, it'll wipe out most of the housing that's left. What will happen to all those people who will be left homeless and destitute?"

"I can tell you what will happen to them, Bob," Toby said quickly. "If this was any other country on earth, the national government might dole out enough to keep them barely alive, or it might not do even that. But this is America, and those people will have help from their neighbors in every city, county, and state across the nation."

"Yes, there's no question about that," the governor said. "We've already been getting telegrams from all over the country, asking what we need."

"The people of this country can be stubborn," Toby added, "and we've needed to be at times. That was what enabled us to break the ties of allegiance to the Old World and build our own nation out of a wilderness. But there are no people on earth who are as generous and as eager to reach out a helping hand to a neighbor in distress. Chicago will have plenty of help."

"I'm sure we will," the mayor agreed. "As Chief Sloan said, Toby, your plan is our only hope of saving part of the city. Before we proceed with it, are you reasonably certain that it will succeed?"

The room became quiet as Toby looked at the map, analyzing the situation once more. Then he nodded. "Yes, I believe that this will work out exactly the way we want it to, Ross."

"Then let's put it into action," the mayor said briskly. "What can we do to help, Toby?"

"Some arrangements must be made to provide the homeless with immediate food and shelter," Toby said. "Jack, if you would ask the lieutenant governor to send all the tents and field kitchens from the state armory up here by train, they'll be here tonight. It would also be good to have a company of militia along with them."

The governor nodded. He went into the next office to contact the lieutenant governor by telegraph, and Toby stepped to the map with the police and fire chiefs. They discussed and agreed upon plans to evacuate the affected areas and for the firemen and policemen to assemble in readiness to set the backfires. As the two men left to relay instructions to their subordinates, Toby turned to the port master, Commodore Alfred Dixon.

Dixon told Toby that the firemen had been commandeering blasting powder sent to Chicago by barge to be shipped out by rail. An ample supply of it remained, and a barge filled with drums of kerosene was in the north part of the harbor. There were more than enough horses and wagons, because two Chicago freight companies had released their animals and equipment to be used in fighting the fire.

"Do we have plenty of workers available, Commodore?" Toby asked.

"Yes, far more than we can use," Dixon replied. "When we first started unloading blasting powder from a barge, word got around at the rail yards that there was work to be done. Within a short time we had hundreds of volunteers at the piers."

"That doesn't surprise me," Toby said. "It would probably be best for you to send instructions to the port for them to begin loading blasting powder and kerosene into wagons, Commodore. It will take quite a while to get all that done, and we'd better get started. Do you agree, Ross?"

The mayor nodded his assent, and the port master left. "I assume that you'll want to be personally in charge of the firemen and policemen who set the backfires, won't you, Toby?" the mayor asked.

"Yes, that's right," Toby replied. "I'll take the backfire on the west side, and Ted will take the one on the north. I'd like Chief Dougan to go with me and Chief Sloan to go with Ted. All of the firemen and policemen know them, and there'll be no confusion as to who is in charge."

"Very well, Toby. What else is there to do?"

"Ted and I have a small map of the city, and we'll draw the exact lines of the backfires on it, street by street. I'd like to have some extra copies of the map in the event we need them."

"I'll go get them from the city engineer," the mayor said, turning toward the door.

As he went out, Toby and Ted sat down at a table and began drawing the lines of the backfires on the map. The mayor returned a few minutes later with a stack of maps, followed by two men whom he had recruited. The men were among those who filled the halls and the courtyard outside, city residents who had come to find out what was being done and to offer their help.

Soon the office bustled with more activity than it had at any time since early morning. Governor Palmer came in with a telegram from the lieutenant governor: Tents, field kitchens, and a company of militia were being loaded onto a train in Springfield. The fire and police chiefs brought in messages from police captains and fire division commanders, while the port master reported on the progress being made in loading wagons with blasting powder and kerosene.

Even more striking than the renewed stir and noise was the change in the atmosphere. There was a resurgence of confidence; people moved about with light steps, their voices cheerful. Although thicker clouds of smoke could be seen through the windows as flames advanced along the streets of tall buildings in the center of the city, in the mayor's office there was a sense of coming to grips with the situation, a feeling that the hours-long ordeal with the fire would soon be over.

The uplift of spirits made Toby even more aware of the heavy burden he had taken upon himself. Once again he was at the center of a momentous event, as he had been in the past, with the outcome resting upon the decisions he would make during the following hours. And this time the fate of the great city at the heart of the nation was in the balance.

The messages from the city reported that everything was moving toward a state of readiness. People were streaming out of the districts to be destroyed by the backfires, and the policemen and firemen were en route to the streets where they would rendezvous with the wagons filled with kerosene and blasting powder.

When the moment was at hand for Toby and Ted to leave, the office became quiet again. The strained wait for the results of the final stand against the fire was already beginning, the tension heightened by the fact that this was the most crucial effort of all. The quiet in the office spread out into the halls, the murmur of conversation subsiding.

The governor smiled as he shook hands with Toby. "I

can't remember another time when I've been at a loss for words, Toby," he said. "Now I am, and it seems that I should have any number of things to say. But I suppose you know what thoughts of mine go with you."

"Yes, I do, Jack. I do indeed."

Then the mayor stepped forward and shook hands with Toby. "Of all the men I've ever met," he said quietly, "you're the one I'd most want to depend upon for this important task, Toby."

"Thank you, Ross. I'll see you in a few hours."

The others in the room spoke quietly to Toby as he went out with Ted, followed by the police chief and the fire chief.

They mounted police department horses and rode out of the courtyard and along the street. The smell of smoke had been creeping into city hall, but outside it was much stronger. Looking at the fire through the office windows had given a sense of detachment; from the streets, however, the destruction and upheaval wrought by the fire were all too real. Scores of drays and wagons filled with salvaged merchandise filed away from the downtown, and everywhere Toby could see the flood of people being evacuated from the city.

Reaching a major intersection, Toby and the others reined up. Here their routes diverged, Toby and the police chief intending to go straight east while Ted and the fire chief would head toward the north end of the city. Toby talked with Ted for a few minutes, giving him final instructions.

"Your backfire will be burning across the wind," Toby said, "and we want it to meet the main fire as far south as possible. So get organized and start it burning as soon as you can."

Ted nodded. "I'll start the men laying the charges and spreading kerosene as soon as the area is clear of people."

"You can speed that up by setting off a couple of charges early. If people hear explosions to the north of them and realize that they're between the explosions and the fire, they'll get a move on."

"That's a good idea. Do you want me to keep you informed of my progress?"

"Yes, particularly if you have any problems. You can send a mounted policeman every half hour or so. Give him one of your maps, and he'll be able to find me somewhere along my route. But don't wait for word from me to set off your charges and start your backfire."

Ted nodded. Then he sighed as he looked in the direction of the fire. "Toby, I haven't seen Marjorie for hours now," he said. "I'm worried about her, and I certainly wish I knew where she was."

"She could be in a lot of places, Ted," Toby replied. "She might be at the rail yards, or you might even see her along the street. But you know as well as I do what she's doing—she's making photographs, because she happened to be in the right place at the right time. But you'd better start learning not to worry about her and to give her plenty of room, or you'll never be able to get along with her."

"Yes, you're right, Toby," Ted said, lifting his reins and starting to turn away.

"Good luck," Toby called. "And don't take any unnecessary risks."

The young lawman and the fire chief began riding away. A few seconds later, Toby turned in his saddle as Ted shouted something to him. The words were lost in the clatter of the horses' hooves. "What was that, Ted?" Toby called.

Ted pointed to the thick, billowing smoke covering the sky and moving out over the lake. "I said that Frank, Edward, and the others at the logging camp will be able to see that."

"Yes, they certainly will," Toby shouted back. Then he waved as he and the police chief urged their horses into a canter.

However, those at the logging camp were now unable to see anything farther than a dozen or so yards away. They were near suffocation from the dense, acrid smoke of a forest fire a few miles to the south that the dry breeze was slowly pushing toward the camp.

Edward Blackstone, breathing through a damp cloth tied across his face and almost blinded by stinging tears from the smoke, carried bags of food and utensils from the Woods house toward the edge of the bluff overlooking the lake. Through the thick smoke, other people were moving shadows as they carried belongings toward the bluff, where rising air currents off the lake were lifting the clouds of smoke.

In addition to Frank, Rob Martin, and the four workers, those fleeing the scene included farm families, homesteaders, and others who had instinctively headed toward the coast and gathered at the logging camp. A short time before, the smoke from the forest fire to the south had suddenly changed from being uncomfortable to being completely unbearable.

Edward bumped into one of the massive, towering trees near the edge of the bluff and almost dropped the bags. Then the smoke thinned in the updraft along the face of the bluff, and he could see more clearly. The families that had sought refuge at the camp were heaving the bundles they had brought with them down the bluff, along with bedding, food, and tools of all types from the camp buildings.

Some were also sliding down the bluff, holding on to ropes tied to the trunks of trees. As Edward dropped the bags he was carrying over the edge of the bluff, he saw Tommie a few yards away, slumped at the foot of a tree. Despite the damp cloth tied over her face, she was almost overcome by the smoke.

Stepping to her quickly, Edward picked her up and carried her to one of the ropes dangling down the bluff. With one arm around her, he gripped the rope with his free hand and started down the steep slope. The rope burned his palm as he descended, the loose soil crumbling under his feet and making him stumble.

When he reached the bottom of the bluff, axes, shovels, mattocks, and other heavy tools were still spilling down it. Edward picked up Tommie and carried her along the narrow bank to where the beach was a little wider. He took the cloth from around her face, walked into the waves and dabbed it in the water, then put it over her eyes. Then he bathed his own stinging eyes.

As she stopped coughing, Tommie sat up and wiped her cheeks with the damp cloth. "I thought I was going to choke," she said, smiling weakly. "Suddenly I couldn't breathe."

"Little wonder," Edward said, standing up and drying his eyes with his handkerchief. "The smoke up there is so thick I could hardly see where I was going."

Tommie looked at the other people, a few of whom were still scrambling down the bluff to the narrow strip of beach that was littered with tools, bedding, and bundles. Most of the people were coughing hoarsely and kneeling in the cold surf to bathe their eyes. "What will we do now?" she asked.

Edward glanced up at the low ceiling of thick, billowing smoke overhead. "We may have to stay here for as long as a day or two, Tommie," he replied. "But at least we can breathe, can't we?"

"I believe," she said quietly, "that your stiff upper lip is getting between me and what you are thinking, Edward. Tell me how you really view our prospects."

As he started to reply, a movement to one side caught Edward's eye. It was a large cinder, possibly the remains of a wooden shingle, settling toward the water out of the dense smoke above the lake. A light husk of charcoal, it drifted from side to side like an autumn leaf as it fell. Then the water steamed momentarily as it touched, turning it to a splotch of black that slowly disintegrated on the tossing waves.

Edward looked back at his wife. "Things don't appear too favorable for us, Tommie," he said gently. "You can see how much smoke there is, and Frank and Rob say the fire is still miles away. It's going to get worse, I'm afraid."

His words confirmed what was in his eyes, and a moment passed while she adjusted to the fact that only hours could be left. Then, her indomitable courage crushing fear, she smiled as she put out a hand for him to help her to her feet. As she stood up, she tucked her arm through his.

"At least we're together," she said. "While I'd like for us to have many more years, most of all I want us to be together at the last moment." Her smile wreathed her beautiful face, and her eyes sparkled as she pointed along the shoreline. "If you like, we could walk down beyond the curve, where we would be alone. We could make love."

Edward smiled down at her and gently touched her face. "That is a most tempting suggestion, my dear," he said. "In fact, more than tempting. But lest the others come looking and happen upon us at a very inopportune moment, I believe it would be better for us to stay here for now and wait for an appropriate time to slip away."

Tommie laughed and nodded as they walked back toward the other people. Most had recovered from the smoke, and Frank was organizing them to stack up the things that had been tossed down the bluff. Tommie joined Kale, Bettina, and other women who were sorting out bedding and bags of food, while Edward helped Frank and Rob gather up tools.

Frank smiled as Edward commented on the variety of things that had been carried to the bluff. "I told everyone to grab whatever was at hand, and it appears that they took me at my word," he said.

"They certainly did," Edward agreed. "By the way, the horses aren't still in the corral, are they?"

"No, I turned them loose," Rob said. "I don't know where they'll go, but at least they're free."

Edward nodded, feeling pity for the horses. At the same time, he reflected, the situation that he, Tommie, and the others were in was hardly better. He stared up at the giant trees lining the edge of the bluff. "Frank, do you think we would be safer if those trees were chopped down?" he asked.

"I'm not sure, Edward," Frank replied, looking at the trees. "But I don't believe we could stand the smoke up there long enough to fell them. Even if we worked in shifts."

There was an outburst of laughter nearby, and Edward turned to see the cause of the mirth. Many of the thirty or so people had spread out in family groups on the narrow beach to find comfortable places. Among them was a young homesteader couple named Raines. The husband was hardly more than a boy, about eighteen. His pretty wife, a year or two younger, had a baby in her arms and was in the latter stages of pregnancy.

Raines was trying to make a fire to keep his wife and child warm in the cool air at the edge of the water, but the driftwood he had collected was damp. His wife, having just fled the dense smoke in the logging camp above, was scolding her husband as she now choked in the smoke from his fire. Raines looked up with a sheepish grin as the other men roared with laughter and went to help him with his fire.

Frank and Rob, laughing too, also went to help. Bettina stepped to the young woman and took her baby, moving her to the upwind side of the fire. They sat down together, the young woman smiling proudly as Bettina held the baby and admired it. Then the fire began blazing up brightly, the men fanning it and adding dry wood.

Flames in the form of unchecked wildfire were a deadly peril in the deep forest, a constant danger. But a campfire stimulated some primeval sense of comfort and security and drew the people to it. They began collecting together again, gathering around the fire and sitting down as the men continued building it up until it was roaring.

The laughter had eased the tension, helping everyone put aside for a moment the impending danger. Almost without exception, these people came from generations of pioneers who had learned to enjoy life while remaining alert for the war whoop from the edge of the forest, for the nearby presence of wolves on dark winter nights. One of the farmers took out a harmonica and began playing a popular tune, and all of the people began singing.

Standing near the stack of tools, Edward glanced around for his wife. Tommie, a few yards away, was looking at him with a mischievous smile. As he chuckled, her

smile became wider, her blue-green eyes dancing gleefully. Edward stepped to her and took her hand.

Tommie laced her fingers through Edward's as they
walked away from the other people and toward a curve in
the narrow beach.

XIV

Toby calmed his skittish horse, then took out his watch and looked at it. "Yes, that's still well ahead of the schedule we set up," he said to the mounted police constable Ted had sent as a messenger. "How long ago did you leave your line?"

"About thirty minutes ago, sir," the policeman replied. "The streets are almost empty of people now, so I made good time."

"All right, tell Ted where you found us so he'll know what progress we're making on this side."

The police constable nodded to Toby and saluted the police chief at Toby's side, who returned the salute. Then the young police officer wheeled his mount back in the direction from which he had come.

Toby and the police chief rode on along the street at a slow walk. Ahead of them were large wagons filled with drums of kerosene and kegs of blasting powder. Policemen and firemen were carrying blasting powder into the empty buildings on the west side of the street, and volunteers from the rail yards were rolling drums of kerosene into buildings on the east side of the street and puncturing them with hatchets.

The preparations on Toby's line were more than three-quarters finished, and it appeared that Ted's line was nearly completed. The police chief remarked to Toby that the work was being done much more rapidly than he had expected. "You used some good ideas to start with, though," the chief commented. "Setting off those charges got the people moving out of there a lot faster. Also, using volunteers to help the policemen and firemen has really speeded things up."

"They've been a big help," Toby said. "But I'm afraid to let them work with the blasting powder. There's too great a chance of an accident."

The police chief nodded. "Yes, even as tired as the firemen and policemen are, it's a lot safer to leave setting the charges to them."

Looking at the policemen and firemen along the street, Toby reflected that they were indeed fatigued. As they moved back and forth between the wagons and the buildings, carrying kegs of blasting powder, their footsteps were slow and heavy.

At the next intersection was one of the pump wagon brigades that were stationed along the route at intervals to assure that the backfire did not spread to the west. The street was wet under the wagons from slow leaks in the water tanks, while the hoses on the sides were patched and ragged. The horses slumped in their harnesses, their heads drooping. Some of the firemen, their faces sooty and scorched, were asleep on the street beside their wagons.

The police chief suddenly stopped his horse and stood in his stirrups as he looked down a cross street. "I see some more people there, Toby," he said in dissatisfaction. "This area should have already been evacuated. I'm going to find the captain in charge of this area and liven him up."

Toby nodded as he looked at the people hurrying toward the rail yards. Only a few blocks beyond them he could see the vast, billowing clouds of black smoke rising over the rooftops. To Toby, it was a scene vividly reminiscent of the Civil War. The people were leading animals, struggling with overloaded carts, and carrying children and bundles. There was a familiar wretched despair about them, the same sense of being caught up in cataclysmic events outside their control. Glancing at the police chief,

Toby saw that behind the gray-haired man's stolid expression were the same remorse and pity that he himself felt.

The last of the people passed the fire line, and the street of tenements and small houses was deserted once more. Ahead, near one of the wagons stacked with kegs and drums, Toby watched a volunteer wrestle a drum of kerosene up a few low steps to a house.

It was a neat, modest dwelling that reflected pride in ownership. The man rolled the drum inside and chopped it open with his hatchet. As he walked back across the tiny front porch, he hesitated. A rag doll, probably dropped by some child, lay at his feet. The man picked up the doll and stuffed it into his coat pocket.

There had been no reported incidents of looting, a credit to the citizens of the city and to the vigilance of the police. The doll was of no real value, but the incident was sufficient to bring a reaction from the police chief. He was on the point of shouting to the volunteer when he and Toby saw the man's face. Walking back to the wagons, the man was attempting to control his grief, trying to smile nonchalantly at the other volunteers as tears streamed down his cheeks.

"That's me and my wife's house," he told his companions. "We finished paying for it and bought some new furniture last month."

The other men murmured sympathetically as the work continued. The police chief, his flinty eyes suddenly watery, looked away and cleared his throat. Then he lifted his cap and pushed his gray hair back as he settled his cap on his head again. "This is not a pleasant task, Toby," he said quietly. "I'll be glad when it's finished."

"Yes, so will I," Toby replied.

A moment later, Toby turned as he heard a horse approaching at a run from behind. It was too soon for Ted to be sending another report, unless he had encountered a serious problem. Worried, Toby watched as the rider, a police captain, reined in his panting, lathered horse and saluted the police chief. "Chief, there's some crazy woman up on the west water tower," the man said. "And she won't come down."

"Then send some men up there to bring her down,"
the police chief growled irately. "Why are you telling me
about it?"

The captain shrugged helplessly. "Chief, nobody can
get up there to her, because she's knocked the ladder
loose and pulled it up. An officer told me that he tried to
order her down hours ago—"

"Wait a minute," Toby said, suddenly all too certain
of just who the woman was. "What's she doing up there,
Captain?"

"Making photographs of the fire," the policeman replied. "She has cameras and other things up there with
her."

Toby sighed, his annoyance mixed with amusement.
"Her name is Marjorie White, and I happen to know her.
I don't know how she managed to get her things up
there—I didn't think she could—but apparently she did. I
guess I'll have to go get her down."

The captain looked doubtful. "I don't think you'll be
able to, Mr. Holt. When anybody says anything to her, all
she does is hold up one of those black camera things while
she keeps right on with what she's doing."

"I can get her down," Toby said, taking out his watch
and looking at it. "Charles, the men will be finished by
the time I get there and back. If you'll take charge and
finish up here, I'll go get Marjorie and catch up with you
on the way back to the assembly area."

"All right, Toby," the police chief replied. "I'll have
the men hold up on setting the backfire until you're out of
danger."

"That won't be necessary," Toby said. "I have time to
get Marjorie and ride back west of the line before the
backfire is started."

"What?" the police chief exclaimed. "No, that will be
too dangerous, Toby. The men on the north end of our
line will start setting off the charges and lighting the
backfire as soon as Ted's backfire is burning. He's almost
finished, so that doesn't give you much leeway."

"I don't need much, and I learned in the army that
it's inviting trouble to change plans at the last minute.

Someone will get confused and make a mistake. I have enough time, so let's let the orders stand as they are, Charles."

The police chief frowned, obviously reluctant to agree. "We could leave a gap in the line for you," he suggested.

"No that won't be necessary. Let's leave everything as it is."

The police chief exchanged a worried glance with the captain, then shrugged. "You're in charge, Toby, so it's your decision to make. Good luck, then, and don't let anything delay you. I'll look for you on the way back to the assembly area."

Urging his horse into a fast canter, Toby rode away from the two men. He knew he had no time left to lose. He hoped he was taking the most direct route to the water tower, but he dared not waste another minute to ask directions or to stop and look at his map.

His decision not to change the orders for setting the backfire had been based on his wartime experience with men laboring at the limits of their endurance. Inevitably, someone would not get the change in orders, while others would misunderstand the change. In an operation that depended on precise coordination, the result would be mass confusion at a time when any confusion at all could be disastrous.

A far better choice was to accept some degree of risk by letting the orders stand. The fire devouring the city of Chicago had to be stopped even at the risk of human life, including his own.

The ride seemed to take forever, with Toby pacing his horse carefully, since he knew the animal would have to carry two on the way back. Street after street passed, the smoke at the center of the city looming closer, until finally he saw the water tower above the roofs ahead of him.

As he emerged into the cleared area where the tower was located, he saw that the ladder was pulled up. He rode through the gate in the wooden fence and around to the other side of the water tower. Looking up at the walkway, he saw that Marjorie was on the side of the tank facing the fire, peering through her camera. She glanced down at him, preoccupied, then turned back to her camera.

"Marjorie," he called crisply, "I'm going to count to ten. If you aren't getting ready to come down from there when I reach ten, I'm going to start shooting holes in those cases."

Her eyes wide and her lips parted in dismay, Marjorie wheeled around and looked down at him. "You wouldn't!" she exclaimed.

Toby waited, counting slowly in his mind, then took out his pistol. "I'm up to five," he said.

Marjorie hastily began removing the camera from its tripod. "Will you help me with my cases?" she called angrily. "Please!"

"Yes. How did you get them up there?"

"I put my belt through the handle, then put it over my shoulder," she replied irritably. "Then I carried them up one at a time."

It was a practical, logical approach to the problem, Toby reflected, but even one of the cases was still too heavy for her to carry in such a fashion. What had got her cases up to the walkway was her determination, nothing else. More than ever, she reminded him of Janessa.

Toby rode around to where the ladder was dangling, then dismounted and tethered his horse to a brace under the water tower. The police department saddle had a breast harness to keep it from slipping backward on uphill rides, and Toby knew the strap was unessential. He took out his pocketknife and cut it off.

Holding the strap and looking up, he waited for Marjorie to come around the walkway. He listened for explosions as he waited, the seconds passing slowly. Finally she appeared. She put her cases down, then hoisted the heavy ladder off the railing and cautiously lowered it into place, Toby helping her once it was within reach.

Marjorie picked up a large stone from the walkway and began driving in the nails that held the top of the ladder. "Police constables disturbed me while I was working," she said resentfully. "But none of them was rude enough to threaten to shoot holes in my cases."

"I needed to get your attention," Toby replied, picking up a stone. Kneeling at the foot of the ladder, he began driving in the nails that held it. "Preparations have been made to set backfires, and one will cross this area. They're due to be lighted very soon now."

Marjorie hesitated and looked down at him; then she began hammering more rapidly with the stone. Some of the nails in the foot of the ladder bent as Toby hammered with his stone. When he had driven them in as far as he could and Marjorie was also finished, he hung the leather strap around his neck, put the stone in his pocket, and began climbing.

The ladder was extremely unsteady, shaking and bowing from his weight. He stopped halfway up to drive in the nails on both sides of the brace that was hanging loose, then dropped the stone and climbed up. The brace helped some, but the ladder remained unsteady. When he reached the top, Marjorie was dusting her cape and hat and putting them on.

Toby began tying the ends of the strap to the handles of the case. He glanced at Marjorie and nodded toward the ladder. "Go on down the ladder, Marjorie."

"No, you take the cases down first," she said. "You don't understand what I have in them. It's priceless— valuable beyond measure."

"I know what's in them, and I know what it means to you," Toby said. "But what are you going to do if the ladder breaks on my way down? These are heavy, and that ladder is rickety."

Marjorie's hands were clasped together, her knuckles white, and her face was pale. "Very well. But if anything happens . . . happens to me, could I get you to send them to my partner in Boston?" she asked quietly. "His name is Clayton Hemmings."

Looking at her, Toby was intensely pleased and proud that his daughter was much like her in disposition. The woman's dedication was extreme, not unlike that of firemen, policemen, and soldiers who viewed some things of greater value than themselves. "All right—Clayton Hemmings," he said. "Now climb down the ladder, Marjorie."

Marjorie turned to the ladder and carefully stepped down to the first rung. As she continued down, Toby finished tying the strap and lifted the cases by it to test the knots. The cases were very heavy, and lifting them took considerable strength. He put them back down and stepped across the walkway to the ladder.

The nails at the top of the ladder were bent, like those at the bottom, and they loosened from the movement of the ladder as Marjorie climbed down it. When she was on the ground, Toby took one of the stones on the walkway and drove in the nails again, as far as he could. He lifted the cases and put the strap around his neck, the cases hanging under his arms. Then he stepped back to the ladder.

The nails pulled out a fraction when he stepped down to the first rung, then a fraction more when he put his weight on the second. He began descending the ladder, cautiously stepping down from rung to rung and trying to avoid sudden movements. The sagging weight of the cases around his neck made it difficult, and he could feel the ladder becoming more unsteady.

The ladder began vibrating dangerously, the nails at the top working farther out. But when he passed the brace halfway down, the shaking stopped. With his weight and that of the cases now on the bottom half of the ladder, which rested on the solid beam, he was able to climb down more rapidly. Then, as he stepped down from the last rung to the ground, he heard a distant explosion.

As it was supposed to be, it was near the waterfront, at the east end of the north backfire line. Another followed it as Toby stood and looked at Marjorie. He knew that the logical course was to abandon the cases, since their additional weight would slow the horse. And from the agonized plea in Marjorie's eyes, she knew what he was thinking.

"That's the firemen and policemen setting a backfire, isn't it?" she commented quietly. "The one to the north of here."

Toby decided that the increased risk was easier to face than the haunting look in her eyes. Carrying the cases, he turned toward the horse. "Come on, let's go, Marjorie," he said. "We certainly don't have any time to waste now."

The horse was a large, powerful Morgan mare, but it had more weight on it than any horse should carry. It cantered slowly along the streets, Toby suppressing his impulse to urge it to a gallop, because he knew it would quickly become winded or go lame.

Only generally familiar with the area, Toby chose a street that led straight west, intending to cross the back-fire line somewhere near its center. The city blocks passed tediously at the sedate canter, and Toby tried to estimate if enough time remained to reach safety.

Echoes of the explosions carrying along the empty streets made it difficult to pinpoint the precise location of the blasts, but Toby knew they were from Ted's line, because they marched steadily westward. Thick clouds of black smoke began rising in a line behind the explosions.

It sounded like artillery barrages—a block of buildings being leveled, a pause, then explosions ripping through another block of buildings. Marjorie's arms were around Toby's waist, and he could feel her turning to listen to the explosions. "Does anyone know you're here?" she asked.

"Yes, but I told them to disregard it," he replied.

A long moment passed, then Marjorie said, "I should have known without asking."

Toby could smell the kerosene along the west back-fire line, but he knew it was still many blocks away. The wind was carrying the fumes along the streets, the same wind that would shortly be driving an inferno along the same streets and turning the buildings into seething masses of fire.

During a long pause in the explosions, the echoes died away. Then Toby heard the first one from his own backfire line.

When the explosions began traveling southward toward him, Toby knew that he was a few minutes short of the time he needed to reach safety. Carrying the equipment cases down from the walkway had taken too long. And now the heavy load on the horse, which limited it to a slow canter, was consuming the precious remaining minutes.

Dense smoke boiled up in a line to the northwest, joining that of the other backfire. As the explosions moved closer, Toby began feeling the concussions sweeping along the streets. And as the rising smoke drifted nearer and covered the only part of the skyline where there was no smoke, he felt a door inexorably closing and trapping him.

Then, at an intersection ahead, Toby saw a street that led diagonally toward the southwest, an opportunity to cut across the grid of streets and move ahead of the explosions, while continuing more slowly toward the west. At the intersection, he turned the horse onto the diagonal street.

The explosions marched closer, each blast drowning the echoes of others that rippled back and forth along the deserted streets. The sounds became deafening, making the ground heave, the concussions whipping forceful surges through the air. A powerful blast only a few blocks away shattered the windows in a house they were passing. Shingles rained down.

The horse had been trained for police duty, taught to remain calm around gunfire, unruly crowds, and in other situations that would normally frighten horses. But the nearby explosions were too much for it, and it began trying to break into a gallop. Toby reined it back, keeping it from running but letting it increase its pace to a fast canter. If it stumbled and fell, they would be doomed.

The street leading southwest ended at a wide square, and as the horse emerged into the open, a set of charges detonated no more than two blocks away. The shattering explosions shook the buildings on all sides. Windows turned into showers of falling glass, dust swirled from doorways, and the air was suddenly full of tumbling shingles.

The horse almost became uncontrollable. Reining it toward the street leading west out of the square, Toby noticed that the stench of kerosene was now thick in the air. Then, four blocks ahead, he saw one of the pump brigades that were posted to keep the backfire from spreading to the west.

The brigades were to wait at a distance of two blocks for the buildings to be demolished, then move forward when the buildings on the opposite side of the street were set afire. That meant the backfire line was two blocks away. Shouting at Marjorie to hold on tightly, Toby kicked the horse as he released the reins. The horse broke into a run.

The firemen pointed in astonishment, then began shouting and beckoning for Toby to hurry. Marjorie clung to him, and the heavy cases bounced against his legs as the horse ran with a labored stride.

When they had covered half the distance, the charges in the block adjacent to the one ahead began detonating. The sound itself was a powerful force pressing in from all sides. The horse staggered. Toby pulled on the reins and controlled the animal as it tried to veer and turn back.

The explosions reached a crescendo. Then there was a pause before the buildings ahead erupted into a mass of debris. Over the ringing in his ears, Toby heard the horse panting as it pounded along the street. Through the dust he saw the firemen beckoning frantically.

An instant later, he saw a policeman run out of the corner building across the intersection ahead. The man, racing along the street toward the firemen, had just lighted the fuses on the charges of blasting powder.

As the firemen pointed and shouted, the policeman looked back. He beckoned Toby to follow him, then cupped his hands around his mouth and shouted ahead. Two other policemen stepped out of a small warehouse, their place of safety during the explosion, and began pushing the wide front door open.

The horse seemed to sense that the crucial moment had arrived and found the strength for a burst of speed. Its stride becoming lighter, it dashed across the intersection and along the street behind the policeman, who slid to a stop at the warehouse door and waved Toby inside. Toby tugged a rein, guiding the horse toward the warehouse.

As the horse ran through the low, dark doorway,

Toby leaned down, Marjorie clinging to him and ducking. She slid off the horse as it stumbled to a stop inside the small, cluttered building. Lifting the cases off the saddle as he dismounted, Toby handed them to her. The two policemen pulled the door shut as the third ran to help Toby hold the horse. Then the explosions began.

It was like a giant fist pounding the building, every timber shaking as the floor heaved and dust spilled down from the rafters. The horse was almost exhausted, but it kicked and tried to rear. Toby and the policemen dodged its lashing hooves and held on to its bridle. There was a long, breathless pause; then the explosions on the next block began.

They gradually became less violent, each succeeding one farther away. The policemen hastily gathered up railroad flares to set fire to the buildings across the street from the demolished block.

Running out, they smiled and shrugged as Toby shouted his thanks. For them, it had been merely one more incident in a long, frantic day. They left the door open, and Toby led the horse outside as Marjorie knelt beside her cases and looked through them. Thick dust still hung in the air as the explosions became more distant.

The fire brigade filed past, taking up their position across from the buildings being set on fire. The weary horses pulling the pump wagons trudged along slowly. The firemen's faces were sooty, their eyes red from smoke and fatigue. They nodded to Toby and touched their helmets. "You cut that one a mite close, didn't you, Mr. Holt?" one of them commented.

"Closer than I meant it to be," Toby replied, laughing.

The firemen chuckled as they moved on along the street. Toby turned as Marjorie came out with her cases. "Is everything all right?" he asked.

"Yes, nothing was broken," she replied. "I have padded slots for all of my plate holders." Dusty and disheveled, she pushed at her hair and settled her hat on her head. "I'd like to make a few photographs of those firemen and their wagons."

"They'll be busy seeing that the fire doesn't spread,"

Toby said, retying the strap between the handles of the cases. "All of the policemen and the extra firemen are assembling at the north end of the backfire, and you can make photographs of them there."

Marjorie nodded as Toby lifted the cases and hung them across the saddle. The horse was still breathing heavily, and Toby led it as he and Marjorie walked toward the next street.

After a long silence, Marjorie spoke. "I knew there was some risk in climbing up that water tower," she said. "But as it turned out, I also placed you at risk, which I had no right to do. I'm sorry for that, and I'm very grateful that you came for me."

Toby smiled. "There's no need for apologies or thanks, Marjorie. I know you were simply doing what you had to do. That's something I can understand and respect. Besides, in helping you today, maybe I've lodged a similar debt against someone in the future. If I have, it was more than worth it to me."

"What do you mean?"

"I have a daughter who's very similar to you, and she'll probably find herself in some tight spots during the years to come. Like you, she'll get out of most of them herself. But if sometimes she can't, and I'm not there to help her, then maybe someone will do it for me."

Marjorie looked away. "I remind you of your daughter?" she asked.

"Yes, quite a lot. You don't look alike, of course, but in many respects her personality is very much like yours."

Marjorie nodded, and for a moment Toby wondered if he had somehow offended her by what he had meant as a compliment. But her expression seemed more thoughtful than offended, and she even appeared a bit surprised, or perhaps relieved. The woman was, Toby decided, very complex and difficult to understand.

The assembly area, near where the two backfires joined, was one of the numerous small parks scattered through the city. Ted, the fire chief, and the police chief were there, along with scores of policemen and firemen.

The police chief was greatly relieved to see Toby. Ted reported that the north backfire had spread in the wrong direction in a few places but that those blazes had been contained. A solid line of fire was now burning southward.

While the others were talking, Marjorie had set up a camera and was photographing the firemen and policemen, and Toby noticed that she was not posing them. Instead, she was photographing them as she found them, the sooty firemen leaning against their pump wagons and the policemen standing with their weary horses.

When the firemen and policemen began leaving, Ted talked with one of the wagon drivers, then put Marjorie's cases into the wagon and helped her up to the seat. As the wagon moved away, he caught up with Toby, the police chief, and the fire chief, intending to return to city hall with them.

Ted told Toby that he had asked the wagon driver to take Marjorie to the rail yards, where she wanted to photograph the people who had been evacuated from the city. "She told me what you did, Toby," he added. "Needless to say, I'm very grateful to you."

"You should be," Toby replied promptly. "When you shot Kellerman, you saved my life. But now we're even, Ted."

"I told you before," Ted said, "that my shooting Kellerman didn't make you indebted to me in any way. But if you think it did, then it was repaid many times over by your saving Marjorie's life."

"Saving her life?" Toby echoed in pretended surprise. "No, I would have done that in any event, Ted. That's not what I'm talking about."

Ted frowned, perplexed. "What are you talking about, then?"

"Carrying those cases of hers down the ladder," Toby replied, laughing. "I told you that was your job, not mine. Doing it scared me out of ten years of my life, so as far as I'm concerned we're completely even."

Ted laughed heartily.

When the group arrived at city hall, there was an atmosphere of guarded optimism. In the upstairs office, the mayor and the governor still stood at the windows, watching the fire. Toby and the others joined them there, telling them what had happened. As they watched the backfires burning toward the fire raging in the central business district, they discussed the prospects that the fire would now be controlled. Everyone agreed that unless there was a sudden shift in the wind or some other misfortune, the outlook was good.

The end came less than thirty minutes later. Toby and Ted called to the mayor and the governor, who had sat down to rest, and they came to the windows to watch as, over the distance of the last hundred yards, the fires leaped together.

In a spectacular display, flames shot hundreds of feet into the air, the intense heat pushing the billowing clouds of smoke upward. Looking at the immense, towering geyser of flames and sparks, Toby nodded to himself in satisfaction. The fire had crowned as he had hoped, dissipating much of its heat skyward. Now it would begin cooling.

While the fire was still crowning, there was a growing commotion in the hall outside the office. A courier had arrived from the fire division commanders in the southern part of the city, and instead of delivering his message to the fire chief in his office, the young fireman was shouting it joyously as he ran along the hall. The fires in the south end had been controlled. The fire was now completely contained.

The cheering in the hall outside rose to an uproar as the mayor turned to Toby and gripped his hand, shaking it warmly. "Toby, it's finally over," he said. "And the credit for that is all yours. How can we ever thank you for what you've done?"

"I've already been thanked, Ross," Toby replied. "Being able to help and to do my duty is more than enough thanks."

"It may be for you," Governor Palmer said, stepping closer and shaking hands with Toby, "but it isn't for us. No, we'll have to think of something, even if it's only a token. Because, as Ross said, the credit for ending this nightmare is all yours."

"Well, I'll have to argue with that," Toby said. "There were many others who did far more than their share in ending this disaster." He nodded toward the police chief, the fire chief, and the port master as they came in. "Those men there, for example."

The three men were beaming for the first time that day. The mayor approached them and shook their hands. "Have all of you passed the good word along to your men?"

"I sent a message to the captains at the rail yards," the police chief said, the other two nodding in reply. His smile fading, Chief Dougan lowered his gaze. "For many of the people there, the fire ended too late."

His remark tempered the cheerful mood in the room. The mayor replied, "We'll have to do everything we can for those people. As Toby mentioned before, we'll have help from all over the country, but we'll have to see that it gets to those who need it." He turned as Donald Phelps approached. "Yes, what is it, Mr. Phelps?"

"We've just received a telegram from Madison, Wisconsin, sir," Phelps replied. "It's from Governor Washburn, and he wants to know if you have any firemen or fire-fighting equipment you can send there."

"No, none in condition to help anyone," the mayor said. "Are they having a large fire in Madison?"

"No, not in Madison itself," Phelps said, unfolding the long telegram. "But apparently the wind carried embers from the fire here and started a lot of forest fires that have become very serious. Several areas are listed here, and a number of logging towns are in danger, with no way for the people to escape."

Toby frowned in sudden concern. "How about the area south of Wedowee, Don?" he asked. "Is that mentioned?"

Phelps scanned the telegram, then nodded. "Yes, it is, Toby," he replied. "Several fires are burning in the region south of Wedowee, and a town called Colmer is in danger."

Toby looked at Ted, thinking about his friends at the logging camp. The main road leading out of the camp went through Colmer. If the town was in danger, his friends were trapped.

XV

It was late afternoon when Toby Holt and the port master reached the north harbor, but the pall of smoke had brought on an early twilight. Ashes drifted down from the smoke and settled over the congested harbor and crowded waterfront streets.

Scores of ships and barges from the main and south harbors were anchored offshore, and the piers were lined with small vessels. Drays piled high with goods were parked beside warehouses that were overflowing with merchandise from businesses in the center of the city. It was a scene of confusion, a backwater of disaster. But the crowds of people milling about were buoyantly cheerful, having received the news that the fire had finally been contained.

On the day that Frank Woods had brought Toby to meet Captain Albert Crowell, the steam launch had been the only vessel at the pier. Now two additional steam launches, a tugboat, and a two-masted sailing ship were wedged together alongside the pier. The captains of the vessels were standing at the end of the pier, talking.

The captains and the port master exchanged salutes, Commodore Dixon telling them what had happened in Wisconsin. "Hot ashes have been drifting across the lake to Michigan, too, although the fires there aren't near as bad," he continued. "The governor asked me to send vessels to the small towns along the shorelines to see if they need help, and Toby wants to go to a logging camp to see about some friends of his. Do you have sufficient coal aboard to go up south of Wedowee, Captain Crowell?"

"Aye, I've just refilled my bunker, Commodore," the portly captain replied. He turned to Toby. "I'll be more than glad to take you to see about your friends, but that will be very small repayment for what you've done for us. This fire has brought us to the point of ruin, but at least you stopped it." He glanced around at the other captains as they nodded and commented in emphatic agreement.

"I'm pleased I was able to help," Toby said. "How long will it be before you are ready to leave, Albert?"

"I have steam up, so not much longer than it takes to get aboard," the captain replied. He nodded in farewell to the others as he started down the pier. "I'll see you gentlemen when I return."

Toby followed him aboard the wide, stubby vessel. The two crewmen were lounging on the deck behind the wheelhouse. At the captain's orders, one of them disappeared through a deck hatch to the engine room, while the other began casting off the mooring lines.

Toby sat on a bench at the rear of the wheelhouse, the captain taking his seat behind the wheel. As the trickle of smoke from the tall smokestack behind the wheelhouse thickened, the drumming of the powerful engine below made the vessel vibrate. It backed slowly away from the pier, the captain turning the wheel and moving a clanging signal lever to telegraph instructions to the man in the engine room.

When the launch had safely crossed the congested harbor, the captain glanced over his shoulder at Toby. "How many friends do you have at this logging camp, Toby?" he asked.

"Three married couples and one child," Toby replied. "There are also four hired men. But if the reports about the forest fires are accurate, we might find others there. There are farmers and homesteaders scattered through that area, and they would go to the coast to escape a fire."

The captain nodded toward the small deck behind the wheelhouse. "We can't accommodate more than a handful, so we'd better take an empty barge in tow."

"Will that delay us?"

"Hooking up will take a while," Albert replied, "and we won't be able to make as much speed. But even without a barge, it would be dark when we got there. There aren't any navigation lights thereabouts, and I couldn't risk going in blind, so we'd have to lay offshore and wait for dawn in any event."

The situation was frustrating for Toby. His friends were in peril, and any delay could doom them to a fiery death, but he realized that there were no alternatives. He nodded in resignation.

The crewman on deck, a gangling youth named Turner, was moving about, securing equipment for the trip. The captain opened the window in the wheelhouse and called to him, telling him to prepare to hook up to a barge.

As soon as the launch had maneuvered alongside an empty barge, the second crewman, a man of about sixty named Jimson, came on deck. Grizzled, wiry, and agile, he munched on a large chew of tobacco and glanced toward the wheelhouse as he helped Turner prepare to raise the barge's anchor. "This is a railroad company barge that we're stealing, Captain," he called. "Did you notice that?"

"Yes, Jimson," the captain replied patiently. "They won't mind our using it, and we'll probably have it back before they notice it's gone."

"Do you think so, Captain?" Jimson said doubtfully. "I'll bet there's a railroad detective at the piers watching us right now. I sure don't want to end up in the city jail."

"I don't want you to, either, Jimson," the captain replied, "because that jail is pretty hot right now. But if you do, I'll come and get you out just as soon as it cools off a little."

Jimson laughed heartily, spitting tobacco juice over the rail. Listening to the two men and looking at the young, rawboned Turner as he grinned and worked, Toby reflected that the three men had taken the disaster in stride. They would undoubtedly suffer financially and in other ways, but they looked ahead instead of behind.

He felt the same himself; his plans for the logging

venture now in a shambles, he would have to turn to other
pursuits. But as long as his friends were in peril, which
was a situation he could not take in stride, the disaster
remained a very real crisis to him.

As the winch whined, raising the barge's anchor, the
captain opened a locker at one side of the wheelhouse and
took out a chart of the Wisconsin shoreline. He asked
Toby about the location of the logging camp. After Toby
pointed it out on the chart, the captain plotted a course to
follow by compass through the darkness.

Dusk was settling when the barge was connected to
the launch by a short cable. Jimson returned to the engine
room, and Turner lit the red and green running lights.
Captain Crowell headed toward the open water, paralleling the course of other vessels the port master had dispatched to the small towns along the shorelines. The
launch began bobbing in the waves as it moved farther out
onto the lake, the lighter barge pitching and rolling heavily.

In the wheelhouse, the binnacle lamp cast a soft light
on the captain as he sat at the helm, occasionally checking
his watch and the compass heading. The running lights of
the other vessels disappeared one by one as they veered
off onto other courses. Then the launch steamed on through
the night alone, its engine rumbling and the waves hissing
past.

Toby rested but did not sleep. It was still well before
dawn when the quiet in the wheelhouse was broken by
the clanging of the lever as the captain signaled Jimson to
slow the engine to an idle. "We should be almost due east
of the place you pointed out, Toby," he said. "As soon as
we have daylight, we'll go in."

"Very well."

The captain secured the wheel with a rope, then took
two blankets out of the locker. He handed one of them to
Toby. "It's a little crowded in the engine room," he said,
"but it's warmer there."

"No, I'll stay here," Toby replied.

"I like to be out in the open myself," Albert said,
sitting back down on his chair and pulling his blanket
around him. "And I've spent more time sleeping on this

seat than I have in a bed." He yawned, settling himself comfortably. "Good night, Toby."

"Good night, Albert."

A few minutes later, the captain was snoring softly. Timbers in the hull squeaked and groaned as the launch rocked in the waves. Toby lay on a bench and looked up into the darkness.

He was weary from the long, hard day, but concern about his friends kept him awake for a time. Then, knowing he needed to sleep, he firmly put all his troubled thoughts aside. Moments later, he fell asleep.

Thick darkness still surrounded the launch when Toby was awakened by the captain stamping his foot on the deck outside. "Wake up, Jimson!" he shouted.

The engine room hatch opened, and Jimson looked out. "Those new boots don't make as much noise as your old ones did, Captain," he said.

"They pinch just as much as the old ones did. Break out some victuals and make coffee, Jimson."

"Aye, aye, Captain. You probably won't like the coffee, as usual."

"I probably won't, but I'll drink it as long as it doesn't have engine oil in it. If it does, I'll pour it over your head."

Jimson laughed, then closed the hatch. The captain stepped to the rail and dipped up water in a bucket on a rope, then knelt beside the bucket to wash.

"The wind has changed to the east and freshened," he said when he came back inside. "The lake is getting a fair to middling good swell on it."

Toby nodded as he put his blanket away in the locker. "The launch is rolling much more than before."

"Yes, it is," Albert agreed. "Barges bounce around when they're empty, so I'm afraid it won't be very comfortable for your friends. It'll probably be tonight before we get back to Chicago, because I'll have to go at a slow speed to keep from making them seasick."

The portly, amiable man's attempt at cheerful optimism in no way relieved Toby's anxiety about his friends, but he felt grateful for the effort. After Toby had washed, Turner and Jimson came up through the engine room hatch with a pot of coffee, tin cups, and food on a tin plate.

Worry over his friends left Toby without an appetite, but he knew he had to sustain himself. He ate his share of the bread, cheese, and slices of gristly sausage, washing it down with the coffee made with boiler water and tasting of rusty metal. When breakfast was over, Turner took the cups and plate out to wash them. Jimson, a fresh chew of tobacco in his mouth, returned to the engine room and shoveled coal into the firebox.

A short time later, the first light of dawn touched the eastern horizon. It slowly brightened, reaching across the tossing surface of the lake. When the green waves were visible twenty or thirty yards from the launch, the signal lever clanged as the captain moved it from idle to slow ahead. The bow began pushing forward through the waves.

The launch was pitching heavily, and Toby put a hand against the bulkhead to steady himself as he stepped to the captain's side and peered ahead. The western horizon was a blur of smoke and lingering shadows of the night. After a few minutes, the outlines of a rocky headland came into view. The captain pushed the lever forward to standard speed.

As the shoreline slowly emerged from the smoke, Toby looked at it and felt a sinking sensation in the pit of his stomach. From north to south, the entire western horizon was a line of angry flames. Toby turned to the captain, whose grim expression echoed his own feelings. No one could be alive in that inferno.

"Exactly where is the logging camp, Toby?" Albert asked quietly.

Toby scanned the shoreline, picking out a distinctive spur of rocks a short distance to the north of the bluff where Frank Woods had intended to build a log chute. He pointed to it. "The camp is about a hundred yards south of those rocks," he replied.

The captain turned the wheel, pushing the signal lever forward to full speed. The muttering rumble of the engine became louder, and the pitching of the launch grew more violent as it picked up speed. The details of the shoreline gradually became more distinct as the launch drew closer.

Seeing a movement at the foot of the bluff, Toby strained his eyes. The captain had also seen something, and he leaned over and jerked the door of a small locker open. Taking out a telescope, he opened it and peered through it. After a few, tense seconds, a wide, triumphant smile spread over his face.

He handed the telescope to Toby, then slammed the signal lever all the way forward to flank speed as he bellowed, "Turner!"

Its engine thundering, the launch put on a burst of speed and began pounding through the waves. Turner ran across the lurching deck and leaned in the doorway of the wheelhouse. "Sir?"

"Get into the barge and stand by to take on passengers!"

"Aye, aye, sir!"

The youth ran to the stern with long strides, then leaped nimbly across the gap to the bow of the barge. The launch was straining, every timber in it vibrating as the hull slammed into the waves. The crests of the waves broke across the bow, and spray streamed down the windows of the wheelhouse. Toby braced himself against the heaving of the deck and steadied the telescope.

Some thirty people, several children among them, were on the narrow beach at the foot of the bluff where Frank had intended to build the log chute. Toby picked out Frank's large, muscular form, Kale's bright dress, then his other friends. He scanned upward with the telescope. The massive trees at the top of the bluff were pillars of raging fire. Toby turned to the captain. "We got here just in time, Albert."

"Not a minute too soon," the captain agreed grimly. "In fact, I'd feel a lot better if they were in that barge right now."

"So would I," Toby agreed, peering through the telescope again. The people were gathered in groups, and they were doing something. At first he was unable to

make out just what it was. Then he saw that they were
digging caves in the soft earth of the bluff, shelters for
when the giant trees above burned through and tumbled
down the slope.

It was pointless, a futile effort. Even a deep cave
would be no protection against the searing heat and suffo-
cating smoke when the huge trees fell, and Toby knew
that the people were fully aware of that. But while it was
pointless, for those people it was a logical course of action.

The same indomitable energy that had built a nation
in a wilderness was still alive in them. Men, women, and
children, they were digging furiously. Death might claim
them, but among this breed it wound find no passive
victims. When they died it would be confronting death,
not meekly accepting it.

Toby felt a catch in the back of his throat as he closed
the telescope and stepped around the captain to put it
back into the locker. "We certainly don't have a minute to
spare," he said. "I'll get in the barge so I'll be ready to
help them in."

"All right, but you be careful," Albert warned. "That
boy Turner jumps around from barge to barge all the time
while they're moving. He makes it look easy, but it's
dangerous."

Toby nodded, weaving on his feet from the pitching
of the launch as he stepped to the doorway. Holding on to
the jamb, he looked along the deck and gauged the distance between the stern of the launch and the bow of the
barge. Dangerous was an understatement—the deck was
awash, and the long, shallow barge was bobbing wildly
behind the speeding launch.

Turner, in the bow of the barge, beckoned and braced
himself to help Toby. Toby picked what he thought was
the right moment, then raced along the deck, splashing
through the water swirling across it. At the stern of the
launch, he planted a foot on the rail and leaped.

The green, foaming water passed below as Toby
reached out for the edge of the barge. He landed on it
heavily, clutching it as his legs dangled and Turner gripped

him tightly. Toby swung his legs up and over the edge, then slid down into the bottom.

The pitching and rolling of the launch were moderate compared to that of the relatively light barge as it sped along, smacking into the waves with jarring impact. It was impossible to stand, and Toby held on the best he could beside Turner and looked ahead.

"The captain has put a bone in her teeth, ain't he?" Turner shouted, grinning excitedly.

Toby nodded, estimating that the shore was now only a hundred yards away, yet the captain had not slowed. Obviously the man was ignoring the very real danger of running aground.

The smoke billowing from the smokestack whipped down toward the barge, the launch picking up more speed as it reached the lower waves in the lee of the shore. The people on the beach still had not noticed the launch; it was approaching from out of the sunrise, Toby realized, and the sound of its engine was drowned in the roaring of the fire at the top of the bluff.

Spinning the wheel, the captain started turning to bring the barge alongside the beach, at the same time yanking on a cord overhead. The brass horn on the side of the smokestack sounded, the sonorous blare carrying across the water and echoing back from the face of the bluff. The people turned, shading their eyes against the sun. They began pointing, waving, and whooping gleefully.

The launch canted to one side as its turn tightened, and for a moment it appeared that the approach would fall short of the beach. Then the signal lever in the wheel-house clanged and the engine reversed, the captain expertly using the forward momentum of the barge to swing it alongside the beach.

The barge slammed into the launch's bumpers when the engine reversed, almost knocking Toby and Turner down. The stern of the barge grated against soil and rock, swinging sideward against the beach. The wave it swept up inundated the beach and swirled around the people, making them stumble and stagger as they rushed to the side of the barge.

Disheveled and distraught, their eyes reflecting the ordeal they had faced during the past hours, the people crowded up to the side of the barge. But they remained orderly and followed the precedence that reached into the ancient past, women lifting children and men lifting women. A young pregnant woman held up a baby to Toby, and he took it, then helped her up into the barge.

The roar of the fire at the top of the bluff was accompanied by ominous cracking noises of wood breaking as the trees weakened and flaming embers spilled down the slope. Toby could feel the heat of the fire as he and Turner pulled others up into the barge. The tall, powerful Frank Woods lifted Bettina and Lucy over the side, then began picking up others and helping them aboard.

Toby took Tommie's hands and pulled her up, and when she was safely aboard, Rob lifted Kale up to him. The women and children safe, men began scrambling into the barge and reaching to help others. Turner directed the passengers to move forward, in order to lighten the stern, and the barge began floating away from the beach. The last men lifted their hands to those reaching for them. Toby pulled Rob into the barge. Then both of them leaned over the side and reached down to grasp Edward's hands.

Edward was the last one in. Toby scanned the beach to make certain no one was being left behind, then turned and waved to the captain in the wheelhouse. Albert pushed the signal lever forward. As it clanged, the stern of the launch settled and the water behind it churned, the propellers spinning.

The slack in the tow cable was taken up with a jerk, and the people stumbled and hastily sat down on the flat, spacious bottom of the barge as it lurched away from the beach. When they had gone no more than twenty yards, several people mutely pointed to the top of the steep slope.

Two giant trees were tilting. They leaned lazily, picking up speed as they plummeted. One kicked sideways as it struck the ground, then it rolled down the bluff like a long, massive barrel of fire, while the other pitched straight down. The entire slope was engulfed in flames, the trees plunging across the beach and into the water. Moments later a huge cloud of steam rose and obscured the view.

The people watched in silence, their eyes wide and their faces pale. Women held their children and men comforted their wives. All of them seemed almost overcome by the close brush with death.

Edward Blackstone broke the silence, speaking with his accustomed dry humor. "You know, Toby," he said, "I fully share your taste for drama and excitement. However, in this particular instance, it wouldn't have diminished my enjoyment of the adventure in the least if you had arrived just a bit sooner."

The comment and Edward's droll tone relieved the tension, and everyone began laughing uproariously. As they laughed, they began gathering around Toby, shaking his hand, slapping his shoulder, and thanking him for coming to their rescue.

A few hundred yards offshore, the captain stopped the launch to see to the comfort of the passengers. The gusty wind had a biting chill of October, and several of the people had been soaked by the wave from the barge that had swept across the beach. With the launch backed up tight against the barge, Toby and the other men helped women and children onto the launch.

The young pregnant woman and her baby went down into the warmth of the engine room, along with several other children. Jimson, torn between concern for them and resentment over having his domain invaded, chewed his tobacco and frowned as he helped them down the ladder. Other women and children crowded into the wheelhouse. Then the launch began moving forward again, slowly towing the barge through the tossing waves toward Chicago.

As the captain had predicted, the return trip took all day. Toby, sitting near the bow of the barge, told the others about the devastation the fire had caused in Chicago. Afterward he talked with Rob, Edward, and Frank about the effects of the fire on their planned logging venture.

Frank was an optimist. "Those are rain clouds," he

said, pointing toward the sky, "and they're moving toward Wisconsin. It might begin raining heavily there."

"Would that do any good now, Frank?" Rob asked. "From what I saw, it appeared that all of the timber for miles around the camp has been completely destroyed."

"No, a forest fire always looks that way," Frank replied. "If it rains soon enough and heavily enough, a lot of timber will be left."

Rob nodded, but both he and Edward obviously thought that Frank was being overly optimistic. Toby reserved judgment on the matter. He had seen forest fires that had been quenched by rain, and sometimes the damage was surprisingly slight. But he also knew that Frank had strong reasons for wishful thinking—the logging venture was to have been his means of support for the next several years.

In any case, Toby fervently hoped that Frank was right. In the months to come, the demand for lumber in Chicago would be greater than it had ever been. Even with strict fire codes requiring brick or stone buildings downtown and a greater distance between wooden buildings, there would still be a great need for wood. And farming families on the plains still needed affordable lumber so they could replace their sod houses.

Near dusk, when they were only a few miles from Chicago, the smell of smoke became strong. As the launch angled toward the north harbor, Toby could see that a few small fires still burned, scattered throughout the immense swath of the city that had been destroyed. Everyone in the barge stared at the scene in silent dejection as the launch slowed, approaching the congestion of the north harbor. Captain Crowell weaved a course through the anchored vessels, the piers coming into view ahead.

As the launch slowly approached an open berth, Toby saw Ted Taylor among the men on shore. The launch eased up to the pier, Turner casting lines to the wharf hands, then scrambling back to the barge with ropes to secure it to the pier.

The passengers climbed ashore, gathering around Captain Crowell to thank him as he stepped to the pier. The captain shook his head, pointing to Toby. "There's the man to thank," he said. "I only went where he showed me to go."

"But you did go, and that's the point, Albert," Toby replied. "You and your men risked your lives in rescuing these people."

The captain shrugged. "Well, I'm glad that things turned out as they did. Do you suppose these folks here can be taken care of at the rail yards?"

"Yes, they can," Ted said. "Boats have been bringing in people for the past hours, and that's where they've gone. There are still plenty of extra tents, as well as hot food in the mess tents. And wagons are waiting to take everyone there."

The people, exclaiming in relief and pleasure, began straggling along the pier toward the street. Toby turned back to the captain. "Albert, will you and your men come along with us for some hot food? I'm sure all of you are hungry, and we would enjoy your company."

"We would enjoy yours as well, Toby," the captain replied, "and a good meal. But I want to get that barge back where it belongs."

Jimson, standing beside Turner at the launch's rail, spat tobacco juice. "Do you want to take her back tonight, Captain?" he asked. "If we stole her for a night and a day, we may as well keep her another night. It would be a lot easier to take her back during daylight."

"No, I want to take it back tonight, Jimson," Albert said. "We might be busy moving ships all day tomorrow."

"If you ain't worried about stoving up the launch against a barge in the dark, then I ain't," Jimson commented, turning away from the rail. "Get ready to cast off, Turner. We'll be able to rest when we're in our graves—as long as the captain don't find out where we're buried."

The captain laughed wearily as he climbed back onto the launch. "Good night, Toby."

"Good night, Albert," Toby replied, laughing as he walked along the pier.

On the street, Toby joined his friends in the last wagon, which followed the others toward the rail yards.

"All of the baggage you left behind is at the tents," Ted said. "I reserved tents for all of you along the row beside my tent, and I put everyone's baggage in their tent."

"Our baggage was saved from the fire?" Kale exclaimed, she and Tommie smiling in delight. "I'm so grateful, Ted."

"Toby had more to do with it than I did," Ted said. "The police stored the baggage for him at city hall, and I moved it to the tents today after the militia got them set up. The tents and the field kitchens from the armory at Springfield arrived by train last night, along with a company of militia. And the lieutenant governor of Iowa arrived from Des Moines today with a company of their militia and the tents and field kitchens from their armory. He's looking forward to meeting you, Toby."

Toby smiled. "It appears that everyone is pitching in to take care of the people who need help."

Ted agreed, telling Toby how the entire nation was responding to the calamity in Chicago. A temporary depot had been set up near the rail yards, because trains were beginning to arrive hourly with relief supplies. Meat packers, flour mills, and various processors of food were donating tons of their products, and other manufacturers were shipping large quantities of needed supplies. Citizens all over the country were collecting food, clothing, and other necessities to send to Chicago.

When the wagon arrived at the rail yards, the efficiency and abundance of the relief effort was evident. Long, neat lines of tents stretched across the level fields beside the tracks, lanterns glowing on poles at intervals along the walkways. Field kitchens in large, brightly lighted tents were manned by volunteer cooks and workers to serve hot food to those who arrived through the night.

Most of the refugees were in their tents for the night, only a few standing about and chatting as policemen and militiamen patrolled the walkways. A few more were drinking coffee and talking at the tables in the kitchen tent that Toby and his friends went into. Scores of long tables and benches were arranged in neat rows inside the huge tent and the handful of people seemed almost lost in the vast enclosure.

After the long day without food, the rich, meaty stew, fresh bread, and hot coffee were delicious. As they ate, Toby and the others discussed plans for the following days, and Ted told Toby that the mayor and the governor wanted to meet with him the next morning. "Yes, I intended to go see them," Toby said. "There's still a lot to be done here."

"How long do you intend to work with them, Toby?" Rob asked.

"As long as they need me," Toby replied. "I'd like to return to Oregon to be with my children and the rest of my family for Thanksgiving Day, but until then I'll make myself available for as long as I'm needed. What do you and Edward intend to do?"

Rob smiled wryly. "Until you showed up with that steam launch, it wasn't a subject that we thought about very much," he said. "Now that we have a future again, we'll have to discuss it some."

"It's much too soon for you to give up on the logging operation," Frank said. "You aren't doing that, are you?"

"No, of course not," Edward reassured him. "Rob and I don't give up that easily. We'll probably remain here for at least a few days, because there may be some way we can help. In any case, we'll be here long enough to see if the logging operation will continue, won't we, Rob?"

"Yes, indeed," Rob replied. "We certainly want to do anything we can to help out here, so we'll stay for at least a few days."

After Ted had shown the couples to their tents, he and Toby talked outside for a few minutes.

"The relief efforts seem to be going very smoothly," Toby commented, explaining that he was curious about why the governor and the mayor had specifically asked for him to meet with them. "Do you know what they have in mind?"

"I saw them for only a few minutes," Ted replied vaguely. "I was here most of the day, working with the police and the militia. But I've done about all I can to help here, so I'll go with you to city hall tomorrow, and we'll find out."

Toby smiled as he nodded. "Very well, but don't expect to get there too early. I haven't had very much sleep for the past couple of nights, and I intend to make up for it."

"You certainly deserve it, Toby. You know, I haven't seen Marjorie since yesterday, when she left us to come here and make photographs of the people. That was the main reason I came here today, because I thought I could help her at the same time. But I haven't seen her."

Toby laughed. "Ted, if you'll just think for a minute, you'll know where she is and what she intends to do. She's either in Springfield or some other city not far away, and she's developing her plates. When she's done that, she'll come back here."

"Do you really think so?" Ted asked hopefully. "I thought she might have returned to Boston. Do you really think she'll come back?"

"Certainly she will," Toby replied. "She'll want to make photographs after the fire is out, won't she?"

"Yes, I guess she will," Ted mused. "Maybe she'll be back here tomorrow, then. I wish she'd said something to me before she left, though, because I'm afraid she doesn't have very much money. She might need some."

"She might not have much money now," Toby said, turning toward the tent. "But I expect that to change very quickly. If I'm not greatly mistaken, the photographs that she made here during the fire will bring her a considerable amount of money. Good night, Ted."

"Good night, Toby," Ted replied, walking toward his own tent.

In the dark tent, Toby struck a match and looked around. His baggage was placed neatly against one wall, and Ted had also put folded blankets on the cot and hung a lantern on the center pole. Toby lit the lantern and spread the blankets on the cot, then undressed, blew out the lantern, and went to bed.

His friends safe, Toby felt an overwhelming sense of relief. But he was also despondent over the events of the past two days. Despite his fatigue, the strong stench of smoke in the air kept him awake for a time. It was an intensely depressing reminder that the proud city of Chicago had been brought to her knees.

XVI

Its breath making puffs of condensation in the cold air, Henry Blake's gelding kept trying to break into a run to warm itself, but Henry held it to a canter, prolonging the ride. At other times when he had taken this route from Vittel to Thieux, it had been with a sense of anticipation. Now it was with something akin to dread.

Normally he dealt with disagreeable situations as quickly as possible, but this one was different. It promised to be the most unpleasant, most uncomfortable scene he had ever experienced. But it had to be done, because he had an opportunity to return home and marry Cindy, the woman he loved. And he had to end his affair with Gisela von Kirchberg.

The road was busy, the normal traffic to and from Paris having resumed, with part of the German forces already withdrawn. Henry exchanged salutes with a Prussian officer at the head of an infantry company. The men were dressed in heavy overcoats.

Smoke trickled from chimneys on the aged, weathered buildings as Henry entered the town and reined his horse back to a walk. A rumpled, heavyset man on the side of the street called to him and waved.

It was one of the German journalists who had been in Vittel. "Did you know that Chicago is on fire?" the man asked, walking toward Henry.

Henry reined up, somewhat puzzled. "What do you

mean Chicago is on fire? Surely the entire city isn't burning?"

"At least a large portion of it is," the man replied, rummaging in his overcoat pockets. "My office in Trier received the news by telegram. I will show you—"

Henry dismounted and led his horse to the side of the street. The man dug papers from his pockets, glancing at them and replacing them. Then he unfolded one and handed it to Henry.

It was a copy of a telegram, containing little more information than what the man had already said. From a correspondent in New York, it stated that the center and adjacent districts of Chicago were being destroyed by a massive fire. The telegram had been sent the day before, when the fire had still not been brought under control.

From recent letters, Henry knew that Toby Holt was in Chicago on business matters, but he was not overly anxious about Toby's personal safety. He knew that Toby was more than capable of taking care of himself. What troubled Henry most was his own reaction to the news about the fire.

It concerned him, yet there had been a time when it would have seemed cataclysmic. Now he had a strange sense of detachment. It was, he decided, past the time when he should have returned home.

Henry handed the paper back to the journalist. "I'm grateful to you for telling me about this, Herr—"

"Holtzen," the man replied, pocketing the paper and taking off a glove to shake hands with Henry. "Frederick Holtzen."

"I'm Lieutenant Henry Blake," Henry said as they shook hands.

"Yes, I know who you are," the man said, smiling. "There is not a journalist here who does not know Lieutenant Heinrich Blake, the Baroness von Kirchberg's young friend. She has rented large buildings outside the town, where part of the general staff was located before, hasn't she?"

The real reason why he had been stopped was sud-

denly clear to Henry; Holtzen wanted information about
Gisela. "Yes, she has," Henry replied.

"She needed large buildings, because many of her
employees are here now," the man mused. "And she
needed her employees here, because many of the wagons
one sees on the road to Paris belong to firms working for
her." He pointed to a large dray rumbling along the
street. "There is one now. Have her profits been substantial, Lieutenant Blake?"

Henry shrugged, making a reply that avoided the
question, but he knew that Gisela's profits had been more
than substantial. Along with the gold and silver that had
been brought out of Paris, art objects, expensive jewelry,
and other valuables had been sent to Germany. By gam-
bling a considerable fortune on a brilliant idea, Gisela von
Kirchberg had become an immensely wealthy woman, and
her riches continued to mount daily.

Henry smiled and shook his head as Holtzen asked
another question about Gisela's financial affairs. "My conversations with the baroness seldom concern business," he
said. "They are usually about such matters as the vintage
of the wine we will have with dinner."

Holtzen laughed heartily. "Of course, and so they
should be between a young man and a beautiful woman.
If you asked her," he went on, "do you think the baroness
would grant me an interview?"

"I'm sorry, but I'm sure she wouldn't," Henry replied. "All inquiries by journalists are referred to her
Saarbrücken office."

"Yes, I know," Holtzen said. "The last time I was in
Germany, I went to her Saarbrücken office, but they gave
me little information. I heard that the office was being
moved to Frankfurt am Main, but they would neither
confirm nor deny it. Do you know if it is?"

The subject was vaguely perplexing to Henry, because he had overheard talk about the same thing among
some of Gisela's office staff. He had never asked Gisela
about it, but neither had she told him about it, and usually
she at least mentioned such matters to him. "No, I don't
know," he replied.

Holtzen sighed heavily, evidently concluding that he was going to learn nothing of value from Henry. But he remained amiable. "You and the baroness are fortunate, Lieutenant Blake, because you have a beautiful companion and she has a companion who is trustworthy. It was very pleasant talking with you, and if you have friends in Chicago, I trust they escaped safely from the fire."

"It was my pleasure," Henry replied, shaking hands with Holtzen again. "I do have a friend there, but he is the kind of man who can deal with any situation. He is undoubtedly assisting the authorities."

As Holtzen moved away, he said, "If I learn anything further about the fire, I will tell you when I see you again."

"I would appreciate that very much," Henry said, mounting his horse. "Good day to you, Herr Holtzen."

As he rode slowly on along the busy street, Henry thought about the woman who aroused such curiosity among journalists, and not simply because of her riches. It was undeniable that part of Gisela's attraction—a great part—was her vibrant, dominating personality. In their disagreements, Henry had found that her will was easily the match of his own. And her quick, hot temper made it certain that a turbulently emotional scene awaited him. Yet he was also very fond of her, and he abhorred the thought of hurting her.

In addition to the other reasons that made it difficult to break off their relationship, Henry had an emotional attachment to Gisela that he was unable to understand. As powerful as it was, it was not love. He loved only Cindy, but Gisela exerted a compelling hold on him that was as intense as love. Breaking that bond was going to be as painful for him as for her.

At no time, however, had he implied any continuing commitment to their relationship. He had carefully avoided any suggestion of permanence between them, and he had told her about Cindy. In every way that he could, he had been honest and fair with her. At least his conscience was clear on that score.

The break had to be made, and for reasons that went

beyond having two women in his life. Through no conscious effort of her own, Gisela was a subtle but potent influence on him, and he was changing. During the brief time he had been involved with her, his personality, interests, his entire outlook on life had slightly but distinctly altered. He wanted to take control again, to end the confusion in his life and fulfill his goal of being a line army officer with Cindy as his wife.

Henry reached the outskirts of the town, and as he passed the last scattered houses, he let his horse increase its pace. It cantered along the road for a short distance, then out of habit it slowed and turned off at a lane. The lane led back to a large farm manor built in typical European style, with barns and the house set around three sides of an expansive stone courtyard.

Henry stopped the horse. Looking at the buildings, he thought about how to broach the subject to Gisela. He had chosen midday as the best time to tell her. Her offices would be crowded with people who would overhear the emotional scene, but that would be better than bringing the subject up in the soft candlelight at dinner or during another of their private moments.

As he flicked the reins and set off again, Henry heard someone call his name. For an instant he cursed himself for having become such a fixture in the area that almost everyone recognized him. He turned to see a carriage approaching from the east, Commander Stephen Wyndham looking out the window and waving. Henry rode up as the carriage pulled off onto the shoulder of the road.

"It's good to see you again, Commander," Henry said, exchanging salutes with the naval officer. "Did you enjoy your visit to London?"

"Not entirely," the commander replied, smiling wryly. "I was asked to explain how someone far less experienced than I managed to bowl all of the wickets while I was unaware that the game had even begun. But other than that, it was pleasant enough." He pointed to the first lieutenant bars on Henry's shoulders. "There's something that was well-earned and that I'm extremely pleased to see. My heartiest congratulations."

"Thank you. I owe you a drink to help me celebrate."

"Indeed you do," Stephen said, "as well as one to make up for the chiding I received in London. We'll have to make it soon, though. I'm being reassigned to Berlin."

"We *will* have to make it soon, sir," Henry replied, "because I'm being reassigned as well. I just found out today."

"Indeed? Will you be going back to the States?"

Henry nodded. "I'm not sure just where yet, but I intend to ask for assignment to the line cavalry."

The commander started to say something, then, glancing toward the driver on the box, he opened the door and got out. Tall and dapper in his Royal Navy uniform, he stepped around the carriage and out of earshot of the driver as Henry dismounted and followed him.

"Henry, I don't presume to advise you on your army career," Stephen said. "But your extraordinary success here proves that you have a natural talent for military intelligence. Your very rapid promotion is evidence of what it can do for your career, so I'm more than a bit surprised that you would want to be assigned to the cavalry. And from what I've seen, you enjoy this sort of work, don't you?"

Henry hesitated, unwilling to admit the truth—that he did indeed enjoy his present assignment and regretted having to leave behind unfinished business. The fragmentary hints about Mauser Arms Works, for instance, had never developed into concrete information; and he could think of a half-dozen other promising leads that he would not be able to investigate. But he had made his decision.

"Yes, I do like the work, sir," Henry replied. "But there are personal reasons—and besides, I'll end up having nothing but staff assignments if I'm not careful."

Stephen nodded thoughtfully. "It's your decision to make, of course," he said. "But I do wish you would reconsider it, Henry. The potential you have as an intelligence officer is of such value to your nation that it seems a waste for you to go into another field, however effective you may be in it." He nodded toward the farm manor.

"And I know someone else who won't be pleased over your decision to leave Europe."

"No, she certainly won't," Henry agreed.

His tone must have betrayed something, for Stephen suddenly frowned. "You weren't by any chance on your way to tell her about it?"

Henry sighed heavily. "Yes, I was," he replied.

"Then I certainly won't delay you any longer," Stephen said, walking back toward the carriage door. "I know that's something you want to be done with as soon as possible, and it's an undertaking I don't envy. Will you be back at Vittel later in the day?"

Henry remounted. "Yes, I should be back there during the afternoon."

"If you'll come by my office, we'll go for a drink," Stephen said. "You'll probably need one, and I'll even host."

Henry smiled wryly, exchanging a salute with Stephen as the carriage moved away. Turning his horse, he began cantering along the lane toward the manor buildings.

The courtyard was congested with wagons, carriages, and tethered horses. A score or more of tradesmen and businessmen from the fringes of Gisela's widespread business affairs were standing about and chatting. The stable boy ran up and took Henry's horse. Henry touched his cap and nodded to the bystanders as the men lifted their hats and bowed.

The expansive front room of the manor house had been converted to an office, with desks and work tables in neat rows. It teemed with activity, clerks moving about with bundles of papers and accountants leaning over ledgers. The subdued hubbub in the room faded as Henry entered, the men pausing in their work to greet him cheerfully. The brooding frown on the face of the manager, Hans Guenther, changed to surprise at seeing Henry so early in the day. The man's thin lips stretched in a wintry smile as he stood up and bowed. "Good day, Lieutenant Blake," he said. "It is a fair day, but it is very cold outside, is it not?"

"Good day, Herr Guenther," Henry replied. "Yes, it is a sunny day, but it is quite cold."

Guenther glanced around at the others as he sat back down. The bustle of activity immediately resumed. Hanging up his cap and overcoat on a rack in a corner, Henry looked across the room at Gisela's office. The door was open, and she had a visitor.

Other men who were waiting to see her sat on benches flanking the wide fireplace at one side of the room. Henry stepped to the fireplace, nodding to the men as they stood and bowed. He warmed his hands, again thinking about how to bring up what he had to tell Gisela. Then he crossed the room and stood at a window near her office door, waiting.

Her voice was soft but very cool as she talked to the visitor; the man's voice was ingratiating and apologetic. Listening to them, Henry thought about the two opposite sides of her temper. When she was angry at anyone except him, she was always cold and composed. It was a calculated, inhuman kind of anger, totally merciless.

With him, however, virtually the only thing that made her angry was suspicions about other women—and these suspicions were easily aroused. On the few occasions when she had lost her temper, she had thrown lusty, unrestrained tantrums, shouting and breaking things. She recovered quickly, however, instantly ready to make peace.

The man in her office was the owner of a drayage firm that had failed to transport the tonnage of food from Saarbrücken to Paris that was specified in its contract. He was trying to explain the difficulties he had encountered, but Gisela was not interested in his excuses.

"Madam Baroness," the man said placatingly, "it is impossible for me to deliver that much cargo in such a short time as—"

"Is this your signature on this contract?" Gisela interrupted, her caustic tone conveying the slashing impact of a whip. "Are you Karl Steiner, or did someone else sign this?"

"I am Steiner, Madam Baroness. But when I signed

the contract, I did not understand all that it meant in respect to—"

"Then you should have sought legal advice, as I have. My attorneys tell me that I can now seize all of your property and commit you to debtor's prison for the penalties in shortfalls you have incurred."

"But the penalties are unreasonable, Madam Baroness. If I am short a single ton, I must haul ten more to make up the shortage. The more I haul, the more I am in debt, and I cannot—"

"Then you shouldn't have signed the contract."

"Madam Baroness, I thought I could fulfill it. But my horses have been going lame, my wagons are breaking down, and I—"

"Take back the presents you bought for your mistress with my money and buy more horses and wagons. Work like one of your horses, as I do. Do what you wish, but fulfill the contract."

"I will try, Madam Baroness. But I have many problems and no one to help me. My workers are—"

"Ask your wife and children to help you."

"My wife and children, Madam Baroness? They are not involved in my business affairs."

"They are deeply involved. If you fail to fulfill this contract, I will put you in debtor's prison, your wife in a whorehouse, and your children on the streets begging crusts. If you explain the situation to them, you will probably find them eager to help."

There was a long moment of silence, then the man's voice quavered as he spoke again. "Madam Baroness, I beg you to have pity. You cannot do this to me and my family. You cannot be so—"

"If you do not fulfill the contract you signed, I can and will do as I said. Get out."

The man came out with slow, dragging footsteps, his face pale and trembling, tears in his eyes. Large and muscular, he had the features of a strong, domineering man, perhaps even a bully. But he had challenged and been crushed by a more ruthless, unyielding strength. As the man came out of the office, Henry went in, half closing the door behind him.

The room was spartan—her cluttered desk, the chair she sat in, and a shelf for ledgers the only furniture. Gisela was pulling a sheaf of papers closer and peering at them through her pince-nez. She appeared to be unmoved, the confrontation with the man already forgotten. Hearing his step, she looked up.

For an instant her eyes remained their normal flat, glassy blue. Then they were sparkling with life. Her strong, Teutonic features, beautiful but forbidding in repose, became radiant with a smile as she took off her glasses and stood up. Shapely in her blue muslin gown, its lacy bodice outlining full breasts, she stepped around the desk to meet him.

Her vibrant personality reached out to him in an embrace that was almost as tangible as the touch of her warm, soft lips to his as she stood on tiptoe to kiss him. Then she stepped back and smiled up at him. "You are home very early today, Heinrich," she said. "If you'll wait until I finish a few things, we can have lunch in our room upstairs. . . ." Her voice faded as she studied his eyes. "No, you have something important to tell me, don't you?"

"Yes, I do," he replied, then proceeded bluntly. "I've been ordered to prepare to leave here. I'll be going to Berlin, then back to the United States."

Gisela's smile faded. "Yes, that is important," she said. "Would you like to go to our room to discuss it, Heinrich, or shall we talk here?"

"I'd rather talk here."

Gisela folded her arms and put a forefinger on her chin. "This was inevitable, wasn't it?" she said sadly. "My loved one is an American, and I must accept the consequences of that. And you need to see your friends and family, Heinrich. How long will you be gone?"

"No, you don't understand, Gisela. I don't intend to return. I intend to go to the United States and stay there, and I'm going to marry Cindy Holt. I've told you about that before."

Gisela blinked and frowned. Then she laughed merrily and patted his arm. "And I've told you before that you're too young to be married. Go and visit with your family and friends, Heinrich. Kiss your young lady and tell her that you love her. Then come back, and I will have a pleasant surprise for you."

"Stop patronizing me, Gisela!" he snapped, annoyed. "You're talking to me like I'm a child!"

"No, no, I am not, Heinrich," she replied, sobering quickly. "And I apologize for making you think that. You are a man, and you have integrity, loyalty, and other virtues that put most men to shame. But you are a young man—too young to be married. If you doubt my opinion, then ask your colonel. Ask my nephew Richard." Waving toward the outer office, she said, "Ask those outside. Everyone will tell you that you are too young to be married."

"Whether or not I get married has nothing to do with those outside," he said. "It has nothing to do with Colonel Brentwood, or with your nephew."

"And I suppose it has nothing to do with me?" she countered, again crossing her arms.

The conversation was not going as he had planned. Henry shook his head in exasperation. "Gisela, I am a man and an officer in the United States Army, and I'm not too young to be married. Cindy Holt and I love each other, and I intend to return to the United States and marry her."

"Then you will destroy that love," Gisela said firmly. "Her father is a general, isn't he? You intend to take her from those surroundings and give her a life of toil and hardship in some hovel on an army base? You are the most handsome and charming man I have ever met, and you are the only man I have ever loved. But you have nothing to offer a wife. Wait until you can give her a position in life and surroundings that will enrich your love. Do not destroy it with poverty."

"A first lieutenant in the United States Army isn't penniless," Henry said impatiently. "There are many others who live on less."

A flush abruptly spreading over her face and her chin jutting belligerently, Gisela turned to her desk. She picked up a heavy ledger and slammed it back down with a resounding boom that reverberated through the room, papers scattering over the floor. She controlled herself with an effort, drawing in a deep breath.

"Heinrich, you are an intelligent man," she said calmly. "Please talk intelligently. You and I both know that most people live in misery of their own making, so don't compare yourself with them and judge happiness in terms of less misery than theirs." She lifted a hand as he started to speak. "No, listen, Heinrich. I said that I would have a pleasant surprise for you when you return from America, and I will tell you about it now. I'm making arrangements for you to be at Mauser Arms Works."

"Mauser Arms Works?" Henry echoed in surprise. "Do you mean that you're making arrangements for me to visit the factory?"

"No, more than that," Gisela replied. "Representatives from the War Ministry work there, inspecting and approving shipments of weapons for the army. Officially, you will be working with them and studying their methods for use by your own army in factories that supply weapons. Some of the manufacturing processes are trade secrets, so parts of the factory are closed to everyone except trusted employees. But you should be able to obtain very valuable information simply by being in the factory."

Her last comment, Henry reflected, was an understatement. He found it difficult to believe that she could actually accomplish what she had said. "How are you making these arrangements, Gisela?"

"Through the factory stockholders and the War Ministry. The wider exchange of military observers between Germany and the United States made it possible, although this is more than a post for a military observer. The arrangements will be completed shortly. Then, when your government makes a formal request to Berlin, it will be quickly approved."

Behind her brief explanation, he knew, lay a multitude of pressures that had been expertly exerted upon key

officials. No military secrets were being compromised, but
she offered something of equal value—a unique opportunity to study at first hand the manufacturing techniques of
one of the foremost small-arms factories in the world. It
would be of intense interest to the Department of War in
Washington.

What the journalist in the town had said about Frank-
furt-am-Main, as well as the rumors he himself had heard,
now made sense. "Mauser Arms Works is in Frankfurt,"
he said.

"Yes. I have an agent searching for a suitable house
nearby," Gisela replied, leaning against the desk. "I will
buy a private railroad car for when I must go to Berlin. Of
course, I would prefer to live in Berlin, but we must do
what we must do." Her tone became affectionate, intimate. "I would gladly endure much greater inconvenience
than that for your sake, loved one."

The situation, Henry reflected, was suddenly entirely
different; a new opportunity was opening for him. Having
access to the Mauser factory was a success on the same
scale as obtaining the information on the capitulation of
Paris. In time, it could prove to be of inestimable value to
his country.

At the same time, from a personal standpoint, nothing had changed. The confusing problem of having two
women in his life would continue, as would the disturbing
changes that he felt taking place within him. He would be
drawn deeper into the web of ties that already bound him
firmly to the beautiful, alluring woman in front of him.

Knowing how much effort she had put into her plans
for him, Henry felt rude and churlish over refusing, but
he shook his head. "Gisela, I am grateful for what you
did," he said, "but I intend to return to the United States
and marry Cindy Holt. I have made a decision."

Gisela was speechless for a moment, stunned. "Heinrich, this is absolutely senseless," she finally said in perplexity. "I cannot believe what I am hearing. . . ." Her
eyes narrowed suspiciously. "Have you met someone else?
Are you trying to leave me to go to her?"

"Of course not," he replied. "There is no one else besides Cindy."

"I have been very busy with my work," she murmured, looking at him from the corners of her eyes. "Perhaps I have neglected you too much, Heinrich. If you have met someone else, tell me about it, and I will forgive you. I may be angry for a moment, but I love you and I will forgive you."

"There is no one else!" he snapped impatiently. "And stop talking as though you were a wealthy old man and I was your mistress. I've told you before not to take that tone with me, Gisela."

"But I am older than you," she replied. "I am also wealthy, and you are a young, handsome man. If you met a beautiful woman of your own age, no one could blame you for being attracted to her. If you have, please tell me about it."

Henry sighed wearily. "Gisela, I said that there is no one else, and there is not. Will you stop asking me if—"

"Then what is it?" she shouted, her face suddenly flushed and her eyes wide as her temper flared. Pouncing on a ledger on her desk, she picked it up and hurled it across the room, the pages fluttering as it slammed into the wall and fell to the floor. "If it is not another woman, then tell me why you are trying to leave me!"

"I told you, Gisela," he said loudly, "that I intend to return to the United States and marry—"

"That is utter foolishness!" she barked furiously. Snatching up another ledger, she threw it across the room. Her inkwell followed, exploding into shards and sending a large splotch of ink running down the wall.

"It is not foolishness," he said angrily, "and it is what I intend to do. Now stop throwing things!"

Glaring at him defiantly, Gisela picked up another ledger and hurled it across the room. As it bounced off the wall, she planted her fists on her hips. "Heinrich, you have an opportunity to advance your career!" she shouted. "And what do you have to say about it? Nothing! You merely continue with this childish foolishness!"

"Gisela, I realize how much time and work you devoted to that," he said. "I am truly grateful, but—"

"I want no thanks!" she snapped, waving the subject aside with a slash of her hand. "No amount of time and work is too much if it is for you. But I cannot bear to see you hurt yourself. No knife or pistol could wound me as deeply. Nothing hurts me the way that does. Nothing!"

Sighing heavily, Henry made no reply. Gisela glared at him in silent, furious exasperation, then looked away. Turning to step toward the window, she bumped into her chair and kicked at it. Cursing, she gripped it by the arms and lifted it, heaving it into a corner. It landed with a splintering crash, a leg breaking off and skidding across the floor.

The normal hubbub in the office outside had died into absolute silence. Henry glanced toward the half-open door. The visitors on the benches near the fireplace were stretching and craning their necks to peer into the office. Gisela stood in front of the window with her back to Henry, pinning up coils of her long, black hair that had fallen loose while she had been throwing things.

Her hair neat again, Gisela turned from the window and stepped toward him. "It is beyond belief," she said, her voice becoming louder with each word, "that you could be this foolish! You have before you a great opportunity, and you are turning away from it!"

"Gisela, I am grateful for your intentions, but you should have asked me first!" he replied angrily. "You do not control my life!"

"I am not trying to control your life!" she shouted in his face, lifting to her toes. "If I were, you would not be in the army!"

"And why not?" Henry retorted. "The army is my career and my life, and I will not have it maligned or listen to—"

"That has nothing to do with our conversation!" she shouted at the top of her voice. Turning and taking a step away, she jabbed a finger toward him. "If you value the army and your career so highly, why are you refusing this opportunity?"

There was, he knew, no good answer to the question. "I have made my decision, Gisela," he said.

"Then I ask you to reconsider it!" she snapped, jabbing her finger at him again to emphasize her words. "And I warn you that I will not allow you to turn away from this opportunity!"

"You *warn* me?" he growled. "You will not allow me to act against your wishes? Gisela, you do not control my life!"

"I know I do not, and I do not wish to! But I will not allow you to ignore this opportunity! I ask you to reconsider your decision!"

"I will not!" he barked. "My decision is final!"

"Then I must do what I must do!" she shouted, slamming a fist down on her desk. "Heinrich, I intend to inform your superiors about the arrangements I have made! You will be ordered to stay here!"

Rage suddenly exploded within him, fury so intense that he was speechless for a moment. He glared at her, his face red. "If I am ordered to stay here, then I will resign my commission! Regardless of your schemes, I will make my own decisions!"

Gisela recoiled a step, her anger fading. "Heinrich, I want only what is best for you," she said quickly. "I want only—"

"You want me to do what you wish!" he shouted angrily. "And I will not! Go ahead and tell my superiors whatever you like, and see if it keeps me here even one hour longer!"

"Wait, Heinrich, wait!" Gisela exclaimed, catching his arm as he turned away from her. "I apologize, loved one. I was angry, and I made a mistake in thinking that you might—"

"Your mistake was in confusing me with the man who was in here before me!" Henry retorted, jerking his arm away from her. "No one on earth can do to me what you did to him, and no one ever will!"

"No, no, Heinrich," Gisela said in alarm as she seized his arm again. "How could I confuse you with him? No, for you I have only love, and I only wanted to do what was

best for you." Pulling his arm, she turned him back to her.
"And I want to keep you with me, but only for a time.
Stay with me in Frankfurt for a few months. It will help
your career, and it will make my life complete."

"No, you went too far, Gisela!" Henry snapped, still
furious. He twisted his arm free. "Even if you were angry,
you meant what you said. You were scheming to control
me. You will never do that, and you will never have
another chance to even try."

"I apologize!" Gisela cried in dismay, catching his
arm again and clutching it as he dragged her toward the
door. "I will never do it again, loved one! Please forgive
me!" She suddenly burst into tears. "Don't leave me,
Heinrich!" she wailed. "Don't leave me, loved one!"

Henry turned back, almost shocked by her tears. He
had never seen her display an emotion that was even
remotely related to despair. "Gisela, I must leave," he
said. "I must return to—"

"No, not now," Gisela sobbed, clinging to him. "Do
not leave me now, loved one. Stay with me for a few
months, a year. You are young, and a year will be a short
time for you. But it will be a lifetime for me. Please,
Heinrich, I beg you to stay!"

His anger completely gone, Henry held Gisela as she
sobbed wildly and clutched him. Hans Guenther stepped
quietly inside, his eyes avoiding the couple as he reached
for the door to pull it closed. His thin, pale face reflected
stunned consternation.

Henry led Gisela to the desk, walking through the
papers scattered underfoot. He held her as she wept, his
former resolve in disarray. His determination to return
immediately to the United States and marry Cindy had
remained steadfast throughout the argument, but now it
was gone.

"You are the only one I have ever loved," Gisela
whispered, sobbing. "I have no one else, and my wealth
and other things are meaningless to me without you."
Tears streaming down her face, she looked up at him.
"Please stay with me for a time. Stay with me for a year.
Only a year, and then I will be content."

Wisps of her thick, black hair were loose again, and she was warm and fragrant with perfume. She had never been more desirable. His need for her, more like a disease or a drug than love, was as intense as the most fervent love. And it was reinforced by his sense of duty. The information he could obtain at Mauser Arms Works would be invaluable.

At the same time, his pure, shining love for Cindy was a powerful force within him, a yearning that demanded fulfillment. Henry felt trapped and helpless, once again fearing the changes that were taking place within him. If he became further entangled with this beautiful woman, he might never be able to resume his former life.

Gisela smiled tremulously, reaching up to caress his face. Her deep blue eyes were pleading as she silently waited for a reply. Torn by powerful desires that pulled him in opposite directions, Henry did not know what to do. But he knew he had to decide. And he had to decide now.

XVII

The sun was warm, but the gusty October wind had a biting chill as Timmy Holt and Joshua Sellars crossed a sloping pasture a mile from the house on the Holt ranch. The deep, autumn-brown grass dragged at their trousers and crunched under their boots, a rime of morning frost lingering in shaded spots under the tufts of grass.

Joshua, nearing sixty, limped on a leg that had been broken decades before when a horse had fallen and rolled on him. He carried three kites under his arm, the paper on them rattling in the wind. "We're getting mighty close to that tree, Timmy," he said, pointing to an ancient dead oak at the top of the rise in the pasture. "You've got your kite string tangled on it a couple of times before, remember."

The boy was carrying a kite that was much larger than the three under Joshua's arm, and he was carefully keeping its leading edge to the wind. Even so, occasional gusts almost jerked it out of his hands. Struggling to keep it steady, he glanced at the tree.

Timmy knew that Joshua was far more concerned with his own personal comfort than with the possibility of a kite getting tangled in the dead tree. As always, as soon as a kite was in the air, the old man would lie down to take a nap—but he would want to find a place that was sheltered from the chilly wind.

"I want to get up to where the wind is strong, Josh," Timmy said.

The old man grunted, pulling his coat collar higher. "She seems pretty strong to me right here, Timmy. Are you sure you don't want me to carry that big kite for you? You're having a hard time with it."

"No, I'll carry it."

Joshua shrugged, reflecting that all Holts, young or old, had the disposition of stubborn mules. He looked at the kite again. Besides being much larger than any the boy had ever made before, it had an entirely different design, wide for its length. "Why did you make a kite shaped like that, Timmy?" he asked.

The design, though somewhat crude, was as close a copy as Timmy had been able to make of a diagram he had seen in a newspaper, from a story about experiments in France. His aunt Cindy had read the article to him, at his request. But it was not a subject that he wanted to discuss with Joshua, for fear that the old man might become suspicious. "It seemed like a good one," he replied vaguely.

"It looks like a funny shape to me," Joshua commented. "And it's awful big and heavy. I think she's too heavy for you to get in the air, even on a day as windy as this one." He reached out and touched the kite's fabric. "You put several layers of paper on it, didn't you? You must have used up a pound of your aunt's flour to make paste. If you took it without asking her, she'll get mad at you."

He had, in fact, raided his aunt's flour bin without asking permission. He had had no other choice, because both Cindy and Janessa seemed to have the uncanny ability to read his mind when he was planning something. And now Joshua was becoming too curious. Timmy moved farther away from him as they walked through the grass. "Don't bump the other kites against this one," he said. "One of them might get torn."

"No, I ain't going to tear one of your kites, Timmy," Joshua said chuckling. "But that kite looks too big and heavy to fly. Maybe you could fly it in a Texas dust storm wind, though."

"What kind of wind is that?" Timmy asked, relieved

by the change in subject and anticipating one of the old man's tall tales.

"Well, it's so strong and blows the dust so hard that it gets into everything," Joshua replied. "You can't eat eggs that chickens lay during one of them dust storms, because the wind blows the dust through the shell. People call them dust storm eggs and just throw them away. You can hatch them, if you want to, but the chicken will be full of dust."

Timmy laughed, then stopped a hundred feet from the dead tree. "This is far enough," he said.

Joshua heaved a sigh of relief as he began looking around for stones to weight the kites down and keep the wind from blowing them away. He and the boy gathered stones, which they carefully placed on the kites. Then Joshua glanced around again. A sheltered, sunny hollow about fifty yards away looked inviting. "I'll go set down there while you fly your kites, Timmy," he said, pointing.

Timmy nodded, taking strips of cloth from his coat pocket to make a tail for a kite. "All right."

"If you need anything, just holler. And stay right here."

"Yes, all right, Josh."

As the old man walked down the slope toward the hollow, Timmy sorted through the strips of cloth. Using the precise judgment he had developed, he tied together strips the right length and weight to hold a kite at the proper angle to the gusty wind. He tied the tail to one of the small kites, then took out his roll of string.

The kite needed only a toss into the air, a gust immediately catching it and sweeping it upward. Timmy unrolled string and tugged it expertly to work the kite higher, watching Joshua from the corners of his eyes. The old man sat down, and Timmy waited for him to lie down and fall asleep, as he always did.

Soon the kite drew his attention away from Joshua. Though made simply, from sheets of newspaper, lengths of light, straight-grained ash, and flour glue, to the boy it became almost magical once it rose at the air. Dancing and trembling at the end of the string, it soared to lofty heights, sending back to him, through the string, an exhil-arating feel of those vast, boundless spaces.

His first experience with a kite had been one he would always remember. In his imagination it had lifted him up to the world of the eagle and the hawk, as kites still did. But a plan he had later devised to see the world as birds saw it had ended in dismal failure.

He had fastened a mirror to a kite and then peered at it through a telescope, in order to get a sense of what the earth looked like from above. But the quivering of the kite had turned the mirror's reflections into a swirling blur. And his aunt had scolded him severely and sent him to bed without dinner for breaking her mirror and taking his father's expensive telescope out of the house.

But now he had another plan, with possibilities so exciting that they were almost overwhelming.

Timmy looked down the slope at Joshua. The old man was stretched out on the grass, his hat over his face, and he appeared to be sound asleep. Keeping an eye on him, Timmy began pulling in the kite and rolling up the string.

Soon the kite was on the ground and weighted down with stones, and the old man still had not moved. Timmy picked up the large kite and carried it to the foot of the tree, then put two stones on it, just on one edge, and tied the string to the frame. He unrolled several feet of string, stuffed the remaining ball in his coat pocket, and began climbing the tree.

Reaching the first limb was the hardest part, since there was almost nothing to hold on to. But he was deter-mined, and, clutching for handholds and shinnying up-ward, he finally pulled himself atop the lowest branch and straddled it.

After unrolling more string and putting the ball back in his pocket, he climbed higher. Some of the smaller limbs had rotted, and they broke when he tested them, but he continued climbing, watching the string and keep-ing it from tangling on a lower branch.

The last large horizontal limb was some thirty feet above the ground. Reaching it, he sat on it and slid out a few feet. The wind was strong, tugging at his clothes. He looked down the hill at the old man, who was still asleep. Then he pulled on the string.

The first tug dislodged the stones on the frame. But as soon as the kite lifted off the ground, the wind caught it and slammed it against the trunk. Controlling his panic, Timmy quickly began hauling in the string hand over hand, pulling the kite clear of danger.

It swayed and spun as he raised it to the limb. Then, as he gripped the frame and snapped off the string, the wind caught the kite and almost dragged him off the limb. Teetering precariously, he steadied himself, gripping the crossbar on the kite and turning the leading edge to the wind.

Lifting the kite cautiously over his head, he held the crossbar with both hands. The slope below was dotted with rock outcroppings, and for a moment fear surfaced in the excitement building within him. But he forced it aside; the slope was covered mostly with soft, deep grass.

Balancing himself on the limb, Timmy took a fresh grip on the crossbar and lifted the kite over his head to arm's length. The wind pushed at it, tugging him backward. But he fought it and leaned forward, gathering himself and poising. Then he heaved himself off the limb.

For a span of two seconds, he flew. During those two glorious, ecstatic seconds, he joined the hawks and the eagles as he glided smoothly away from the tree, the ground passing swiftly below.

Then the front of the unstable kite nosed upward, stalling. It came to a standstill in the air, and Timmy and the kite plummeted. As he fell, he saw Joshua spring to his feet and begin racing up the slope. Then the mass of dark, jagged rocks was close.

He struck, feeling himself bounce. Excruciating pain shot through his head, his leg—everywhere. Then darkness closed in.

The kitchen windows were covered with condensation, the air thick with the smell of cinnamon and the apples that Cindy and Janessa had been canning. Icy fear gripped Cindy as she helped Janessa clean off the kitchen table, while Joshua stood holding Timmy, trying to explain what had happened.

The boy was pale and still, a blood-soaked rag around his head. The fear within Cindy threatened to turn to panic, but the way Janessa acted helped her retain control. The girl was a blur of movement as she cleared the table, her face expressionless. Then she broke into what Joshua was saying and gestured impatiently toward the table.

"I looked away for just a minute," the old man said, on the verge of tears as he put the boy on the table. "I looked away for only a minute, Miss Cindy, and all of a sudden he was jumping out of that tree with that big kite. And then he fell on them rocks."

Wanting to scream at the man, Cindy knew that it would only be venting her feelings for no good reason. Joshua loved Timmy and would willingly risk his life to protect the boy. "Yes, I understand, Josh," she said, pushing the old man toward the door. "We'll see to him."

"I should have known he was up to something," Joshua said, backing away reluctantly. "He had that funny-looking kite that was wider than it was long, and he didn't want to talk about it or to—"

"Yes, yes, we'll discuss it later, Josh," Cindy interrupted him, hurrying him out the door. "We must see to Timmy now." She closed the door and turned back. "What do you need, Janessa?"

Bending over the boy and methodically examining him, Janessa moved her hands up one of his arms and squeezed gently. "Get clean rags and cold water," she replied tersely.

Cindy stepped to a cabinet and took out a roll of bandage rags. As she was filling a basin at the sink, she suddenly remembered an incident of several days before, one that was now all too meaningful.

Timmy had brought a newspaper to her a second time and asked her to read the same article to him again. She had become suspicious, but not suspicious enough. The boy had quickly dropped the subject when she had questioned him. Later she had glimpsed him prowling around the barns with a folded newspaper. Now she realized he had been looking for a ranch hand who could read the article to him once more.

The article had been about an apparatus built by a man in France, a glider that had enabled him to soar down to the ground from tall buildings. There had been a diagram of the apparatus, which was similar to a kite but wider than it was long. The last paragraph in the article, which she had failed to emphasize sufficiently to the boy, had been about the man's death when the glider had failed during one of the descents.

Cindy put the basin and rags on the table, then watched Janessa. As the girl moved her hands up Timmy's left leg, she hesitated. She gingerly pressed just above his knee, feeling through his trousers. Then her hands moved on up his body. At his chest she hesitated again. She unbuttoned his shirt and slid a hand inside, cautiously feeling for something. "We'll need Dr. Martin, won't we, Janessa?" Cindy asked.

"Yes we will," Janessa said, sliding a hand under the boy's neck as she continued her examination. "He has a broken leg and two broken ribs that Dr. Martin will have to set. That's bad, but it isn't really dangerous, since the bones aren't through the skin. His neck feels all right. That cut on his head might be the worst." She dampened a clean cloth in the basin and untied the rag around Timmy's head.

As she lifted the blood-soaked rag, more blood began welling from a deep, four inch gash on the boy's forehead. Looking at it, Cindy felt numb with fear. Then she saw that Janessa's composure was starting to crumble. The girl's face was ashen, and she blinked back tears as she pressed the damp cloth over the cut. Her fingers trembled as she felt around the cut and opened Timmy's eyelids to look at his eyes.

Realizing that she was allowing the girl to bear too much responsibility, Cindy stepped around the table and put a hand on Janessa's shoulder. "I'll send for Dr. Martin," she said.

Still looking at the boy's eyes, Janessa said, "Tell the rider to send a telegram to Dad. He must come home."

"Is it that serious, then?"

Her eyes filling with tears, Janessa looked up at Cindy. "He might have a fractured skull, Cindy," she said, her voice quavering. "I can't tell whether he does or not. But if he does . . ."

The haunting fear in the girl's eyes completed the ominous sentence. With a sinking feeling in the pit of her stomach, Cindy turned and walked toward the door. "I'll find one of the men."

"Tell him to hurry, Cindy."

"Yes, I'll tell him to saddle the fastest horse we have."

"No—I mean tell Dad to hurry," Janessa said, her voice breaking with a sob. "Tell him to get here just as quickly as he can."

The feeling of somber depression with which Toby Holt had gone to sleep was replaced by a lighter mood the next morning. He woke much later than he usually did and felt well rested. Outside his tent he could hear children shouting gleefully as they played. People were laughing and talking as they passed the tent.

As he walked to the field latrines to wash, shave, and change into clean clothes, what he saw lifted his spirits. Women were moving about busily, seeing to their children and hanging up washing. Men were constructing furniture and other needed items as they discussed plans for beginning their lives again. The hardy American fortitude in the face of adversity was very much alive among these people.

All of his friends were gone from their tents when he returned. Toby walked to the kitchen tents alone and went through a serving line. The cooks filled a plate for him with fried potatoes and thick slices of bacon, and at the end of the line were bins of hot biscuits and a coffee urn.

When he had finished breakfast and was drinking another cup of coffee, Toby saw Ted Taylor crossing the tent toward him. "I thought you might be here," Ted said, sitting down to join him. "I was looking all over for you."

"And I was looking for you. Where did you go?"

"It's raining heavily in Wisconsin, and Frank and the others are trying to find out if the fire at the logging camp has been extinguished," Ted replied. "They're at a telegraph office that has been set up near the temporary train depot. From what they've heard so far, it looks very favorable for the logging operation."

"That's certainly good news," Toby said, immensely pleased. "It's good news for us—particularly Frank—and for a lot of other people. There will be a big demand for lumber during the rebuilding here."

"Yes, there's no question about that," Ted agreed. "There's some bad news as well from Wisconsin, though. Some people were killed in the forest fires there, but I haven't heard how many."

Toby's expression was grim. "I expected that, because a lot of the camps and towns there are completely surrounded by forests. Frank and the others were fortunate that our camp was on the lake. You say they don't have any casualty figures?"

"Not when I left—but I wasn't there very long," Ted replied. "I've been at the train depot most of the morning, watching the incoming trains to see if Marjorie was on any of them. She hasn't been so far, but there's a train due in from Springfield in a few minutes. Instead of waiting for it, though, I thought I'd better get back here and go with you to city hall."

"We could meet that train first."

Ted shook his head. "It'll take us a while to get there," he said, "and the governor may be leaving today to return to Springfield. We should leave as soon as possible. I can look for Marjorie later."

Ted's urgent desire to get to city hall and his sudden relative unconcern about Marjorie's whereabouts appeared strange to Toby. But he nodded and took a last drink of coffee.

The unusual warmth of the past days had given way to more seasonable weather, a raw chill of approaching winter in the air. The sun was behind clouds, and the wind for which Chicago was famous was making the tents billow and sway as Toby and Ted went outside. The change of weather would be uncomfortable for the tens of thousands of people whose extra clothing was now part of the tons of ashes covering Chicago.

But the clothing was already being replaced. Families were standing in lines at wagons filled with bales of garments, and militiamen were breaking open the bales and searching for things to fit the people at the head of the lines. The clothing had been hauled from the train depot, where it was arriving in carloads from all over the nation.

The street leading to the tents was crowded with wagons bringing more clothing, food, bedding, and other relief supplies as Toby and Ted walked toward city hall. Ted talked about the organization and management of the relief effort, which was an undertaking of enormous proportions. A council of citizens had been appointed by the mayor to oversee the distribution of the supplies; sufficient quantities were already on hand or en route to last through the winter.

The pall of smoke ahead grew thicker as the two men walked through the outlying districts of the city. Like the area near the piers, the streets here were a backwater of the disaster. Littered with ashes, they were congested with people and vehicles. Buildings were crowded beyond capacity with goods that had been hurriedly hauled out of the burned areas. On every side was evidence of the catastrophe that had struck the city.

At the same time, on every side was evidence that the people were organizing themselves to recover quickly. The bustling activity was purposeful, not the aimless milling about of defeat and despair. In the crowded buildings and even in wagons along the street, tradesmen, craftsmen, and merchants were resuming activities that in their multitude would gradually bring the city of Chicago back to her feet once more.

A carriage for hire passed, then slowed and stopped. Hearing his name called, Ted smiled widely and hurried toward the carriage. "Marjorie!" he exclaimed. "Where have you been?"

"I've just returned from Springfield," Marjorie replied, leaning out the window. "I went there to develop my plates and to send them to Boston. Are Kale, Tommie, and the others safe? I heard that over a thousand people were killed in forest fires in Wisconsin."

"A thousand?" Ted's smile quickly vanished. "Yes, Toby went for them yesterday in a steam launch and brought them back. You say over a thousand people have been killed?"

Marjorie nodded somberly, looking at Toby as he joined Ted beside the carriage. "Several journalists were on the train from Springfield. They said that the town of Peshtigo was completely destroyed, killing eight hundred people, and other smaller towns were also destroyed. That's many times more than were killed here, isn't it?"

"Yes, far more," Toby replied. "About two hundred were killed here, the last I heard. Ted told me the rain was extinguishing the fires in Wisconsin this morning."

"I heard the same from the journalists on the train," Marjorie said, "but it'll probably be several days before we know the full details. If you're going to city hall, you can ride with me. Perhaps we can find out more there."

She opened the door, then moved her equipment cases to make room for the men. As he settled in his seat, Toby noticed that Marjorie's financial state had improved much sooner than he had expected. The cases were new, made of expensive leather bound with brass, with Marjorie's name and profession printed on each side in neat, bold letters: M. WHITE, PHOTOGRAPHIST.

Her dress, hat, and short cape, in the same subdued color and style as before, were also new, and the carpet-bag containing her personal belongings was bulging. But the lines of fatigue on her pretty face were the same as before, and her eyelids were heavy from lack of sleep.

As the carriage moved slowly along the congested street, Ted commented on the new cases. Marjorie looked at them in satisfaction. "I've needed new ones for quite a while," she said. "These are just as strong as my old ones, and much lighter. The dealer worked on them through the night last night, painting my name on and making padded partitions for my equipment."

"Did you sell your photographs in Springfield, then?" Ted asked.

"No, when I arrived there, I sent my partner a telegram to let him know what I had. He contacted the catalog company that sells our slides, as well as a few publications that make etchings, and they advanced him money. He wired part of it to me, and after I paid for using the darkroom and shipped the plates by express freight, I had plenty left over."

"It certainly appears that you did," Ted commented. "But you look very tired, Marjorie. You must not have had much sleep since the fire started."

Marjorie shrugged. "I slept on the train going to Springfield, and I took a nap on the way back. I'm a little tired, but I still have work to do. There'll be time for sleeping later."

"And now you'll be a famous photographist, won't you?" Ted said. "I'm really pleased at that, Marjorie, because you deserve it. Everything turned out just right for you."

Although Toby kept silent as his friends talked on, he was also intensely pleased by Marjorie's success, and for several reasons. One was because he liked Marjorie, and, as Ted had said, she deserved it, for she was totally dedicated to her profession. Another reason was because of the pleasure it gave Ted. The young lawman beamed with satisfaction as he talked with Marjorie.

Looking out the window as the carriage moved slowly on, Toby spotted a familiar face among the others along the street. He called to the driver to stop, then shouted and waved to Aaron Ward. The young merchant was carrying a bundle of papers under one arm, and he smiled and waved as he strode rapidly up to the carriage. Toby got out to shake his hand.

"Toby, I was worried about you and the others when the fire first started," Aaron said. He looked into the carriage, lifting his hat to Marjorie as he greeted her and

Ted. "But word soon got around about what you were doing, so I knew you were safe. But how are your friends in Wisconsin? I heard that the forest fires there have been disastrous."

"They were picked up by a steam launch, and they're all safe," Toby replied. "Did you manage to save the merchandise from your store?"

The amiable young man smiled philosophically as he shook his head. "I didn't get there in time to save even a needle or a spool of thread. It was a complete loss."

"I'm very sorry to hear that, Aaron, because I know that store represented years of work. When will you be able to start another business?"

"I've already begun one," Aaron said cheerfully. "I have the merchandise that was in my warehouse, and I've found a partner, a man named George Thorne. We've set up shop over a livery stable on North Clark Street."

Toby nodded, pleased. "I'm certainly happy to hear that. It doesn't sound like the ideal location to attract customers, but it's a beginning."

"Oh, we don't intend to have customers in the store," Aaron said. "Nor do we intend to display our merchandise. We're going to take orders and ship by rail." He separated one of the papers from the stack under his arm and handed it to Toby. "Here is our list of merchandise."

"The customers will write to you and tell you what they want?" Marjorie asked, intrigued. "How will you get paid?"

"They'll send the money with the order," Aaron replied, handing her a copy of the list through the window. "The instructions are on the list, and we guarantee satisfaction, or we'll return the money. And we'll ship to any point in the nation. I'm sending the list to railroad stations all over the country, and people can write to get their own copies."

"What a marvelous idea!" Marjorie exclaimed, showing Ted the list. "People who live on remote farms will be able to buy things without having to leave home and travel for miles."

"It certainly is a good idea," Toby agreed. "And the

prices on this list are hard to believe. There's no question in my mind that you'll have plenty of orders." Toby handed him back the paper.

Aaron smiled and waved it away. "Keep it, Toby— you may want to order something," he chuckled. "I must get these lists to the train depot, but I hope to see you again soon."

Toby shook hands again and got back into the carriage, Marjorie and Ted calling out in farewell.

"By the way, Aaron," Toby said out the window, "where did you get the name for your new company?"

"Oh, that's my middle name," Aaron replied. "Goodbye, Toby."

As the carriage moved off again, Toby sat back and nodded to himself in satisfaction as he glanced over the list once more. In time, he reflected, the list would undoubtedly include more items and expand to several pages. He looked at the name at the top again, then folded the paper and put it in his pocket. He had no doubt that he would soon be hearing more from Montgomery Ward and Company.

The courtyard in front of city hall was congested with vehicles, tethered horses, and men. Toby got out of the carriage, then lifted down one of the equipment cases. Ted took the other case and helped Marjorie down the step. Suddenly a man in the crowd pointed and shouted in a stentorian voice, "That's Toby Holt! That's him there! He's right there!"

The people, many of whom had been at city hall the previous day, surged forward. They surrounded Toby, Ted, and Marjorie and shouted greetings and praise for what Toby had done on the day of the fire. Hands reached out to shake his and to slap his back, while those who couldn't reach him whooped and cheered.

People on the edge of the crowd pushed forward in excitement, and Toby was jostled and pressed tightly. He shook hands thrust out at him as he smiled and nodded, slowly making his way through the crowd. Ted followed, shouldering and elbowing men to make room for Marjorie.

The crowd thinned near the steps in front of city hall, and the whoops and cheers grew to a bedlam as Toby mounted the stairs.

The policeman on duty at the entrance touched his helmet as he opened the door. Toby nodded to him, then waved to the cheering crowd as he went inside. Ted and Marjorie followed, the three of them laughing about the rowdy welcome they had been given. Businessmen in the entrance foyer gathered around Toby to greet him and to shake his hand. They were not as boisterous as the crowd outside, but just as sincere.

A tall, natty man of about forty stood to one side until the others finished greeting Toby. Then he stepped forward, and Ted introduced him.

"Toby, this is the Honorable Howard Bixbee," Ted said, "the lieutenant governor of Iowa."

Toby shook hands warmly with the man. "Ted told me that you were here, Mr. Bixbee, and I've been looking forward to meeting you. The men, equipment, and supplies you brought have certainly been of great value in easing the hardships of the homeless people here."

Bixbee smiled. "Governor Merrill and I are more than eager to do what we can, as are people from all across the nation. But I don't want to waste your time, Mr. Holt, so I'll tell you right off what I have in mind. Since my arrival here, I've heard over and over about how you kept the city from being completely destroyed, and quite frankly, our state is looking for someone like you, to help out with a problem we have. If I may be so bold to ask, what do you intend to do now, Mr. Holt?"

Toby grinned at the unexpected offer. "Well, in the days immediately ahead, whatever I can do to assist Governor Palmer and Mayor Mason," he replied. "And I'd like to return to Oregon to be with my children and the rest of my family for Thanksgiving Day. After that, it depends on conditions in Wisconsin. I came here to set up a logging and lumber business, and I'd like to continue with that if the timber around our logging camp hasn't been destroyed."

"Yes, I see," Bixbee mused. "The reason I asked is

because we have a problem in Iowa that our law enforcement agencies haven't been able to resolve. The governor and I have discussed setting up something like an independent temporary agency to deal with it. Gangs of train robbers have made several attempts to stop trains and rob them, and the last one was successful. Worse still, we've heard rumors that the James gang has moved into our area."

"It sounds like you do have a problem," Toby said. "Your state police agency and the United States marshal's office haven't been able to handle this?"

"No, because to them it's only one of a number of law enforcement problems. The governor and I decided we needed someone to work with the railroads and the state, to concentrate solely on this. But if your family and business affairs demand your attention, I can understand that."

"I'd still like to help out," Toby said, "and in this case perhaps I can. I believe this man beside me would do better than I could with your problem. Ted Taylor is one of the finest lawmen I've ever met."

"Yes, I'm sure he is," Bixbee replied, smiling at Ted. "After I met him, I decided that I might discuss this with him if you had other commitments. We do want to bring in someone from outside the state so that he would be completely independent of the other agencies. Actually, we had in mind someone with statewide experience. . . ."

"Then Ted's your man," Toby said confidently. "He's simply better at being a lawman than he is at blowing his own horn. He's worked with the attorney general of California and with the railroads there. I don't think you could find a better candidate."

Bixbee lifted his eyebrows at this surprising information. "I'm inclined to agree with you, Toby. Do you have any plans for the coming months, Ted?"

Ted glanced at Marjorie, hesitating; then he shook his head. "No, sir," he replied. "I haven't made any plans at all."

"In that case, would you like to come to Iowa and talk with Governor Merrill and the attorney general about this?" Bixbee asked. "If they're satisfied with your qualifications—and I see no reason why they shouldn't be—then we can discuss specifics about compensation and so forth. The position would be one of special law enforcement assistant to the attorney general."

"Yes, sir, I'll be glad to come to Iowa and discuss it," Ted replied. "It sounds like it would be very interesting."

"I'm sure it will be—and I'll look forward to seeing you in Des Moines, Ted," Bixbee said. He took out his watch and looked at it. "Well, we'd better get upstairs to the mayor's office, hadn't we? We don't want to make you late for your appointment, Toby."

It was the first Toby had heard of having an appointment, and he frowned in perplexity. Then he recalled Ted's vague reply the previous evening as to why the governor and the mayor wanted to see him, as well as Ted's unusual urgency to set out for city hall. "It appears I'm the only one who didn't know that I had an appointment with the mayor and the governor," he said. "What have you been up to, Ted?"

"I've only been following orders, Toby," Ted replied, laughing. "The mayor asked me to have you here at eleven, and that's what I've done. I believe he and the governor would like to express their appreciation for what you did during the fire."

"That's what I was afraid of," Toby said, smiling in resignation. He picked up the equipment case he had carried inside. "Well, we may as well go on up and not keep them waiting."

As they walked upstairs, the lieutenant governor, mindful of Toby's planned logging business, told him of the latest news that had been received from Wisconsin. He said that all of the forest fires in the state had been extinguished by the heavy rains, and the damage to the best timberland appeared relatively light. Unfortunately, there had been a heavy loss of life.

In the echoing stairwell, Toby could not help but overhear the conversation between Ted and Marjorie. Ted invited her to go to Iowa with him, pointing out that she might have an opportunity to photograph notable outlaws. Marjorie's reply was friendly, but it was negative. She told

Ted she would have to work with her partner for a time in Boston if the demand for the slides of the fire was as great as anticipated; after that she had several opportunities to explore, including a whaling expedition.

In the upstairs hall, Toby saw the mayor's secretary peering out a doorway. The man disappeared, and a moment later a hubbub of conversation coming from the mayor's office faded into silence. At the end of the hall, Toby and the others filed into the secretary's office. Howard Bixbee took the equipment case from Toby and motioned him ahead into the inner office.

The mayor's spacious office had been restored to its former neat appearance. Gone were the large wall map and the extra tables and desks. The mayor and governor stood in front of the desk, and some twenty men stood along the sides of the room. Most of them were senior city employees, including the fire chief, police chief, and port master. The remainder were businessmen—Charles Horton, the chairman of the Board of Trade, was among them.

A murmur of greetings broke the silence as Toby entered the room. Ted, Marjorie, and Bixbee stopped at the door. The mayor and governor started to walk forward to shake hands with Toby, then paused as a spontaneous outburst of applause broke out.

Beaming in approval as they looked around, the governor and the mayor joined in the applause, clapping enthusiastically. When it began dying away, they stepped up to Toby, shook hands, and exchanged greetings.

After a moment the governor stepped back, his manner becoming more formal. "Toby, as you know, we're just now beginning to assess the damage and plan steps to recover from this disaster, so circumstances don't permit a ceremony that is truly worthy of what you did here. Nevertheless, we wanted to make a gesture of appreciation while memories are fresh. So we'll proceed, and I'll ask you to speak first, Mayor Mason."

"Thank you, Governor Palmer," the mayor replied as the governor stepped back to the desk. "This is an instance when one should either speak at length or say very little," he continued. "I'm tempted to the former, since we are deeply in your debt, Toby. But everyone here is aware of that, so I'll be brief. We have suffered a devastating blow, and it will take us years to recover. However, we will be able to recover, because we still have several major districts of our city to build upon. And it is due to your efforts, Toby, that we will have those districts."

A murmur of agreement rose from the others, and the mayor held up his hands for silence. "Having said that, I'll finish. I was approached by a committee from our Board of Trade, who wish to make a tangible gesture of appreciation. I therefore yield to Mr. Charles Horton. Mr. Horton?"

Charles Horton, spare and as immaculately neat as he had been on the day Toby had visited him in his office, stepped forward. "Thank you, Mr. Mayor," he said in his soft, dry voice. "I'll strive to be similarly brief." Taking a long, thick envelope from his inside coat pocket, he cleared his throat. "Mr. Holt," he said, then smiled quickly. "Toby. The business community of Chicago is basically in the same state as the rest of the city. We have suffered a severe blow, but thanks to you, we have a base upon which to rebuild. The members of the Board of Trade, sharing the cost equally, have decided to enroll you by a very direct means as a businessman of the city. It gives me great pleasure to present you with a deed to two full lots of waterfront property in the section where you expressed a desire to set up business."

As he took the envelope, Toby was at a loss for words; the property was extremely valuable, and the cost of waterfront land for a lumber mill was to have been one of the largest expenses of the entire venture. "This is so completely unexpected that I hardly know how to begin to express my gratitude," he finally said. "I'm deeply grateful, of course, both for the land and for such an extremely warm welcome into the business community of the city."

"Speaking for the Board of Trade and for the business community," Horton said, "you're more than welcome. We're honored to have you among us." Smiling, he pointed to one of the bystanders. "And if you're still intending to build a sawmill on that property, that's Daniel Sanders, the chairman of the planning commission, and he approves building permits."

"Toby will get his permit, Charlie," the man said, laughing. "You really didn't have to single me out in front of the mayor and the governor in order to get a commitment on that."

Others laughed, too, and Charles Horton returned to his place among the men. Then silence fell once more, and the atmosphere became formal as the governor picked up a parchment scroll from the desk and stepped to Toby. "Within the last hour," he said somberly, glancing around, "we have been informed that the death toll in Wisconsin may exceed fifteen hundred souls. Ours here is something over two hundred. Each one is a tragedy, but I must ask myself, how high would our death toll have been if Toby Holt hadn't been present?"

"Hear! Hear!" the mayor called loudly, applauding vigorously.

The others echoed the mayor's shout of agreement and also clapped. The governor lifted the scroll, unrolled it, and began reading aloud.

"Whereas on October 8th, 1871, a calamity occurred in the City of Chicago that will hereafter be officially referred to in the State of Illinois as the Great Chicago Fire; and whereas on that date Mr. Toby Holt did, at great personal risk, render invaluable service in the saving of lives and property; we do therefore confer upon him the most sincere and deepest gratitude of the people of the State of Illinois. Signed and presented by John Palmer, governor of the State of Illinois."

The governor rolled up the scroll, tied it with a ribbon, and gave it to Toby, then shook hands with him. There was an expectant pause, the people waiting for Toby to speak. He nodded to the governor. "Thank you, Governor Palmer. I am deeply honored by this," he said. "I will keep it very proudly as a reminder of the time when I was privileged to serve the people of Chicago, the city at the heartland of my nation."

"Well said, Toby!" the governor boomed heartily. "Well said indeed!"

The other men gathered around Toby, offering their thanks. As he shook hands and exchanged comments with them, he noticed that Ted had moved Marjorie's cases to the center of the room and was helping her set up her tripod and camera. Police Chief Dougan, eyeing the camera with a wary frown, was moving unobtrusively toward the door to leave.

Marjorie quickly stepped after him and caught his arm. "Sir, just a moment, please," she said. "We'll need you in the photograph. Governor Palmer? Mayor Mason? Gentlemen, could we have the photograph in front of the desk, please? The light is strongest there. And we'll need the fire chief and port master in the photograph as well."

The mayor and the governor looked at each other, a bit startled by Marjorie's peremptory tone. Then they obediently moved toward the desk. The fire chief and the port master, scarcely more eager than the police chief to be in the photograph, followed them. Toby braced himself for the ordeal and went toward the desk with the others.

Marjorie reached into one of her cases and took out a mirror, comb, and can of pomade for the men to tidy their hair and mustaches. Turning toward the bystanders, she said, "Gentlemen, would you stand at the other end of the room, please? And I must ask you to be absolutely silent. The light is poor, and the exposure will take a full minute. There must be no noise to distract the subjects and make them move."

The men gathered at the opposite end of the room, silently watching the preparations for the photograph. When everyone's hair and mustache were neat, Marjorie straightened collars and flicked lint from the coats as she positioned the subjects in front of the desk and posed them around Toby.

The fire chief, police chief, and port master, each holding his uniform cap on his stiffly crooked left arm, stood behind Toby. Marjorie placed the governor and the mayor at Toby's sides, with their right hands tucked in the front of their coats, and their left feet a half pace forward. She turned Toby's scroll to display the seal on the ribbon and instructed him to hold it at chest level.

Ted, standing beside Marjorie as she began focusing the camera, grinned at Toby's discomfort. Toby glanced at him grimly, then steeled himself to look at the large, glaring eye of the lens. Marjorie made her final adjustments, placing the cover over the lens and inserting one of the large, black plate holders.

The soft murmur of conversation among the men at the far end of the room died away as Marjorie glanced in their direction. Turning her attention back to her camera, she pulled out the dark slide and placed her hand on the lens cover. Lifting it, she began counting.

A minute seemed to take forever. When it was finally over and she had replaced the lens cover and the dark slide, the men around Toby laughed and sighed in relief. The governor stepped toward Marjorie. "Would it be possible for me to get a copy of the photograph?" he asked.

"Yes, sir," Marjorie replied. "I'll ask my business partner to send copies to you and to Mayor Mason."

"We'll certainly appreciate that, won't we, Ross?" the governor said. "That sort of thing can be very helpful when election time rolls around."

"It certainly can," the mayor chuckled. "Especially if Toby Holt is in the picture."

Toby laughed, and the men at the opposite end of the room moved forward again, resuming their conversations. After Ted and Marjorie replaced her camera and tripod in the cases, they joined the discussion. Toby noticed Donald Phelps, the telegraph office manager, coming through the crowd toward him.

"It's good to see you again, Don," Toby said. "I understand you're back in business, with an office near the temporary depot."

"That's right, Toby," Phelps replied tersely, taking a telegraph envelope from his pocket. "This is for you. It came in only a short time ago. I decided to bring it right over myself."

His tone and expression were somber. The mayor and the governor glanced at him, their smiles fading as they fell silent. Quiet spread through the room. The rustle of the paper was loud in the stillness as Toby opened the envelope and took out the telegram. His face turned pale as he read the message.

His lips taut, he put the telegram back into the envelope. "Thank you, Don," he said quietly. "Gentlemen, my son has been seriously injured, and I must leave immediately for Oregon. Please excuse me."

"Of course, Toby," the governor said. "Is there anything at all we can do to help?"

"No, but I appreciate the thought," Toby replied, as the mayor's secretary handed him his hat. "I'll keep in touch."

"I'll go with you, Toby," Ted said, intercepting him at the door. "You'll have a long trip ahead of you, and I'm sure you could use some company."

Toby shook his head. "It's good of you to make the offer, Ted, but you have other things to attend to."

Lieutenant Governor Bixbee followed them into the hallway and said, "A week or two either way isn't crucial as far as the proposal I discussed with Ted," he said. "Don't let that be a consideration."

"I'm going, Toby," Ted said firmly.

Placing a hand on Ted's shoulder in a gesture of thanks, Toby nodded. As he led the way toward the stairs, he felt almost overwhelmed by anxiety. He knew that it would take days to reach Oregon and find out what had happened to his son. The brief telegram contained no hint of the cause, nature, or extent of Timmy's injuries, but his being summoned home at all haste was ominous.

READ THIS THRILLING PREVIEW
OF A BOLD NEW SERIES
OF THE AMERICAN WEST
FROM THE AUTHOR AND THE PRODUCERS
OF WHITE INDIAN AND PONY EXPRESS

RIO GRANDE

BOOK ONE IN
THE TAMING OF
THE WEST

BY DONALD CLAYTON PORTER

The time is the early 1860s; the place is the desert country of Arizona and New Mexico, where U.S. Army forces face not only the incursions of rebel war parties bent on conquering the West for the Confederacy, but also hostile Indians determined to drive out all white men.

Lieutenant Kevin O'Reilly, U.S. Army, had been sent into Navajo country as part of Major Emery Church's advance unit. This assignment delighted the big Irishman since it meant he would most likely see again the beautiful Navajo girl who had captured his heart. But so far there had only been the endless patrols into the countryside, chasing down bands of Navajo, parleying with them to get them to move to the reservation. There had been no sign of the girl . . . until perhaps today.

Kevin yanked his horse to an abrupt stop. The distant crackle of army carbines was shattering his concentration on the tracks of the Navajo band he and his six-man patrol had been following. The sound of the rifle fire alarmed O'Reilly, for among the footprints beneath his mount's feet were the small, dainty impressions left by the passage of a young woman—and the tracks led in the direction of the rifle fire!

He turned to Private Mike Connor, the broad-shouldered Irishman riding alongside. It was Mike who, at the last meeting with the Navajo chiefs sometime ago, had prevented O'Reilly from striking out at the ugly Navajo brave that had accosted the lovely Indian girl. Kevin now noted that Mike's face wore a frown as he cocked an ear to the slight northerly breeze.

"How far away is the shooting, Mike?" O'Reilly heard the tension in his own voice.

Connor glanced at his friend. "Mile and a half, maybe two miles. Sound carries far on a day like this. Now, Kevin, we don't know what it means. Could be a hunting party. And even if 'twas a skirmish, we don't know your Navajo maiden is in it. Try to relax and have some faith. Believe in the luck o' the Irish. After all, there be many Navajo women." His voice trailed off as O'Reilly touched spurs to his horse and moved at a swift lope toward the sound of the gunfire. Mike kneed his own horse into motion, waving the other troopers forward. "By the saints, let it not be his Navajo," Mike muttered to himself. "If Kevin is to find her, let it not be this way."

They covered the distance in a very few minutes. Kevin already was off his mount and moving among the huddled bodies in the shallow ravine when Mike and the other troopers caught up. The scene before them shocked the veteran soldiers. Eleven Navajo bodies, including four women and two young children, were sprawled about the ravine. Two of the adult men wore the robes of tribal chieftains.

Kevin looked up, face pale. "She's not here, Mike. But, my God, why? We were supposed to parley with the Indians, not wipe them out. Yet here are eleven Navajo slaughtered like so many sheep—and not one of them is armed." O'Reilly sank to his knees, gently lifted the dead body of a young girl, perhaps eight years old, and cradled the bloody head against his jacket.

Mike Connor stepped from his horse, moved from first one body to another, then straightened. "I know the two chiefs," he said, aware of the tightness in his own voice. "Cuello and Castellito. They sought peace. They were going to come to the reservation willingly. And this is what they ran into. . . ."

Kevin O'Reilly carefully placed the dead girl on the sand, then covered her with a blanket that had been wrapped around the frail shoulders. He felt the tightening in his chest as the sickness inside him gave way to a growing fury.

"I'll know who did this, Mike. And when I do . . ."

Connor saw the powerful hands of his friend clench and unclench. He knew that when the explosion came, someone would pay. "All the work we've done," O'Reilly said through lips drawn thin, "all the effort to convince the Indians to come in peacefully. Gone in a volley of rifle fire in an ambush. The rest will never come in now, Mike."

" 'Tis the truth you speak, my friend," Connor said. He turned to a pair of white-faced young troopers. "Bury them as best you can," he said. "I'm going to ride a small circle to see what I can find."

Connor returned in less than a quarter of an hour. He slid from his mount in front of the lieutenant, who was wielding a trenching tool alongside the troopers.

"Kevin," Connor said, "I'm no threat to Kit Carson at reading sign. But this was an army patrol that did in the Navajo. And it don't take no expert scout to put a name on a horse that moves with a left hind foot turned out so sharp."

Connor sighed to ease his own growing fury. "I didn't see it happen, Kevin, any more than you did—but that hind foot belongs to a Tennessee walker that's rode by just one man. It appears that our Major Emery Church was the man who set this ambush up."

Kevin straightened. "Then, by God," he said, the edge on his voice as keen as that of his trenching tool, "the major will pay!"

Mike sighed. "Hold up a minute, you hot-tempered Irishman," he said. "Do you think Church's report will be the truth of what happened? Will General Carleton take your word and mine—a junior officer and a single trooper—against that of a major? No, my friend. Trouble you don't need, you or your young Navajo maiden."

Connor fetched his own trenching tool from his pack and turned to digging hard and deep as he talked, welcoming the exertion. It would help to burn away his own disgust. He tossed a spadeful in a growing pile at the mouth of the small grave. "No, Kevin, let us not speak of this to the major, as we have no proof. The damage has been done."

Kevin straightened after placing a tiny bundle in the bottom of a grave.

"There's fact in your words, Mike. But, by God, someone will know of this besides us. Colonel Carson is on his way to take over the Navajo campaign, I hear. And Kit Carson will need no proof!"

Assuming full command over Major Church's smaller advance units, Colonel Kit Carson moved to Fort Wingate, located just on the fringes of Navajo country in Arizona. General Carleton, meanwhile, remained in Santa Fe, eagerly waiting for Carson's reports about the patrols that were being sent out to subdue the Navajo and bring them to the reservation.

"Our plan," Carson told his subordinate officers, "may seem harsh on the surface. But in the long run it will save lives on both sides and bring a relatively quick end to the Navajo problem. Our purpose here is not to kill Indians, but to subdue them. Thus, by destroying their homes, burning their crops and orchards, gathering their sheep from them, and providing them food, medical aid, and clothing, we can get them to surrender."

Carson meets with the chiefs of the Navajo and sets forth terms of peace. Some of the chiefs want to accept, but others, including one named Gallegos, angrily reject the terms.

Following this meeting, the colonel and his immediate subordinate, Lieutenant Colonel Ted Henderson, adjourn to Carson's office.

A knock sounded on the door. "Come in," Carson called.

The door swung open. Ted Henderson noticed that the tall lieutenant who entered almost had to duck to clear the upper frame of the doorway. The broad-shouldered young officer saluted, his fingers trembling slightly against the campaign cap.

"Lieutenant Kevin O'Reilly, sir, respectfully requesting an audience with the commanding officer.

Carson casually returned the salute. "Come on in, Lieutenant. Sit down. What's on your mind?"

O'Reilly swallowed, his nervousness now obvious to Ted.

"Sir, I could be—brought to court-martial for

this, but—well, my conscience just couldn't take it any longer." O'Reilly cleared his throat. "Major Church," he said, "is guilty of serious crimes against the Navajo."

Ted saw Carson's eyes narrow, and he waited for the lieutenant to proceed.

"There was the matter of an ambush, sir—two chiefs—"

"Wait a minute, Lieutenant O'Reilly." Carson reached for a paper on his desk and handed it to Ted. "Colonel Henderson, will you please read for us Major Church's official report on the incident for the lieutenant's benefit."

Ted read the report aloud, watching as the husky lieutenant's eyes widened in disbelief.

"But—but sir, that's not how it happened," O'Reilly stammered.

"Then why don't you tell us what did happen," Ted said.

O'Reilly shuffled his feet. "There was an ambush, all right, sir. But it wasn't the Navajo chiefs who were responsible. Cuello and Castellito were not even armed! It had to be Major Church's patrol that staged the ambush, not the Indians!"

Carson sighed, sank heavily into a chair. "Will you swear to that under oath?"

O'Reilly scratched an ear nervously. "Yes, sir. And so will Private Connor. But it would just be the word of me and Mike against that of an officer commissioned in the United States Army. But if you ask, sir, of course, I will testify. And I will have the satisfaction of knowing I've told the truth, even if no one else does. But, Colonel Carson—"

"Yes, Lieutenant?"

"There may be even more mischief afoot, sir. Just before sunset, sir, Major Church and about thirty of his men rode out on patrol. I—I'm afraid they have something more in mind than just checking out the country."

Ted saw alarm flash into Carson's eyes. "Which way were they headed, Lieutenant?"

"North, sir."

Carson turned to Ted. "Any chance of catching up with them, Colonel Henderson?"

Ted shook his head. "There's no moon tonight; we would be searching on blind luck. And they have fresh mounts and a head start."

"Then," Carson said with a sigh heavy with dread, "I suppose we will just have to wait until sunup." He turned to the young officer and held out a hand. "Lieutenant O'Reilly, you did the right thing in coming to us with your story. It took courage for a junior officer to complain about the field conduct of his superior officer. I thank you. And when Major Church returns, your name will not be mentioned in our—uh—discussion."

In the soft gray light of early dawn, the bedlam of yells, whoops, and fast-moving hoofbeats jarred Ted Henderson from a fitful doze. He hastily pulled on his boots and, strapping his pistol belt about his waist, stepped from the small room which served as his quarters near Carson's command post. Ted felt the muscles in his jaw tighten, the hair on his forearms stiffen, as he watched a mass of riders whipping their mounts across the parade ground. He glanced at Carson's quarters. A light burned in the window, and Ted was sure the colonel had been awake the entire night.

With long, angry strides, Ted crossed the few feet to Carson's combination office and living quarters, fighting the growing tension in his stomach. He stepped onto the small porch as Kit Carson, his blond hair askew, opened the door.

The two officers stood rigid and silent as Major Emery Church, heading the detail riding in, brutally yanked his lathered horse to a halt before them. Ted's heart skipped as he saw the blanket-wrapped bundle clutched in Church's right hand.

Church tossed the reins of his exhausted mount to a nearby trooper, then delivered a sardonic salute in the direction of the two officers. Neither Carson nor Ted returned the gesture.

"Come into my office, Major Church." Ted heard the flinty edge on Carson's voice. Waiting until Carson had stepped into the room, followed by the major, dusty and grinning, Ted entered and carefully closed the door. The heavy wood muffled the babble of excited voices from the parade ground outside.

"Explain yourself, Major. I ordered no night patrols." Carson's controlled voice did not match the expression in the narrow eyes illuminated by a single oil lamp on the commanding officer's desk.

Ted noted the ill-concealed glitter of contempt in the major's eyes. Knowing a clash was more than possible between the two, Ted casually stepped off to one side, placing himself a pace away from a point between the two men.

"Somebody had to do something besides talk," Church snorted. "So I did it."

With a flourish, the major flung open the blanket, spilling the bundled, grisly contents on the floor at Carson's feet. Ted heard his own sharp intake of breath. A gory pile of Indian scalps lay at his feet.

Church casually flipped a small scalp over with the toe of his boot. "That," he said, "is the only way to tame Indians."

Ted moved by instinct, catching Kit Carson's arm in a powerful grip as the colonel drew back to swing at the major. "Kit! Don't do it! Striking a junior officer will cost you the command, and we need you now more than ever! This animal isn't worth it!"

"Well, well," Church's sarcasm rang in Ted's ears, "the famous Kit Carson has a bodyguard now."

The slender thread of control that held Ted's own temper snapped. He whirled to face the major and advanced a step. Church instinctively retreated. Ted glared into the smaller man's eyes, pinning him to the spot like a bug nailed to the floor.

"Major Church," Ted said, surprised at the even, conversational tone in his voice that belied the fury now churning in his belly, "but for the fact that we are both in uniform, I would give you the damnedest beating you have ever seen in your miserable life." He noticed Church's hand ease toward the holstered pistol at his hip.

"Go ahead, Church! Try it if you've got the guts! You'll find out you aren't going against weak old men and kids. Go ahead, please. Pull a weapon on a superior officer, and I'll kill you on the spot!"

Ted advanced a step, then another, until the retreating major's back came into contact with the wall. Ted found a small measure of satisfaction in the sudden flash of fear in the major's eyes as Church suddenly realized the infuriated officer before him meant every word. Ted pushed his face close to Church's.

"Major, your stupidity is equaled only by your gutless taste for Indian blood. This butchery has turned what could have been a negotiated peace into a long and bloody campaign that will cost many lives!" Ted reached out and plucked Church's pistol from its holster. "You wanted blood, Major," he said, cocking the weapon, "well, by God, you have it. And it might very well be your own."

Church's eyes, now bright with fear, followed the path of the pistol muzzle as Ted raised it slowly from waist level, pointing it at Church's forehead. Then, deliberately, Ted lowered the weapon.

"Major Church, you are confined to quarters until your superior officers decide on your punishment," Kit Carson commanded. "As for myself, I would prefer to hang you in the center of the parade ground to show the Navajo how white man's justice really works!"

Kit stalked to the door. He flung it open with such force it almost left the hinges. "Get Sergeant Major Armbrister over here, on the double!" he yelled to a nearby trooper.

He stepped back into the room, noticing that some color was beginning to return to Major Emery Church's face. "If you so much as poke your nose from your quarters, Church, I will personally bite it off. Do I make myself clear?"

Church turned to Ted. "You haven't heard the last of this, Henderson," he said, hate dancing in his eyes. "I'll get you for this."

"Any time, any place, Major—but out of uniform

I'll not disgrace the United States Army by smashing a snake in blue!"

Frank Armbrister, stepping through the door, took in the situation at a glance.

"Frank, I want you to escort Major Church back to his quarters. Arrange for a guard at his door at all times. If he wants to go out for anything other than the latrine, I am to be informed at once," Carson said.

"Yes, Colonel. I'll take care of it."

"And Frank," Ted added, "should Major Church make any attempt to escape or ignore your instructions, I would not be at all surprised to receive your report that he had met with a severe accident."

"Yes, sir. A man can get hurt real bad around here if he isn't careful," Armbrister said, one eye closing in a slow wink. "Now, Major, will you come along with me?" Armbrister took the major's arm.

At the door, Church turned and glared at Ted for a moment, eyes flashing hatred. "I'll kill you for this, Henderson—mark my words."

"Sergeant, did you just hear this officer threaten the life of a superior?"

"Yes, sir. Spoke right up and said it, he did."

"Don't forget that, Sergeant. You might have to repeat it under oath one day."

Armbrister nodded, then escorted Church through the door into the light of a new day. Ted turned to Kit Carson, noting the hot fire still burning in the colonel's eyes. "So what do we do with this loathsome Indian scalper, Kit?" he asked.

"I know what I'd like to do—hand him over to the Navajo as a gesture of goodwill," Carson said, "but we might as well face facts. No court-martial panel is going to take action against him. In their view, what Church did would be an action against an enemy in time of war." Carson sat heavily in the rawhide chair behind his desk. "But if you will write out the report stating exactly what happened and its probable impact on the campaign against the Navajo, General Carleton should find it interesting reading."

A tentative knock on the door brought Carson's

voice to a halt. Ted called, "Come in," and Kevin O'Reilly, face lined in worry, stepped into the room.

"Begging your pardon, Colonel Carson—I heard what happened. I—I must examine the scalps that were brought in. I understand there were women and children killed by Church and his men."

"Certainly, Lieutenant," Carson said, "and from the tone of your voice and the expression on your face, I hope you do not find what you search for. After that, would you please see that the remains are given a decent burial?"

Gingerly, O'Reilly picked his way through the scalps, hoping he would not be sick in front of his two commanding officers. At length he looked up.

Ted could see the relief in the young officer's eyes despite the pale face.

"It—it isn't here, sir," O'Reilly said. Carefully and with a reverent touch, the big Irishman began placing the scalps back onto the blood-stained blanket in which they had arrived.

"For your sake, Lieutenant, I'm glad to hear that," Carson said. He turned to Ted.

"Colonel Henderson, we have a most unpleasant but necessary duty before us. I need you to assemble some messengers, people the Navajo may listen to. I must send my personal apologies to the various Navajo chiefs for this atrocity and all other committed by Church—and my personal promise it will never happen again." Carson sighed. "I don't think they will listen," he said, "but I must try. I will go in person to the chief of the band massacred in this most recent incident. You take charge here. Your patrols can work in the vicinity of the fort."

Ted nodded "Myself, Yellow Crow, Frank Armbrister, and Albert Jonas will carry your message. I will find others as well."

"Sir?"

Ted looked up as Kevin O'Reilly stood, the blood-stained bundle held respectfully in his arms. "Yes, Lieutenant?"

"I would like to volunteer to deliver one of the messages."

"Do you speak Navajo?"

"Pretty well, sir. I've been spending a lot of time learning."

Carson nodded. "Very well, Lieutenant. Take no more than a couple of troopers with you—and you realize, of course, that the Navajo may kill you on sight?"

"I'll take the chance, Colonel Carson. And thank you." O'Reilly turned to go.

"Lieutenant," Carson said, his voice soft, "if you tell me which Navajo you search for, perhaps our other men might be of help."

The lieutenant paused at the door. "I don't even know her name, sir," he said, "but I have reason to believe she is with Gallegos's band, possibly a relative. She's—the most beautiful woman I've ever seen."

"Then go with God, Lieutenant. And I hope you find her."

Wind Flower gently brushed a stray strand of black hair back into place behind an ear. She breathed deeply the crisp, cedar-scented air of the secluded branch of the Canyon de Chelly, and she felt the spirits which guarded the sacred place flow about her, bright comfort.

Pride swelled in her breast as she listened to her father near the conclusion of his speech. Few bands of the Navajo, she thought, were so fortunate as to have as strong and just a leader as her father, Gallegos. His rich voice carried easily to where she sat, a respectful distance from the circle of braves around her father.

"You have heard the words of the white soldier," Gallegos concluded, "and they are the same words the Navajo have heard before, words that mean no more than the passage of wind through the trees. Now the Navajo must prepare for war! The spirits shall guide his arrows, and from the scared grounds of this canyon he shall ride against the soldiers, strike hard and fast, and drive the blue-coated ones from the land of the Navajo!"

Wind Flower heard the mutters of assent from the

braves, then suddenly felt a discomfort deep within and knew she was being watched. Fifty feet away, the squat, ugly figure of Choshay stood, his eyes glaring at her. Wind Flower felt a chill settle about her shoulders.

Choshay had become obsessed, she thought, since her father had banned him from the ranks of his warriors and warned him never again to approach Wind Flower. So far Choshay had kept his distance, yet Wind Flower continued to carry the thin, razor-sharp skinning knife in its sheath strapped against her thigh. The old ones, the gossipy grandmothers who knew more of tribal intrigues than the leaders themselves, had spoken of Choshay's growing band of warriors—mostly outcasts like himself—and their killing of white women and children on frequent raids from the holy canyon. His cache of big guns, even horses, continued to grow, and the whispering ones said he had accumulated much dried meat and corn in a spot known only to himself.

Wind Flower knew that she was wise to worry, for one day Choshay might become strong enough to challenge Gallegos for control of the Canyon de Chelly and its inhabitants; only his fear of Gallegos had kept him at a distance so far. But when Gallegos led his warriors from the canyon to defeat the soldiers, then Choshay might seize the opportunity to gain control. She suppressed an inward shudder. Choshay, she vowed, would never touch her body; Wind Flower would plunge the skinning knife into her own breast first. Death would be more welcome than his filthy touch.

Wind Flower rose, brushing the loose sand from her soft deerskin dress. Gallegos had finished his oration, gaining the enthusiastic support of his braves, and now they would be planning the details of their war against the white man. That left much for a woman to do. Meat and parched corn must be prepared for the warriors, crops had to be gathered, sheep had to be tended, blankets had to be made to shield the Navajo bodies from the cold that would come.

Making her way back to her own hut, she paused at her grandfather's lodge to see if he were in need of anything. But the sight that greeted her stilled her tongue.

The old man sat hunched over the sacred sand paintings, wrinkles of many years deepening in the weathered, tired face. Wind Flower had seen that expression before, and she knew the sand paintings spoke to the revered old one of troubled times to come.

Lieutenant Kevin O'Reilly forced his leaden legs to carry him the final few steps to the top of the high mesa overlooking one end of the Canyon de Chelly. He raised a hand, signaling the footsore and bone-tired infantry company behind him to halt. He scanned the countryside with care and saw the smoke from numerous fires, the blackened, charred land where fields of corn once stood.

Satisfied at last that no Navajo warriors lay in ambush, he waved his soldiers forward. Tall stalks of heavily eared corn stretched over several acres before them. This was the Indian corn that grew late in the season and remained on the stalks right up until the first snow.

Kevin O'Reilly did not need to tell his troops what to do; by now they were ruthlessly efficient in the destruction of Indian crops. At his hand signal, they deployed in the familiar skirmish lines at the edges of the cornfield. Within minutes, flames licked at the sun-dried stalks, and with the gusting winds, the field soon would become a short-lived and raging inferno. All that would be left would be another scar on the face of the land.

A glimpse of movement within the cornfield caught his eye. He stared through the steadily growing circle of flames, hoping an innocent deer or antelope had not been trapped in the ring of fire.

His heart leaped in dismay as the movement suddenly snapped into focus through the heat waves shimmering above the field—a slightly built figure, long hair swirling, raced from one point to another, seeking a way to escape the nearing flames. It was a woman trapped there, O'Reilly realized.

The lieutenant reacted without thinking, tossing his rifle aside and plunging through a small opening in the ring of flames into swirling, choking smoke. He stood for a moment, confused and disoriented by the smoke and shimmering heat, eyes watering in protest. Then he spotted her again, only a few feet away.

O'Reilly squared his bull-like shoulders and plowed through the cornstalks. The slender figure, taken by surprise, tried to twist free of the powerful grip on her arm. O'Reilly shouted in the Navajo tongue above the growing crackle of flames. "Man help!" He momentarily realized his grip, stripped out of his greatcoat, tossed the heavy garment over the small body, and scooped up the girl. He glanced about, feeling the first wash of fear, looking for a break in the circle of flames. He found none, and there was no time to search. Running at top speed, he dashed toward the nearest flames, felt the slap of fire against his body, and then broke through into the fresh clean air, stumbling into the arms of a sergeant.

Ignoring the hands that slapped at his smoldering clothing, O'Reilly whipped the greatcoat from the slender figure.

Recognition hit him with a jolt—the high cheekbones, chiseled face, brown eyes wide with fear—the girl from Salt River! Unable for a moment to speak, O'Reilly simply stared. The object of his long search was now within his arms! The woman's eyes softened as she touched his face and his forearms, and O'Reilly became aware he had suffered some minor burns in his dash through the flames. The touch broke his trance.

"Daughter—daughter is safe now," he said in his good Navajo. "No harm will come to her from the fire or the soldiers."

She bowed her head slightly, and O'Reilly was pleased that the flames had not scorched the thick black hair which fell almost to her waist. He reached out as though to stroke it, then checked the impulse as the girl once more raised her eyes.

Wind Flower felt her heart pound within her breast as she looked into the strong but gentle face before her.

"Twice now," she said, her voice musical in the flowery Navajo tongue, "white brave has saved Wind Flower. Once from the ugly one, Choshay, and now from the fire. The daughter of Gallegos thanks the brave soldier not once, but twice, for the gift of life."

Through the daze of a swirling brain almost overwhelmed by the beauty of the woman and the just-ended struggle to save her life, Kevin O'Reilly heard a low whistle at his side.

"The daughter of Gallegos," the sergeant repeated. "Lieutenant, you don't realize what a prize you have here."

"Sergeant," O'Reilly replied in a choked voice, "no man alive realizes just how much of a prize . . . " He could not seem to pull his eyes away from her face, her beauty, the tenderness he saw in her large, long-lashed brown eyes.

"If Gallegos will negotiate for anything," the sergeant said, "it's this girl. He'll pay almost any price to get her back."

"No!" O'Reilly's sharp tone surprised even himself. "It will be her choice; I'll not hold her captive!"

"But, Lieutenant!"

O'Reilly cut the protest short with a quick wave of the hand. "Wind Flower is free to choose," he said in Navajo. "It is white brave's hope, his dream, that Wind Flower will come with him, that she will join her people who have already come to the white settlement. But if she wishes to return to her people, no white hand will be raised against her."

Wind Flower looked steadily at this big soldier in blue. She knew what she had to do.

Coming in 1987 . . .
WAGONS WEST
VOLUME XIX

WISCONSIN!

by Dana Fuller Ross

As a new Chicago begins to rise from the ashes of the Great Fire, the lives of the Holts and the Blakes undergo new trials.

Struggling to build his fledgling lumber operation in Wisconsin's forests, Toby Holt confronts the opposition of wealthy lumber barons in Milwaukee—and in particular one man whose obsession is to destroy the Holt enterprise once and for all.

In Germany, Henry Blake faces the hardest decision in his life—the choice between Cindy Holt and Gisela von Kirchberg. Nothing in his experience has prepared him for this—and nothing can protect him from the violence of his family's reaction to what he decides.

Others come to the northern woods to share in the wealth of Wisconsin, including a master brewer's widow and her young daughter, who bring to America all the secrets of Old World beer-making. Their pluck and enterprise ensure them a new life on the Wisconsin frontier.

Read WISCONSIN!, on sale May 4, 1987
wherever Bantam books are sold.